broken
ground

also by
KAI MARISTED

Out After Dark

Fall

Belong To Me

broken ground

a novel

by
KAI MARISTED

SHOEMAKER & HOARD, *Publishers* • WASHINGTON, DC

LIBRARY OF CONGRESS CATALOGING-IN-PUBLICATION DATA
Maristed, Kai.
    Broken ground : a novel / by Kai Maristed
        p. cm.
    ISBN 1-59376-005-1
Title.
PS3563.A6597 B76 2003
813'.54—dc22   2003014109

Text design by Amy Evans McClure
Printed in the United States of America

 SHOEMAKER & HOARD, *Publishers*
A Division of the Avalon Publishing Group
Distributed by Publishers Group West

10 9 8 7 6 5 4 3 2 1

to Gregory

CONTENTS

You have no lasting city here,

and wherever you may be you are always a stranger and a pilgrim . . .

Thomas à Kempis, 1379–1471

broken
ground

PART ONE

arrivals

INCOMING FLIGHTS

A ding-dong chime, like a celestial doorbell, announces their descent. The plane's left wing tilts toward a vast steel-gray disk nubbled with high-rises, sliced by speedways and canals, and scarred by a canyon of raw excavation: the gaping grave of a demolished wall. *Quick end to a long beginning,* thinks Kaethe, and then: *What if I don't even recognize the place?* Her seatmate, a glossy-cheeked, charcoal-suited businessman who throughout the flight hasn't wasted a glance on her older and all-too-single fellow traveler, now leans across her lap to grimace out the window. "Scheiss Berlin!" he confirms.

The city. Six years ago, she thought she was finally leaving it for good. But six years are dropping away now, swiftly, free fall, leaving only an icy void in the pit of her stomach. It occurs to her that for all her coming and going she has only once before approached the city this way—by air and from the west. Her first arrival. She was a young girl then, only sixteen. As today, traveling alone. Then, the jerry-rigged stages of her journey from North America had taken eight days. Then, the final crescendo came as a patched prop airplane roared low over bomb-crushed, only partly and cheaply resurrected Berlin, its shadow crossing saplings that had sprouted in the rubble of roofless buildings. At the plane's approach the young trees bowed and blanched. Now resurrected memory, an equivocal thrill, grips her.

Loss of altitude. She pictures a cat swung round and suddenly dropped. Engine drone resumes. To her sideways glance the business-man looks remarkably fresh and alert for someone who has worked throughout the flight, tapping inaudibly on a slim, saturnine computer, which in the night cast a silvery sheen over his absorbed features. And how does he see her? A crumpled green traveling suit. Stale aura of lilies-of-the-valley. Weather-darkened patches on the backs of her hands. On the vanity side Kaethe has stayed slimmer for example than that stewardess, at most half her age, butt-wagging briskly down the aisle. In fact Kaethe, having lost courage during the 'meal service,' feels her body verging on the insubstantial, turning translucent inside the green suit. Why not? The businessman, of course, doesn't see her at all.

His tufted, manicured fingers lower the lid of his computer so gently, so considerately, they might be latching shut the door to a nursery.

"If you'll excuse me, sir . . ." He sighs. Waits. But where have her shoes run off to? With stockinged toes she probes through the litter on the floor beneath her seat—the London and Hamburg newspapers, a Paris fashion magazine, a paperback *Faust*. The Peruvian poncho her daughter gave her long ago, nylon carry-on bag, zippered makeup case, and everywhere the pebbly eucalyptus bonbons spilled during take-off—to find her shoes, black pumps she forces on feet fat and numb after nine hours of flight. "Excuse me!" she repeats with urgency, half-rising.

"Too late, lady. Verboten, now. Tough luck." Her seatmate's off-hand German sounds like a correction to her automatic choice of English—that meta-language of commerce and migration, of terminals and fresh starts and also of the country this plane took off from. He taps her arm as she tries to squeeze past. He points to the red signals blinking all the length of the cabin like holiday decorations in a bar. "Strictly forbid-den, to walk in the aisle during landing." Sardonic lowering of his voice. "Naturally, too *dangerous*."

The plane sinks like a shot bird. She falls back in her seat.

"First visit to Berlin?" he asks.

She shrugs. "Hardly."

"Ah. So for you I expect it's like in the old Dietrich song? You can't resist the allure of the city?" He tugs her safety belt tight: an odd inti-macy, after thoroughly ignoring her so long. *"I still keep one suitcase in Berlin, da da de dum de dum . . ."*

"No. It's only a stopover."

"Curious to see the world's biggest construction site?"

"Not at all. I'm looking for someone."

"Looking for . . . I see!" Spoken quickly and lightly, to fend off a suspected lonely heart. "Suppose nowadays, with the big money moving in, Berlin's as good a place for that as any."

She shuts her eyes. No use: clouds of heat continue to rise through her body, to explode, heat into light behind her eyes. *Halogen,* she thinks, *neon, freon.* She presses her dry lips together to hold in a sudden excess of saliva. Swallowing this liquid requires all her effort.

"Lady, you feel unwell? Should I call for some water?"

Her hand lifts and circles in a dismissing gesture, as if flipping a coin into a well. She can't even muster anger at his sudden badgering.

Never motion-sick. Not here, not in that first, jolting plane, not on trains or ships, in careening cars, on motorcycles, roller coasters. Never. To be motion-sick would be for her as out of character as letting white roots show in her hair or taking religious vows or developing a taste for slapstick comedy. So she tells herself, to quell the nausea.

"Frau Schalk? Thousand pardons! But look here, hold this, the paper bag, you know, in case of an emergency . . ."

A rough paper edge nudges her calmly folded hands. She refuses to open her eyes. Self-contained. She is German again.

On the wind-scoured plain of the Mark Brandenburg, June can be cold as November. The moment she passes through the terminal's electric-eye doors, a bruise-blue cloud over Tegel Airport starts to release sharp pellets of rain. Her fellow arrivals scramble into waiting taxis, followed by imploding umbrellas. Kaethe is in no such rush. No one is waiting: who would know she's come back? Standing at the curb, scanning passing faces in the refreshing rain, she can feel her heartbeat quicken with excitement. Her stupid heart! A fearful hope leaps up, one she's reluctant even to name at this moment, although she can't escape its sibilant suggestion in a swirling rain gust: *Sophie Sophie Sofchen—*

Be on guard, she tells herself. It's only because you've been living where weeks go by without any human contact, where any new face is food for days' worth of conjecture, that you dream it could be so magically easy, that she might be *here*—as if this crowd were all the city holds. Be reasonable!

She focuses on checking her belongings: suitcase on its wobbly little wheels, overstuffed carry-on, Nikon dangling from a cord around her neck, purse. *Things,* she thinks, possessions, how they expand and con-

tract, one day you are suffocating in responsibility to *things* and the iner-
tia of their mass, but next morning, after a fire or flood or maybe a trap-
door divorce, you stand stripped to your shivering skin.

In her purse are Kleenex, two passports, a bank envelope chubby
with new D-mark notes, and the canceled plane ticket—one-way,
because she didn't and doesn't know when she will want or need to
leave again, or where she will go from here.

She looks around for a bus. The cheap ride downtown. She does not
trust her relationship with money and knows how quickly this parched
city leaches gold, silver, copper from its guests. She means to watch her
pennies, to make a good start for once.

Her former seatmate stumbles past, headlong. "Taxi! Wait, you bastard, for heaven's sake!" Athletically he slings his laptop and a navy-
blue case such as pilots carry into the nearest cab. Before, during the
flight, he annoyed her; now she has an impulse to wave. How strange,
she thinks, to spend nine hours joined at the hip with someone, to eat
and drink beside him, under tender night-lights to surrender to sleep
together—but only trade a few stingy words and then part forever. She
guesses that this businessman, traveling so light, must have everything
waiting here in Berlin: an apartment bright with modern furnishings
and art, an eager girl or boyfriend, or wife ... perhaps a child. He snaps
down his umbrella. Door slam. She sees him stiffen blindly against the
gravitational force of acceleration as the cab splashes past her.

With that lash of cold gutter water across her ankles she feels completely alone. This is the arrival of invisible Kaethe. Of the former
Countess von Thall, for that matter—the name still printed in her
German passport, although for everyday use she's long since reverted
to a simple, generic Frau Schalk ... *But he knew me, in the plane. How
did he find out my name?*

A shared ocean of hours. While she slept (drooling in her exhaustion
on the airline's pillow, as a damp spot testified) had he bent down to
read her luggage tag? Had his hand even dredged for the ID inside her
purse? Or could he be someone who did know her, having observed
her here before, in her former life? *Don't go looking for trouble. Those
days are over. Life in Berlin is different now.*

All the taxis are Mercedeses, all creamy blond. The drivers assert
their personalities with crocheted seat-covers, steel cloverleafs and
horseshoes screwed to the front radiators, and sentimental toys (plastic
crucifixes, stuffed toy dachshunds, velveteen soccer balls) tied to the

rearview mirrors. As she nears the line, one taxi peels loose from its companions and draws up so close that when the window rolls down she sees a single hair sprouted from a mole on the driver's inclined ear.

"Where to?" A guttural accent. Turkish? Bulgarian?

"The Pension Kurfürstin. Near Charlottenburg Palace, you know that neighborhood? How much is the ride?" She has never seen this pension, booked from an agent's list with some misgiving—often the grander the title, the seedier the real thing.

The driver flies around to take her suitcase. He looks hardly old enough to have a license. Furry brown hair grows low on his forehead over a premature wrinkle of concern. She smiles, an American habit. His blank response reminds her of babies in orphanages who are starved of playful contact. A shuddering roll of thunder is followed by rain hammering on them with conviction. "Climb in, lady! I'll make you a nice price, don't worry. Climb in!"

Warm, inside. Ashtrays sealed by Please-don't-smoke decals. Tasseled beads swing from the mirror. Leather and lemon, garlic and mint— welcoming smells, as if she's been ushered into a private home, a hospitable parlor somewhere in the Near East. Her driver shoves a tape into the slot, a quarter-tone pop song wails, he hums along. One is, she admits to herself, a little nervous these days about Muslims. Is this a song of new love, or lost love? Or religious fervor? She leans back, glad to be ignorant. Branches, the thick young rain-burdened leaves of a cold June, wipe across the taxi's furled windows.

Between branches, flashes of the old survivors: stone buildings with shell-holes artfully filled in and ornamental stucco restored. Beyond soar blue and yellow construction cranes, steel sketches of skyscrapers. She thinks: it's a fake, collective amnesia. You'd think nothing ever happened here but the unbroken progress of prosperity. Nearly a decade since "unification," yet she still isn't entirely comfortable in Berlin-West, which *is* still the West despite revised maps that deny a wall ever existed —no deep scar, no crosses for the ones who failed to make it across, not so much as a faint dotted line . . . Well, but how comfortable was she ever in the East, then? Or in the States, these past few years? *The cat that walks by his wild lone/And all places are alike to him.* It's the echo of her father, who liked to add: "That suits me and that's you too, admit it, Kaethe-Cat!" A Marxist-Leninist who quoted Kipling, wasn't that just like Max Schalk, a man who flaunted his own contradictions. And

why not? Contradictions are above all a way of escape. Her father still
reminds her of a character in a chase movie, who by running into the
house of mirrors splits instantly into so many facets that his panting
pursuers can't guess which one is the flesh-and-blood man.

She straightens up for a better view of the boulevard. It's the lunch
hour. Office workers trot with clipped steps to restaurants, shops and
noon rendezvous—and here comes her improbable hope again. Slow
down! she wants to cry to the driver. Let me study the face of each person remotely the right age. *Twenty-two* is Sophie's age. Twenty two win-
ters since a birth under a new moon in the sign of the Archer, in this
city . . . that particular year closed with a memorable thaw, lakes of
melted snow submerged the cobblestones, birds sang in the stark trees
of the old hospital's inner courtyard, a nurse hooked the tall windows
open to let a spring-like breeze comb the long muslin curtains across
the lying-in bed . . .

"What route are we taking? Are you sure you know where to go?
It's in Charlottenburg, didn't I mention, near Westend, up off Span-
dauerdamm." She recognizes enough streets to know they are heading
toward the wrong part of town. Here's the Tiergarten and a glimpse of
canal. They're heading east.

"I go a detour for tourists. Show you some Berlin sights first. No
charge."

He twirls the wheel fast, like a cowboy spinning a six-shooter, and
they enter the next enormous boulevard: Street of the Seventeenth of
June, designed for a full regiment marching abreast. Ahead looms the
Reichstag, all scaffolded over like Gulliver among the Lilliputians.

"This is intolerable. We're clearly going the wrong way. I insist you
turn around." Her Countess von Thall voice. The style of self-assurance
stays on long after all conviction is gone.

He turns right along the bed of the Spree, into harsh, unrecon-
structed no-man's-land. Here the epicenter of the city is reverting to
country. No pedestrians. Scant traffic. Only billboards shading empty
lots, weeds, bushes, low crumbled remnants of foundations. Kaethe is
surprised to see a refugee woman, veiled in black, squatting on the
grass-fringed sidewalk. A hand-lettered sign dangles from her neck:
Bless you for any Penny. Nine my children killed. Killed in war, of course.
Where? Albania, Macedonia, Kurdestan? Here? Old woman black and
curved like a thorn, hugging her rag-cushioned crutch. A mask of
wrinkles. The Muslim headcover slipped down to the weather-crisped
bridge of her nose.

"Stop just a minute, I want to give her some change...." But the taxi continues, as if the driver is well aware that Kaethe has no German coins yet, only the unbroken hundred-mark bills she swore not to squander on impulse. When she looks up again the beggar-woman has passed from sight. Instead, up ahead, she sees a recently slapped-up poster showing a male and female executive smoking cigarettes and making eyes across a conference table. Her mind freezes, hypnotized as if recognizing the first stage of a recurring, inevitable nightmare.

This image invades when she is least prepared. It may leap out like this, from a billboard advertisement for brandy or cigarettes or a movie. It can crystallize, a pool of silence, out of some cheerful gathering of strangers. Not an image any rational person would summon voluntarily. Although the image has never in fact come in the guise of a dream (for there is no action, and the only change is the gradual discernment of detail) sometimes it fills the dislocated moment on the brink of sleep. First she sees the outline of a man seated at his desk, at home. The man has his back to the observer, who cautiously moves closer.

The man at the desk has made himself comfortable. Stockinged feet thrust into a pair of scuffed leather house-shoes, suit jacket unbuttoned. He lets himself slump, as though near the end of a long day. The desk is cluttered with papers and correspondence, a fountain pen leans against an ashtray bristling with crushed stubs. Near his elbow, a traveler's magnetized chess board supports a brandy glass with only a brown film left in its bowl.

It is afternoon in late November. Despite lace-curtained windows the room is dim. The lamp-bulb has burned out. Only the angle of the man's head, cocked acutely forward and sideways, as if struck by a startling idea, suggests alertness. His left hand dangles down beside his chair, the other rests on the desk. When the observer clicks on a flashlight (these discoveries progress much faster than words convey) these hands stand out first in its jumping beam. They are a garish blue-purple color, as incongruous as a Bozo-nose on a middle-aged, dignified man.

"How again is name of hotel you want, lady?"

"Hotel?" She blinks, finds herself looking out a cab window at a passing, rain-cleansed square. Shudders with relief. Released for now. In the eight or nine years since the apparition's first occurrence her reaction has muted from stark terror to the queasy, helpless chill that overcomes someone forced to drive close by an accident. There is no other way past. "Where *are* we?"

"City Center, dear lady."

Scaffolded old buildings shrouded with flapping linen. Towering steel skeletons. Torn-open pavement of strange-familiar streets. She feels like a stroke victim with only half a memory left, the elusive moment of recognition always around the next corner. "Look, isn't there a police station nearby? Jaegerstrasse. Does that still exist?"

Widened brown eyes and the worry-wrinkle flash up into the rear view mirror.

"Drop me off there. Forget the hotel for now, that's too far. The police station will be better. I have to file ... an errand to do there."

"I wait outside for you, lady. Then drive you to hotel. Easy, okay? So you leave all baggages safe with me. Amur." He raps the laminated portrait on his taxi-driver's I.D. "City license! You trust Amur."

She doesn't. And relies on her father's teaching, that mistrust is an instinct never to be ashamed of, even at the risk of affronting a virtuous, hard-working immigrant. "I'm afraid you'd be waiting far too long. It's the bureaucracy, after all."

But Amur the boy driver insists. He is still arguing as he pulls up with a jerk of the handbrake, and the rearview mirror captures his milky-tea forehead and the dramatic eyebrows working in frantic sincerity; he *is* hurt, and she feels terrible, and the worse she feels, the surer that her instinct is right.

Swiftly, like a bailiff evicting a deadbeat tenant, he piles her things out on the pavement in front of a stone portal. Kaethe hurries to follow. Her left leg buckles at a twinge of pain; it's all she can do to stand upright. On the gray wall facing her is the ubiquitous government emblem: a black, emaciated bird of prey stretched out on a yellow shield. *Bezirksverwaltung Polizei.* She fumbles for money. The fare amounts to robbery, directly on the police's doorstep. "Change?" her driver barks. She nods, then hands back a five-mark note. "You need receipt?"

"Not necessary ..." Surely the tip was enough to satisfy him? Only as the cab spurts away, tires squealing, does she remember that to Berliners, generous tips signal some kind of weakness. Normally, a few small coins will do.

REUNION

Max, her father, used his face like a virtuoso—to lace emphasis, mockery, regret, even outright contradiction into his flat voice. That voice was always monotone, more nasal in German than English. On the day of her arrival, while showing her through his apartment in the Szredski-strasse (a battered and tired-looking lane, an oasis in the rubble-garden of central Berlin), he turned to his daughter and said, "This place will suffice for two, my dear, don't you agree? If we're careful, we won't get in each other's hair." Without inflection, like someone reading from a train schedule, or suspicious of other ears listening in. But meanwhile his smile spun up, creasing the right side of his face, drawing down the eyelid above in a wink. The smile and the closing eye were briefly linked by a long, deep dent in his right cheek. An old scar? A wised-up dimple? Already, her stale, hoarded memory of a father was being blotted out by this living man.

"Isn't it just like a train of box-cars?" he said, as one long, high-ceiling room opened to another. "All aboard, Fräulein: the Orient Express!" The cavernous interior kitchen was windowless. Dominating the three largest rooms were massive, ornate altars covered with mermaid green tiles. *"Coal* heat," he explained, "our famous Berliner ovens. They stink of sulfur and puff out black soot and come January you'll thank God for them." There were chairs, boxes and books stacked everywhere but, except for the first, front parlor with its lace-trimmed windows to the street, the place didn't look remotely furnished.

"All the flats in Berlin are built to the same plan. All alike. You can thank King Frederick the First, he *made* this city. Literally, out of sand, straw and backbreaking taxes. Crowned himself the first King of Prussia, declared this windflattened settlement of donkey-traders and mercenaries and refugee heretics his capital. He unified the villages, called them all Berlin, bribed Italian artists and Parisian actors to move in—that's power! Fritz inherited a lousy tumbleweed garrison and hired himself a genius of an architect and city planner and forced free lots and lumber and cheap loans on every citizen. Condition: they had to build houses to his specs. Boomtown! Did I say houses? *Tenements,* same as they are today, dozens of these flats per building designed to last till Armageddon. Past Armageddon, as it's turned out. In only three years, over 600 of these blockhouses sprang up. This was back in what? Seventeen hundred or so, not much by way of population explosion back then. Mostly poor weavers and soldiers. So of course, because no one could afford all the fancy real estate, most of the King's new capitalists went belly-up. Bankrupt. Couldn't pay back the royal . . . Oh hell, look at poor you. Are you exhausted, Kaethe? My God, you grew fast. Big girl. How about a splash of tea?"

She was staring at him, hard, as if she wanted to drink and swallow him. She marked certain words he used, phrases no one used in the Yankee hills where she, and he too, had grown up: *flat. Splash of tea.* Lightly, playfully, he swung the suitcase she had been carrying for so many days that its weight had become her natural companion. "Well! This will be quite an adventure: getting to know you." The suitcase was dapple-blue pasteboard with brass-colored locks. It held nearly everything that had value to her. She had ducked back, instinctively, before letting him take the case. Afterward her whole arm tingled and stung as feeling returned.

His own parents had shouldered most of the job of raising her. Born in wartime England nine months after an encounter between a young German refugee and a peripatetic serviceman, she was shipped off with her mother as soon as feasible to safer America. They arrived on the farm that Max Schalk himself, she later realized, had throughout his school days schemed single-mindedly to escape. Max's "love-child," she overheard her grandmother call her, and small Kaethe's pride rose up at the title. Max's rare visits dwindled, ended. He was rumored to be in Austria, or Yugoslavia, or Germany. After her mother's death, Kaethe, age thirteen, was sent off a second time, to board at a girls-only school in mild, genteel Chapel Hill, North Carolina. At Gore Academy she was neither happy nor unhappy. If anything, she suffered from a lack of gravity. She found a teacher capable of keeping up her German, and willing to take her in over the vacations. The rhythm and rigor of studies helped quell upsurges of restlessness and even occasional panic. In her school all the girls were waiting, but she was waiting more fervently, and in deeper ignorance, than the rest. So three years had passed.

When Max's summons came—along with his regular payment, the hefty packet of tickets and documents, a letter to the Head requesting special leave, and sealed, detailed travel instructions for Kaethe alone— she didn't hesitate. An overnight train took her to New York City, then a Cunard steamer for five days across the Atlantic to Southampton. Trains and ferries brought her diagonally down the continent to Vienna, where the only serious delay occurred: on the way to the airport, her taxi snagged a small boy. Minutes later, surrounded by gasped prayers from a swelling crowd, the boy pushed up on his hands and feet, miraculously intact, having fallen exactly between all four whirling tires, still and small like a possum playing dead. When the police arrived Kaethe pleaded to be allowed to go on to the airport—there were plenty of witnesses to the accident, and she herself was on her way to be reunited with a parent lost after the war, *Bitte, meine Herren,* lost since she was little. She must not miss her plane! The boy's indignant mother ran up to scold Kaethe, the taxi driver, her dirt-smudged son, the crowd. The policemen ignored her: Kaethe's tale moved them more. Kaethe, speaking the precise high German she had learned in America, wearing her Ami-style plaid skirt and loafers, amused them. Gallantly, they chauffeured her to their airport.

There, the interrogation by border officials about her visas and unpopular destination and purpose and sanity was long and unnerving. First stars were twinkling when, finally freed, she left the customs' shed to cross the tarmac. She was surprised to find her two uniformed protectors still waiting outside the fence, waving goodbye. She saw their hands drop, uncertainly, as she turned and trotted, juggling her blue case, toward an isolated, battered plane newly painted with bold Cyrillic letters. She was humming with relief at having made it to this last stage of the journey. So close now! She waved back at the comical crushed looks on the policemen's faces as she clattered up the Aeroflot's silver steps.

Her first time inside an airplane. The fuselage was dusk-dim, like a ship's hold, and nearly empty. The only other passengers were four men who sat equidistant from each other, as if at the matinee of a smutty movie. She sat down in front of the left wing, looking out. Not afraid of flying. Her palms were dry. In two hours the plane would be landing at Schönefeld Airport, in the Soviet sector of Berlin. Last stage. Almost there, she could allow the dream-film of their reunion to run through her mind—but now with a surge of anxiety she saw herself not remembering her father well enough to recognize him. She would lurch up to the wrong man while staring indifferently through Max Schalk.

In her suitcase was a faded snapshot of her parents, Max and Barb, taken back when she herself formed a mere pale smudge in a stroller. The brownish snapshot with deckle borders was tiny as a favor from a popcorn box. Max, though he sent her museum art cards a few times a year, had never responded to her written wishes for a newer, larger photo. A likeness of him. But then, in all the years before tearing open the additional, sealed instructions, she hadn't even known where he lived—where, in an emergency, she could have found him. She had sometimes guessed at East Germany, or farther east, or possibly as close as Vienna, which was sometimes the *poste restante* on his cards and payments, invariably sent registered mail, express.

Berlin. *Soviet* Berlin. He trusted her now. *Szredskistrasse, 70a.* She had memorized his address. No one could take this from her again.

The engines woke up and throbbed. The solid propellers turned lethargically, each in a separate rhythm. Someone tugged the web belt tight across Kaethe's lap. She leaned forward, holding her breath. The propellers caught wind, sped up, beating air, converging in tempo and blurring to ghosts.

Past midnight they stayed awake. Max asked questions. He was aware of both less and more about her past than she would have guessed. Kaethe heard herself babbling, stumbling between two languages, eager to offer answers, to show herself in the life she had left behind only days before, which she already looked back on as strangely two-dimensional, flat as the backdrop for a stage play that has folded or left town. . . . Then they stared at each other with open curiosity, and fell into silence over the strong black tea. She wondered whether this man with the one-sided smile and bristly, brindled hair would demand a goodnight kiss from her. A cuddling hug. She was not used to touching people. She watched; he made no sign. With a start she recalled having seen only one bed, in his neat, book-lined back room. Where would she sleep?

She had nothing to worry about. For the time being, Max gave her his own room.

RECONNAISSANCE

Once inside the bustle and hum of the police station Kaethe passes Property Crimes with a shrug at her own incompetence. She can't recall the cab's license number; a first name isn't enough to go on, and by now the serial ID will have been filed off the Nikon left in Amur's cab; within an hour it will have changed hands three times over. Theft was his dreary purpose from the start. Obviously she has forgotten how to move about alone in a city. She enters Missing Persons.

The wait is long. Too restless to read, she watches the other petitioners waiting, as they watch her. The image of an unidentified man slumped at his desk trembles at the edge of her mind. She leaps up, absurdly eager, when a uniformed clerk motions her to a seat in his cubicle, facing the back of his computer. Her palms are slick and hot, as if she's about to be interrogated about some fresh crime. She balls them into fists. "Let's have a look," the clerk drawls to his screen. "Quappen, Quitznow, Rabenhuber, Tzevanotschke. We have no von Thall. Illustrious name! Good news: no incidents, no arrests. There has been no report whatever filed on a person of this name. You wish to file a Missing Adult? What is your legal relationship to this individual? And the precise reason you have come to the Berlin municipal police?"

She stutters, unprepared. But why even attempt an explanation? Simply assert, "Well, I'm the *mother,* you see—" in the belief that *mother* projects gravity and credibility.

"Mother of this person Sophie. Who is not registered in Berlin. A twenty-two-year-old adult female."

"Exactly! Here, I have pictures . . . I should mention, she's a tall girl. One meter seventy-two, in fact. Taller than me, obviously. And she stands tall—noticeable in a crowd—like her father in that. Her eyes . . . probably gray comes closest, but hers are really much, much darker than what you might think of as gray. Except in sunlight. Her hair, well, she likes to change it, often. Sleek to curly, red to straw, short to long—and that may complicate finding her. Odd, isn't it, how something as superficial as hair can work as a nearly complete disguise? Sophie can afford to experiment, though. Her natural hair is wonderfully coarse, Asian you might think. She tans like an Indian. We used to say that before it became so wrong to say. . . . She has beautiful skin. She really is quite beautiful. No, I'm being objective, believe me. Even when she is sad—nothing out of the ordinary, but we are all sometimes sad, aren't we, despite pressure everywhere to deny it—even then a sort of half-smile hovers, because of the particular shape and curve of her lips. . . . Do you see what I mean?" She stops. He hasn't written down a word. Why go on? As if hoping to prove her claim by meticulous description. As if in hope that by advertising the missing girl's stunning physicality she can arouse this beige-shirted officer's personal desire to launch a search.

"Any street drug history? Prostitution? Kleptomania? Other psychosocial instability?"

Kaethe stares, having nearly forgotten what kind of mind police work shapes.

"You mentioned the father. Count von Thall, I take it? He doesn't show up on our residency rolls either."

"No, no, he wouldn't. He lives in Munich now. We don't—"

"You're separated or divorced?"

"I'm . . . the latter." Her mouth still goes stiff around the actual word, as ugly as it ever was.

"How long?" Now the officer is writing something down.

"Oh . . ." Not a question she ever asks herself. She finds her brain paralyzed, unable to add or subtract. "Fifteen years?"

He looks up sharply. Half his lifetime, could that be why?

"Remarried?"

"Me? No. No."

"Is *he*? Your ex."

"Yes, in fact."

"Can't have two countesses, can we? So you are legally no longer titled. You need to have your passport updated."

"Probably. I really don't care."

Another sharp glance. "Custody? Of the child? To you?"

"Well, that depended. . . . But you could say no, I suppose, in the narrow sense. He kept . . . control." Deep in her pocket she fingers the letter from the "ex," creased to a square. The letter that pulled her back to this city. Its contents would hardly help her case here.

"Right. So then as for you, you've been living some time now back in the U.S. of A. Nice life over there! I myself have a brother in Atlanta, engineer with VW."

She finds no reply.

"This daughter often has visited you over in Oosah?" *Oosah?* Usa. U.S.A. It takes Kaethe a minute to catch on.

"Well, no. She won't. We haven't exactly been—" For a second time, hand against mouth, she stops herself from blurting another word. *A mother who met with her daughter for only one day, in all of six years. . . . Exactly what kind of mother is that, Frau von Thall?* "But we always kept in touch. I wrote stacks of letters! This photo, you can look at the date, it's from less than a year ago! Listen, Officer . . ." She peers at the name shield under the green epaulet, but it's a blur.

"Povold. Hans-Jorg."

"Officer Povold, please, I've come all this way because I'm afraid for my daughter. I believe she's here in this city—"

"Not exactly hardship duty: a visit to Berlin!" He grins. There are little gaps between all his upper teeth; they look like a stubby fringe of bone. Kaethe remembers a time when she found Povold's sort of Berlin-boosterism endearing. Much earlier, when the city was maligned and adrift and half-deserted, she'd talked that way herself.

"Sophie is . . . in some ways very innocent, for her age. She could be in some trouble. Or in a dangerous situation. Or about to enter one." Perhaps she *should* bring out the letter. "I sense this strongly, remember I am the mother, after all."

But now Hans-Jorg Povold leans back, nodding amiably, smiling more broadly. His relaxation implies that they both know how mothers show up here all the time, fussing and costing man-hours and taxes, when all someone in the family needs is a little slack.

Under the circumstances as represented, he informs her, the State lacks sufficient grounds to activate a search. The State regrets.

Out in the street again, she hesitates. Office workers on flex-time stream toward the underground, homeward. But now she is reluctant to hurry to the predictable hotel-pension where she will sleep for the next days or weeks. Reluctant to sit alone on bed's edge and contemplate this first day's rebuff. It's the mutating East side that draws and tugs at her now. What's left of the old bog-capital, as Max would have said. *Imagine, Kaethe-cat: this dreary haunt started up as a camp for reindeer hunters, early stone age! And later built up to a five-gated citadel. The Brandenburg is the only souvenir gate left—but never through all those ages, until the Soviet brothers came, did Berlin come under anyone else's boot. Even the Romans spat us Eastern Allemani out. Too tough to chew. Too sour.*

"Us?" But as she sets out walking, her heart brims with anticipation, a sort of agitated longing, the way an eye brims with tears. Call it freedom: from now on she can hunt for Sophie on her own terms, in her own way. Her suitcase bumps along behind her, over cobblestones and makeshift bridges that span ditches, mudfields, underground caverns filled with hammering machinery and the puny shouts of men. A half block away from the Alexanderplatz she enters a temporary stand-up snack joint and spoons in a large bowl of green pea soup, surrounded by bums and addicts. Firmly, she mops up the last of the soup with a heel of bread.

Definition of a miracle: the mutation of yesterday's moonshine into fact. Kaethe is not alone in her greedy amazement; despite the recent years of "normalcy," other passengers in the sweetly rocking double-decker bus still gape at the reunited mid-Berlin landscape as if half-expecting the scenery to burst apart like a broken film reel. The route loops, as bus routes do: from the Alexplatz to the Opera—and now offers a straight, unobstructed view down Unter den Linden to the Brandenburg Gate. All in one eyeful, one moment. The wonder is, what is *not* there.

The bus wallows left, sways past a few boutiques and wurst stands. Sandpits. Office towers so new the glass plates are still taped. Her breathing turns shallow, some physical sense of geography having recognized, before her mind does, that they are approaching Checkpoint

Charlie, that broom-swept, white-washed electric space. Guns trained
on it from turrets on both sides. Checkpoint. Point of deliverance
or point of corruption, depending on where you stand. Where you stood
. . . From up on this bus she almost missed it. Along with one of the old
warning signs—*Achtung!* in four languages—only a small guardbooth
has been preserved, a torn-off fragment like the glassy, glossy wing of a
beetle. Museum dust. Ha! She laughs out loud. A man in front of her
turns with a disapproving scowl.

"Point Charlie Chaplin!" she says.

It is evening in the unending daylight of June by the time a final bus
disgorges her with a group of Korean tourists at a corner of the palace
park. The sun's reddish glow turns the gray city to bronze. Excited,
frail-looking women help lift down her suitcase. In the snapping wind
and the glare, Charlottenburg Palace is merely a long wavering shadow.
She turns her back on it, heading into the surrounding cat's cradle of
residential streets.

These are fine burghers' houses, made of massive stone blocks, six
stories each with shops on the ground floor and dozens of offices and
flats carved above and within. Pre-war, the wide, wooden side-gates let
carriages pass through to the inner courts. Brass business-plaques still
surround the main entrances. On number twenty-three: "Wippel &
Kopke, Tax Advisors 2nd Fl," "Dr Phil Bettina Strub, Child Psychologist 3rd Fl," "G. Cecci, Wigmaker 6th Fl Rear," and the largest, most
ornate: "Hotel-Pension Zur Kurfürstin, Proprietress: Rahel Loewnfus.
5th Fl Front."

"What took you so long?"

"I had no idea anyone would be waiting. Excuse me."

"You're the only newcomer this week. This is Boris. Boris, shut your
muzzle, please. After today he won't growl at you—"

"Wolfhound?"

"Part, part. He has a terrific memory. You'll never be forgotten."

"I like these, what, original lithographs, this, what, opera poster—"

"Hand-signed. You notice such details? Everything here is original.
One of a kind. Like my guests. At present I have a Russian sculptor, a
family of string musicians, a Tibetan acrobat, and a completely unlicked
babe, an actor from Los Angeles . . . I hardly ever have an ordinary
tourist, I don't know why. Here, Countess! Umbrellas, in this jar behind

the door. I buy them for a mark apiece at the flea market, for any guest to take—to each according to need, yes?—in case of rain. Which appears perpetual this spring, no?"

"I'm no expert about furniture, but this mirror, it's so . . . humorous. All the vines, faces . . . Is it Jugendstil? And the small table?"

"My father was a collector. I love Jugendstil. You too, I take it? If one has fine things, why not share them? I must trust my guests. Boris, shut *up*. I'm glad you appreciate the Hotel. Wait until you see your room, Countess. I expect you—"

"Oh, won't you please call me Frau Schalk? It's Kaethe Schalk. No title. That came and went the way married-on names do. Long since irrelevant."

"Here you see my office. I confess to saving some nice things for myself. Isn't it a lovely space? Southern light! I'm in whenever the door is open, and you should always feel free to . . . Ah. Here comes my Lies."

"Pleased to meet you, Lies."

"*She* knows her way around Berlin. Anything you can't find, ask her. Lies, dear heart, take the suitcase on ahead. *Cave,* Boris. Go to your cave! That's his cave under the telephone table. Do you mind just completing this form, Countess, for the police?"

"I never had a dog. But almost everywhere I've stayed a cat or two has found me. The farm where I've been living—I seem to share it with a wild cat. Not a starveling, she has a thick, shiny coat. But feral. Comes when she wants to. No one can approach her."

"And here is the breakfast room. Seven-thirty to nine-thirty, we serve. Should all five tables happen to be occupied, simply ask to join someone."

"Oh, the balcony! All the flowers!"

"I can't live without flowers. No, of course that's an exaggeration, one can go on without just about anything except food. So come over here, come, look under the nasturtium—chives! And these tiny strawberries, here, taste one! Sweet? Mm. Come, come along, you must be exhausted, flying direct from the States—"

"A little tired. I would like a bath."

"Understandably. The w.c. is across here, and here is one bath, another bath is just down the corridor. Across from your room. Come along! Each room has some unique characteristic, but to me this particular one is the sanctuary. Here. Your larger key is for the main door and the smaller one fits this lock. . . . Oof. Ah! Now do you see? The windows open to the courtyard. It's so quiet you won't even know you're in the city—and there's the big Jugendstil bed, the armoire, writing desk. Soap and towels by the sink. Well? Do you object to black furniture? Too austere?"

"It's a grand room. Huge! For only one person."

"But the travel agent's fax said you intend to stay for a while, Countess."

"Oh, please. I can't bear to hear that. It makes me uncomfortable."

"Kaethe von Thall. Isn't that the name on your reservation, on your passport? Not so terrible! I assume, the same von Thalls as in the history books? Virtuous soldier-advisors to a long line of Prussian kings? And am I wrong, or isn't a title by law now simply part of the name? What a sideways blow for democracy! But a name isn't a thing one can simply walk away from, is it? Not like a house or a nationality, or even for that matter a dog. A name becomes part of one's essence, one's identity. But of course I will call you however you like."

"You won't mind my saying, Loewnfus sounds fairly exotic. For here and now."

"And there's the front doorbell again. Some forgetful fool has locked himself out again. *Lies, see who is there!* Excuse me, please. *Coming!* Oh, and for heaven's sake, always take your room keys with you, no matter where...."

When she wakes the light in the room has dwindled to smoke-blue. She lies fully clothed on the bed, looking up from the bottom of a well: the dim ceiling is fifteen feet high. Long gauze curtains shiver and coil in and out of the two tall windows on the evening breeze, tripping a memory she can't pin down. Hasn't she lain in this room before? Impossible: she entered it for the first time only a few hours ago.

Midafternoon, by her watch, still set to U.S. time. Nine-ten, by the clock on the nightstand. Nine o'clock at night is mere children's-hour for Berlin. She should get up and bathe, make her first phone calls, afterward forage out for food.

She moves. The letter rustles in her pocket. From her shallow nap a puzzle piece of dream floats into mind and she latches on, letting it drag her back.

So: to see herself walking away from the charred farmhouse and down a sandy track to the paved county road. Miles, past the yellow clapboard church and past the Grange, on into the General Store. None of the usual local carpenters, dropouts, shepherds were there, only gentian-eyed Joe the owner, and a newcomer-woman, dressed in white, browsing the wood-floored aisles. Kaethe found the assortment of goods on the shelves subtly altered: instead of canned tomatoes and bags of beans, there were jars of preserved body organs, unlabeled but clearly visible through the glass—a small liver, a pink conundrum of intestine, other items recognizable but unnamed. The woman in white, with a nurse's authority, had prepared a makeshift table for Kaethe to lie on. Joe encouraged Kaethe: this was an emergency, she would be doing him, doing the universe for that matter, an enormous favor. Lying on the table, on her side as commanded in the fetal position, she realized that the stranger needed something from her. A part would be taken. She hoped the nurse was skilled, experienced. She lay bare from the hips up. Hands gently widened her shoulders. A four-inch boning blade sank to the hilt between her breasts. But it was the anaesthesia slowly, thickly entering her spine, that silent, rising, inescapable agony of the spreading anaesthesia, that woke her.

She gasps, lowering her thighs into the bath. Billowing steam escapes through the narrow window, hooked ajar. An electric bulb overhead shows her body flushed below the waterline, which laps a tangent at the upper rim of her nipples. Outside, a bird expands its five-note theme in fantastic variations. A Drossel, so she identifies it—but does Drossel translate as "lark" in English, or as "thrush," or does this large, plain, absurdly gifted bird not exist in the New World? Seldom that her language ability stumbles, but when it does, then over such lowest, irreducible terms. The Drossel sings on anyway, in the near-dark courtyard.

Under the water's surface her hand explores her anatomy the way some trusted other person might: the floating rejuvenation of her breasts, the buttery slack circling her waist. Although she's not far away from sixty, she still has a waist if not the one she began with. The body is changing from the moment of conception until long after death. A single birth hardly leaves a mark. What is the French saying? 'The first baby for health, the second for beauty—but the third takes it all away.' Health, then. One true birth gave her a slight broadening of the hips, and muscles thickened from carrying. Her stomach, smooth and hardly rounded when she lies back like this, supine, is lined just above the mound with two curved wrinkles draped like thin necklaces low across her hips. Like smiles drawn by a child. Pubic hair is called "Schamhaar," literally "shame" in German, the more shameless, inquisitive language. Her Schamhaar floats in the current like silky moss, hazelnut brown, twined now in her fingers that slip and comb as someone else's hand might. As her hips relax, her flushed knees fall apart, letting the warm water flow further inside her. It's her resurgent hunger and the warmth of the bath, of course, and new surroundings, and the lifting of time's rules called jetlag, that coming together make her feel a little drunk. Solitude, and its solace. A virtually frictionless small pressure, under shimmering water. With a tremor the hips rise slightly, out of habit. The body's natural expectation. The body doesn't know, is blind to everything but touch. Finger-play. A translucent beating, like a hovering dragonfly's whirr. Pleasure crosses to pain and back again, well-trained. Somewhere in this city, perhaps, tonight—there is a man who used to be able to stop her breath like this. But how many years have gone by since his body, any body, man or child, weighed down on these muscles and bones?

Her imagination fails to summon him. Instead it lets curious strangers wander in: Frau Loewnfus with her rakish, hennaed hair and protuberant, witty eyes, and her teen-aged reincarnation, Lies, the wiry hair snipped even shorter and colored a shade darker, a sassy steel ring snapped into one nostril. Unsmiling, the women bend closer.

"No." Kaethe stands up so abruptly that bathwater sluices down like a wave off a rock. For a light-headed moment the white walls turn black. The Drossel has stopped singing. Hurrying for a towel, dressing in clean but wrinkled clothes, she steps barefoot over bundles of dirty linen stacked in front of a washer-dryer—Lies's work cut out for her tomorrow, she thinks, already presuming that Lies does all the work.

Doors, her own included, are clinking open and shut. The corridor walls of the pension are covered with mirrors, prints, playbills, low-watt bulbs in iron-flower sconces. Guests brush past her on their way in or out, murmuring good-evenings.

The communal phone sits in its pool of light in the breakfast room. She peers below the desk for the shaggy, brindled, calf-sized hound—not generally partial to dogs, she nonetheless wants to make peace with this guardian of the fifth floor, enchanted shambling beast from some hoary tale. But its lair just now is empty.

Frau Loewnfus has explained her honor system: guests log each call with its duration in an open notebook. Theoretically, any cheat can ring up Tasmania, say, or Shanghai, without paying. There is a challenge, Kaethe thinks, almost a calculated temptation, in the proprietress's ostentatious display of trust.

She dials a number in east Berlin.

"Hullo. Leytenfeger speaking."

"Mathias! How *are* you?"

"Hullo? Who's there?"

"It's me. Kaethe. I know it's been a while...."

"Kaethe? No. Kaethe Schalk? That is impossible. No. But wait, wait a moment! All right, I'm back—I had to turn the gas-ring off. I'm back now. Is it you? Are you there? What has happened, what's wrong? *Kaethe?"*

"It seems so funny to be able to call you on the phone, like this. Remembering what we used to go through."

"Keep talking. Where *are* you?"

"Here. In the city. West. I found a decent, cheap room. Near the Charlottenburg Palace. Remember when—"

"No. *No.* And why have you come back? Why are you calling me? It's been *years,* Kaethe ... Christ Jesus in heaven! It is you. Your voice. You are all right. Why are you *disturbing* me?"

"Well, I thought by now that we ... Mathias? While I'm here we could, I'd like to at least, simply go out for a coffee, or a beer, together. I think about you. Often. I keep imagining how you're getting along here, now everything's gotten so much easier..."

"My letters. Did they reach you? Where are they? You never answered, not once. Do you know what I have been through? How I agonized over you, the things I imagined. Whether you were. So. But you are alive."

"Mathias, why? I mean, after what happened—what I did, what you ... accused me of doing. You can't have expected—"

"Later I tried to call you. No phone listing—is that possible, for six years? Going on seven. I wanted those letters back! I hate to think of you reading all that shit I wrote, and laughing. So is this your next joke? In the name of God, why are you *calling* me?"

"I'm sorry. I—I was in fact wondering if you happen to have heard from Sophie. Recently, that is."

"The kid? Soph?"

"Um. There's a chance, I think she might have come back here—"

"You don't know where she is? You lost her?"

"Please! I tried the police."

"Hold on, let me think. She did send a Christmas card. From Munich. Not this winter, maybe the winter before. A Giotto Annunciation. I was touched. Probably I cried. A piece of you, so to speak. And so, now you've gone and lost Sophie? *Again* you've lost her? Extraordinary! But maybe not so surprising. Maybe there is such a thing as divine book-keeping, after all."

Kaethe's thumb, swiftly and of its own volition, jams down on the telephone's twin horn-stubs, breaking the connection.

Every subway system gives off its own unmistakable breath. Even if blindfolded, Kaethe would know she is somewhere beneath the streets of Berlin, when the tunnel air blows moist with shag tobacco and chocolate, hashish and 4711 cologne. From Richard Wagner Platz to Zoo Station is only a few stops. She climbs up the long flights of stairs, part of a jostling crowd. Finally the short summer night has fallen, close to eleven o'clock, and the city is beginning to wake up. Pimps and croupiers, strippers and jazz players, are eating breakfast under the stars and the awnings of outdoor cafés.

The habit of walking. A person can walk forever here without reaching the limit or crossing her own path. Her legs remember that the distances are unlike those of any other city ever known. "A scatter of lousy isolated villages," according to Max in one of his impromptu history lessons, "shotgun-married to each other by the Hohenzollerns. But by 1935 the worker from Schoeneberg still wasn't likely to have ever made the trip all the way to Spandau, and vice versa. Chauvinist, insular villages. That's why this more recent division works so well, you get it?"

As a teenager Kaethe used to get around the city by bicycle. She loved her black bike, her iron donkey, the way a cowboy loves his plug-ugly horse. Now with her jacket buttoned to the neck against the wind, hatless, paper money stashed in her jeans, she feels like any aimless tourist, another lone Ami past her prime and on the prowl. But her stride, despite a touch of stiffness on the left side, stretches out to a distance-eating Berlin pace. Through the pattering shadows of sidewalk plane trees, into the shadowless dark under the stone struts and overhead rails of the S-train, which even in the coldest cold war decade went on running empty-sealed cars over the Wall, connecting the city's farthest corners.

Here under the tracks, despite the late hour, small art galleries and bookstores surge with customers. A few hundred yards ahead jaunty lights glow in the trees of a flowering square ringed by cafés and bars. Strains of dixieland and bouzouki music and women's laughter and a tango drift on the wind, turned locally warmer. Savignyplatz! Automatically she has chosen a direction, conscious only of the need to push exhaustion so far that when she returns to the hotel, sleep will claim her.

Savignyplatz. There was no garden here when she stumbled on it almost forty years ago. Nothing to notice but a slab-sided, bomb-pitted movie house and a cluster of smoke-filled, sour, beer-and-bockwurst pubs.

One of those pubs became her first home, after her first defection. Home, though tonight she can't resurrect its name. In that cellar everyone was "du." Intimate, anonymous. All the student-comrades. They were thin and quick, sucking on hand-rolled smokes, burning with disillusioned sarcasm and revolutionary intent. She was their freshest star from the East. She told how the Young Pioneers had let her down, newly hatched bullies swaggering in the schoolyard in their gray uniforms, the tight scarves like blue scabs around boys' slender necks. In Savignyplatz, the talk was about rebirth, solidarity, convergence, resistance. About finding a "Third Way."

In the cellar pub a few steps under the cinema she played chess with masters, borrowed books of poetry and philosophy, was sketched in charcoal, showered with advice. She slept on the hardwood pub benches, was cured in time of body lice and of bronchitis, of naive presumption and unproductive fears. Food, epiphanies, blankets: everything important was shared. She shed the shackles of technical virginity with a boy from Savignyplatz—a passionate political economist, *Chinese,* they called him—whose other name she felt no need to ask. More than ten years later his haggard face with the jutting, Mongol-like cheekbones would blaze at her from a checkerboard array of suspects on a Post Office wall: "Sought for Armed Terrorist Conspiracy." That shock came in a December; a few days later she would discover she was pregnant. As she stared at the poster a wave of queasiness caused her carefully addressed holiday cards to slew from her hand to the mud-and-ice trampled floor.

By that morning in the post office, luck and instinct had already long since brought her far from the squalor and transcendence of Savignyplatz. She might have passed near it in the daytime with her mind fixed on something else, but nothing ever brought her back inside until tonight.

It's still a territory of the young, but young turned rich. It's less like the catacombs, more like a festival. The couples meandering by in lumbering embraces are too stylish to be students. Pay attention, she tells herself, *look* at them! Instead she faces a shop display window (The Book Witch, trendily in English) to buy a book as defense against the awkwardness of eating dinner in public, alone.

"Hello hello! You found us, finally. Welcome, sister!" A massive, gray-haired, dreadlocked woman, shouting in American, bursts from the bookshop. "Come on in, darling, *ganz* Berlin is on fire to meet you!"

"Sorry, I'm not anyone who—" Kaethe is being drawn inside.

"Sister, I've read every line you wrote since *Grandmothers of Revolution.* And now you're on world tour with *Cloning the Goddess!* Simply *fantastisch,* as we say here . . ."

A dozen or so oversized art photographs hang suspended like theater drops from the ceiling. One shows nude female torsos confronting each other, touching only with the tips of their nipples. Another memorializes four nude black girls lying on a blanket, sardine style, a single stark Caucasian squeezed in between them. These posters strike Kaethe as innocuous, unlike the close-up photo of a bald woman (smoothly appetizing as are all the camera's subjects) inserting her remarkably slender tongue into another girl's navel ring. Tasting? Tugging? For a second Kaethe envisions the hotel girl, Lies.

"Come meet and greet! The fans are all waiting in the back room."

"But you've made a mistake. Sorry. I can't stay—" Avoiding the owner's bewildered disbelief. "But I did want to buy a book . . ." eyeing the displays for an eligible title, one that she can hide her face behind in a restaurant tonight. Some are in English: *The Metaphysics of Masochism. Gin and Cherries. Das Homosexuelle Jahrtausend. Gay Grandparenting. Sappho's Memoiren.* "Here. This one, how much is it?" But the owner has dashed into the street again, and is clutching at someone who bears no resemblance to Kaethe at all, who blushes and smiles and nods. The real author, no doubt.

An hour later, forking up spaghetti by candle-gloom from a dim plate, Kaethe regrets not having stayed for the author's reading. She should have ventured into the back room. Taken a good long look around.

Struck up conversation with young strangers. She will have to begin this sort of thing soon. Why not tonight?

Kaethe—
I write to you strictly because of my concern about Sophie. She has been missing for twenty days.
    Please inform me when and if this letter reaches you. You leave no traces. Sophie did once mention to us that you have moved back to America, to Glass River. This choice appears perverse as I recall you often saying you wanted

It doesn't matter that there's not enough light; she knows the letter in her pocket by heart. She reaches for her wineglass. The small, single table wobbles. All around are banquet-sized trestles thronged with party-makers—the ruthless schickeria of Europe: duelling club boys, Hermès girls with capped teeth and Mallorcan tans.

I won't find my Sofchen in a place like this, she thinks, not likely.

Now and then one of the sleek women nearby tosses a glance back over her shoulder, as if irritated by Kaethe's mere presence. This hostility forces her to look away, toward the mirror-tiles that line the walls. *Pompeii* is this restaurant's name, painted mossily on the mirrors. In the large monocle of the first P she is shocked to find the intrusion of her reflection. Disheveled halo of hair, furrowed loose skin. Hooded amphibian eyes. Slack, bardolino-stained lips. She raises her glass, pursing those lips to send herself a complicit smile.

You have to get used to being out among people again, she reminds herself. The wine is ballooning to her head, bearing its sympathy and rosy expectation. She drank no wine all her time on the farm. She met with no one, save on treks to the store. Alone on the high hillside she metamorphosed gradually from a prodigal outcast picking out space in charred ruins, to an anchorite, to a sort of maenad—but who could see her run out into the livid center of a hurricane, smash ice, keen with the hawks or mumble with the rain? She clambered among the hills until sundown, day after day. At least there were lively apparitions to keep her company. Here in the city the living are less tolerant. She drinks, shuddering and wagging a finger at her reflection. *Imagine how tough, if you had to survive* here *again.*

"Tomorrow's news, tomorrow's opportunities! Jobs? Apartments?

Steal a jump on the competition! Buy your *Daily Mirror* right now!"
Black sweatshirt. Beard stubble and in a hurry. This one fits her idea of
a student. He's doing a job she once did. She signals. He pulls a paper
from his bag and folds it with a deft one-handed slap. "Mark fifty, lady."

He is staring at her, she senses, while she struggles to tug loose change
from her pocket.

As he backs off toward the open door, flinging papers and catching
coins in midair, a passing waitress lifts away Kaethe's plate.

"Crying shame, isn't it?" comments the waitress. Her long nail taps
a front-page photo.

The photo is subtitled "Street Children," but the somber three caught
in the camera's range (boy with a fine metal chain fixed in eyebrow and
lip, boy sunk in hooded sweatshirt, butch-shaved girl with delicate
swastikas tattooed round her neck) all look past childhood, twenty or
older. To decipher the text Kaethe has to set her sticky candlestick
directly on the page.

EMERGENCY ASYLUM
Berlin, (dpa). Every year the Children's Emergency Service takes in
1500 cases. Most stay only one or two days. Nobody can or wants to hold
on to them. The Service is no lock-up institution. Nights, around two or
three o'clock, the street kids turn up, the homeless and prostitutes, boys
and girls, all in all an estimated 7000 of them living today in Berlin—

It is truly late. If only the old pub were still here in Savignyplatz, she
would walk no farther than the corner, then dive down five stairs to
sleep on her bench. Kaethe is refolding the paper, pocketing her glasses.
She thinks, *seven thousand!* An army of aging children, drifting loose in
this city, is that number possible? But at least this is June. Month of sunshine and roses. The army of seven thousand have the whole summer
ahead of them . . .

When Kaethe stands up her left leg suddenly buckles. She struggles
desperately to stay upright, performing for all disapproving onlookers
a comical, desperate dance with a mismatched partner—gripping the
little table as it reels under her like an inspired ouija board.

the currency
of stories

BEYOND THE RAINBOW
COLLECTIVE

Sophie von Thall knew she wasn't what they had expected—though no one said what that was. A boy, perhaps. Her father, lumbering down the hall on hands and knees with Sophie astride, her fists twisting his necktie and collar, called her "Wild Amazon," sometimes the "Gypsy Changeling." When ladies in shops bent low to examine her, prepared to coo about family resemblances, they soon straightened up in disconcerted silence. Even her mother, while tickling Sophie into helpless shrieks of bathtime laughter, murmured, "What star did you fall off from?" smuggling kisses past Sophie's flailing arms. "Who sent you, Little Stranger?"

What difference, what they called her? A surprise or not, she belonged fiercely to her parents. And certainly by the age of four she seemed to possess some sort of answer to the question: *who are you?* Sophie: what there was of her then. By age four, about the height of a three-shelf bookcase. A tallish, sway-backed child with out-curved tummy, high-hunched shoulders, dimpled elbows, unevenly angled feet. The suggestive blue-gray of her irises was only revealed in bright daylight, generally her eyes appeared improbably black, and would settle on people with a shining, motionless gaze that led her grandmother to predict a bent for moral philosophy, and provoked unease in strangers. Her hair was rust-brown and coarse and impossible to keep combed.

Her mother, she noticed, couldn't bear much confinement. Mamma (Kaethe in Papa's Prussian drawl, the long "aee" following by a tongue-flick of "teh!") kicked off her winter blankets, refused to wear warm stockings or sweaters, and would sometimes scoop Sophie up and burst into a run (gasping with satisfaction, her net grocery bag swinging like a bell as she swerved through the indignant crowds) for no reason other than impatience with the limits of walking. To nosy strangers Mamma explained that she was a foreigner, recently arrived, about to move on. Their sour faces accepted the fib as "we thought so."

Sophie launched her own experiments in moving on early.

The very first time she ran away (by scrambling up onto the Rose-neck bus behind an unwitting maternal backside, to ride all the way to the line's end in the scorched, spired heart of West Berlin) her aim wasn't so much to leave home as to explore the Outside, that hard-to-picture world that absorbed and returned her parents every day with matter-of-fact regularity, but returned them nonetheless changed—either electrified or bone-tired, joyful or disturbingly sad.

Climbing down from the bus she recognized the entrance to the Zoological Garden from former, family outings. A sense of destiny flooded her, of harmonious benevolent forces visibly at play. She easily ducked under the zoo turnstiles without paying, as a momentary member of a large, chaotic family. She wandered the paths between model habitats, feeling as the shadows stretched out increasingly thirsty and lightheaded, revisiting rare animals that looked less sleek and happy than she remembered. They stared directly at her as if intent on conveying an urgent message, now that she had managed to come here alone, able to linger and give them her full gaze and attention.

The paths were emptying when a uniformed zookeeper squatted down to ask Sophie her name. The moment she answered he took her hard by the wrist. Into an office. Two policemen joined them in the stuffy little room. She pursed her lips against the offered cup of Orangina because she needed badly to pee and saw no bathroom anywhere. Mamma and Papa burst in together and tried both to hug Sophie at the same time, and snapped at the police. The police growled back. Papa accused the police of "ignorant mistreatment"; they shot back with "criminal neglect." Sophie, near to wetting herself, whispered her difficulty. Mamma led Sophie out into the dark and stood guard while Sophie tugged down her underwear and squatted between the bushes. She watched a full moon tangle itself in the branches. Mamma asked low, "Why? What was the trouble? A problem at school? Or did you simply miss me? Did you go looking for me, was *that* why?" But Sophie held silent, listening to the small patter of her urine on leaves. Then, with a shiver of delight, she heard the lioness roar.

Mamma, of course, was the one who ran away. Not every day, but often. Everyone knew she had 'come from America'. Sophie understood that America was quite close compared to a star, was that where Mamma went some weekday mornings? She set out after Papa had gone to work, after putting on slithery clothes and spraying her chest with a scent that smelled like crushed peonies. Mamma's good-bye kiss was light and glancing, as if she feared that Sophie would delay the departure. But in late afternoon Mamma's return hug was boisterous, as though in the Outside she had won some terrific battle or prize. Papa wasn't supposed to know. Not about dangerous adventures, nor that Sophie had been left in the never predictable care of the old lady who kept a little apartment in the back of their house. By suppertime, when Sophie's own gleeful anticipation of Papa's return kept her hopping and cartwheeling from room to room, the delicious smell on Mamma had faded and all Sophie's clowning could earn from her was a nervous, absent smile. Her eyes looked inward.

These were to Sophie the unmistakable signs that Mamma had been running away, instead of going where she was allowed to.

Sophie's interest in the Outside grew voracious. Sometimes she managed to slip away and explore new streets for hours without the old-lady-in-back or anyone else having any idea she'd been gone. Only once did she become hopelessly lost; a neighbor delivered her home on the back of his bicycle at dusk. Again there was yelling. Papa shouted, "All right, stick her in the damned kindergarten, if you can't or won't live up to your responsibilities!" Mamma shouted back, "You spoil her rotten! You worship her in all the wrong ways. How will she ever learn to figure out the real world—unless she's with *other children?*"

Other children.

Mamma and Papa, arm in arm for the special moment, blew good-bye kisses to Sophie through the locked gate of the "Rainbow Anti-Authoritarian Children's Collective." Mamma looked so stricken over getting her own way that Sophie felt guilty too. Once her parents had driven off and all waving was over, she turned to confront people her own age. A tall, slippery, spiked iron fence kept everyone inside the play-yard, which surrounded a low building painted with rubbery, grinning stick figures and huge flowers. Inside was where the teachers stayed. They were gentle, long-haired young men and women ("Hop-heads and draft-dodgers," said Papa with a laugh) whose efforts to talk like four- and five-year-olds made them incomprehensible.

They were blind, as she soon found out. Blind as if struck by a spell.

The yard was raked dirt, punctuated by islands of rank bushes, and "imagination equipment." The Rainbow children ran around crazy with boredom, screaming or whispering; they had almost no regular voices left, and were always hoarse and phlegmy from lingering colds. They divided into Hunters and Prey. The Hunters, self-titled, were all boys, and they Preyed on weaker boys and the girls. The victim was chosen apparently by sheer random group impulse—that was part of the rules—and chased by Hunters round and round the Hut and up and down the climbing structures until she fell down from fear and exhaustion and they piled on to dig and twist and pinch. Sometimes, as if disgusted, they untangled themselves and pulled away, and left the Prey merely dirt-smeared and shaking.

On Sophie's third day, Kommiss (that was one Hunter's play-yard name) pointed to her. "That girl's a Blackie. Take her!"

But when the Hunters closed in, chortling and poking forked fin-gers at her eyes, she barely blinked. And when someone touched her she grabbed his grimy arm with both hands and dug stubby nails in. He shrieked, exaggerating his pain. Three or four Hunters jumped her to the ground and grabbed blouse, skin, hair, a fistful of cheek, what-ever they could get of Sophie. She made no sound. She kicked their legs, punched with her elbows and sank her own throbbing teeth into someone's salty-tasting palm, while the other children looked on, hud-dled in a screening circle.

Suddenly everything stopped. Kommiss and his team turned their backs on her, wiping their fingers on their leather pants as though she had disappeared. In wordless agreement they moved toward a boy whose yard-name was Schmaltz.

"Schmaltzie!" Pebbles ground in Komiss's throat. "Schmaltzie, Schmaltzikins, come over *here* to me..."

The Prey spurted off. They chased him, crowing, exhilarated. When they eventually grabbed Schmaltz with eight hands at once, they dragged him into a man-high stand of rhododendron bushes. They ordered him to take off his shirt and shoes and socks, and they tied him to a leafless but still strong trunk-stalk. His suspenders round his wrists, arms raised over his head. It was a hard job of tying-up. Schmaltz's thin ribs heaved with suppressed sobs. His nipples were a bright red: like lipstick spots, said Kommiss. Schmaltz tried to avoid seeing anyone; his pale eyes stared up through the bud-heavy branches as if all that mattered was the shapes of moving clouds. In ones and twos the Hunters drifted away, went into the Hut for their milk and fruit snack. They forgot him. It was a while before Schmaltz began to babble and cry.

Sophie walked to him through the screen of glossy leaves. When she set to undoing the rope-knots, Schmaltzie watched her working fingers with a look of hatred.

She ran away again. With a toy spade she dug a depression under the iron fence, behind the rhododendrons, and wriggled to the Outside on her belly, like a dog. What she wanted was to catch up with her Mamma. To find out whether on these mornings alone she was staying in the house, or still running away. They could run away together ... but standing now on the hushed, tree-arcaded street like her own but not the same, she realized she didn't even know the way home.

She skipped fast, then cut into a path between houses, to escape the sight-line of the Hut. The narrow path led steeply downward, turning into stone steps. Sophie bounced down, flew down, holding to an iron rail, singing songs from America her mother liked to sing to her. "Big Rock Candy Mountain." "I've been working on the Railroad." Sophie could pronounce most of the syllables in the right order; she had pictures in her head of what they meant. The steps twisted. In German she sang the song of a game her father had taught her. *Taler, Taler, Du musst wandern / Von der einen Hand zur and'ren* ... Players sang this while passing a coin secretly from one hand to the next behind their backs. When the song ended, the 'it' person had to guess who held the wandering coin ...

Ahead loomed woods. Sunbeams striking through thickets. A stretch of damp brown sand, cerulean water beyond. The path widened, inviting her to the lake's very edge. The shore looked deserted: Mid-September was cold for swimmers, and Tuesday was a workday. She heard the slap-suck of small waves as they tossed soapy foam up along the muddy land's edge. Black-velvet ducks with round blue eyes zig-zagged on the water. She noticed another movement further down the sand. A young man, naked except for a wool scarf he'd forgotten to take

off with the rest of his clothes, faced the lake. He was rising and folding, rising and folding head to knees. Without interrupting these exer-
cises, he waved. Sophie waved back.

In time the figure approached. Sophie saw him age with each step:
despite suntanned, broad shoulders and strong, knotted chest and thighs
the beach-man wasn't young, but ancient. He did after all wear an old
man's drooping, scanty brown bathing bikini. His long hair wasn't
blond but a yellowish white. And he had no scarf; it was only a tangled
beard that blew back over his thin, corded neck.

"Diver ducks." He pointed.

"Yes, I know they are."

"What do people call *you?*" He had an echoing voice, as if his wide
chest was completely empty inside. The ducks thrashed up tiptoe on
the surface of the water as if to fly, then settled back again.

"Sophie."

"*Sophie.* Been out tramping this wilderness long?"

She nodded proudly.

"Hungry, then?"

"Not so . . ."

"Not *so?* Wait here. I have just what you'll like. Seek and ye shall
find. You wait here."

The man strode off into the woods, and returned toting a gray, frayed
rucksack. He sat down crosslegged, pulling his callused bare feet up to
rest on top of each gnarled knee, and gestured for Sophie to do the same.

She worried that his food would be inedible. Instead it looked delicious. There was milk in a metal canister, and roughly carved oval sand-
wiches of brown bread and mild butter-cheese.

He offered a share. His beard fluttered along the stringy outstretched
arm. "Not afraid of me, girl?"

"No!" She laughed, and so did he.

He watched her eat. He asked, "Are you a princess, girl?"

"No. Probably a countess, when I grow up."

"Hah. You come from the fine folk."

When he asked where home was, exactly, she shrugged. It wasn't
correct for a grown-up to ask her address, Papa had said, only the police.
Papa knew all about correct. She mumbled merely "near Roseneck."
The bearded man paid no mind; he told her he lived by the lake all year.
She envisioned his lumpy, bare feet stomping through snow, and shiv-
ered. He needed the peace, he said: he was a practicing hermit.

"Practicing for what?"

"Practicing . . . for a *Saint*." He laughed as if laughing hurt his hollow chest. He pitched out crumbs to entice the wary ducks closer. "To live among the angels. 'Last year's poverty was not yet perfect. This year poverty is absolute.' Ach, you call yourself Sophie? But you don't understand."

Sophie recalled pictures on the walls of Grandmother's bedroom. Saints with their eyes rolled up toward heaven. The blood drained from their greenish faces. (*These are icons,* Grandmother said. *Symbols of mankind's transcendent faith.*) "I saw a saint, actually," said Sophie. "Yesterday."

"So. And what did this guy look like?"

"A boy. Young, not all strong and bumpy like you. They stabbed him in the chest and tied him to a tree and left him there to suffer and cry. For the sins of mankind. He prayed to the Heavenly Ghost to come down with a two-sided sword and release him."

"Well. My, my. *Sum ergo cogito.* Christ only knows what you saw. And heard. Sophie."

The ducks were growing bolder. He had tossed out all his own breadcrusts when a different creature appeared, scuttling along the water line. As the intruder approached, the ducks arrowed to deeper water, leaving bread to float near shore, untouched.

"Wise girl. Share out some of yours, now," said the man. "Feed the kitty. . . ."

Sophie looked at him closely. He didn't smile. Only rude children with no upbringing would tell an adult he was flat-out wrong, or crazy. At home Sophie had been pleading for a pet. A kitty seemed her best chance. But Mamma, although she always paused to stroke and talk to cats they met on the street, refused to allow one of their own.

"*Anima mundi.* Don't you be a stingy girl."

She shrugged, and flipped out a shred of cheese, which the visitor snatched in its undershot jaw. Anyone could see that this creature, with its long, sloped head, twitching nose, high humped gray rump and naked, scaly tail, was no sort of kitty.

She whispered, "He certainly is hungry."

"In perpetuity, Sophie. The gnawer. Ever insatiable. That's his fate. Blessed are they that *do* hunger and thirst . . ." He was drawing in the sand with a triangular stone. She began to recognize the lake's shape, scratches for trees, a snaking path to the diamond of Roseneckplatz.

"Is that a map? For me to go home?" Suddenly tiredness did grip her. And fear, along with a piercing longing for Mamma's laugh, for Papa's strong lifting hands. "The way to go *back?*"

At her changed voice the long-tailed visitor rose on its hind legs, rigid with suspicion.

"Feed him more. Continue so. *Omnes et unum.* Let your light shine, Sophie!" She tossed another morsel, and another. The beach-man went on drawing, while rocking forward from his waist, firmly back and forth as if swayed by music nearby. The ducks paddled at a wary distance. The sky danced swiftly across the lake and from there sparked to the surface of the rat's ruby eyes, which took in Sophie's every move.

PROLOGUE TO
THE NIGHT

The undying light of these June evenings shimmies as if refracted through ice. Latitude circa 52 degrees north. In more southerly parts of the world, Massachusetts for instance, even in summertime darkness blows in between the stars by eight or nine o'clock. In the solid dark a person feels warmer, centered. In her half-ruined farmhouse far out in the country, Kaethe felt less exposed than she does here: there, the moody weather gave companionship; even violent storms set trees creaking, branches flying. But here she is city-alone, in the *anomie* of urban sociologists (Horkheimer, Weber, Reisman and the other black-listed texts displayed in casual defiance on the shelf by Max Schalk's bed): mute and ringing with echoes, scrutinized and invisible.

The brilliant stamina of this light forces her to press on for twelve or fourteen hours a day riding the bus lines, the high parabolic S-Bahn trains, the underground U-Bahn trains. And to keep on walking. The city encompasses 883 square kilometers. Every day its legal population of over three million swells by an uncounted flux of war refugees, smugglers and anarchists, dropouts and runaways. Her search for one and only one among them isn't completely blind: she has a method of sorts if nothing so complex as a strategy. She pictures the city laid out like a living map, glowing in certain corners and intersections above or under street level where the uncounted illegals gravitate to each other's company, cadge food and survival tips, entertainment and laughter, cheap drugs or free medical aid. Quadrant by quadrant, she's filling in the map.

She's a stranger who has lived well over half her life here. Her anonymity now is a tribute to the size of the city. Or has everyone she used to know also left? Of course there are some districts she has yet to revisit, where someone—an old classmate, a former neighbor, or perhaps assistant pastor Mathias Leytenfeger leaning out his window to knock dottle from his pipe—might give her a piercing squint or even shout out her name. She has not gone back to Szredskistrasse. Or to Magdalenenstrasse or Königsallee, not to the Grünewald Lake, nor out to Potsdam, not yet . . .

In this extended twilight (sky spookily invigorated by the tantric embrace of moon and sun, although the earth and shrubs below have turned to black silhouettes) Kaethe on sore feet threads her way through tables and chairs set out on the pavement. There is hardly a block in the city that doesn't host one or more colonies of round metal tables, and by evening they are all occupied by customers who eat, or drink, or merely argue with swooping movements of arms and neck. Grinning, they holla at each other, at children patrolling the gutter on scooters, at friends spotted across the street. The groups multiply, meld into clans, spill toward the center of the cobbled streets.

Romany children and Ukrainian fiddlers and masked clowns work the crowds for pocket change and mocking applause. The clowns bow, upping index fingers at tightwads. In the sweep of their sizing-up glances, Kaethe is an unperson. She sits down at a crumb-strewn table on a nameless side street to order a salad, and bends with difficulty to loosen her shoes. While she waits the other tables fill three rows deep, children crawl on fathers' legs, men kiss women perched on their laps, women embrace women.

From a demobbed Russian soldier working the Reichstag flea-market Kaethe has bought a green canvas bag, a capacious buckled pouch that she wears slung across her body to foil pickpockets. Inside are her wallet, address book, certain letters, pencils, pens, the city map, a few newspaper clippings, face powder, reading glasses—and the two photographs sheathed back to back in plastic that she pulls out now carefully, as she has done many times this day and the days before.

Suddenly dusk is dropping quickly. She stands and brings her photos to the nearest table. "Excuse me! May I bother you a moment? I wonder if you can recall having seen this young woman anywhere?"

A Brecht-imitator, wire glasses and gray stubble-hair, pinches a corner of the photo-sheath for intent scrutiny. Kaethe holds her corner tight.

"Original," he announces. "Pretty, in a dry way. She's called?"

"Sophie."

He looks around his table to shaking heads. "At least not the Sophie *we* know," he says. Someone chuckles.

She shows the pictures to a pan-pipe player, and to a clown who points to his own painted tear. A woman asks with cold suspicion, "How do we know you aren't a spy or cop, after the kid?"

Kaethe tilts the photo to catch the last light. The girl in close-up is looking straight at the camera. A squarish face: the wide jaw and full lips seem to promise a quip or a quirk. The lips are generously curved, ebullient, like those of an Attic Apollo. Her eyes are wide-spaced, deep-set, opaque. Her exposed ears lie furled tight to the skull, pale as the insides of oyster shells against whirlwind chopped hair: reddish black with yellow streaks, the colors of smoldering straw.

"Sorry to have disturbed you." Kaethe returns to her own place. One by one the spare chairs have been subtracted from her table, which she continues to have all to herself. The waiter finally brings the wrong salad. He lights a candle. The clowns and musicians have drifted away.

It's a quarter to midnight and drizzle hangs in the air. Her hips are stiff, her ankles swollen from walking. She's hungry again but there will be no more food tonight. The brass plaque lettered "Pension Zur Kurfürstin, Prop. Rahel Loewnfus" sweats rain under the streetlamp. Kaethe trails numb fingers over it on her way in.

In the corridor she carries her shoes in her hand. As she passes the kitchen a husky, laconic voice rings out, already familiar. "Up so late, Countess? Do come join me!"

For a room that churns out twenty or thirty heaping breakfasts every morning of the year, the kitchen is improbably tiny. Prewar white enamel stovework lines one wall (the window above opens to the courtyard where the Drossel sometimes sings). Sinks on bulging legs and cabinets fill another wall. A blue-washed farm table covered with an oilcloth occupies the rectangular middle of the room. Now, under concentric wheels of light from one hanging bulb, a moist sheen of recent attention is evaporating from every surface and object—the iron burners have been scrubbed by a sooty toothbrush, the floor-mopping rag rinsed and laid folded at the threshold for a shoe-wipe, the peelers and parers and graters hung from hooks.

Kaethe plants her chin on cold fists, her elbows on the tablecloth (faded roses climbing faded blue lattice). She inhales the scent of herbed soap with a rush of nostalgia. Homesickness: a resurgent anticipation of pleasures past...

But homesickness has no business with her. In times gone by she might have called this country, or at least this city "home," but she wasn't born here and has since, having lost the last shreds of protective ignorance, chosen to leave. Moreover this is a hotel kitchen, nobody's home. Its cloistered smells of nutmeg and soap, boiled milk and green onions, and the specific *German-ness* of a crude woven mop-rag and glass jars of preserved carrots and beans, and the long, tong-shaped igniter which, when squeezed with determination, flashes a spark into the stove's sweetly leaking gas pilot—all this, she thinks, merely reminds her (with the force of ambush) of a Kaethe who once was. It's not the old apartments (Szredskistrasse, Königsallee), and their cavernous, tiled kitchens she's longing for. It's simply to be their Kaethe again. In the same way, she thinks, the stumbled-on photo of a discarded lover can surprise you to tears, not because you're sorry to have lost track of him (a callow cad then, probably an over-ripe, paunchy cad now) but because in his silver-film eyes you glimpse a girl he saw: irreverent, stubborn, broke, with as many futures radiating from her as threads from a spider's web.

"I have my nights," says Frau Loewnfus, smiling hermetically around her cigarette. "Same as you, tonight. Music doesn't help. The television makes me nauseous, all that hypocritical gesturing. I can't read, but sometimes I flip through the illustrateds, only the trashiest stuff. I become insatiably hungry! For spring strawberries—here, please taste some of these, *please,* they won't keep, look how scarlet, not chemically ripened for the store, I picked them myself this morning. In the fall I gorge on hazelnuts. In winter, oranges. Simple. I am a simple woman. Some nights, I find myself talking to Lies, if she's been out late and stops in here. What a luxury, to have someone who will merely sit and listen. A passing stranger makes the ideal listener. An employee is second-best. God knows what Lies makes of the stories I've told her. But don't be misled—she has her depths, our Lies."

"She isn't related to you?"

"Lies? My God, no! Oh, that *would* be funny."

"Somehow I thought she might be your daughter, or niece. Well, the red hair . . ."

"Top-grade Nile henna. Obviously she has her own source. Acquaintances say she mimics me but I can't see a trace of resemblance, myself. When I was younger, back when we were living in Belgium, my hair used to be dark brown, with a shine like a brazil nut. My son's curly locks, exactly the same."

"So do you come originally from Belgium . . . Rahel? May I say Rahel?"

"May I say 'Countess'?"

"No. You're making fun."

"And would a Belgian ever make fun? There's your answer. No, I was born here in Berlin, right in that sunny front room that is now my study. However, soon after my debut in the capital of the Third Empire my parents found it necessary to pack up and leave town. Luckily they had the means to scrape together the bribe needed to keep two adults and a toddler out of the Grünewald KZ transport, and then managed to stay one jump ahead of the SS, across borders and hidden, thanks to Socialist solidarity. Or more bribes. But they lost sight of each other. I have no first-hand memory of my mother. After forty-five my father couldn't muster the heart to move back to Germany, let alone Berlin. And of course his only fortune was this building, which the Nazis had confiscated. Papi didn't have enough energy or faith or anger left even to attempt to prove ownership. These days I no longer blame him. But *then* . . . Well, of course I married, in those days all good girls married, didn't we? My husband was a professional altruist. A dull, kind man. I followed his career from Antwerp to Brussels and eventually back into Germany. To Hamburg. I was a supportive wife—well, not always, but I embraced that worthy goal, starting out, at least. I didn't know yet that self-sacrifice is a form of vanity. But listen to me, rambling on! I think it's your turn, now."

"So you have a son?"

"Aaron. Yes. Our only child. He's not—but that's a separate story. Maybe for another time. Right now, I'm curious to hear how your research went today."

"My what?"

"Lies keeps me posted on the little events that occur here. Lies said that at breakfast you showed her photos of a young woman you are looking for."

"Yes, that's true. My daughter. I only asked Lies because they seem about the same age."

"Lies is such a fabulating goose! She's convinced you're on the trail of the 'other woman.' Of course, in some families a daughter does play the 'other woman' part, no? So, is she a von Thall offspring? Judging by the illustrateds, they're all over West Germany. A fertile bunch, no offense. Sponsoring this, inaugurating that, accepting a post as—"

"The family's had since the thirteenth century to propagate, after all."

"Lizards don't change their scales. Which one was your husband? From the rich branch of the family, or the heroic branch?"

"I was married to Achim Friedrich Johannes von Thall. Who I mostly called Joe."

"Achim . . . The one down in Munich? But isn't he married to the Bavaria Beer heiress? A chesty, photogenic blonde. Whereas he has the noble profile."

"Yes."

"So, the heroic branch, but *with* gelt. Perfect. One always assumed the beer-Brunhilde was his first wife. Not you. Why hasn't anyone ever heard of you?"

"My good luck. It's terribly late, Frau Loewnfus. Time that I turn in."

"Oh, please, forgive. Forgive me, Kaethe Schalk! It *is* late. So much talk makes me tipsy. I only wanted to show you hospitality. You see, I'm used to having guests arrive here with tales in their baggage, confessions they're dying to unload. With me they are in luck—because I don't remember worth a bean. I listen deep into the night, brew this rosehip tea fresh (everything has to be fresh) but later I can't remember. The stories mix up in my head like those tri-sected picture books we had as children, remember? Goat's head on top, giraffe's torso, chicken feet. Scrambled. So all secrets are safe with me."

"But I'm not hiding any secrets."

"Of course you're not. Oh, will you look at Boris! When his legs jerk like that he's dreaming. In dog years my old friend is near eighty, after all. His breath is dreadful, nothing to be done, it's either his stomach or his teeth. Look, do I seem pushy to you? Nosy is the last thing I want to be. Please be frank. All my life, I've detested such people. And clearly you're not in the habit of talking about yourself. I respect that."

"Nobody phoned here for me today, did they?"

"Not today. Not a single call since you arrived. More tea? When did you last see your daughter?"

"This is some special variety, isn't it? Thank you. I saw her ... last August. Nearly a year ago. Only for one day. In a beer garden, in Munich. She had moved back into her father's house. Before that she was living on a sort of collective farm. She refused visits from outside. A 'biosphere' they called it, everything 'alternative.' Where they weave wool from their home-raised sheep, grow and grind their own grains ..."

"Probably dig their own latrines. Sounds like a resourceful girl. I'm sure she'll come up fine, wherever she is. Here, let's drink to her health with a drop of Trappist bitters!"

"I shouldn't. I want to be out early again tomorrow."

"Don't go yet. Why be in such a hurry to go back to an empty room, to lie down all agitated and upset, praying for sleep? *This* will help you fall asleep."

"Half a drop, then."

"Wise decision. The first thing a newborn learns is how to fall asleep, and how to wake up. Yes? Crossing those simple thresholds. But somehow I've lost the knack. Can't sleep, can't wake up properly either. Have you ever had the sensation of waking up with no shimmer of an idea where you are? Yes? I'm almost used to it, I wake—and don't know where, or when, or *who* I am. I go to the mirror and meet a face: this nose, this pale mole, these gouged corners of the mouth—these eyes that look back at me like those of a stubborn serpent being prodded by a stick.

"It's only when I begin to paint on my make-up—all laid out on the dresser like a reminder from the night before—that my role here in the pension returns to me.

"Yes, my role, that's how I think of it. I *won* this part! It was pure coincidence. I was still living, if you could call it that, in Hamburg, shortly after my husband's suicide (no, please don't say anything) and without a purpose, when a lawyer from the Restitution Office in Berlin called. The Loewnfus house is intact, he said, and belongs to you. It's your duty to come to Berlin. This *house*. In Hamburg, I had been sav-

ing up pills, sedatives from a prescription. There are idiot-proof recipes
for how to succeed at ending yourself, you know; you can pick them up
as flyers in an *alterno*-shop. I needed only another month worth of the
prescription but in the meanwhile I couldn't sleep lying in a bed, at best
I dozed propped up, like a horse or a stork. That was six years ago—"

"Only six years? What took them so long?"

"Well, see, the Wall had come down, which at the time I scarcely
noticed, and apparently some observant beetle chewing through musty
files stored in the East-zone war archives found a Third Reich Document of Dispossession bearing my parents' names—as well as mine, for
legal thoroughness. All in impeccable order. Stamped. Fingerprinted.
Print of my baby-hand, too. Heil Hitler!

"While the lawyer waited on the line I heard someone laughing. Me!
You understand? It was such a relief. No more decisions to make, not
even about when and how and where to swallow sufficient pills . . .
Instead, to have a paperpusher call up out of the blue and in that bored,
bureaucratic tone simply *tell* me what to do next! Myself, I hadn't
spoken a word or heard a human voice for weeks. The telephone was
about the only thing left in the flat, since it couldn't be sold. . . . The
lawyer pressed me till I croaked an answer. 'I'll make it to Berlin, naturally, yes.'

"My promise meant snap. I could still have ducked out. But that
blissful shake-up was a catharsis. It's hard to die laughing! I felt as weak
and unconnected as if I'd swallowed the pill-hoard and slept straight
through a lifetime. Maybe that's how death is: an enormous, silent shift
in awareness. A new role to play. Were you raised in any faith, Kaethe?"

"Raised looking on, if you like. By my grandparents. Strict duty-
idolizing Lutherans. But not raised *in*."

"Listen. Rahel . . ."

"Your glass is empty again."

"Suddenly so tired."

"I perfectly understand."

"I have nothing to hide, understand? No secret. On the contrary.
Find. If you can help—here. Her picture. See? My sunshine. Sophie."

"She's lovely."

"She's missing."

"Children do go missing. Often for years. Tell me, did you quarrel?"

"No. Her father had the legal custody, until she became *grown up*.

Nice distinction but what does it mean? Sofchen . . . can be stubborn.
Like me. On her own since sixteen. Sometimes her father sent her
money. I tried. A few years ago she went to live with him. With *them*.
Two weeks ago he wrote to me. Never did before—that's a measure of
desperation. He is perpetually busy—he always disliked the vacuum of
a quiet evening, a free hour. He hired detectives to trace Sophie but they
turned up nothing. He always has worshipped experts but I, well, I
know what detectives are. So I came here myself."

"Why to Berlin? Just because every lost kid seems to end up here in
the Calcutta of Europe?"

"No. It's because here is where we lived together, we were happy
here! Of course, Sofchen might be in Calcutta, for all I know. And I'd
be wasting time."

"How is time wasted? Does she want to be found or not, isn't that
your question? Is she lost to herself, or only to you?"

"Oh, damn! Look what a mess I made! Clumsy—I'm sorry, I stood
up too fast!"

"The cloth is plastic, Kaethe. Everything washes out. No problem.
We'll leave it for Lies, in the morning. Forget it."

"All right. I'm going, now. To sleep. Thank you, Frau Loewnfus."

"Nothing to thank!"

"For your stories. For listening. For the drops."

"I'll walk you down to your room. Ready? Tzak-tzak! Out goes the
light."

"No! How can the sky already be so blue, so bright, how can that be?"

"Have you forgotten, Countess Kaethe? There is no real night, this
time of year."

Again fully clothed on the bed. Goosebumps. A dawn breeze inspires
the quartet of curtains to float and entwine. The unseen bird intones
his nightsong backwards. Kaethe sleeps waking, or else wakes inside
her own dream. There is the weight and presence of someone sitting
beside her, although the doorlock is plugged from inside with the giant
key. The smoky voice of Rahel Loewnfus proceeds without words:
there's only the rise and fall, an ongoing stream of inflections as she and
Kaethe go on fanning out their pictures and confessions.

THE STORY OF A
SELF-INVENTED MAN

Max, for the time being, gave Kaethe his own room. His whitewashed walls and posters of the Moscow Zirkus, his hard mattress on the floor.

For his daughter, longitude conspired with latitude: a time lag of six hours played into the hallucinatory early light so that she woke each morning, before the impatient bells of trams and the first delivery bicycles, to the intense muttering of mating pigeons. Under the eiderdown she stretched, stroking frayed fingernails down her sixteen-year-old ribcage and belly, the body that was in constant flux and change, much like the rest of her life. But she knew exactly where she was. She had gone from the high snow-and-rock fields of her grandparents' New England farm to a southern girls' boarding school, Gore Academy, and now from the heat and red earth and indigo nights of North Carolina across an ocean and half a continent, to rediscover her father. In the chilly brilliance of Berlin.

She pushed off the featherbed. Out on the hall landing a narrow door opened smack on a streaked, cracked porcelain toilet with a dangling wooden flush-pull. Back in the windowless central kitchen of the flat was a clawfoot tub; Kaethe stood upright and naked in it to sponge her goosepimpled skin with tepid water. She dressed in the semi-uniform of white cotton blouse, blue serge skirt. Only her underwear, gone slack and gray from washings with the suds-less socialist soap, was still

American-made—even Max couldn't locate an underground source for Playtex bras.

She set out breakfast for two. Chicory ersatz coffee, farmer's cheese smeared into fragrant rolls she bought downstairs from the bicycle vendor—paying with a few of the slippery gray East-marks stamped with hammer and sextant that weighed less than plastic toy-coins used for games in America. Max never exacted meal-fixing or any other specific chores from her but he beamed to find the table arranged: murmuring *schoenen Morgen, mein Liebstes,* he kissed her cheek so swiftly and expertly that her ear buzzed. She inhaled the baking soda and mint he used to brush his teeth.

More and more he guided her toward speaking only German. The language was familiar to her mind, from infancy and mother's songs and from her school lessons, but not to her body. During the first weeks the muscles of her throat and tongue and lips had ached from this unaccustomed exercise, the effort to make vowels and consonants exactly echo her father's—twirled *auch* reopening abruptly after its end, *der Weg,* the path or way, looping away from firm "g" to finish with the most tentative lisped "ch," *bisschen,* the little bit, briefly baring the lower teeth. (Although imitating Max, she heard in her own conversation the wry smiles and inflections of her mother.)

School began at 8:05 A.M. With a twitch of ministerial strings her father had enrolled her midterm in Obersekunda, as the eleventh year at the Lise-Meitner-Comprehensive School was called, and though she and Max treated her attendance there as a kind of experiment, it was a crucial experiment. He needed her out and away, far from his flat and his daily sphere of action. On a regular schedule. In a safe, known place.

She took classes in Geography, Mathematics, Composition, Chemistry and Physical Culture, dropping Russian as hopelessly unprepared. If her German was adequate for school, her degree of socialization was not. In a not unpleasant way she felt seen by teachers and pupils as a sort of barbarian, an historically and culturally impoverished personality, potentially dangerous unless she could be reformed. They were more wary than hostile; in fact some made tentative efforts to draw Kaethe closer, to tutor her by unspoken example. She enjoyed, they noticed, too much choice. In the bone-cold, bomb-scarred warren of a Gymnasium, under vaulted halls and ceilings that dwarfed the students hunched over their flat-armed chair-desks, her freedom clung to her like radioactive dust.

Whenever a teacher entered the class (Instructor of Geography Herr Doktor Drabke, say) students clattered to their feet, greeted formally in unison and stood at stiff attention until Drabke (say) barked, "Seat yourselves!" before turning his spitz-beard to the map of Siberian natural resources. Kaethe was always out of step, late to stand up. She possessed no natural salute. She tended, without conscious cause or intention, to suddenly grin. In Physical Culture her clumsiness on the Horse and the Rings and the Balance Bar led to her being sidelined as a risk to herself and her classmates—while they, performing a hierarchy of stunts, streamed over these leather-skinned obstacles in close formation like a herd of leaping deer.

She was notorious for questions. More than once during her first naive weeks she corrected a Professor's assertion. ("Wrong, sir: Eisenhower is *not* the chairman of the Ku Klux Klan.") At girls' recess, classmates lisped questions about Mickey and Goofy and Elvis. (They strolled in small circles close to the building; the playing fields were off-limits because of undetonated bombs under the thriving weeds.) Did she have jazz records and could she show them how to dance rock-and-roll? No, she regretted: no.

On the other hand, she discovered that certain phrases left in her head by books, poems and essays were texts that no one else here had or would likely ever have access to, and by her move into this school were transformed from loose baggage to charismatic contraband. In the recess-yard, casually, she dropped such names as Orwell and Sartre, Hemingway, Eliot and Pound. At lunch—often lentil soup, else 'Griess Suppe' a granular blubber-white paste, or cabbage stewed with shreds of luminous pork—Kaethe some days could pull from her bookbag a fat fresh orange tucked there by Max. ("Business thrives, Kaethe-cat. Eat before it rots!") The galvanizing scent of orange oil spurting from the ripped greenish skin made everyone nearby look up sharply, though not directly at Kaethe who held the fruit cupped in her right hand. None of her classmates had been in the same room with an orange before. She passed the segments around feeling both elevated and embarrassed, not noting who took them and saving only the last dewy piece to stuff in her own mouth. As long as "business was thriving," as Max put it, there would be mounds of oranges at home on the kitchen table, in a disintegrating jute bag stenciled *Haifa* or *Tblisi*.

In part from a handful of passionate teachers, more from reading her father's books and listening to his rambling, mental stone-skipping across the waves of history and the dialectic, she was discovering new heroes. The ambitious, erratic young Jew Karl Marx, nicknamed "Moor" by his wealthy socialite friend Engels, tearing the lid off bourgeois society to reveal its moral bankruptcy and convoluted seeds of self-destruction. Another Faust, as Max said, unable to hand Knowledge and Philosophy back to the devil, even when he wanted to. Karl Liebknecht and Rosa Luxemburg, the young Spartacist leaders murdered in the *German Revolution,* winter of 1919. And Bert Brecht, who set it all to music. Reading Brecht aloud, the clipped sardonic worker-slang of Berlin, Kaethe found a voice—sentences uncoiling their meaning nimbly and precisely—and even a harsh, assured laugh that she would never have heard nor imagined coming from herself before, at Gore Academy.

And unlike the Gore girl, whose bobbysocks had slumped down sadly into her saddle shoes as often as her barrettes lost their grip on her oily hair, who had no "pocket money" from "home" to stand treats with at the Ice Cream Dream, and who warded off all personal comments with a certain look, Kaethe in Berlin had a friend.

Jutta Bumcke was long-waisted, flat-chested, buttermilk-blond. Her hair curled up below her ears, thickly; her hair clips stuck in place even when she bounded from the Horse to the Rings to the sour-smelling rubber mat. After school, nearly wordlessly, she led Kaethe onto the tram, down streets still impassable with erupted pavement and chunks of masonry, to the smoked-brown stucco building where she lived with her mother, aunt and brother in three rooms. Father Bumcke, a railroad brakeman gone to Engineer Corps in the war, had vanished at Stalingrad. Now Jutta's smoldering brother had a room for himself.

Kaethe understood herself as Jutta's trophy. Shimmering with exotic colors, like a circus star or a North American bird, an oriole or bluebird—the birds of Germany being so drab. "Does your mother know where you are, child?" inquired Frau Bumcke.

"I live with my father. He doesn't expect me back until six." Her freedom sparkled like rodeo rhinestones all over her.

"Ach so! And what does your Herr Father *do?*"

This was perennially, from the first asking in a time before she was at all sure she had a father, a difficult question. That original moment had been in England; Kaethe was four, living with her mother in a DP-occupied asylum-castle called Babel by its inhabitants who worked in the surrounding fields, who spoke German, French, Yiddish, Dutch, and slept four or more to a room. Kaethe believed that her mother, called by everyone merely *Baerbel,* must be a close relation of the castle Babel, and she herself therefore a living, breathing descendant of the huge slab-hewn stones and parapets—from which platforms they all, the ragged rule-less children, pelted the honking, spurting, piebald geese in the moat with spoiled cabbage heads, until some old person, gabbling goose-like, chased them away from the fun.

"What does your father do?" A tall boy, with gray stubble-head and snot-glossed chapped lip, blocked her escape. *Was macht dein Papi?* Silence. "Is he a soldier? Is he dead in action?" Shrug. "Is he a Nazi?" The boy followed her all afternoon. "Nazi. Nazi-Kind. Nazi. Nazi." Like a dull cracked bell, while Kaethe walked ahead, not looking back at the voice until the moment nazinazinazi when she felt a burning deep below her mind. Going up in flames she turned and rammed her fiery head into the boy's long narrow stomach, so his air drifted out: Naaaah...

"My father," she told Frau Bumcke, who peered out of slanted gray green eyes identical to Jutta's, but set in a skin-maze of wrinkles. "My father works for the State." This was her first invitation to a Berlin home. Her first invitation into a friend's home, anywhere. "He works with the Ministry for the Interior."

Jutta sucked in her breath, thoughtfully, as good German girls are taught to do.

"Ach, so!" said the mother. "The Ministry! Interior . . . So is your father—?" Knuckles pressed against her mouth, she pondered her daughter's guest. Eventually she finished. "Oh, dear. My son says I'm a terror with idle questions."

She allowed the girls to escape together into the women's bedroom. Jutta shut the door. Kaethe was free of expectations but remembered what girlfriends at Gore often would do, afternoons in stifled silence, if chance gave them a closed door. The engrossing "games" of exploration carried out in hot, breathless concentration. *(You be the boy this time . . .)*

Jutta settled crosslegged on the floor, between high cliffs of twin beds. Kaethe imitated her. She wasn't a real Berlin schoolgirl yet, not like the genuine Jutta who all her life had hurried home punctually from the last class, who aspired to become a chemist or pediatrician, who wore, beneath her white short-sleeved blouse, nothing but a boy's thick-ribbed undershirt.

They worked on trigonometry. They labeled and colored their maps.

Kaethe was a last-minute understudy, mimicking every gesture, feeling her way into the diligent-Socialist-pupil story.

"Did you know we're having a week off in June, to work harvesting the strawberry fields? The whole school gets to go."

The whole school, squatting in flat, buggy fields. Work without pay. For the second time in a day Kaethe had a flash of Castle Babel. "I don't know if I can make it."

"You have to come, Kaethe Schalk! It's not voluntary."

"All right, so I will then. Sure!" Grinning into the lie. Her friend seemed impenetrably younger. Of all the things Kaethe could confide, was there one she would understand?

"Oh, *good.*" Jutta trapped Kaethe's shoulders in an impulsive squeeze. "And my mother approves of you, Kaethe. Honestly."

Imitation was exhausting, and on all subjects Jutta continued to be mysteriously boring. But Kaethe would come home with her again to study, and again, drawn by a deep, happy vibration she felt on entering the Bumckes' apartment—at being trusted, allowed to witness the mundane particulars of their photographs and Party tchochkes, cracked dishes and hopes, mended shoes and blankets. At penetrating her friend's home.

One of Kaethe's strengths, tutored by Max, was a tolerance for apparent contradictions.

Like every serious Communist she ran into, Kaethe despised apparatchniks, along with the proliferating nomenklatura who were busily commissioning their hideous, stark villas in the "garden district" of old Pankow. She despised equally the bootlicking bitchery of the Young Socialists, but most of all she despised the faithless. The "Zone-crossers." Myopic egotists, selling out for a mess of pottage . . . By the way, she asked Max, did you know that Esau's pottage in the Bible was really lentil soup? We get it nearly every day at school. . . .

At this historical turning point, as the Soviet Union prepares to grant our Democratic Republic complete sovereign recognition, we are hemorrhaging hundreds of workers each day to the West. So Max, reading to her from the paper *New Germany* over their supper together. *This State has no alternative but to take counter-action. We must by all means retain our educated, productive*—Deserters. Bribe-takers.

Oh, let the bastards all go, she said. Good riddance. Her teeth clacked hard, biting happily through black bread. Max didn't mind if she spoke with her mouth full. *We'll be that much stronger. It's a new kind of country, see?*

The Meitner School was too hidebound and conservative for Kaethe Schalk; she was running ahead.

In their beginning together, Max was a stranger. An intimate stranger, granted: the first man other than a doctor to lay his hand on her, a gracefully muscular man who kissed her goodnight and goodmorning with a possessive squeeze round her hips, who taught her to cook his favorite meals, who brought his women-friends by for brief, light-hearted introductions before leaving Kaethe to a night in their flat alone, and whose severe, squared hairline and quirked brows and fine-textured skin fascinated her. The original of her mirroring self.

Kaethe had experience in pleasing people she hardly knew.

She overheard him lament that the flat looked out of date, makeshift, too bohemian for his rapidly increasing responsibilities. What was needed was a more 'representative' home environment, a place where international colleagues would feel at ease. Kaethe ventured out lugging bags of citrus fruit and Lever soap powder, and returned lugging furniture: Jugendstil chairs, a veneered table, Persian rugs. Meissen plates and cups. Bags clanking full of silverware . . . Their dinner parties were about to begin.

"Horribly hot, tonight. Unusual."

"Isn't it the truth? Look, that candle flame doesn't stir! Not a millimeter. Too bad . . . All these goodies and I honestly don't think I can stomach a bite of anything tonight but fruit."

Max, at the head of the table, turned a blank, affectless gaze on the chatterbox to his left. This young woman, Kaethe bet, would not be invited again. Berlin, where the decimated stock of males tended to sport artificial arms or legs, justifying the yellow *handicapped* armband so eerily reminiscent of a certain earlier at-a-glance identifier, was swarming with her potential replacements. Even the women whose prettiness had improbably survived the war years and hunger years had a desperately available look in their eyes, and might be satisfied with nothing more than the gift of a fine meal in the company of a man who was well-spoken, and washed, and more or less sound of body and mind.

"Geisha," Max called them. The geisha on his right, beside the

Egyptian attaché, wore a sleeveless, full-skirted gauzy dress that made Kaethe sneeze. Across from the attaché, on Kaethe's right—from the foot of the table she faced her father—sat the tall, angular, wildly popular Russian poet, Dmitrov, who was pensively plunging a pair of cherries into his vodka glass.

In guttural, resonant Oxford English he said, "Winter or summer, fools never recognize their own happiness." The lights had been left off for an illusion of coolness. Only the one candle and a band of red horizon from the open casement behind Max illuminated the front room. Dmitrov's eyes scanned the dark walls. "If only I were back in Moscow I would not care how hot or cold the weather."

The two geisha pouted at each other, wide-eyed.

"For me," said the Egyptian, whose small potbelly made a natural cushion for his laced hands, "summer is the season of happy infatuation. In a lantern-lit boat floating on the Nile, at night—"

Kaethe frowned at the poet. "But you *do* live in Moscow. Don't you?"

"Sure. But is *quotation,* little angel. Is Meister Chekhov, darling. *Three Sisters.*" Dispensing forgiveness, his vodka-moist forefinger brushed the arch of her wrist.

"Even at your age," said Max to the plumply smiling attaché, "I would never have termed an infatuation 'happy'."

"Infatuation? Always ends in misery." Dmitrov held up a dripping cherry and slowly brought it closer to Kaethe's face, like a cajoling parent. "Come, little angel . . ." The alcohol singed her lips. She opened her mouth barely wide enough to accept. "So, Ekaterina. Beautiful. To the eternal Russo-German romance!" He tossed back what was left in his glass.

Max and the attaché did the same with theirs. The chatty geisha wordlessly sprang to her feet, to top up all glasses. Kaethe drank too, to drown the burning, swallowed the cherry in more cool fire. The Egyptian stood to propose honor to "General Gamal Abdel Nasser, and his drive for our national liberation! Freedom for Suez!" They all did the sentiment honor. It was this Suez-partisan, after all, who had brought the vodka. Settling back, the Egyptian cried, "Please, my friends, call me Hossan!" Max stood up next, a featureless outline against the night-purple western window. "To strengthening the bond between our working classes. To the solidarity of workers everywhere—our bulwark against the war-mongering strategies of international capital!"

"Bloodsucking profiteers," growled Dmitrov. "Hear, hear, hear!"

Glasses smashed on the dark walls. Hailstorm. One sailed through the open window to a tinkling end five stories below. The two geisha laughed self-consciously, uproariously, like children left up too long past normal bedtime. Kaethe, calculating the replacement cost in soap flakes and cocoa, went to the kitchen for fresh glasses. When she returned to the room a lamp had been turned on. The male guests clustered in loud conversation around Max, slapping the table for emphasis, while the women waited apart, smiling forlornly, brightening when Kaethe joined them.

"You still stuck in school, Schatz?" The gauze skirt rustled like a sheaf of wheat.

"The Lise-Meitner. But now we're on summer break." "Break" implied a return, but could she bear to re-enter that farce, the grim tedium, not to mention the approaching ordeal of exams she wasn't prepared for? Even less could she imagine herself returning to North Carolina, to the locust groves of Gore. During the four months of her "visit" neither she nor Max had broached the question of how long it would last. Arriving, she had assumed the reunion, however blissful, would be brief. But more recently Max had tossed off remarks that implied a longer future together. A shared life. She lived in a free-floating bubble of time, threatened only by the shadow of "What next?"

"I can hardly believe it," said the other geisha. Sad creases under her rich brown eyes. "Is it true you're really an Ami? You talk perfectly normal!"

"My mother was German. And, at school, I had a sweet biddy of a German teacher who—oh!" Kaethe clapped both hands to her mouth. Her sneeze exploded. The attaché laughed. Sad-eyes flinched, hissing *Gesundheit,* as Kaethe sneezed again. "Prosit!" Dmitrov called. Kaethe wiped her eyes and nose, apologizing.

"No harm, Schatz. You look cute when you sneeze! So—where were you born? Who was your Mutti, hm? Where did you grow up?" Germans, Kaethe thought, had a knack for bold interrogation.

"I was born in London, actually." Generally this claim raised her status. "Right in the middle of the War." She glanced up and over to Max for corroboration, but he was immersed in a conversation of his own. "After the Blitzkrieg started my mother and I were evacuated to the countryside. For farm work . . . She was still a German national, see—"

"Interned was she? Your poor Mutti? P.O.W.?"

"Well no, nothing that bad. I mean, the others weren't exactly prisoners. Baerbel—my Mutti—was more like a political refugee. Not that she ever had politics that I knew of . . . Her father was political, I think. He died before I was born. Pneumonia. She wasn't political. . . . Anyway, she must have been so young then. Hard to imagine." Kaethe looked out toward the window, the night, Dmitrov. His unblemished, waxen complexion in the heat. "Actually my mother was, she was hardly older than I am now. School-age. When she had me."

"Happens every day, sweetheart. And the poor girl left to fend all alone? So how did she maneuver your Papi back into the picture?" Following Kaethe's example, the sadly mascaraed eyes swiveled to the far end of the table.

"What front did your Papi fight on?"

"East or West?"

"Wait. I don't think you understand—" Again she stopped. Did these guests have any inkling that Party office-holder Max Schalk, unlike his German wife and their mixed daughter, had been born and brought up a Yankee? *Bite your tongue, Kaethe-cat.* It was the fault of vodka and the heat wave that she was babbling, trying to make herself important to a pair of gossipy geisha.

How much of Max's life was she free to tell? For that matter, what did she know for sure? How much of what she *thought* she knew for sure came from Max's edited public version of his history, or sprang from the quicksand reminiscences of her grandparents? Finally, how much was her mother's sometimes wishful, sometimes vengeful, embroidery?

"Max was off fighting fascism." What statement could be safer? "Only in his twenties, but he saw the disaster coming. He volunteered. Totally committed to the struggle."

"He couldn't very well drag a family along," mused Sad-Eyes.

"Max? No kidding. A hero of the Resistance," concluded Gauze.

Kaethe didn't blink. No call for pedantic correction. She kept a photograph filed in her memory of a razor-faced boy in a double-breasted uniform; RAF, according to Baerbel, who propped the photo in its cracked leather frame on bureaus of one rooming-house after the next. *It was your father's Mut, his confidence I fell for. But everyone did. Nothing could stop him—he ran off the farm to Canada to join the war effort early, before the U.S. finally kicked in. Not many did that. The Canadians loaned him to British Intelligence but then the Amis claimed him back. He was precious, on account of his background he understood some Deutsch. Your father ended up wearing more uniforms! It was on account of his brain-power, not only his talent for languages, they all wanted him to translate, to interpret for the prisoners.* Remembering, her expression lightened, as if the boy-soldier had nothing in common with present-day reviled Max Schalk wherever and whatever he might be.

"My mother went to the Red Cross and found an address. She wrote him about me. After the war, he came to find us—"

"So honorable! Did he get a medal? He should have got a medal." With a burp, the geisha finger-combed Kaethe's straight, blunt hair. "A Hero of the People."

That word was beginning to irritate. Kaethe could feel vodka perco-lating edgily in her forehead. So was Max a hero, then? At seventeen, escaping Glass River, he had joined the RAF, and later, while still in Allied uniform, secretly signed on to the International CP. Eventually he defected, first undercover and then openly and irrevocably, to the German Democratic Republic. *(And that, Kaethe-cat, perforce ended my paternal visits to you.)* But didn't 'hero' require some soul-shaking crisis, decision, sacrifice—and hadn't Max emphasized that he never saw any viable alternative to the direction he took? It had unfolded itself to him through war and war's aftermath as the only liveable reality. A hard rebirth. "The political is the basis of the personal, Kaethe. Of the whole life." She loved him for this. Even as a boy in Glass River, Max once told his daughter, his dominant mood had been simmering rage: watching valley farmers being squeezed to bankruptcy by the strategies of Kraft and Nestlé and A&P. And the millhands and quarry workers whose relief ran out, scrawny men with big-eyed brats, while big industry, not much hampered by the holding actions of that suave patrician, FDR, swapped their labor elsewhere—to the Negro South, to Mexico— wherever muscles came cheaper. Even as a young recruit, Max had begun to see Fascism as no more than tumor-outgrowth of capitalism. And then the *dialectic* entered his life: While interviewing German pris-oners for the Brits and the Amis, he said, he grew unbearably conscious of the German in himself. He was the translator, split in his own blood. The accountings and self-justifications of captured Wehrmacht soldiers echoed his impenetrably self-righteous parents. He translated others: passed on words of older men, a bitter reduction like black bile. Their twisted confessions in his mouth. How to get clean, ever?

Kaethe, skeptical and starving, took in Max's every word. She pressed him: But after the war? You could have come home—

"Not then. The Occupation needed me more than ever—within Germany. There was money, too. For us all! But eventually I couldn't *not* understand what was going on: the point of the questions I put to senior officers and officials, their answers about organizational structures, production capacities, patents, chemical formulae.... War is business. Business is war, but only to a point. The winners offered clean slates, fresh starts or, where a whitewash would look simply too bizarre, new passports and passage out. I was the deal-maker. A trusted asset to both sides."

So by then, wherever Max had looked, only one direction gave off any light. East. Does that make a hero?

The two geisha, Kaethe suddenly realized, had been chattering at a swift clip. Now, as if oppressed or offended by her silence, they stopped. They studied her as if she were one of those schoolyard bombs: maybe dangerous, maybe dud. A random hush infected the room.

Once again Dmitrov was looking at her aslant, with the suggestion of a smile on his long lips. This time she met his stare, bold, curious, her throat filling with some viscous emotion she could not have analyzed if she wanted to. He let one arm (black sleeve, large hand) drop to his side, where Kaethe could see it clearly. Then his unfolding palm turned to her slowly, as if she should join him then and there. Stand by him.

"Well, I think it's all madly romantic," Sad-eyes declared to Gauze. "London, the Resistance and what have you ... don't you wish you had lived in the olden days, instead of catching hell as kids for what the NS-bosses did here? I don't care much about heroes. I care about *love*. We're up to our kiesters in heroes now, all those Heroes of Socialism, they're listed in the papers every week, but—" She glared at the men's backs. "Love, and war. The fateful brief encounter! I mean, Schatz, what a fabulous start in life you had. Destiny, and all that stuff."

Black as the bottom of a dry well. At the fade of each sizzling cloudless day the sky over Berlin gradually thickened with a starless night haze. Despite the laboring "rubble-women," widows who cleared the city of war debris, and the overtime of exhausted utility crews, some old neighborhoods like Szredskistrasse remained unlit, dark as the Pleistocene. (According to Max the disappeared streetlights, harvested by the Soviet occupation along with cars, cooking pots, public statues of Bismarck and any other remotely portable scrap metal, were now rusting away on some railway siding in Minsk.) Kaethe liked to lie in unbroken darkness, opening and closing her eyes to test the lack of difference. Close, open: it was like sliding into water the exact same temperature as the air.

She lay bare-ass on top of her featherbed, back turned to the invisible open casement, willing a draft to swipe over her shoulders and buttocks and the sweat threads behind her knees. Waiting, as she this summer had sometimes fantasized herself waiting—sixteen after all, primed with regular menses, her imagination gorged on the contraband paperback fiction only an arm's length away—waiting for an ardent, adult lover. This lair of a back room was so remote from the front of the flat that she could hear no voices, couldn't tell if the party had broken up yet. Max, if he stayed home, would as usual sleep on the firm-stuffed sofa in the front parlor. The geisha, along with the Egyptian who was an official guest of the Republic, would drift off to their various destinations. But Dmitrov, being the sort of floater her father welcomed under his roof—Dmitrov had been offered a rat's nest of blankets in the central kitchen.

Mattress quills pricked her skin.

She heard the doorlatch drop, like a soft clearing of the throat.

She listened, and the person who had opened her door also listened, and she made her breath drag like a sleeper's, while suddenly, helplessly smiling in the dark.

There was only a slight sigh, and dry creak of the parquet floor, as he eased himself down onto the mattress beside her. The surprisingly cool touch of the visitor's searching fingers lit at random near her navel, on the upper right thigh. Explored the cowlick on the crown of her head. *Be still,* she ordered herself. A foreign, delicious smell of pine and sandalwood was filling the room: freshly applied cologne. In East Berlin not even geisha could afford a good cologne.

Don't move. But could he hear the rough thudding of her heart, insufficiently muffled by the featherbed she lay sprawled on? Her heart, a shy liar, contracted. But fear brought a kind of pleasure—because along with the swirling menace of the unpredictable, she felt here in her own bed, as if in a seat in the murk of a movie hall, resolutely safe. In a few hours she would wake up in another, daylight world. Beyond harm.

His hand grazed the side of her breast, as if confirming her. Kaethe, moaning the childish moan of groggy sleep, half lifted her torso and turned in his direction. He paused to gauge the unimpeachable regularity of her breathing, before his hand returned to the freed breast. A thick finger, callused where it must have clenched a pen, brushed across her nipple. Kaethe shivered in the night heat. Shifting his weight, the poet, her father's house guest, passed his other hand like a cup of warm air down over her buttocks, as if soothing a skittish, sensitive animal. She tried to imagine how his thoughts sounded in the sibilant rush of his language. The hand dove down to her crotch. A finger pressed lightly, curiously, against the lips. Proved to her the slickness there. I'm asleep, thought Kaethe, no one can help what goes on when she's asleep. Bunched fingers now, rotating, teasing open her legs. She allowed herself a confused whimper, and moved against his hand.

Then there was an absence beside her, although she had heard nothing. To her relief came the click of a shoe being set on the floor. The slither of undressing. He came back. His skin was so much cooler, and as silky as Kaethe's. A hand found and held the side of her neck, lightly, while his other hand, still wet, slid back knowingly between her legs. The panic struck up in her again, less like a movie.

Kaethe whispered, *"Ich bin Jungfrau."*

No answer. His whole cologned body rolled heavily against her. Weight. The hand insisted.

Wrong language. In English, hoarsely, "I'm a virgin," she repeated. "A virgin. I never yet—you understand?"

He folded her hand in his. In the unbroken dark she recalled his humorous, slanted eyes, their secretly shared smiles during the party, and felt some of her faith return. He steered her hand to touch his erection. Its wet snubbed tip pressed against her hip. She had never seen a real penis, only the painted or sculpted versions; strange now, to be touching one before seeing. The only erections she had ever seen were etched on the sides of ancient Greek figured vases: she recalled the satyrs' particularly long penises, thin and up-curved like scimitars— exactly the shape she was guided to hold now. Smooth as mother-of-pearl, swelling and lunging in the loose loop of her hand.

"How could you!"

"Could I what?"

"My own—my own *daughter.*" When Max skipped shaving even for a single morning he looked as if he'd spent a month in Siberia. They had both overslept. Raspberry stains of rage sprang out below Max's cheekbones. "With my own goddamned invited guest. In my own flat. My bedroom!"

"I was sound asleep. You know the door doesn't lock. How was that my fault?"

"You were asleep. You slept through *that?* Permit me to laugh." He laughed, a high-pitched theatrical cackle. Then he fired his cup at the wall. Coffee unfurled like a brown banner; the cup exploded, shards falling into the sink.

"You made me drink three glasses of vodka last night. I was sick. Nothing was real. Everything was like a dream."

"The hell with your lies!"

"You should stop throwing cups. Max, you know they broke five of our glasses last night?"

"Hah. That's not all they broke."

"Max. Nothing *happened.*" Kaethe was sure. As far as anything is sure. The pale yellow pool had soaked into the featherbed instead of into her insides. A wistful, neglected ache had accompanied her into the dense bird-cooing dawn, into dreamless sleep.

"You'll have to go back. This situation is intolerable."

"Back? Where?"

"To your grandparents! Or to that school. I'll *gladly* pay! To the States. I can't afford this craziness. I have too much at stake here. There's no time for this insanity."

"Max? Time?"

He squinted, peering sideways at her, exaggerating his incredulity at her willful ignorance. "I've only *begun* my work here. Haven't you figured that out by now? So much left for me to do . . . It's musical chairs. The international game. Universal. Marching round and round to the music. Faster and faster. Winning—but at some point the music is cut. And then if you're not quick and ready you're out. In mid-march, mid-sentence—"

"Haven't I been some use to you?"

"Kaethe. You and I, we don't . . . really know each other. It's too late. My fault. I had an impossible, sentimental idea. About the two of us—"

"I am not going back again. *No.*" She stood up and drained the last drop of her own coffee. It wasn't bitter enough: her mouth still tasted of sandalwood cologne. Staring at Max, she flung her arm out sideways, releasing the cup. It appeared to explode in midair. "I'll go! I can live with my friends here, okay? Fine! But you can't send me back again."

"What is this 'again,' please?"

"First you sent Baerbel and me back from England."

"In forty-five, you mean? Damned right. Broke my butt to get you off that bankrupt island, into the States. Everyone knew the Soviets were sending their Mongol shock troops in to snipe, loot and rape Berlin, and, no surprise, I was about to be posted to where? Berlin! A ghost town: four million people before the war, two million ghosts left over after. A graveyard in progress. Do you know that in the winter of forty-six another thousand people froze to death? Wolves prowled these streets. This street, yes! They fought over carcasses with the cannibals who were starving in these shells of houses. Do you think I had a choice?"

"Later. Later on you could have sent for us."

"When? Should I have brought you here in time for the embargo, while we watched for Clay's C-54's to start carpet-bombing our side of town over again? For the next couple of years we still had damn-all to *eat.* And no time to sleep. We had a city and a Party to build up—the new Germany, remember? *When,* later? Just when it looked like we were drawing ahead, in fifty-three, the counter-revolutionaries launched their illegal strike. Soviet tanks cleared the streets. Another five hundred casualties within hours . . . But you don't think I ever wanted to lose you, Kaethe-cat?"

"I grew up only half-believing in you. You sounded like someone Baerbel and the grandparents made up."

"Look. Whatever your mother's miserable luck was, it started long before she met me. Give me credit: I did manage to visit you both, on the farm. That wasn't easy."

"I don't remember it straight, Max! They talked about you two ways. First what a great student you had been, your Sunday School awards, your 4-H prizes, how proud they were of your war record . . . and then how you had lied to them and always looked down on people in Glass River and ashamed of your parents who you abandoned and later for good measure dumped Baerbel and me on them—"

"For your safety. So you both could *eat.*"

"Those were wonderful dinners. Omi and Opa liked to grind Baerbel down into tears. They all screamed at each other. It was about Max: were you a traitor, or a super-agent working for Hoover, *where* on earth you were, whether McCarthy was going to send G-men to arrest us as red collaborators, whether you had sent money and who was hiding it, what your secret plans were. Whether you'd come back. Oh, God. Those were some dinners."

"We're rather far from the subject of last night."

"How could you leave me? You knew *her.* You knew *them.*"

Max stood up. She followed him to the front room, threading among the dregs of the dinner party. Max pushed the window's lace aside. They saw coal-streaked house façades, sugary white where the noon sun filled mortar scars. "I had to save myself," he said. "I was sure that with time—you older—would understand. That's what I held on to."

Kaethe's eyes stung. For all her fury, here were thick tears. One splashed onto the plate that had been Dmitrov's. A troika of his scented cigarette butts lay squashed on its rim. She had noticed that all other traces of him—rucksack, notebooks, the rat's nest on the kitchen floor—were gone.

Max paced the parlor. "If you have anything meaningful to say to me, please do. Otherwise, we start making arrangements."

"I can't. I won't go back."

"You won't stay *here,* not after last night. *Damn* it. I'd have at least hoped that once you started to screw around you'd show some selectivity. But to let that imbecilic parasite Hossan touch you—"

"You mean Dmitrov."

"Yes, he's the one who *told* me, he could hardly get to sleep for all the coming and going, but it was Hossan in there with you, damn it, and if you at least showed—"

She was deaf to him. A last greasy tear and her crying was over. The Egyptian? No. But how complete the darkness had been. Now her skin crawled, she brushed all over herself as if beset by insects: arms and legs, face and hair. Along with nausea a small laugh rose in her throat: you stupid girl. Don't you know already that no one is who you take them for.

In the end Max let her stay, on a few strict conditions. First, she was to give up his room.

BORDER RAIDS

Waking into the heat of the day. Lashes of sun across Kaethe's bare calves. She imagines herself in Carolina age fourteen; in sleep she has kicked the featherbed to the floor. How late? She sits bolt upright into a silence underscored by the occasional clank of pans from across the courtyard, the whine of a pupil's violin bow being dragged along its scales. This is the somnolence of the German noon break, after a long morning's work. She pictures the breakfast room with its five tables stripped bare and ashtrays set out for the afternoon magazine readers and evening card players who never materialize, perhaps because the room is too perfectly prepared (a polished ship rising into the Berlin firmament, its balcony-prow banked with flowers) or else because it's a fishbowl that anyone entering the hotel is bound to glance into. Or because of Boris, panting in his cave under the telephone?

Despite their late night, Rahel must have been up again at six to serve the breakfast. Kaethe frowns sideways at her reflection in the long mirror of the armoire, a mirror so streaked and splotched that whatever it frames resembles an expressionist painting, full of exaggerations and omissions. Sometimes her reflection has been a Klimt, sometimes a Schiele . . . But today, the nude recumbent at midday in a burst of bedding feels unusually rested and relaxed, "well in her skin" is the German expression. But to think that Rahel may never have gone to bed at all. . . .

She rises. Washes rapidly at the corner sink. Dresses while trying to decide how to save what's left of the day. Her plan had been to ride the S-Bahn out to its southeastern terminus, Potsdam, to explore Friedrich's once-brilliant summer resort. She's heard that in the shadow of Sans Souci Palace, where Voltaire once played skat with the Kaiser, colonies of young squatters have sprung up around the headquarters of the new/old Communist Party, the PDS. She had intended to search Potsdam from morning till dark, although the prospect of lingering in a PDS enclave makes her uneasy, as picnicking by a precipice would. As does the possibility, the implications, of Sophie in fact living there. (And who else might a person run into? Seamy and sunken but nonetheless still unnervingly memorable faces from the old bosses' strongholds of Pankow or Lichtenberg or Weissensee? The man at the desk shimmers in the peripheral vision of her mind, unbidden and unwanted.)

Anyway, she's slept too late for Potsdam. And it's time, she thinks, automatically taping new plasters over old blisters—yes, *time,* eight days gone already and the money wad thinning fast—to do something more, something beyond the "personal" placed in the *Tagesspiegel* and the pilgrimages to parks and bars and satellite suburbs. What then: push harder with the police? Or turn to someone else for advice? Who is left? Mathias refuses to see her. Try to get a call through to Achim? After all the betrayals, reach across the bitter ice?

Without locking the room she goes out to use the toilet. When she returns Lies is standing at ease over her desk, gazing down at photos, letters, scrawled notes, addresses. All the muddle.

"Well rested, Frau Schalk? I saved you some fruit."

"Oh Lies, good heavens, you didn't have to. This is so kind—"

"I noticed you like apricots. Muesli? Cream? You don't look like a person who should skip too many meals."

"You're tempting me."

"Eating is not a sin, Frau Schalk."

"Well, no. That is true."

"I've been checking around. About that girl in the photo. So she's your daughter?"

"Yes. But it's such a long story. I didn't want to go into details, burden strangers."

"But she is obviously the only reason you came here. One doesn't catch you shopping at KaDeWe or out to the cabarets at night. So if you need help, why didn't you at least tell me her name? Sophie von Thall. Have you thought about the possibility—I mean, with a juicy name like that—"

"Kidnapping? Of course I think about it! But the police don't. They say no one's received any threats or demands. They say all the old Red Brigade types are dead or in prison. The anarchist movement is stone-cold and the world is safe for—"

"Your coffee will be stone-cold."

"Anyway, 'von Thall' may not be the name she would go by, here."

"I get it. Maybe she's not 'Sophie' either. Everybody has a handle of her own. It's better. Makes you more you. Not for disguise, like with your anarchos, but to expose. To reveal your essential nature."

"Interesting."

"My friends are called Pig-ear, Mosquito, Krishna. For example."

"Ever hear of 'Chinese'?"

"No. Sounds nasty, though. Racist."

"Ah. And what's the name of your essential nature, Lies?"

"That's private."

"And mine?"

"Not for me to say. Your name will find you."

With the professional focus of a nurse, Lies watches Kaethe pick food from the tray set on the desk. There are apple slices and apricots in a flowered bowl, biscuits and cereal, and a cup brimming with tepid coffee. Lies wears a red-checked shirt that clashes with her dark-claret hair, and tight, pristine white denim shorts, and military-style leather boots that lace above her ankles. Her sturdy calves are shaved, stippled. Her silver nostril-ring trembles like a suspended tear.

Kaethe, slurping coffee, remembers the lugubriously rollicking sound of "Tarantula" as bubbled up through the mucus-ridden throat of a former superior.

"Actually, I had a handle once too, you know."

Lies twitches a dimpled, patient smile.

"Give you a hint? Italian folk dance. 'Trampling the Spider.'"

Lies shrugs. "I'm no good at guessing games." She reclaims the empty cup, lifts away the tray. "I've got the afternoon off, Frau Schalk. If you want, I'll take you to meet some people. Over on the East side."

"Who?"

"Just friends of mine. They're just people. But they're young, they get around."

"Of course. Of course I'll come!"

"Don't dress too fancy. But also . . ." Reaching the door Lies pauses, considering. "Don't forget to bring money."

From a double-decker bus they gaze down on the sandy gash, over a mile wide in places, where the rolls of wire, the bricks and cement and every scrap of nearby asphalt or vegetation, as if contaminated, have been dug out and hauled away. Hauled to where? Even the river Spree, once a convenient extension of Wall, has been diverted by master engineers from its natural bed into giant pastel-hued conduits, to allow construction of the deeper and higher new metropolis to come. Without turning to Lies Kaethe says, "Back then, when deserters tried to swim across the Spree, machine gunners in the towers used to pick them off like ducks. Suppose the dead can see us, see what we do, their river disappeared, sucked away in a giant pink straw."

Lies's forehead is flattened on window glass. "It's just a big noisy show. They'll never finish digging, it's just an excuse to tear up the past. I don't believe in the 'new Berlin' happening. None of us do."

"What do you think is the point, then?"

"Politicians wanting to distract us!"

The Info-box glides by. A giant replica of a contractor's headquarters-trailer, it's a real-time museum of the construction site's projected future, with movies and dioramas, café and gift shop. An unexpected star tourist attraction. Kaethe has read about the Box in the hotel's event guide, but feels no urge to spring for a ticket. Lines of tourists snake around the base of the now receding Box, which roosts high on a metal tower in order to provide the widest possible view. "It looks," Kaethe tells the girl, "a lot like an old Vopo guards' station. Up on the Wall." She remembers afternoons as a young, idle wife, sunbathing on the West side, out on the grassy weir toward Wannsee, how the blond boyish Vopos—the People's Police—two to a tower, would wave and flash grins and raise their binoculars to her. Not a memory to be shared with Lies. "Distract whom from what?"

"What they're really digging for. Mummies wrapped in gold, like the Britz Maiden. Magic amulets and swords. Powers from the ancients, the genuine Druid-Germans who lived here, back before Tacitus discovered us. When Germanni were reindeer-hunter-people, from even back between the Ice Ages."

Tacitus. The Britz Maiden. Spoken in the clipped urban dialect, bits of Kaethe's old-style education, indissoluble as heavy metal, are floating in Lies's mind. This close to the girl, in daylight, Kaethe can see that the parting of her claret-red hair if left undyed would grow out pale brown. The blasé arch of her eyebrows is as obviously painted as her cyanide-blue nails. "Are you being sarcastic? Or do you believe this story, Lies?"

"Sarcastic? I stay open minded. A person should be able to hold more than one aspect of reality in her head."

"Well, yes. I completely agree with you." Smiling, relieved, she adjusts her bag. A recorded conductor-voice chants their next stop.

"But there are the sacrifices," Lies adds. "Deaths. One every few days. *Human* sacrifices."

The slick plastic bus unloads at Potsdamerplatz. After their next transfer, the train wagons pulling them deeper East will be rickety industrial antiques. Kaethe hurries after her guide, who weaves through the throng into a tunnel, down a curving throat of stairs.

"Come on, now. Whose deaths are you talking about?"

"The fallers. What do you think happens, up on one of those cranes, if someone puts his foot left instead of right? Straight shot down into the pit, huh? But these days the fallers hardly ever get reported in the papers. Too many kids smashed. Bad for politics."

"Construction workers . . . They know what they're doing."

"Kids, mostly. The builders hire any sucker they can get."

Lies walks fast, almost skipping. Kaethe has no idea how far below street level they are; she has no mental map of this station. Stairs and corridors, punctuated by bright-lit cells selling roses, pretzels, ties and socks, open up continually to the right and left.

"See those guys over there? The three squatting under the symphony poster? With the monkey? I know they take a walk on the sky for day rates. It's fast money."

One of the trio rattles a McDonald's coffee cup out toward Kaethe. His pet, dressed in neckerchief and shoulder harness, looks like an organ grinder's dwarf accomplice: black pug face, white tufts at groin and armpits. The boys might be anywhere between eighteen and twenty-five. Ponytail, home-made tattoos, raging acne, a lavender mohawk cockscomb. One spits and hisses, "Shit Wessi, gimme a fiver," to Kaethe as she passes.

"When a body falls that far, Frau Schalk, how can anyone on the ground even tell who it was a minute before? Me, I can't imagine going up so high. The cranes sway, too. Not centimeters. Half a kilometer, in the wind. Sometimes guys have to shoot up before they go up. It's called New-Berlin courage."

"That's asking for it."

"What isn't? You think needles are more suicidal than whoring?"

"Not quite the same, is it? At least the girls can use protection."

"Girls? Are you a sexist? Equal opportunity, Frau Schalk! The boys sell, too. If anything, they're more in demand. And maybe better at it? And naturally, plenty of girls shoot up. By the way, Frau Schalk: Girls sign on to sky-walk, too. Quick money."

Kaethe looks up at the nodding arm of a crane, high as a jetliner. *Oh God. No. Sophie.*

The friends are called Toboggan and Astarte. Pig-Ear and Mosquito. The two females are perched on top of an iron climbing cage; the hems of their long skirts waft through the bars over the heads of the four who are seated around the rim of a disused sandbox. Sweet hashish mingles with the scent of lilacs. A joint is circulating. Lies sucks in with a flourish and passes the fat hand-rolled over to Kaethe, who draws and feels the burning joint ascend from her fingers as she blinks back tears. Lies croons, *"Taler, Taler, du musst wandern—"* The others smile knowingly and hum along. It's a nursery song for a game in which a coin passes secretly from hand to hand. Good song for a playground, thinks Kaethe, and is granted a sudden vision of a ruddy-cheeked child laughing in the heady pleasure of directing her parents in a game. Slowly Kaethe opens her eyes, not to the expected blue sky but to Astarte's long, muscular yellowish thighs and triangle of dingy underwear.

"It's Pig-Ear," says Lies, "who wanted a look at your pictures."

Kaethe gropes in her bag. Hands over the plastic-protected photos, sees Sophie's image palmed from hand to hand, dropped in the weedy sandbox, brusquely dusted off. Pig-Ear's own huge soft hands are dappled like a camouflaged jungle soldier's with bruises that march up into his long loose sleeves. "Oh, I think," he says.

"You think what?"

"I might have seen her." His lips remain parted after speech, as if breathing is an habitual problem.

"You have? Where? When?" Kaethe leans forward, one hand already inside her bag clutching the money she wants to offer Pig-Ear right now, in front of these witnesses, to claim him and bind him. "Was it Sophie? Or what name did she give?"

"Did I say I talked to her? And where is the question, right? Could've been the TV Tower. Could've been the Medic van. Lotta women hang around the van, looking for DepoProvera. Could've been in Tiergarten, over where those horny Turk johns cruise in their busted-down Trabis. Listen, Frau: suppose you run into thirty, forty people on the street in a day. You can't remember every face you run across. Your head would overflow from it, right?"

"But *her*, you do remember. True? Why?"

"Why . . . Real tall. I always like a strong-built woman. This one looked so straight into my eyes like—at first I thought maybe once we made it together. And I noticed the rats, I guess."

"Rats?"

"Her hair is way longer than in this picture. Super dreads, she has now. And the rats going in and out, like hide 'n seek." He shrugs. "Just normal rats."

Once, on the long bus ride that returned her to Glass River, fifty miles per hour up a hairpin road, Kaethe had let her gaze roam down the mountain's pine-furred flank into a bowl of infinity, blue haze. She felt then the terror and embrace of falling, as if the bus had already pitched over the edge, out of time in a single instant. Now she is pitching into blue shadows toward the white mass of Pig-Ear, paralyzed but wanting to tear him apart, extract whatever he knows.

"Holla." He lifts her by both wrists. "Don't you go and faint on me."

"Lies? I need you!" Kaethe calls out. She twists like a hoisted cat in his grip. Apparently they are alone in the sandbox; the others seem to have wandered off. "Where is Lies, Pig-Ear? Where did they *go?*"

"Wanted to leave us our space to talk business in? Look, if you're back to rational, tell me what's the mission objective with the girl? I've got time, but not much time. Plenty of businesses needing my attention."

"I feel all right now, Pig-Ear. Please. You can let go of my arms." From her soldier's bag she pulls a twenty mark bill. "No mission. Only to call me. If you see her again—or if you hear anything—the smallest thing—about her? Here's for telephone charges. Fair?" He shrugs, watching a sparrow fluff in the dust. She holds out another twenty. "You can call me day or night. You have the number, where Lies works?"

"Call you up anytime, Frau? Hey, thanks for the invitation!"

They leave the park, entering a cobbled square. The others, rising from a table outside a green-walled pub, swing into step around them.

Kaethe's mind is silent, suspended between real hope and fear of her own gullibility—until she looks up to a street sign, to find herself crossing the intersection with Szredskistrasse. She hardly turns her head yet registers the long canyon of chipped stucco housefronts, their mouths agape to inner courtyards. How could she not have recognized? The jumble of signs identifying small storefronts (laundry, vegetables, used electronics) as dingy and basic as ever, though some are now lettered in Turkish, or Vietnamese. How it would amaze her young companions, especially Lies, to know that she once lived here. That children from the mandatory socialist day-care program mined golden sand in the playground, back while she fetched beers for Max from the green-walled pub.

Mosquito announces he wants to host a party. They are passing a variety of street fêtes—an art sale, an impromptu tango demonstration—and he wants everyone to come back to his bunker. To mellow. He squints at Kaethe, measuring the decades between them. The bunker's not so far, he says, but it's a climb, nearly straight up. Up top I've got more *stuff,* he says, than you could dream of. More dope, she assumes he means, but Lies explains that Mosquito is a taxi-fence: he makes a market for stuff drivers bring him, after shift. It's fabulous, says Mosquito, the junk people leave in the back seat! Wedding rings and gold watches. Wigs and false teeth. Crutches—can you picture that? Passports, only the passport market's gone lousy. Computers, cameras, cocaine.

Kaethe admits she herself lost a camera on her last taxi ride.

"Exactly! You see?" says Mosquito. "Not to mention the live cargo. Parrots, dogs, snakes. Alligator eggs! Exotica's so hot. Plus a human baby, now and then." He laughs. "Those I turn in to the clinic. You don't think I'd fence a *baby?*"

"Go on along to your party," says Kaethe to Lies. "I'm tired. I should head back to the hotel."

She doesn't want to watch the girl playing with stolen goods, or going from dope to harder stuff. Chubby, tough Lies in her sausage-skin shorts arouses in Kaethe an involuntary current of concern.

Lies strokes her arm. "Come with us, we'll look for your camera there! Any camera! Mosquito gets incredibly generous in his party mood."

"I don't need the camera after all."

"Well then. At least I'll bring you something, okay? What do you need? Make a wish. Hairdryer? Video player?"

"I could use . . . I don't know. Possibly a typewriter?"

"Honestly! Oh, Frau Schalk, how can you be so old-fashioned?" Overcome by laughter. In the next moment her friends, teasing and scolding her, have pulled the girl away, and only Pig-Ear waves.

Through much of Kaethe's life there have been episodes, intervals, when her thinking seems to completely stop. Her mind seizes up like a ruined engine. "Thinking," the whole process of juxtaposing phrases, sending words up to pour down on and ignite other words, an unwinding chain of inner events as constant as a heartbeat—without it, time stops too.

She has been walking, but for how long? She has a memory of crossing Szredskistrasse, and later of looking up at a random corner building to get her bearings and with a shock (the shock of premonition, as in a repeating dream) reading the street-sign Blankengasse. Somehow she had arrived at the entrance to Mathias's alley. Was he at that very moment staring down from his fourth-floor window, observing her hesitation?

She broke and ran. She broke away from the temptation to enter narrow Blankengasse and climb the crumbling tiled stairs inside entrance 5A to bang on the apartment door of Pastor Mathias Leytenfeger. Not for her now, to turn to a preacher. Which way did she turn instead?

How late is it? Dusk, unending dusk, but she's not hungry. She doesn't recognize her surroundings as part of the old neighborhood. The curving narrow street she's been following suddenly emerges into a wider boulevard, deserted and steep-sloping. Last rays of sun glint richly on doubled lines of trolley tracks. "Where the blue of the night/ Meets the gold of the day . . ." This voice—a crooning tenor, suavely American—emerged from Baerbel's maple-cased Magnavox radio, on weekend afternoons when the grandparents had allowed Kaethe to go visit her mother. In her bed-sitter room in the Pittsfield Gardens Baerbel would sing along, swaying and simpering, pronouncing "the" as "zah" and "gold" as "colt" *Where the blue of the night* warbled out over the tarry-hot main street. Not one garden nor blade of grass. The theme music was the signal for a glass of schnapps to be poured. Two glasses. "Trink du doch auch, mein Schatz! Do Mamma the decency, sweetie, everyone knows a lady shouldn't drink alone—" but Kaethe was twelve years old and her throat closed tight at the kerosene-like fumes of brandy.

During those years after the grandparents forced their daughter-in-law to move out, Baerbel, who had earlier acted ashamed to admit her origins, spoke German more and more. She dredged up old games, she sang folksongs off-key, she wanted to resurrect the language of infancy in her daughter. But there wasn't much time. By the end of the blue-gold summer Baerbel would be gone, cremated to off-white ash, the urn taking minimal space in Glass River's Lutheran cemetery. ("Dead by her own hand," the grandmother intoned, with a breath of I-told-you-so.) In the October to follow, Kaethe would be riding in a pullman across the Mason-Dixon to Gore Academy, as arranged from far away by her father, semi-mythical Max.

It was at school that her episodes of not-thinking began.

Kaethe blamed the war of languages. The two languages struggling for space in her brain, at least two, English and German, not counting British and hill-Yankee, Swabian farmer-immigrant and the glass-pearl, high-German notes of Rilke and Goethe. They traded ascendancy from time to time as circumstances required. One thought canceling out the other. Match. Checkmate. Leaving Kaethe without any words, no language, only images as hard to hold as ice slivers, melting away.

You should drink too, my treasure. "Trink du doch auch, mein Schatz—" Later, Baerbel, later I will. *Mees zah co-olt of zah day . . .*

A fresh tinkle of broken glass. Kaethe looks down at her shoes scuffing through shards of a smashed schnapps flask. This boulevard is deserted, shadowy houses and office fronts set far back from the wide sidewalks. Streetlamps flicker on like a ribbon. Gold of the night. No trolley stop visible either uphill or down. Which direction leads back into town and which would take her farther out, to the east?

The man at the desk had been drinking. Rust-brown dregs of brandy congealed in the glass. Window propped open to the crisp November breeze. The inquisitive, darting O of the flashlight pauses on the dark-stained, dangling right hand. Below the hand, apparently dropped on the dusty parquet floor, lies a fountain pen. Gold and green lacquer, heavy and dented, a handsome pre-war Pelikan. The observer crouches for a quick examination but refrains from touching the pen. There is no sound from the night street; no sound in the room except his own slow breathing and the crick of his knees as he straightens to get a clearer, closer look at the man at the desk.

"Hallo! You there, lady, you have the time?" A figure strolls out in front of her from nowhere, following its own voice, then there are four of them, all slender and alike in jeans and tee shirts.

"Of course. Just a moment, wait . . ." Kaethe steps toward a street-light, to read her watch, squinting, a little embarrassed by her poor eyesight. No glasses. The others move closer, two walking backward so that all four constantly face each other. The two girls switch long glossy dark hair like horses' tails. Turkish girls, Kaethe assumes. "I think it's ten forty—"

"You think ? Don't you *really* have the time for us?"

"Hey, that's a pretty watch."

"Oo, I could use a watch like that."

"You drive a Mercedes? No? BMW? Where's your Mercedes parked?"

"What are you looking at here?"

"What's in the big bag?"

"She's leaving. Oh oh. She's got no time to spare for us!"

"You're some Wessi tourist, aren't you? Are you crazy? You think you can come around here, stare at people and show off all day?"

"Hey, lady. Yes, you! Let me try that pretty watch on!"

"Who gives you the right? You don't belong here."

"Give it!"

"No time for us."

"Oo-hoo. She's in a hurry now!"

"I touched her—"

"You *tripped* her—"

"Put that shit blade back out of shit's sight."

"Look at her. You're *scaring* her."

"So?"

"I think someone's coming—"

"Shit! Let's move it! Someone's coming!"

A dachshund's dog breath. Cold-grape nose. The dog's master bends close, reluctant to touch a total stranger, especially one sprawled flat on the ground. Kaethe pushes up on her hands and knees, assures him that she is all right. Filthy foreign thugs, he says. Aliens. What the world is coming to, since the Turning. I'll say this for Honey Honecker, he at least kept order in our public streets!

The dachshund's owner leads her limping up over the hill's rise to the trolley stop. She will have to wait alone for transportation, his wife is expecting his return, my best half has a heart condition, nervous if I'm late, understand? Yes, she understands nervousness alone after dark. Her skin is clammy. Stinging pavement grit ground into her elbow and palm. *Komm, Pucki! Jetzt gehen wir nach Hause!*

Alone, she keeps reminding herself to breathe. The rectangle of light jolting this way may be her trolley. Yes, there's the old pagoda-shaped streetcar, the uniformed driver. Two wan passengers. She feels a smile begin to break over her face, broadening as if in recognition of a long-awaited beloved. This has, after all, been a good day. An enormous day! Now she knows, *oh, for sure,* that somewhere in this city Sophie is living through her own version of night without darkness. Her own searches and encounters. *Where the blue of the night / Meets the gold of the day / Someone … waits … for me …*

The lock mechanism of the pension's main entrance tumbles like links of chain as she twists the key. The only light burning is the small lamp by the telephone. Boris yawns pinkly as she passes. Rahel's door is shut. Tomorrow, Kaethe reminds herself, with all the money from her bag stolen along with her watch, she will have to make some arrangement about her bill with Frau Loewnfus and move somewhere much, much cheaper.

Entering her own room, Kaethe finds two surprises waiting: a note pushed under the door asking her to call a number she doesn't recognize. And on the desk, gaping open on its hinge, a giant black clam: a laptop computer. Already plugged in, it makes a faint, continuous roar like the ocean in a seashell; the screen glows like mother-of-pearl. Kaethe can't help but begin to play with the keys. The tracing pad responds to her clumsy fingertip with runes and polite inquiries and scrolls of commands, her tiredness evaporates. Eventually the symbol of a notebook appears. She taps; it blooms open to a page, blank except for the hovering arrow awaiting her bidding, and one unfinished sentence.

"I have made an irredeemable mistake"

the brief history
of a great idea

THE TORCHES
OF TAUNUS

Her dress was like a glorious animal that wore her. A heavy, nacreous satin, it hugged her arms and wrists, her collarbone, breasts and hips. Its hem brushed the arches of her feet. It was undecorated except for the pinned-on, severely wilted corsage of white freesia. A crown of drooping freesia had also been knotted into her hair. She sat beside her husband of eight and a half hours, occupying with him the head of the central table in the receiving hall of a hunting castle: the sixteenth-century Jagdschloss Eber, a half-timbered retreat in a remote forest corner of the Taunus hills.

Though the hall was murky, so dark that its edges and exits were lost behind the smoke from wall sconces and other sources, she saw white everywhere, in its varying moods and qualities. Down the length of the table multi-armed candelabra oozed yellowish wax that shriveled on starched linen. The silver platters and bowls reflected the candle flames in flashing white. The youngest girls wore infantile white gowns laced with green ribbons. The men's plastrons, wives' and widows' hard-clicking diamonds, the cream sauces (horseradish, béarnaise, dill) napping foods so rare and rich they might have been stolen from the hoard of a troll, the chamber players' quarto pages of sheet music, the talc complexions of the very old—all white, bridal white.

She had never been looked at by so many people, for so long. This attention—completely out of her experience, she had nothing to connect it to—had expanded and intensified since the morning, when at the local town hall she and Achim showed identification documents and medical affidavits and signed the heavy book of records and slid their respective gold rings off the left, temporary betrothal hand onto the right, the permanent one. Only the bridegroom's closest family members witnessed those procedures, then guided them to the Jagdschloss's chapel where many more guests waited, swiveling to stare at the von Thall heir and his bold (to some, inexplicable) choice. A bride without clan or background or definitive place of origin. A defiant, even mutinous choice, and so their instinctive, best response was to close in on the pair in an ineluctable embrace. The rheumy stone walls exuded wintry moisture even in May, and a choir of the musically inclined von Thalls harmonized in "A Mighty Fortress Is Our God" followed by Bach's wedding cantata, with Achim's youngest brother rocking away at the organ pipes, before the pastor led Achim and Kaethe through the promises that would bind them unto death.

Now they laughed. Eyed by the guests at their table (those at other tables stretched backwards frequently for a glimpse, or clashed fork against crystal before standing to shout an incomprehensible toast) like icons or a pair of painted statues, but hardly spoken to throughout the five courses of the wedding meal, they drew together inside the bubble of observation. They leaned their blond heads together—his hair an ashy absence of color, hers bleached gilt. In near-whispers they made fun of the sawing, squeaking musicians, defeated by ricocheting echoes, and of the barbaric spectacle of a trio of wild boar sucklings (trophies of their host, a distant cousin) sizzling elliptically on spits over a fire pit in the middle of the hall. Beneath the table Achim's forearm pressed across Kaethe's lap. She felt nothing: the heavy dress protected her like a spell. He drew her hand up into the light, into everyone's view, stroking her wrist with his thumb. His own hand was square as a stonemason's, the nails chewed down flat.

"My children. What a blessed day this has been—*is,* at this moment. This holy sacrament. This joy, for me. Joy of a lifetime!" Seated on her son's left, magnified by candle-glare, the Countess Ana Luise von Thall beamed fondly. Her long, sturdy teeth were flecked persimmon-red (she had no practice using lipstick); her tall frame was made even stronger and stiffer by a glistening black and green gown, splendid as the carapace of some huge night-beetle. Although she had encouraged servants to heap her plate full again and again, it now shone as if licked by a bear, as clean as the untouched dishes beside her that corresponded to the empty chair reserved for her husband, the late Count Ernst von Thall, Captain of Cavalry, slaughtered with his Junker honor intact, according to eyewitnesses, at the head of his troops of the Sixth Army in the dawning days of 1943—"Just in time," Ana Luise would console herself and the fatherless boys, "to be spared at least the horrors and shame waiting around the corner for those of us who remained."

"You'd better make a speech." Achim leaned to his mother, urgently. "Otherwise Uncle Harro's gearing up to, and look, he's soused as a kulak and his trousers are unbuttoned."

Ana Luise glanced at her brother-in-law, who had done eight years in a Soviet prison where he escaped neither shame nor horror, a former P.O.W. gone native in the steppes, who started his day with a belt of vodka and wept easily, and whose semi-employment in a government office monitoring trade with Eastern Europe was generally considered an act of patriotic generosity. "But my dear son," she said. "You're the one always telling me I can't express myself sensibly."

"Don't be shy," said Kaethe. She hesitated before adding, "Mother."

"Oh, I don't care if they find me funny! I only want you, you children, to know how happy I am. Oh! To witness the two of you in the chapel, together. In God's sight. Given to one another, in his care."

Her new mother-in-law, Kaethe had already decided, was not a hypocrite. On the contrary: if bitten by a base feeling or thought she would thrust it away with revulsion, and completely embrace its opposite, no matter what that was. In this way her convictions and outlook took some truly unorthodox turns. To look past the candle-flicker into Ana Luise von Thall's large, prominent, seldom-blinking eyes brought an unexpected sense of peace; tonight, with the ever-increasing din of the wedding party (the lewd wagering had begun, spontaneous dancing had broken out in a smoky corner) Kaethe found that meeting Ana Luise's eyes was like looking into a lake surrounded by the rumble of a thunderstorm, and finding reflected there only mild white clouds and blue sky.

And what did the mother-in-law see, as she beamed, brimming with indulgence, at Kaethe?

There was the dress she had sewn, working for hectic weeks with two aged companions, maiden sisters who had served the von Thall household since their First Communions, and without a wage since the fall of Berlin. The magnificent dress: if zookeepers rub orphan tigers with the hides of tribe members, Kaethe thought, to encourage acceptance by a nursing mother, was the real function and beauty of the dress its ability to cover Kaethe with this tribe's texture, the singular right smell? But could Countess von Thall alone still make out, inside the dress, the waif who had rung at her door over a year before? That bold, ingratiating girl, offering a visitor's bouquet of hothouse tulips, had presented herself: *Good afternoon! I'm a former student of your childhood friend Gerta Eisblum. She asked me to give you her fondest regards.* And if Ana Luise that day had suspected that Kaethe Schalk was sick of peddling papers and waking in ice-cold squats, that she had invested all her spare change in the overpriced flowers, that at twenty-three she had discovered tiny wrinkles under her eyes and had as good as forgotten her old German teacher's introduction to 'the right sort of people' until this wealthy-sounding villa address turned up in the pocket of an old school jacket—if so, Ana Luise gave nothing away. She invited Kaethe in. And if she herself could no longer surely place the classmate Gerta— perhaps Eisblum was not her maiden name?—along the convoluted routes of her memory, she gave nothing away. She bent to kiss the girl on both cheeks, as those who have friends in common will do. And invited her into the house.

What if Ana Luise could look through the wedding make-up of powder, rouge, and mascara to Kaethe's unmasked skin, sallow and tending to infection, in the German word, *impure?* Or deeper still? Could she see into Kaethe's skepticism, the crossed fingers in the chapel, the conviction that to turn this adventure down would have been a graceless snubbing of life's possibilities? Was Ana Luise capable of grasping a person so completely unlike herself?

"*Liebe Damen und Herren!*" Uncle Harro banged a knife-edge on his wineglass; Ana Luise lunged to catch the glass from falling, Harro hawked phlegm and swabbed his face with his napkin while fighting to free his legs from under the table. "Dear Family!" He stood, successfully. His smile stretched wide, displaying the gaps between stumpy teeth. "Dear cousins, in-laws, grandfolks and great grandfolks. Dear girls and boys. Well-wishers of the musty old von Thall tribe, and *friends!*"

Kaethe glanced around.

"Dear God," murmured Achim. "Spare us."

"Here's to you, Achim! Your long life and happiness! Standing in for your father, I raise my glass—who the devil took my glass? Here's to you, my brother's son, and to your bride! We can see you're bursting with pride that you hooked her. About time, eh? New blood, new blood's what this inbred pack requires. Well, and here's to *you,* my dearest Ana Luise, not exactly new blood but you do sparkle like a million tonight, fine as I've seen you in years! Now I wonder, why are you relatives out there looking at me like you swapped your backsides for your faces? Is this a wedding, or a tax court? Say, if you think I've had a drop too many, you should see my camel! Ha har. Joke, kapisch?

"Ach, Ana Luise, you're blushing. If only my brother Ernst could see you tonight! You'd about raise him from his grave, darling. All right—I don't have the slippery tongue for speeches but I haven't heard anyone do better today either.

"Well, what I want to say is—somebody's got to make noise, right? What I want to tell you two is this: hope. I know a few things about hope. Hard to hold on to when a guy is alone. He can coddle it, feed it lies. One moment into the next it deserts the post. Also thank God I know about finding hope. At first you don't remember what to call it. It's tiny, like a single atom. It's strong as the damn atomic bomb.

"You two tonight. Each of you is the hope for the other, right? Hang on to that.

"Dare I hope a few of you beloved relatives remain awake? And you've all got wine in your glasses. Ready? This is to the new blood. When this girl woke up this morning—were you scared, sweetheart? We can be a scary tribe. Ha har! Damn it, what am I saying, you don't scare easily. She was Kaethe Schalk, fresh out from East Berlin, had the good sense to cross over, Uncle Ulbricht's loss our gain, eh? Eh? Smart girl, read more books than I know the titles of. I guess like me she's traveled the world some, she did time early on in the States, ha har, ha *har*—that so, Kaethe? All right, dear relatives, up with your glasses now! Here's to the marriage of East and West! Here's to the start of a Great Idea! East embrace West. Out with the old, in with—Comrades! Here's to all the babies you'll be having—damn, we can use some innocence in this tribe! Here's to you, our new daughter: Kaethe von Thall!"

He tossed the wine back with his face screwed up, as if missing his clean, unscented vodka. When his eyes opened to fix on Kaethe there was no drunkenness in them. Hurled with force and sure aim, his empty glass spun past her head to explode on the rough plaster wall. Children shrieked and the men stomped and cheered, and Achim's youngest brother barked like a dog.

Outside, Kaethe gulped cool air. Rich odors of cow dung. Trampled clover. She threw her head back to rest her gaze in wells of stars rimmed by moist night cloud. After a few steps the earth started to heave and buckle beneath her feet. Pulling Achim to a stop, she buried her head against his arms.

"Are you smashed?" he asked in a gentle voice.

"No," she lied.

"Look at me, then." His hands pressed her arms, forcing her to stand straight. Then his kiss fell on her mouth so warm and welcome, after all the stares of strangers, that she only vaguely registered the silhouettes flowing out through the Jagdschloss gate, behind and around them. This long, unrelenting kiss, pressing deep into her mouth, unleashed a drunken, unbearable mix of lust and nausea. *Stop,* she wanted to beg. When he let her free she felt his saliva smeared on her, wet and fresh in the night. "Bear up a while longer," he said. Tone of wry apology. Breathing hard. "This tribal circus won't last forever."

"Achim. What's going on now? What are they all *doing?*"

Two by two, the wedding guests had begun to climb up a long, curved, treeless hill. Those who emerged on the ridge stood out distinctly against the night sky. They carried long sticks, like ceremonial weapons, upright before them.

"Already? Come on! We can't be late—" He gripped Kaethe's hand, pulled her stumbling up the slope in the dark. Her ankles twisted. The dress's hem caught on thistles and thorns. Far ahead, some of the climbers began to set their sticks on fire, lighting one from the next, passing the bloom down along the line. More than a hundred torches sprang alive in yellow-red, huge dirty flames that jumped and merged erratically. Kaethe longed to hear Achim say something wry, or dismissive, or blasphemous. Break the spell. He was dragging her eagerly uphill; grass clumps and rockslides slipped away but in his grip she couldn't fall. Lit by the brassy torchlight his face (the large rough-cut features not unlike his mother's) looked utterly determined. Singing rose from the celebrants as the bridal pair took their place in line as its leaders. A chant she didn't recognize. Farther away, she thought she

heard gunfire or drumrolls, or was it only in her drunken imagination?
She glanced backward: the marchers advanced slowly, heads held high.
Their faces appeared serene, rapt, unfamiliar in the torchlight. There
was an ur-innocence about this night procession, she thought: it was
like a group of ancients playing childhood games. Even the children
in the line looked ancient now. She thought that the unreality of her
marriage—no, *her* unreality within it, her lack of substance and intent
—had caught up with her with a vengeance. She tried to push out a
laugh. But who would hear her, as she faced into the indifferent night
with the procession of bobbing black-smoking torch-bearers moving
behind her?

It's what tradition demands, the men insisted. They were panting like
foxhounds after a fast course, spitting and coughing, bursting with
hilarity at their own ribald allusions: to nuts and cherries, eggs and figs,
to hardness and crispness, ripeness and mingled juices. The abduction
of the bride—it's required. Because you're one of *ours* now, don't you
see that's the idea? Long after they had set her down she felt the
imprints of their arms and chests, muscles and bones. The dress that
had protected her was gone.

She had taken it off herself, following the torchlit march, and returned
to her bedroom in the Jagdschloss, where like a post-midnight, exhausted Cinderella, she had pulled on plain shirt and slacks for one
more outing which haggard-eyed Achim promised with a rueful smile
would be "The last act. A late-night snack with friends, down in the
village pub, it's staying open just for us—" Now she pictured the wedding dress spread out on the carved Jagdschloss bed, like a body without a soul.

She had no idea where she was. Someone had dropped a soft but suffocating blindfold across her face the moment she stepped out of the
pub to look for Achim, who had gone in search of cigarettes for too
long. . . . Someone else had pushed her succinctly into a car and the car
accelerated long before the idea of being afraid, of calling out for help,
had taken shape in her. Now, hunched on a musty sofa in a dim slope-
roofed room that reeked of mouse droppings, she couldn't put a sure
name to any of her milling captors, knew only that neither Achim nor
his brothers were among them.

"The groom's job now is to find you," someone explained to her as if
she were a half-wit.

Kaethe felt an unreasoning spurt of fear.

"He's such a smart ass. The Herr Doktor-Octer-Wocter of what's-it-called, neurophysics. More like Doktor Draft-dodger, huh? So where was he when we all did our time in the barracks? Can't find his woman? Bet he can't find his own prick! All I can say is, he'd better come looking soon."

They wouldn't dream of harming her, she told herself. These men, cousins or schoolyard playmates of her husband, were merely compelled to go through the motions of an antique farce. Like Kaethe herself. They tried to tease her into a better humor. They brought in pear juice and fresh cigarettes. Achim was way too old for her, they said: soon, when she got bored with married bliss, she'd know whom to call. A gray pre-dawn began to define the attic window. Oh leave, she begged them. Leave me alone! They looked let down, exasperated, even angry. All right, then; they would stand guard out on the street. Their boots shook down wooden stairs. If she had not been so tired, she would have wept.

In her mind she rehearsed a witty, future recounting of these events to her father. She saw his sharp features folding into incredulity and outrage, and eventual I-told-you-so. She missed Max.

You should be here, she thought. *You should have found a way to be at my wedding.* Everything would have been different. How? She imagined Max charming Ana Luise and disputing politics with Harro. Achim, too, had yet to meet his father-in-law, whom Kaethe herself hadn't seen in twelve months, not since her formal engagement, a decision Max stamped with approval during one of her infrequent visits by S-Bahn to the Eastern Sector.

She had become a routined border-crosser, during the laxer days before the Wall. But after it went up she became—like everyone else who landed on "West" in that crazy game of Red Rover—an official refugee to the Allies, and to the GDR a deserter of the Republic: a felon. Lucky, according to common wisdom. It was Max who crafted her luck and eased her decision. On the day the Wall began to materialize with thunder of brick-laden trucks and roar of cement mixers and crackle of rumors and radios, furious shouts of Vopos as the panicked and the adventurous, the agile and the suicidal, sprang from roof to roof and out of third-story windows into the amateurishly linked arms of strangers, there was never any overt discussion of which side Kaethe should land on. Where she should make her life next.

She had become something of a burden. Max found Kaethe at age twenty less tolerant and malleable than she had been at sixteen. Max was prospering, had acquired Finnish furniture and a housekeeper; Kaethe no longer provided much amusement to his friends and associates, nor an adoring echo of his views. After graduation from the Gymnasium (grades too marginal to secure a place at the Humboldt University, and in this matter for once a tight-lipped Max refused to pull strings) she jobbed along with her friend Jutta, helping in a day-care ward. "I never suspected you'd like wiping little snot-noses," he said, and Kaethe answered, "Right, I don't." But when Max mentioned an opening in his department, translating classified documents and reports, Kaethe refused. She had taken years to grow into Berlin, to let Berlin grow into her. She moved and joked and sounded like a "Goerre" from Szredskistrasse, and had no wish to go back to being rocked by the seesaw of two languages, two worlds less compatible than ever. She said none of this to Max. Still, he took to contemplating her with eyes narrowed and lips compressed, until he commented without inflection, "You remind me so much of your mother." Too much, she understood him to mean. They quarreled: about Mao versus Lenin, Fidel Castro, the viability of "Socialism in One Country." Max quoted Bismarck and Lao Tse. She denounced his pragmatism as hypocritically self-serving. He found her idealism borrowed and half-baked.

When the Wall appeared—literally overnight, like a joke left by a malevolent sorcerer—they were almost relieved. It offered a tactful way out.

Max was one of the privileged few who heard rumors about the sealing-off in advance. He had pre-arranged for Kaethe a second set of identity papers—to avoid potential future embarrassment, as he phrased it. The documents included a Vermont driver's licence; they continued and brought up-to-date one Kate Shalke's American persona, as if an anti-matter version of Kaethe existed in some parallel universe. The passport, genuine in the purely technical sense, would allow her to come and go through the Americans' Checkpoint, as well as Friedrichstrasse S-Bahn Station, for Germans the only remaining point of East/West interpenetration. The papers, he warned, should not be over-used.

She should tell no one. Certainly not Jutta, who was excitedly organizing a week-long holiday for the two of them, hiking in the Harz. As far as acquaintances on the West side went, Kaethe the border-hopper already had her bunk, literally a pantry off the kitchen of Chinese's apartment commune. Most of her personal items (books and clothes, high school photograph album, hi-fi records) were already stowed in that shallow cave. On her last day, the seventeenth of August, Max accompanied her downtown to the station. She wore her outgrown Gore Academy uniform, bra-less because the jacket was already strained tight across her chest. People in the streets either scurried blindly to their destinations or stood stock still; disrupted in its rhythm the city smelled of sulphur, desperation and fresh cement.

They shuffled in line through the rat's-maze of steel barriers in Friedrichstrasse Station. Max, who had the bachelor ex-soldier's skill with a needle, had sewn three hundred West Marks into her plaid hem. Her dowry, they joked.

"This is the right time to go," Max assured her. "Make your move before things settle into a routine." One more of his lessons in first-strike, in the power of risk-taking to disarm and deceive: Kate S., an exchange student at the Free University in the West Sector, handed her papers to the controller and turned away, laconic and awkward as any young American, to embrace her host, a stiff and tweedy Professor. *Smile politely,* he had told her. *Auf Wiedersehen! This is no farewell. I'll be in contact. You can be a considerable help to me from over there. I'm looking forward to that. And we will be together again.*

"Greetings to the colleagues!" he cried now. "Have a safe journey!" She was brusquely waved forward through the gates and turnstiles, answered all questions in Yankee-flavored broken German, turned at the last moment with an urgent need to throw a goodbye kiss. But no one she recognized was there.

Guards holding machine guns at ready patrolled the platforms and catwalks of the station. They avoided looking directly at her, as if she was bad luck. She was the only civilian. Waiting, she wondered if a new Central Committee emergency decree had canceled all trains. Finally a blazing engine bound for the West roared in; she wrenched desperately at a door till it opened, and stepped up into a nearly empty car and sat on the wooden-slat bench staring down at the tips of her Eastern-made shoes which, she now realized, all along could have given her away. The train gathered speed, a hellish speed, howling at full throttle through the blanked-out East Berlin stations, through the old tunnels whose isolated lamps whirled away backwards like torches thrown into the void.

White fog concealed the village streets and houses. A rooster crowed nearby, conjuring for Kaethe a picture of tingling metallic feathers, long coppery tail-feathers quivering with sound. The cock's crowing soared into churchbells that clanged over the cobbled square. Five tollings. Except for the bell-ringer, they, last night's bridal couple, were the only people abroad so early. Achim's long right arm protected her shoulders from the cold drizzle. His knuckles were neat red ovals of scraped-away skin. He had, as one of the abductors complained, shown a total deficit of humor. Friendships were broken that night. A door and a table-leg and a lamp were broken. When Achim burst into the room where she lay half-watchful and half-dreaming his face was livid, knotted, swollen. Only his limp ashen hair, colorless as driftwood under water, was instantly familiar. For an unreasoning moment she thought he might hit her. She sat up, braced, in one quick silent motion.

The boys had crowded in behind him then, first congratulating, then criticizing, jeering. How had he found the hiding-place? Was there a snitch? A tip-off, finally, Achim said. He'd been to five villages and used up a tank of gas. There's always a snitch, someone said. Has to be. Part of the game, damn it! The wonder is, why this time the snitch held off so long.

Spoke-like streets radiated upward from the square. Now and then a breeze stirred the fog for a glimpse of the forest-furred side of one hill or another. They made out, a mile or two away above the village, a jut-ting half-timbered wing of the Jagdschloss.

"You should rest and wait for me here," he said. They had paused in the middle of the square by a two-tiered fountain crowned with a torqued, spouting trout. "You could rest a while and dangle your feet in the fountain while I go get us another car, or a can of gas." He pressed with his thumb between her brows as if to erase a smudge of dirt. Or a frown. She sniffed the tang of blood and caught his hand and licked the abraded knuckles one by one. Not tired, she swore, not at all. He bent to wash in the fountain, splashing his ruddy cheeks, hair, neck. Dull coins, worthless tiny pennies, lay clustered like mere embryos of wishes under the bubbling water.

"Taler, Taler, du musst wandern," Kaethe chanted in a hoarse, dawn voice. *"Von der einen Hand zur anderen."* Just as permutations of white

had animated the smoky hall of the evening before, the dominant color of this fog was red. A narrow red ribbon had been trodden into the groove between stones. Red geraniums swam on balconies surrounding the square. The brass trout had bulging eyes of red glass. *This,* she thought. *This moment! I never guessed* . . . to be on the cusp of a new life, beside her handsome, fiercely possessive young husband in a fog-transformed square. She had a sense of being a fully aware, fully present observer of her own infinite moment of happiness. It was as strange as the dream of being aware and present at one's own death. She wanted to sing at the top of her lungs, race across the square, hurtle cartwheeling to seek out the magical rooster. But Achim pulled her closer by the damp cloth of her blouse, and began to unfasten its buttons. "No one can see us," he assured her. "And if some lucky peasant did see, so what?"

She stood before him bare from the waist up. He scooped water from the fountain and dripped it over her neck, shoulders, between and over her breasts. "You told me you aren't sure you were ever baptized," he said. She shivered. "Now you're purified for good and certain." He crouched, an awkward, large-boned man grinning and trembling with the effort, to kiss, first, her navel. She looked down at his moving head, at her dark pink whorled nipples, and the tip of his lapping tongue drawing random designs.

In the Jagdschloss, the wedding guests slept heavily. Kaethe and Achim encountered no one. He pressed close behind her, up the stairs, into what until now had been her off-limits room, and bolted the door from inside. They whispered. What they were about to do, alone together, felt illicit, despite all the times they had had sex before. To be married felt illicit, she admitted. Achim laughed along with her. These walls, he reminded, were thirty centimeters thick. No one can hear us, he promised, as before he'd said: No one can see. The pearly dress lay spread over the bed, lively and graceful. Hers, but she would never wear it again. Hers in what sense then? Already her past. What would happen in years to come, to this dress? Where would it end up?

Move the dress, said Achim. Hang it out of the way.

Gathering up the folds of satin she found them still warm in her cold arms. One corner of the room was monopolized by an enormous Biedermeier armoire. All the furniture was outsized and funereal black. When she had finished looping satin over hangers and had closed the armoire's doors, Achim took her by both wrists and pressed her toward the turned-down bed.

The bed was oak, old-style, no wider than necessary, with high sides like a box. The mattress was soft and experienced; when Achim rolled his weight on her she sank deep, while imagining the ghosts of couples who had used this mattress for the same purpose before them. Achim covered her mouth with his hand: he didn't want to hear words. With a practiced twist of his knee he parted her legs. Only her mind was ready for what would come next. Her body felt brittle and chilled, and suddenly, in the suggestive sheets, tired beyond endurance. She wasn't supposed to speak, so to ask for more time she tried to shift away from under his weight. He pinned her in place while reaching, groping for something under the scattered pillows. He drew out a silk necktie striped navy and green. Quickly, like a soldier securing a potentially treacherous prisoner, he crossed Kaethe's hands above her head and whipped the tie around and between her wrists. She didn't resist. She smiled up at him, incredulous. There had never been this play-acting between them before. He tested the knots; they held. You have the narrowest hips, he said, like a boy. That's what I love about you. He set to work on entering her. It hurt as it never had before; *this must hurt him too,* she thought. Please stop, she said. Come on, oh, come *on,* he muttered. His penis rammed coal-hot and smooth as glass. She imagined fever. She was too dry. Come on, it's all right, let go! he said. With a cry of satisfaction he broke into her.

Every thrust he made now burned inside her. She had no chance to join in his movement. No man had ever done this to her. Achim never had. She didn't know him.

"Wonderful. Oh, my sweetest, sweetest. *Wonderful.*"

Tears pooled cold in corners of her eyes. She didn't want to beg or cry and spoil his pleasure. It was only her body he pounded at, after all. She had lost sense of how long. Her mind drifted back to Szredskistrasse: to the question of the exact order of the books on her father's bedside shelf. Achim lifted his bride's hips to slide pillows beneath her, changing the angle of entry. His flushed face hung over her like a setting sun, grimacing with a kind of joy. When he let her go—rolling away smiling, disengaging his stiff, engorged penis which was now finally, dripping with slick, he said, "Wonderful, oh God, isn't this worth all the damn shit, the best fuck ever. Isn't it?"

Bright voices and a fresh giggle passed by outside the door. She came back to the room, the present. Soon there would be the morning-after breakfast to attend, and she would sit bathed and dressed in full daylight at a table with the relatives all around....

"I'm crazy about you, Small Hare," said Achim, "crazy crazy crazy. I better watch out. It's frightening. Do you know the power you've got over me?" But this old mattress, he swore, was a loss, a frustration-device, a fun-killer. He drew Kaethe by her bound hands down to join him on the floor, where he spread out a quilt, and now with the hard wood beneath her there was nothing to prevent her from receiving the full hammering force of his delight.

THE MANDARIN BRIDE

They were poorer than the jobless, who at least had the government's security net to break the fall. Poor enough to drink tap instead of bottled water, to hoard the butts of hand-rolled cigarettes and to cheerfully stoop to pluck a ten-pfennig piece out of the muck in a gutter. Yet "rich in the things money can't buy": a phrase Frau Albus, their landlady, savored in her Saxon drawl on evenings when she invited, then insisted that her "lovebirds" sit down to her oxtail soup, her sorrel with ham, her jewel-red currant preserves. The lovebirds both existed in a state of almost incessant hunger, a subconscious gnawing that did not interfere with energy, lust, or ambition, but could be muted by the smoking of Dutch hand-rolled shag tobacco, so that hunger acquired a pungent flavor of its own. Apart from the landlady's charity, on all days but Sunday their one full meal (rough lumps of gravy-glossed potatoes, brown bergs steaming like fresh horse manure) came cheap at the University canteen. On the long Sundays, when the canteen as well as all city bakeries stayed shuttered, they snacked on bruised apples, Polish chocolate and yesterday's rolls.

Serving them in her kitchen, Frau Albus alluded pertly to the extra calories required by newlyweds. She enjoyed running her sinewy, detergent-scarred hands over Achim's arms and back as she wheeled round the table, guffawing at herself and winking at Kaethe. "Frau von Thall, you remind me of myself! Madcap like I was then, a girl in

my twenties," she said. All three of them knew it was only a wishful
misremembering, although poor Albus was mad all right, had been
driven into her present ecstatic, un-Teutonic madness by a series of early
losses she would reveal in limited doses, over a glass of schnapps, only
when wild with loneliness.

They were poor, and already owed a few hundred marks to relatives
and friends, to Albus and the corner grocer. Achim wore darned Savile
Row hand-me-downs from more securely established relations, Kaethe
dressed in velour jeans and hippie cottons from the Turkish market.
They would walk ten kilometers to save bus fare toward wine and
movies on his assistant professor's dribbled salary and her occasional
windfall from an academic translation. Achim refused to see her take a
"dumb girl" job, such as kindergarten assistant. She was his wife, and
younger; in all tenderness and respect it was his rightful responsibility
to structure her future. Moreover, kindergartening paid beans. She
should focus on continuing her education. "Plan for the long term,"
said Achim, "and the present will take care of itself." This was one of
the incongruously weighty pronouncements that emerged at times
from his soft, mobile mouth.

He wasn't aware that toward the end of each month Kaethe stopped
in at the new Self-Service market on Roseneckplatz to slide packages
of frozen rabbit legs, tins of prawns and sardines (his favorite delicacy)
into her quilted jacket. At checkout she paid only for the oatmeal and
sugar visible in her sagging string bag. Her hands sorting out coins
sweated at the prospect of being seized at any moment by an outraged
citizen. Her heart hammered with the desperation of a hounded,
zigzagging hare or fish. Minutes later, mingling on the sidewalk with
the other housewives, she felt lightheaded, victorious and virtuous, as
after a long day's work.

Dear Max!
The system here in the West is corrupt and immoral and insidious
as hell. I am loving every minute of it. You know, a ten-minute
stroll down the Ku'damm infects you with all the greed you never
knew you had. The itch to consume is a parasite, it inflames the
blood, you can't shake it. All those watches and purses and silk
scarves displayed like untouchable fine art in those lit-up glass
cases. Though when you wipe your eyes and look close the things
are just opulent-ugly. Doesn't matter. EveryTHING is here but

hardly anyone can get at the stuff; people work fanatically just to get a little piece of a THING or a copy that pretty soon falls apart. Here the politicians all talk about "choices" right?—picking this THING over that THING as the means of self-realization. It's pathetic. There are a few opportunities, however. There is a splendid institution called, so correctly, the Self Serve Market. It is a great equalizer. Don't worry, I'm not being suckered. I can handle some temptation. Believe me, I still can't imagine staying here for good.

She wrote to her father every Sunday morning, when their piously emptied, villa-lined street, the Königsallee, fell so quiet she and Achim could hear, in summer, a cat lolloping through the grass; in winter, the creaking of ice on the Grünewald Lake, almost a mile away.

By "rich" Albus meant they had youth, laughter, erotic satiety. But they were rich, too, in things that usually only large amounts of money can buy. Their bow-windowed pair of furnished centrally heated rooms, dusted gratis by the curious landlady, had been the ornate reception rooms of a vanilla-stucco villa in this fine "garden quarter" of the city. Even now the only sign of war having ever blighted the neighborhood was the unsolved, long-term absence of some homeowners (mostly Jews) as attested to by boarded windows, blasted façades and weedy overgrowth. The official solution to such neglect was "temporary occupation" by fortunate refugees who managed to stumble into the right line at the right time. Contrary to her usual luck, Frau Albus had done so. Her socially useful business of illegally subletting rooms to hard-up students required discretion in the Königsallee, which tolerated no radicalinskis, no working-class brats, no couples living in sin and, above all, no foreigners. To have the newlywed von Thalls passing through her iron gate was a wonderful advertisement, a balancing credit against such times when Albus had to shelter, say, a broke bouzouki singer, or a pair of girls up from the country hoping to meet dance-hall soldiers—or even, briefly, a bluish-black, scarified Ethiopian medical student, whom she let in or out only at night, or in suffocating disguise. These things happened because the woman was actually as anyone could see stark raving mad, generous to a fault and soft-witted from loneliness. And so Achim and Kaethe lived for pennies a month in a patrician refuge with parquet floors and stucco cupids on the ceiling, because a noble name looked so appropriate under the doorbell.

And Frau Albus took pride and spoiled them like the children she had never had with goodies she couldn't afford, because they didn't shake off her sudden swooping caresses, and because along with her they looked down on the ambulatory, nattering dead outside.

Marriage, as in a tale from Grimm, opened up for Kaethe a world of everyday magic. At the laundry, Countess von Thall's husband's mended shirts were bundled and ready before anyone else's. She could buy sold-out concert tickets at student rates. Strangers addressed her formally, with *gravitas,* as if she were an adult equipped with a full set of coherent opinions and an unshakable outlook on life. Printed invitations to gallery openings, State cocktail parties, christenings and other celebrations piled up on Achim's desk next to the stained and eraser-flayed draft of his dissertation. Most nights they went out somewhere, invited, on the town. Kaethe learned to waltz, to surrender to the speeding abandon of a full-blown waltz. There were smoky nights spent in scrofulous Wall-side pubs, sucking hashish with Achim's friends. They all, boys and girls, seemed happy to include Kaethe. They let her in on their jokes, teased and flattered, and propped her up by the shoulders, laughing, in the rainy, reeling dawn alleys next to no-man's-land, when she'd had more beer and schnapps and dope than she could take.

No matter how late they returned, Albus, in print housedress and mules, was waiting up. "Just to double-lock the gate behind you, my dear Count." She wore a paisley kerchief over thinning hair and gripped her mop like a lance. Soon she would press her ear against the wall to catch the sounds of their lovemaking. They knew this; they were used to her.

Fools betrayed themselves over her new name. In a letter to Max she described a recent foray to the Free University, where prior to marriage and soon after her move West, her application had been turned down. "Records incomplete and unverifiable." Now she was reapplying, aware of the irony and redundancy of her chosen specialty, to the Department of "Amerikanistik." The senior department professor lowered his platinum eyebrows (silky and long as insect feelers) over the hand she stuck out for shaking. He scooped her fingers up to his lips and exhaled, across her knuckles, the syllables of her predicate. *Liebe Frau Gräfin, Willkommen bei uns ins Institut!*

Those hand-kisses smacked of courtly ancien-regime conspiracy and defiance. At the University, revolutionary factions had begun to spring up in one department after the next. The young buccaneers,

Revoluzzers, slung red banners out of administration windows, protested the "U.S. puppet" Shah of Iran, "refunctioned" classes, and
addressed the University Chancellor himself, through makeshift bull-
horns, as "you ass." "This crop of toadstools," as the silky-browed professor called them, "brats nourished by the warm rain of Economic
Wonder. They are all color and no roots! A decisive kick by the authorities and we'll be rid of these rotten Reds! *Nicht wahr, liebe Gräfin von
Thall?"*

That predicate. Her name. Until the celebratory day and night of
her wedding she had almost ignored it. It wasn't lost on her that Achim
found her faith in the individual Rousseauian nobility of any person *(a
mind is a mind is a mind)* disarming. Her vanity insisted that no name,
whether fabulous or horrible, could ever alter or augment her. That
this particular name, if anything, was lucky to attach itself to her. But
after marriage, the name imposed its practical, irrefutable existence.
She had to learn to answer to it, and to write it fluidly. When she made
the mistake of scribbling her former name on a check or application,
she felt as if she had gone out on the street half-dressed. In the unspoken tradition of newlywed women she compulsively practiced the loops
of her new signature on scraps and napkins everywhere. Rows of repe-
tition, like a schoolchild's dumb training. The female ambience of Gore
Academy came back to her, the incandescence and pallor of girls, girls'
faddish passions and passionate fads. There had been a lasting romance
with signet rings and sealing wax.

Achim promised her a signet ring as soon as they could afford one.
"Gold and lapis, that's always tasteful, don't you think?" carved with
the seal of the von Thalls. The family shield bore a Crusader's cross in
the upper left, an acorn on the lower right. "For loyalty. And, I guess,
fertility," he laughed. "The simpler the design," he explained, "the older
the family. That's a dead giveaway." She noticed that the other women,
her new friends and relatives, all wore signet rings. The encoded outward emblems of a complex secret society. How casually the rings
enclosed soft, unlacquered fingers. She wanted to study the signet
designs up close. Were the others as ancient, as quintessentially noble,
as hers would be?

There was a reverse declension to her new name. The overly awed
dragged it out for egregious embellishment: "Most gracious Countess
Katharina Mrs. von Thall." (She was often being upgraded from hum-
ble Kaethe, a name suited to millworkers and milkmaids, to a four-

syllable *Katharina*.) Even "Most honorable and gracious Princess Katharina zu und von Thall," for the speaker's own glory, and extra measure. (The few princesses she'd met all seemed to make ends meet as photo models for *Vogue*.) At the other end of the spectrum, among the name's aristocratic coevals, she was dubbed in instant class cousinage simply "Frau Thall." An arousing intimacy, a stirring in the newcomer's blood.

Within the family she was Kaethe. She enjoyed her surprising power there to raise high spirits, a mood of promise. Ana Luise laughed throatily whenever Kaethe reappeared on her doorstep, "darling daughter, come to indulge an old woman." The brothers flirted gallantly. Harro raked her cheeks with his torn furrowed lips and sniffed her hair, praised her Yankee custom of washing daily, head to foot and no matter how gelid the water. "You'll show 'em all up! Force us to high standards! A new broom sweeps clean!"

They overlooked and covered up her errors. One by one they came to her, confessionally, as if they had finally found the true and righteous listener, to explain or protest or cry about where they had been and what they had done during the "NS Time." They brought gifts to her of small revered items—a silver thimble, a beribboned braid of Achim's baby hair. All icons radioactive with significance, selected from the meagre hoard of non-necessities the women had saved from pillage, oblivion, conflagration, on their trek in forty-five, under smoking skies seeded with bombs, from Russian-invaded Prussia to the dying, surrendering West. Kaethe mattered. She was the wife of their oldest son.

SOME FACTS
AND ASSUMPTIONS
ABOUT ACHIM

He first saw light in the hectic flame-tongues of tapers arranged like a makeshift altar around his mother's quaking adolescent body. Still the midwife yelled for servants to bring more light. He was delivered—as would be his four brothers in years to follow—on a rubber-sheeted daybed in a ground-floor room of his father's ancestral home. Minutes later outside in the stable-yard a housemaid, choking with excitement, hammered the news on a gong for the villagers to hear, causing the father's prized pair of black Trakehners to squeal and buck in their stalls.

He was the longed-for first result of the union between Ana Luise von Thall, née von Bohrmacke, and Count Ernst Friedrich Achim von Thall, then Lieutenant of Cavalry, whose relatively prosperous estate adjoined the smaller holding of the Bohrmackes. Despite his youth, Count Ernst was a diplomaed agronome; more meaningfully, as the oldest son of the oldest son in an unbroken patrilineal chain documented back to the first Crusades, senior male of the dominant branch of his clan. In 1934, the year of baby boy Achim's birth, the von Thalls comprised approximately one hundred and sixty kin, almost all living within the rural territory of East Pomerania. After 1945 an informal family census would tally thirty women, twenty scattered children, and fourteen adult males. With a few notorious exceptions, and for all its six-centuries-long record of service to the State, the family looked down on politics as a variant of hooliganism, while exemplifying the local virtues of frugality, intellectual modesty and voluntary military service. In wartime the flag-bearers die young.

The Bohrmackes were different: famous throughout the region not for service to the Empire but for their *inwardness*—a fierce, unbending piety, a dedication to charity and ascetic self-denial which found apotheosis in a bachelor uncle: a shy, psoriasis-plagued church organist who endured mystical visitations and had cured hoof-rot and scours with his stuttered prayer. For all the material benefit of a match between Count Thall and Ana Luise, a tall, big-boned, dreamy girl, her family's internecine schism and resistance had nearly spoiled the betrothal. The Bohrmackes were not charmed by Ernst Thall, who had been over-heard arguing free-thinker ideas, who had lived in the notorious bar-racks of Berlin and certainly while in that same swill-hole of a capital had danced polka and waltz with women of every imaginable origin, before returning to claim his neighbors' undefiled daughter.

And so, too, the first eighteen months of marriage, with Ernst fre-quently away and Ana Luise under the tutelage and scrutiny of women of both households, had been a harsh disappointment and awakening for her. She wept over her mistakes: the bumpy, knotted embroidery, rye loaves so charred even the pigs wouldn't eat them. The servants had a right to despise her, she thought; her clumsiness made extra work. She wept each month in new anger at herself, and in despair over the reappearance of bloodstains in her underwear: the barren stain, the worst of her failures. In secret she went to her uncle, the music-maker, the recluse. She rose above shame and did as he told her. Her belly swelled, changed from soft to hard, grew enormous and hot to her rev-erent touch.

The baby was born blue. "Slid out blue as a boiled eel," marveled the midwife later. In her foresight she had planned for the delivery couch to stand near the kitchen, and as soon as she'd uncoiled from around his neck and cut the massive, turquoise, serpentine cord she hurried to the oven, carrying the blue boy, his skin covered with white birth wax, his sex resting like a large squashed flower between the wrinkled blue thighs. She laid him swiftly, alternately, in a tub of cool water and a nest of over-heated linen. Back and forth. Rubbing and pleading and mut-tering. "It works with hound-whelps, it works with the lambs," she prayed. In her own Polish she entreated the Virgin Mary and her own father in Heaven as well, the shepherd Ladzlo who'd taught her how to make dead lambs wake. In her grip the blue newborn warmed to lavender, then bloomed ruddy pink. "He whimpered is all," said the midwife. "He never once did cry."

He had a happy childhood. He thought so, and so he would later tell his friends and his wife. With her rapturous nature his mother loved him to the point of folly; the other women were quick to point out her "child worship" and remove him whenever opportune from her inexperienced, spoiling hands. Achim in turn worshiped his father. Captain von Thall's duties kept him mostly far away—*with his men*—so that when he did return home on brief leave—*to the lap of the family*—his instinct to assume the part of strict and demanding parent was completely stifled by a heady mix of sorrow and exhilaration, nostalgia and presentiment, so that grubby little Achim, swarming up Papi's riding boots and gray twill uniform, past knobby hazards of belt and scabbard, eagle buttons and ribbon-pins, for a breath-robbing whiskery typhoon of a kiss—Achim knew himself in the arms of the true spoiler, the placated yet unpredictable source of power.

Nine months after his father's visit on leave (unless Ana Luise had happened already to be pregnant) another brother would come crowing into light.

It was his brothers whom he loved best. Loved and often wished dead or, much more satisfactory, absorbed back into that mystery of fecundity, their mother. The brothers demanded all his eyes' and ears' and wits' alertness. With each new birth any pretense of supervision over the boys diminished. When war burst out into the open, in September of 1939 (Achim felt pure relief expand in their household, as when after rolling thunder the hard rain finally begins to fall) supervision dropped to a minimal evening count and check. The boys were growing up together, so their father liked to tell fellow officers, like a damn natural litter of hounds. Achim was in charge. His brothers challenged him, all fighters, and each one seemed to him like a different piece of himself. On the other hand he had to shepherd them constantly. They were smaller and "cute." They soaked up the mother's attention. They took the food.

"Aristocrat," he assumed when he was little, was a catchphrase for "poor and uncomplaining." Peasants and villagers could complain to

their hearts' content, yet wore wool jackets, and kept apples and potatoes and cabbages piled under the eaves of their cottages. In the Great
House rags were re-sewn into underwear and sent to poorhouses. In
the Great House the three, four, five brothers each clutched a boiled
potato in a scrubbed fist and filed by a board onto which was nailed a
pig crackling, or a carp skeleton—and rubbed their dinner potato on it,
for nourishment and flavor. At table they held scrubbed hands and sank
their flaxen heads and thanked the Lord for his bounty. Amen.

He became a good student. He had to keep a length ahead of the
brothers. Goethe and Schiller were pompous bores, English was tricky,
but mathematics came easy: a system of tautologies, yielding and trans-
parent. He was happiest designing and dismantling machines—radios,
clocks, a broken loom—cracking the code of how parts slotted together
to perform a complicated task. He dissected birds and snakes with
hands cold and steady, face hot and flushed with concentration. He listened to music in the same way. He was powerfully drawn to harmony.

Although change was slow in coming to the countryside, by 1939
most of the local school's original teachers had been let go and replaced
with certified National Socialists. The handful of disgraced pedagogues
who had not fled, been conscripted or imprisoned took shelter with the
Bohrmackes, famous for turning nobody away. (Later an older Achim
absorbed the idea that it was such sheltering that led to his father's arrest
in Berlin, in June of 1938, for "antifascist activities"—and that arrest,
kept secret from the children, explained the adults' relief when war
came, a development which would require the Captain's military skills,
would restore his value and return him to the healthy fellowship of men
like himself, principled members of the warrior caste.)

But for Achim and his brothers at home, those idled schoolteachers
were a flapping black plague. They had no honest work; they itched to
justify their existence; they pounced on the boys to sour every free
moment with Latin verbs and long division. Achim detested Grandmother for taking them in, along with all her other "cases," the refugees,
both villagers and absolute strangers who arrived after dark. The house
swollen by morning. Beggars. "Pleaders" was Grandmother's word for
them.

All during the glory days of the Third Empire the word "Jew" sig-
nified little to Achim. Never uttered at home, it was just another smutty,
low-class Nazi word. The "pleaders" were bundled into makeshift

beds, with nonexistent wounds bandaged up hilariously whenever an SS commando would make a sweep through the territory. Unrecognizable, scarcely human bundles. "Come, let me show you gentlemen our Field Hospital!" Grandmother insisted. Achim noticed that the crisp SS fellows didn't like hanging around with fanatical charity women of the Bohrmacke type anymore than he did himself.

He teased the grandmother. She had a long face the color of rendered butter oil and a jaw too big for a woman. When she smiled you wished she wouldn't. It was a controlled, pious smile, always with an unswerving intent. He and the brothers once filled the drawer of her writing table with grasshoppers. They neighed behind her to mock her grating voice and long, ivory teeth. Using a basting tube, they force-fed potato schnapps to her Doberman bitch.

He mocked anyone who offended him and anyone whom he feared. He also teased his brothers, who tormented him back, everyone almost always laughing fit to burst. The more the cut stung the harder one was expected to laugh; together the five possessed a rich culture of insults and face-saving, even more savage self-mockery.

Sometimes their mother paused nearby, bewildered, as if hoping her presence might soothe and affect them. They ignored her. She was powerless, rudderless, a person oddly devoid of firm convictions, incapable even of finding enough food for her children. Why had she allowed herself so many, then? Achim by age eight discovered a dip in his sternum, a sort of sinkhole where the ribs came together, half as deep as a fist. *Rachitis*. Rickets. None of his brothers' bones were bent by rickets, though: the little ones had always been fed first. "My dear, dear boys!" Ana Luise hovered in doorways, watching them with an uncertain smile as they shouted and gouged and laughed with each other. Her smile so unlike the grandmother's, so purposeless, she seemed not to know it was there.

There were no men left in the villages. With time the teachers were gone, the clergy were gone, the older schoolboys and even Achim's diffident, miracle-working, musician uncle had been called away. Cattle, pigs and horses either requisitioned or slaughtered: there was no sense trying to keep anything alive.

He was ten when someone broke into the empty stables in the depth of a rain-swept night. This wasn't uncommon; the family didn't fear thieves so much as the ravaging fire that refugees might kindle with remnants of straw. Achim, as acute of hearing as his vanished uncle, pulled on his clothes and went out to investigate.

By height and beard the stranger seemed to be that curious, almost exotically rare figure: a grown man. Hunger and wind had pared his face so close that Achim could not begin to guess his age. His feet were swaddled in muddy rags; he wore an unidentifiable, bleached and bloodstained uniform under a belted, brightly striped blanket. "Snuff out that light, boy," said the stranger. Achim obeyed. "You don't frighten easily, do you? Which one of the brood are you then?"

Even in the dark there was a welcome bracing quality to the stranger's voice, like a brisk rubdown after you've been out too long in the cold. "My name is Achim Friedrich Johannes."

"Right. Good. The oldest son, then?"

"Yes, sir!"

The man commenced coughing. Small noises at first then racking, as if something big was stuck in his chest. Achim could hear how he tried to muffle the racket in the folds of his sodden blanket wrap. When he could breathe again he said, "The Captain—the Count, your father —sent me."

"I thought so." Achim's father, so everyone said, was leading troops in Russia. Was he still? How many kilometers away is the Front? Achim wanted to ask, but instead he waited.

"Bring your mother to me. And then fetch your grandmother here. She's a resourceful woman, isn't that so? Don't tell anyone else, or we're all in deep trouble, understand, don't . . ." The warm voice trailed off as if drowsy, fading into sleep. "Don't alarm your brothers yet. There'll be time enough before you leave."

"We're leaving? For where? When?"

"For the West. Before cock-crow," the man said matter-of-factly, and now Achim had proof that this was a messenger come from a far country. The man didn't even know yet that all the cocks in Pomerania were long since slaughtered or starved.

Grandmother Bohrmacke resolutely refused to join them. "*Someone has to watch over the estates until you all return.*" She smelled strongly, sickeningly to Achim, of the beetroot soup kept boiling in her kitchen. She wore a pair of pistols crossed over her apron; she stood surrounded by female suppliants who no longer bothered to hide even in daylight. Ana Luise begged uselessly, pressing a knuckle against her large lower

lip to stop its trembling. Achim felt his body humming with the excitement of leaving. For the first time he recognized the yawning enormity
of Chance. He foresaw that they might never meet with Grandmother
again, after the trek began.

Things were falling apart faster than even a messenger from the
Front could anticipate. Once the von Thall group had reached the main
Stettiner road, they discovered that there was no longer any need for
secrecy. As the rainclouds cleared their two carts merged with a steady
westward trickle of traffic. Ana Luise called out to cousins and dance
partners she hadn't seen in years, freeing an arm from the leather traces
to wave. She and the midwife and midwife's sister pulled the first cart.
Two brothers walked alongside. The second, smaller cart, loaded with
sacks of beans and various treasured objects and three-year-old Leon,
the youngest brother, was spanned by Achim and the grunting, spitting
messenger. He had kinfolk far to the west, in the Taunus hills, he said,
as did the Captain himself. "One has reason to believe that region will
be relatively secure after . . . (voice down to a coughed whisper) the End
has come and gone. God knows. God knows we deserve a place to rest."

So Achim as an adult clearly remembered the beginning of their
trek, but little of the days and nights in between. Monotony of hunger
and sore legs and back, gut cramps, fevers. Ana Luise's irrepressible
triumph and pride in her *usefulness* at trading all her jewels and serving
silver for a serviceably healthy ox. Achim coming to the strange, uncom-
forting realization that no one, not even the brothers among themselves,
bothered to quarrel anymore. The arrest of the messenger by a squad
of errant Gestapo. The theft of the ox by a gang of women, at night, at
knifepoint. Small Leon, his blond curls acrawl with lice, reclining like
a prince on the flattened sack of beans as he regarded the bombers that
streaked the sky, oohing at their extravagant offerings of color and light
and screeling noise. "There, look, another flyer, another *great* big flyer,
look Achim, look up!" And, over a month after setting out, their arrival
in the clattering, already overcrowded courtyard of a Taunus hunting
lodge . . .

"You see," he murmured to Kaethe, as they lazed in bed together on
a wintry Sunday morning, "we have so much in common. I grew up
partly in a castle full of ragged, nothing-left-to-lose refugees, and so
did you."

"I hardly remember, though. And I didn't stay long. And for me it
was in a foreign country."

"Well, for me West Germany was foreign enough. Comical accents, funny food. They called us the barbarians. At first all we had to survive on was Care packages—remember those awful things?"

Strong winds moaned around Frau Albus's solid house. Reflections of snow rippled across the ceiling. "No," Kaethe said. "I was too little."

"Powdered milk. Uck. And corn, corn, corn. My God, I hated the slimy taste of canned corn! But in one box I hit the jackpot. I found a complete tuxedo. Even the patent leather shoes. It all nearly fit. I took that for a sign."

"Let's be careful about signs. We both had the curse of religious grandparents."

"Militant Lutherans, threatening us with angels."

"Puritanical angels..."

"But they didn't succeed, did they? I don't find you suffering many inhibitions! Listen. With our children it will be the opposite, right? We won't manipulate them. Nothing forbidden on mere flimsy principle."

"Trust me. I'm utterly amoral."

"We both are. We're so alike. Here, look at our *skin*. Raise your arm next to mine, like this, in this light."

"The air's freezing. Brr. Cover me back up!"

"But first, do you see? Our skin is the same exact tint—"

"Silvery. Fish-white with a tinge of yellow."

"Now touch. Touch me. Here, up along my ribs. Slowly... silky, isn't it? With your eyes closed you can't tell the texture of you from me. Try it. An experiment. Close your eyes. Stroke here, and here. What do you say? Of all five senses, touch is the hardest to deceive. Do you feel it? We're indistinguishable, so alike. Like brother and sister. Almost twins. Every time another one of my brothers was about to be born, I was praying for a sister. A girl for me to hold, to adore. I promised I would get her everything she needed, and protect her forever. Stop. No, better not stop yet. Go on. Oh, come up here to me now, forget the cold, small Hare. Kiss me. Make me hard."

A THEORY AND PHYSIOLOGY OF PERCEPTION

He was luckier than some, having had to switch the topic of his dissertation only once, following the devastating discovery of a "scoop" published through Johns Hopkins University. Over a year's work wiped
out, but he knew of worse cases—balding, stooped "students" kept
shackled to their lab benches for twenty semesters or more. Candidate
von Thall's revised, defensive thesis design was both more general and
more particular than its torpedoed predecessor.

"A Theory and Physiology of Perception" with its string of subtitles
would zero in on the concept of the JND, the *just noticeable difference,* a
key concept in fields ranging from decision theory to market psychol-
ogy and live-subject experimental design.

"Let us define 'Perception' as the registration of stimuli by any of the
five senses. For reasons of time and economy the study's extensive, original, experimental explorations will be limited to the phenomena of
visual and auditory perception, and augmented by a thorough review
of the literature.

"Throughout, the JND provides a powerful conceptual tool for
establishing pragmatic threshold values in perception, as well as for
modeling function and 'switchover' or 'trigger' points in the synaptic-
neural cortex."

He received "fishing expedition" queries from firms such as Siemens,

Messerschmidt-Blohm, Ciba-Geigy. Their poverty was temporary, he told Kaethe. An interlude they'd look back on with nostalgia some day. Once this thesis was finished he'd be earning thirty thou at least. There'd be money for an apartment of their own, good new suits and a car.

"When?"

"For God's sake, Small Hare. I've only just started the new project. And this is science, so it's uncertain by definition, right? By the way, we *are* talking about brain surgery. Literally."

He sounded happy rather than annoyed. She couldn't see his expression. They lay in bed side by side on their backs in the place and position where most of their real conversations occurred, and this time it was evening, the room lit only by one guttering candle stuck to a saucer on the floor. The fatty smell of wax reminded Kaethe of slightly rancid butter. She was hungry; they hadn't had had any supper yet.

Achim brushed his arm across her breasts. He was fond of quoting Martin Luther: *In der Woche Zwier/Schadet weder Mir noch Ihr*—the coy rhyme of the churchman translating roughly to "Two times in the week/does me neither harm nor her"—but they did it far more often than the Church founder advised. At least daily, sometimes twice on Sundays. And sometimes, as tonight, her inner labia felt swollen and hot even before they began, before his first exploratory, diagnostic touch. Achim liked to have her that way.

He liked to fuck her when she had the start of a fever, too, but would then be careful not to kiss her mouth.

"Maybe you shouldn't," she said now.

"Shouldn't what?"

"Take an industry job," she said. "Maybe what you want, what satisfies you, is to go on doing pure science. Not give up research for the money."

"Is that how you see me? A lab hero in the white jacket?" He rose, shook off the covers, his magnified wavering shadow almost covered the ceiling.

"Don't know. Anyway, not just for the money."

"Who'll support us? You?"

He bowed between her raised knees. She felt the warm saliva, the same temperature as her skin, before she felt his lips or tongue. He would kiss her there—only when she was a little abraded and reddened would he kiss and lick her sex—*to make it feel better.*

"You could divorce me," she said. "And marry some dumb rich girl."
"Like I should have in the first place?" Briefly, he raised his head.
"One of those pearls-and-twin set heiresses . . . They're all over you
at parties anyhow . . . and you'd have all the money you need, and could
stay with science. And—*oh.*"
"Go on," he said.
But all sensation was concentrated between her legs, in the space
covered by his mouth and testing, probing tongue. The rest of her body
lay like an unmapped continent, limitless and nearly numb.
Kaethe drew a breath. "A gigolo. You'd have everything you want."
She smiled. This struck her as a brilliant solution.
"And what would you do? Go on. Talk."
"And then I could become your mistress, you'd set me up in a secret
lair and come spoil me like this and we would never become bored or
take each other for granted and we both could always . . . *oh. Oh.*"

Only Achim still remained pure. Or, as he put it: a scientist is, if not
utterly pure, at least a political virgin. The rest of his immediate family
(remarkable for their swift adjustment to exile) had moved into the
western power structures like liquid seeping into a dry sponge. One
brother would soon clerk for a Supreme Court Justice, another was in
Bonn as an adjunct on the Chancellor's staff. Uncle Harro, not unnatu-
rally, had been taken up by the Christian Democrats as an "expert" on
Soviet economics. Even Ana Luise had found her speaking voice, to
her sons' astonishment, on the influential Ecumenical Council of the
Lutheran Church. True that Leon, the youngest brother, deep in his
faceless world of harmonics and the rhythms he tapped compulsively,
day and night, had no status other than substitute organist. But no one
gave him much thought.
Despite political demonstrations swirling down the main avenues
nearly daily—anti-U.S. imperialism above all, also anti-Shah, anti-
nuclear, anti-Vietnam, anti-neo-Nazi, pro-Palestinian, anti–capitalist
tool press, anti–police repression, anti–entrenched reactionary-
faschistoid professorial hierarchy—most departments at the Technical
University continued to function. Experiments went forward in labs
locked against errant anarchists; PhD candidates such as Achim continued to flatter their all-powerful "doctor fathers" and work for them
as gardeners, child tutors, car mechanics, wife amusers and house
painters, in hope of eventually ascending to a position from which they

could distribute the same genial abuse to later generations. Most students had been lured from the more conservative states of western Germany by Berlin's draft-free status. Most were dedicated to the idealism of physics, chemistry, astronomy. Most were miserably lonely. Leaning out the windows to watch chanting, banner-swinging marchers below, the young scientists shouted encouragement and sometimes ran down to join the rally for a few kilometers, for the snapping fresh air and chance of flirtation and uplift of a cause, whatever the cause and however fuzzy (to young scientists) its theoretical underpinnings. It was clear enough, and enough to know, that virtue and uprightness lay on the Left side. Farther and farther to the Left, as time went by, lay justice, and the only chance of ever curing the unspeakable and unspoken disease of history, and also emancipation from stuffy tradition and its unwholesome prohibitions. To the Right lay the unfathomable past. To the Left lay joy. It was worth stealing a few hours off from the lab, for a brightened conscience, and for joy.

What Kaethe witnessed was different. The Free University had been established—after partition, as a sort of quickly erected dialectical counterpart to the East's trophy Humboldt University—deep in leafy, prosperous, suburban Dahlem, in the heart of the American sector. The scattered low buildings felt insubstantial, like a camping ground or barracks. Far from the milling downtown staging area of the main demonstrations, the students fermented in discussion groups, Red Cells, anonymous commandos.

In mid-May of her fourth semester, Kaethe walked between pale pink rose hedges up to the house of the professor with long eyebrows. A Doberman charged up to the other side of the iron-barred, glass door. Its full throat quivered. "Hush," she mouthed, "you know me." Her professor preferred, in such unsettled times, to hold his appointments at home.

"My gracious Countess von Thall, how delightful to see you, come in, do come in!" He trapped her hand and knee-kicked the dog. She winced at the hand-kiss (recognized now his mocking adoration, or was it adoring mockery?) and glanced back to the street, wary of witnesses, radical spies.

Black tea stood ready on a tray in the shrouded, curtained parlor. All the windows were shut and latched tight.

"You shivered," remarked the professor. "You find this room chilly?"

Kaethe smiled, examined the tea leaves that formed a swaying cross at the bottom of her cup, and explained that she had come for advice on how, in which direction, to continue her studies. "Things are falling apart," she said. "'American Studies' are not popular right now. It's difficult to finish a course when students boot the faculty out of the lecture hall and refunction the subject and abolish all requirements and grades. It's difficult to get official credit."

"Indeed. Quite so." His thin lips tightened.

"Do you have any suggestions?"

"Time. Give them time. Let them guillotine each other. The revolution will eat its children."

"I don't have so much time. I want to write a thesis, get my diploma—finish up."

"Do you need a diploma?"

"What do you mean?"

"You have a husband. He is well situated. To take care of you. You're a fetching young lady! It's not as if you were a man." He slipped a lemon biscuit to the dog.

"Excuse me? I'm not sure I follow." Her mind momentarily groping. She stared into her cup.

"Alternatively . . ."

"Yes, Professor?"

"You *could* come here. To me. For private instruction, I mean. I have the ear of the higher administration, as you, Countess, may well imagine. Of course I can see to it that you receive the proper credit and proper documentation of same. As to the little thesis, we could chose a subject that is less theoretical, less demanding, more of a data-gathering nature."

"Private lessons?"

"By private contract. A simple honorarium. To me, under the circumstances, an honor. I would hardly charge what my time is worth. With some diligent application you can earn your diploma, dear Countess, in express tempo, so to speak—to do with as you will."

He chuckled. He drew the dog by its russet forepaws up onto his knees. The animal whined in a note so high as to be almost inaudible. Achim would be interested in that sound, she thought.

"Well, Countess?"

She imagined how the Professor's kiss would feel on her mouth: that it would be long and excursive, simultaneously dry and sticky, like his lectures. She saw them paired in an eighteenth-century engraving: *The Philosophy Lesson.* She imagined his thin arm and tickling hand wandering up under her lacy skirts. She set down her cup, sputtering laughter.

Somewhere in the house's recess a telephone rang. At the same moment the dog scrambled free, bounding toward a window. The professor swore, swatting furiously at red hairs on his trousers. Glass imploded into the room, showering the frantic Doberman: through the glass a stone wrapped in paper tumbled along the Persian rug until it reached Kaethe's toes.

"Give me that damned missile!" ordered her professor.

She obeyed. He snapped off the rubber band, unfolded the paper and read, while Kaethe edged closer to the broken window.

"Whoever threw it seems to have run off," she reported. She wondered if that person was someone she knew.

"*Naturally.* The cowards." His face was suddenly marbled red. "Pardon me, Countess! I must retract. I can no longer offer you—I can offer nothing. . . . Nothing is as I had hoped. I will be leaving this Godforsaken place. The Rector will grant me a leave of absence. I shall demand full compensation!" His voice scraped like a rake. "You—you better come away from that window. Come over here, now!"

The dog obeyed. Kaethe nodded but stayed where she was, turning toward the rose-perfumed, inward rush of spring air.

In Berlin there was no place left for neutrals. Achim chose sides. Because the name Achim Friedrich Johannes von Thall might send the wrong signal to fellow progressives, he began to introduce himself as plain "Joe" Thall. He signed up with the Young Socialists, the activist, junior wing of the SPD. Uncle Harro, from his conservative perch, approved. "You could do worse than get in thick with that steam-engine Willy Brandt. The man sups with the devil himself." The Tech Uni's YuSo chapter was an earnest, mostly male band of students who gathered on folding metal chairs in a basement rental hall of a pub. They waited in vain for a visit from the Mayor. The air was stale and the comrades unwashed. The room next door boasted a bowling lane; YuSo speakers often were drowned out by the huzzas of beer-swilling bowlers and the thunder-rumble of their pitches. Kaethe's thoughts drifted, during the initiatives and debates of the YuSos, from the ponderous apostrophizing of the class struggle and socialism's March Through the Institutions to the story of Rip van Winkle. She recalled it to memory by whispering phrases in English: the *discontented wanderer, bowling* contests of the cantankerous, hard-drinking Catskill *dwarves,* and the *twenty-years' sleep.* And when she woke, would there be a New Economic Order on the planet? Socialism with a Human Face? Justice?

Achim nudged her (on purpose?) as he stood up. When speaking to an audience he consciously pitched his voice deeper than normal, while glancing down frequently at the card of cramped notes fitted into his palm. This was their third YuSo meeting; he had risen to speak at each, and at these moments a frown bulged between his blond brows, and a trace of spit gathered forward between his lips. Tonight Joe's subject seemed to be the question of how to popularize a campaign for increased public investment in pure scientific research. As the floor shook she wanted to press his frown smooth with her thumb. Bowling balls smashed against pins and a cheer penetrated the dividing wall.

For Kaethe, to recall her first life—the life before Berlin and before her reunion with Max—was like dreaming open-eyed, in images as trivial as Washington Irving's portrait in a textbook, as homely as the bucked teeth of an eighth-grade teacher, as haphazard as crossing over the broad, wind-crimped Hudson River on an outing with yowling schoolmates in a yellow County bus. It was like being the keeper of secrets that could never be communicated, because the key to their code had long since disappeared.

Her father was literally deaf to his own "Ami" past. In a sense she admired the thoroughness and discipline with which Max had progressively erased huge swaths of time—events, places and people. Clutter. She had learned on her infrequent, always too-short visits East to avoid mention of his parents, or the land and landscape where he and Kaethe had both spent their childhoods. A dead, expressionless glance would be the only reaction to the name of her mother. And this last fact, the more she thought about it, struck her as such a radical claim to freedom that his refusal to engage memory seemed almost rational. He taught her by example how little memory a person needs to carry, in order to survive and thrive.

No one else knew about her visits across. In this she deferred to Max: nobody on this side of the Wall, not even "Joe" Thall, knew about the U.S. passport. She kept that oversized, gold-embossed document of her pale, fleshless alter ego, the American Katie Schalke, stored in a *Lebkuchen* tin along with a few emergency dollars and a train-and-streetcar schedule for the Soviet Sector. Her own sweet secret.

Applause jolted her. Pallid, sparse-bearded engineers and scientists nodded fiercely and drummed the floor with their heels. Everyone here warmed to Joe. They grinned up at him hungrily. How he attracted allies! It was a knack, partly physical, like getting cream to whip, or staying upright on skis. He wanted to teach her to ski with the best, and also how to ride horseback; they had, after all, standing invitations from friends on country estates. As he took his seat the tweed of his trousers brushed her arm, bare though the month was November. There were men in the room who admired Kaethe, and this pleased him; he liked to choose her dress, sure of his own taste. It's good to be envied. He noted the lurking, longing glances of other men, and after meetings would ask her whether she would consider going with any of them. Maybe as a threesome? Or if one had his own steady girl, a mélange of all four together? *Think about it, Schatz. Simply an experiment, we need new experiences, what do we have to lose, we trust each other more than anyone—so wouldn't that be fun for once?*

In a corner of the hall stood a battered metal beer keg. Soon, after formal adjournment, the chairman would hammer loose its wooden plug and warm foam would spurt and spray anyone who stood too close. Then Kaethe and the few other women would pass around slopping half-liter paper cups while the talk reverted to business: to dissertations, scholarship funds, the stress limits of metals, proton accelerators, limits of infinity.

But for this moment, as she watched Joe Thall beside taking the comrades' questions (smiling at the comrades, gratified of course, but also beaming with idealism and so young, suddenly, in her eyes) she was overcome by a sudden up-welling of emotion. Desire, fierce possessiveness, but not only that. This was something richer: both pride and humility played in an ardent yearning to merge absolutely with this man. And yet she could weep over the challenge of ever bridging the distance. It was as if the husband looming over her was wrapped in brilliantly reflecting mysteries. By being loved by the others he had become, again, a stranger.

The first Sunday of Advent. Fading mercury sky of afternoon, when the sun after a few hours' uncertain appearance has rolled back down below the horizon. Ana Luise, whether from the habit of parsimony or to refute the night for as long as possible, had lit no lamps. She hurried to greet and embrace her oldest son. She was beaming and making watery sounds of delight.

"Children! That you've come after all, when you surely have so much else to do." She was consciously, splendidly dressed for the occasion in a rustling, cobalt blue silk dress, with the rakish accent of a tasseled red shawl. Just as her house came on loan from the State ("temporary use, term undefined") so admirers in Berlin and elsewhere brought her gifts and refused to take no for an answer. "And so punctual! Enter, enter, Harro is already here. Your brothers are en route."

A glad teariness was magnified by the older woman's glasses. Caught in the embrace, Kaethe inhaled the aura of her mother-in-law's body: 4711 cologne, and the gamy smell of her iron-streaked hair twisted in a thick bun. Woman's sweat. Spearmint and laundry starch, and the brassy, iodine whiff of blood that trailed her everywhere, reminding her son, so he too often complained, of those early war years when his mother was ever pregnant or giving birth. Always milk and blood, the combination of fecundity and hunger. *Now she's got running water, if she would learn at least to* wash, he said. *But she's oblivious.*

Kaethe ducked free. She didn't exactly shy from the smells of Ana Luise—they seemed irrepressible, natural rather than unclean. But she wondered if the blood smell was an unavoidable aspect of a certain age, connected to the mysterious female event she had heard referred to as "the Change." In the normal course, she presumed, a young woman would by now have learned the details of this future fate from her mother.

Achim, on his turn for the embrace, closed his eyes. "Yes, Mother. Enough please, Mother." He twisted away.

Ana Luise, who tended to laugh more out of a sense of pleasure than a sense of humor, laughed deeply.

Harro rose in the dim dining room as they entered. "Finally. Sit here by me, my girl!" He pulled out a chair.

The pine wreath lay flat on the table. Embedded in it were four unlit beeswax candles in metal cups. "No, remain standing, please," Ana Luise begged. Her voice shook with excitement. She called for the maids, the old nurse and her sister, to come hobbling from the kitchen. *A household of crippled babushkas!* Achim whispered, squeezing Kaethe's hand.

"We should wait for my brothers," he said out loud.

"But now is the moment. Nightfall," countered Ana Luise. "They're too late." Twisting her hands in the fine dress, she struck Kaethe as both nervous and implacable.

"Hairsplitting, dear sister," said Harro with an affable shrug. "In His birthplace Palestine I reckon it's already tomorrow."

Ana Luise had placed on the table in front of her a cream-colored leather Bible and a box of wooden matches. One match bloomed, throwing everything else into darkness. Guiding one shaking hand with the other, Ana Luise bent low to ignite the first candle. It sprang alive.

"He is on His way," she quavered.

"He is on His way," they all responded, raggedly. Kaethe felt hands fumbling for her hands. In six distinct voices, joined together in a rough ring around the table, they intoned the Lord's prayer. *Das Vaterunser.* And if Ana Luise knew about the scenes during Kaethe's growing-up, the threats and storms over her childish refusal to pray to God the Father (dopey dumb superstition, my real parents are atheists remember? You can't make me!), what would she think of Kaethe? Hardly the worse. She would forgive. *Christ is in the heart, my daughter, in the impulse and the act; the spirit will be revealed in His own due time.* So she would say. Ana Luise could lead a person to the brink. Then she could make the leap look easy.

By candlelight, through misted glasses, Ana Luise read from the Prophecies. Then she handed the Book to Achim, pointing to the open page.

"Where?" he asked.

"'And beside this...'"

"'And beside this.'" He shot a humorous, helpless glance upward, to disclaim any allegiance, before he resumed. "'Giving all diligence, add to your faith virtue; and to virtue knowledge; and to knowledge temperance; and to temperance patience...'"

His voice slowed. Earnest and beseeching in the small parlor. The candle flame broadened as he read on. Its light outlined his full, moving lips softened in shapes she'd never seen before. In her calm state of boredom and incomprehension Kaethe was surprised by a stab of lust. A starry flicker deep inside her.

"'And to patience godliness; and to godliness brotherly kindness; and to brotherly kindness charity. For if these things be in you, and abound, they make you that ye shall neither be barren nor unfruitful in the knowledge of our Lord Jesus Christ.'" He closed the book.

Lust, thought Kaethe, is the emotion that doesn't lie. Her sight blurred, close to tears. Gratitude for lust, that invites forgiveness, generosity, even divinity. All manner of thing will be well. Where had she heard that?

"Thank you for reading," said Ana Luise. "Let us pray silently now."

Heads dropped. Harro's bald pate collected the last light from the window.

What does prayer feel like? How is it done? By rigid concentration, like recalling a memorized sonnet or the quadratic equation. By slipping into a practiced trance? How desperate do you have to be, for your prayer to get through all the other prayers? What do people pray for? The abstract goodies such as mercy, charity, peace on earth? The things most people spend a lifetime striving for are presumably laughed out of Heaven.

Ana Luise looked up first. She gazed directly at Kaethe, seeming still to hold a complete, fully formed prayer in her eyes. Without blinking she removed her glasses. The candle flame jumped between them.

Kaethe looked away, obscurely intimidated. Uncle Harro grasped her elbow.

"Amen!" he boomed.

Finally the lights were lit. The brothers arrived boisterously. The second oldest brought along his fiancée, a daughter of minor Dutch nobility. The third oldest, on a week's leave, preened in his new, nattily tailored Bundeswehr uniform.

"I detest having to see you wear that," said Ana Luise. "A uniform looks to me like a death-shroud."

The sons groaned. Leon sing-songed, "Ladybug, ladybug, Pommerland is all burned down, fly away home."

"The next war," said the second oldest, "will only last about fifteen minutes. No need for shrouds."

"Cynical pups," said Harro. "When you are *old* dogs you'll see how sentimental life can make you. Funny—in my experience it's the guys who get dished out the worst breaks, who end up sappiest. Now why is that, I wonder?"

"And what about you?" asked Achim. "Are you a sap?"

"Nah. I'm the exception that proves the rule. Ask your mother!"

Ana Luise poured coffee. The maids, reeling under the weight of the tray, brought out the Baumkuchen, a massive, iced tree-trunk of a cake. All the von Thalls ate in fast, large bites, grinning up around mouthfuls as if mastication itself was a form of conviviality. The Dutch girl, lisping impeccable German, kept up a stream of agreeable platitudes. Kaethe picked at the dry cake, preoccupied with what had passed between her and the Mother after the wreath-lighting, before the others came in. An imploring look? A command, or an attempt to inject her will and her vision into another's mind.

But now Ana Luise had crumbs stuck on her lips and was laughing appreciatively at some rude exchange between her boys.

"And so, how long have *you* been married?" asked the Dutch fiancée.

"Three years."

"And no babies yet? Goodness. Well, I can't *wait* to have children. I want at least four or five. It's the goal of my existence."

Harro landed his arm on the back of Kaethe's chair and leered at the visitor. "Kaethe don't have time for kiddies. Our brainy girl, this one is. Keeps us on our mental toes. Reads Kant and who is that guy? Adorno. Goes to the *University.*"

"Really?"

With his free hand Harro poured rum in his coffee. "So what will it be, Kaethe my Schatz? Once you get the big degree, a 'Doctor' to match your husband there, hear hear—what's the job to be? *Kak rabater,* girl?"

The room had suddenly quieted. The brothers all turned, hoping for a fresh laugh, toward their uncle.

"I'm not sure what I'll do." She set down her cup. "Translator?" For that she would need only to pass the State qualifying exams, not finish up a diploma, let alone a PhD. The finishing line had receded further and further into the fog of student-revolutionary chaos. "Maybe."

"Simultaneous? Like in the UN? Now there's the job must pay a mint."

"Really?" asked the Dutch girl.

"If she wants to, she can translate like a parrot!" Again, Harro spoke up for her.

Achim leaned forward. "My wife," he said with a deprecating smile, "is a closet scribbler. She's going to be the next Jacqueline Suzann."

Her stomach contracted as if she'd been punched. The brothers guffawed. Achim blinked at her, indulgently. Kaethe held out her rattling cup and saucer to her mother-in-law's coffee pot. "I'm not against the idea of children, at all . . ."

The second brother chucked her under the chin. "Then why do you run around all over the place? Look you've got *us* now. This is your family. Aren't you ever content?"

"Do we have any beer?" said Ana Luise dreamily, pouring the coffee. "Beer helps a woman conceive. The hops as well as the yeast. Vitamins!"

"Don't forget," said Harro, "the need for early bedtimes. Plenty of r and r!"

"And watch the brain strain." The third brother smoothed his uniform.

"My doctor friend," said the second oldest, "told me the anti-baby-pill can make a woman infertile. It happens."

"Hush," Ana Luise warned.

"I've heard," offered the Dutch girl, "about some phenomenal caves in Hungary, where you can go bathe and the magnetic radiation has an incredible boosting effect on the ovaries. Really miraculous."

Swallowing with difficulty, Kaethe drank down coffee she could no longer taste, couldn't have said whether it was hot or cold. The morning after her wedding she had thrown her pills away—risk made sex more exciting, she found. Now she stole a brief look at her husband. Sometimes they fucked standing up, he pressing her against a convenient wall, raising her slightly by a grip under the arms so she teetered on her toes, to fit the height of his upward tilting hips. And sometimes (only this morning, in fact) on the bed he would reach back around to hold her thighs and squeeze and insist until her legs pointed straight up to the ceiling, leaving every place inside her open to his thrust, and the flood-bath of semen. Three years, she had thought until this night, was not yet long enough to worry about. Other things mattered to and distracted them both, at least for the time being.

"Radiation? Superstitious nonsense!" said Harro. "Whether the business clicks or not is all up to a woman's psychological state. She can block, or receive—the power's in the *mind.*"

Plates clattered as the two ancient sisters began to clear away. This was a painful sight to behold: one trembling dish at a time, a fork at a time. The halting, slurping shuffle of felt slippers, because shoes no longer fit the women's tiny, gnarled feet.

Ana Luise patted the hunched shoulder of the old nurse, who had pulled all five von Thall sons into the world. "The power is love," she said. "Dear Harro, *love.*"

"Ach yah. That dementia. That bloody irritation you can't get rid of, can't scratch off or cough out—it sticks in your craw like a peach-pit! Suffocating. Makes your eyes water worse than in a coalmine. Ha har."

"Oo," said the Dutch girl, "you are really a dreadful cynic, yourself," and Harro looked pleased, and gave Kaethe a comradely squeeze on the shoulder.

In the kitchen, as she scraped dishes, Achim came up close behind her.

"Don't kiss me when I'm washing up."

"You're mad at me."

"You simply let them think . . ."

"Think what? Anyway, it's not up to them, right? Forget them."

Piano notes seeped through the closed door.

"Is that Leon, playing carols?"

"Don't begrudge, for God's sake. This whole ritual is for Mother, after all."

"I don't begrudge. He plays so well."

"For a guy with only one oar in the water, sure he does. So come on. Come warble with us! You shouldn't set yourself apart."

Leon, struggling to extract music from this piano, which was a loan like all the rest of the furniture. He scowled, spit bloomed between his lips much more thickly than on public speaker Joe Thall, his torso oscillated, large head bobbed, and his feet stomped the pedals. He looked like a clown trying to row and bicycle simultaneously in thin air. He played *Kommet, Ihr Kinder* and *Es Ist Ein Ros' Entsprungen* and *Stille Nacht, Heilige Nacht.* The notes sprang out pure, with little tender innovations of timing and suggestions of counterpoint. There was no trace, in the sound, of the player's visible rage and frustration. The other von Thall males stayed seated at the table, eyes half closed, crooning baritone and bass with their legs stretched wide in front of them. The women clustered around the piano. The Dutch girl's trained voice soared confidently in the *Venite Adoremus,* while Ana Luise's torso swayed along with her youngest son's, and her expression grew beatific, a mask of ecstasy.

Leon raised both hands from the keys. In the pounding silence Ana

Luise tried a few uncertain bars of a song that had been sung through already. No one followed her. Harro called out, "Kaethe! What do they sing in far-off America?"

"All the same tunes. Just a different language."

"No—give us a cowboy Christmas song! A folk song!" The single advent candle, half-consumed, lit his broad face from below.

"Maybe... 'Go Tell it on the Mountain,' then?" She remembered the tune, though not all the words. The verses she offered were pieced together. Her voice was small but tonight it held true and everyone smiled encouragement, while Ana Luise swayed as she had for her son's magnificent music. To have all their eyes focused on her, to be the center point of rapt attention, and the air rushing in and out of her, made her warm and light-headed. Her blood hummed. She sang *over the hills and everywhere* and pictured her grandparents' snow-laced fields in the village of Glass River. Reaching for an *hallelujah* she felt a wave of heat chase up through her body, engulfing her, faster than sound.

Leon had abandoned the piano. The keyboard was now shut. Kaethe sat on a chair and all the family had changed places in the room while the room itself, throbbing, seemed much brighter than it had a moment before.

"Is she all right? Should we give her some rum?"

"Don't raise her head up yet!"

A hand pressed her neck, pushing until she was bent forward again from the waist, head bowed between her knees.

"My God in Heaven. She scared the daylights out of me, going down like that."

"Yes, yes. A doctor, do you think?"

"What would a doctor do?"

"She's never sick. Never! Kaethe has the constitution of a horse."

"Let her up now. It should be safe enough. Here's a cold towel..."

She was helped to sit upright. She felt the towel's icy smack across her brow.

"You fainted," said Harro.

"No. Never have." A swift, nameless apprehension squeezed her heart.

"Always a first time for everything."

"So. She's all right now, looks like?"

"Probably never been better."

"You know, my dearest, you really must begin to take more care of yourself!" Ana Luise, stroking her hair.

"Can I bring you anything? Water? A nice fresh beer?" The Dutch girl's eyes sharp with speculation.

"What's the matter? Tell me what's going on, somebody! Why's Kaethe down on the floor?" Leon, distraught.

Achim gripping her hand in his, and the protective, proprietary glint of the gold ring. "Nothing so terrible. Sometimes, women faint."

In freezing winter, Kaethe and Frau Albus set milk and left-over herring out on the garden walk for the strays; some mornings these offerings lay frosted and undisturbed, other days every trace had been consumed, though whether by cats or rats or some other nocturnal prowler there was no telling. The gaunt, high-shouldered toms undulating beneath the hedges and through the brittle grasses kept their distance: they wouldn't be petted, nor coaxed toward the warm breath of the open door. "And thank God for that," said Achim. "Anyone can see they're feral and full of vermin and a dozen diseases."

"Such a hazard!" Albus mocked in a piping, puppet voice. "The Government ought to step in and protect us!"

"I mean it. I don't want my wife, in her state, to touch those animals. Best solution would be a dose of arsenic on those tidbits out there."

"Brum brum brum. You'd never dare, Herr Count! You've a soft heart like the prizes in the shooting gallery. Those big, stuffed, scarlet satin hearts—"

"Call him *'Joe,'* not Count," Kaethe prompted.

Joe Thall had recently won election, unopposed, as district representative for their YuSo chapter. At the same time his thesis research was turning up results so tantalizing that his professor appeared to be scheming to publish extracts under his own name, in a flattering, classic sort of betrayal. Recently, Thall was keeping his drowsy wife up past midnight with excited debates about the rewards and risks of academic pioneering versus a political career. There was something portentous about his phrases and the promises he held out that made her uneasy.

He brought her treats and surprises, sometimes coming home by bus during a long lunch break. He transported dripping maraschino-cream specialties from downtown cake shops, copies of the *Herald Tribune* from Zoo Station, hothouse flowers in wobbling cones of paper. All far too expensive, they needed to save pennies now more than ever. But he also needed to spoil her and encouraged her to express extravagant wishes, to set him difficult tasks. She slept and woke in a bovine, queasy haze and wished she could simply vomit. She ate crackers in homeopathic nibbles as recommended by the midwife. Once he brought her kumquats—tiny concentrated versions of the oranges she had shared years before with her Gymnasium classmates—and she found they alleviated nausea. She had never felt this kind of happiness before. So quiet, lucid and limpid, abiding like air around her.

But among all the gifts there would be no signet ring, they agreed. It was hard to believe there had been a time when they had been too ignorant to recognize that anachronistic fetish for what it was: elitist, anti-democratic. All across Western Europe the rings served the ludicrous-sinister aim of preserving the oligarchy of ancient tribes. A network of power clans, basically unchanged since the fall of Rome, torn but not destroyed by two world wars, and now in the ominous process of restoring itself. Weighty gold rings encased heraldic jade or lapis, onyx or bloodstone. Weight of their tradition ignored such flimsy pop constructs as nation-states, the Enlightenment, emancipation of the working class. The rings were mating signals between bloodlines so etiolated and inbred it was a wonder the women still bore fruit. Poor Leon, Achim said with a regretful shadow of a smile, wasn't exactly a unique case. Achim put away his own carved ring in the back of a drawer, in the dented silver cigarette case that held four buttons cut from his father's cavalry uniform, and he kissed his wife's undecorated fingers with a signature smile of wistful sarcasm and self-knowledge.

"Here's something to keep you out of trouble," he announced on Christmas Eve, after their return from the ugly, modern church they were patronizing only for the quality of the choir.

"I can't believe how the Count spoils you. Open it!" Frau Albus had barged into their room under the guise of offering a huge bottle of blue Bols liqueur. She knew what was in the ribboned box almost as big as their sprout of a tree, stolen from nearby Grünewald forest. Her cheeks bunched up in a hectic cherry-dark burn.

They emerged struggling, tiny claws sticking like pin-sets into cardboard, purring with ragged energy into the light. Two kittens. The strong sweet odor of urine rose from inside the box. With two hands Kaethe plucked them both loose from the box's walls and settled them in her crossed arms where the claws scrabbled to raise miniature ribbons of blood on her skin and to jab holes in her blouse. Their bulging possibly sightless eyes were gray-green overlaid with a bluish sheen. One kitten was gray-furred, with hair long and wispy as an old man's beard; the other felt more solid in her hand, a brindled tabby stripe.

Kaethe was babbling kitten-talk while fending off Albus's attempts to swoop in and grab a kitten away.

"As Landlady I should forbid you to keep them," said Albus with a piratical wink. "Against House Rules."

"They're very tiny," judged Kaethe, "to be taken from the mother. Weaned already?" She didn't ask where the mother was.

Achim shrugged. "Beyond my expertise. But they look like survivors to me."

Kaethe's breasts, already a good size-and-a-half larger, often tingled, and especially now under the clawed-up blouse as the kittens butted and squirmed blindly against her.

"Earlier I lifted their tails. A boy and a girl," said Albus, nearly succeeding in a raid. "I suppose we realize what that means."

Achim said calmly, "We'll have them neutered in due time." He leaned in and scooped up the tabby. It hung limp from his hand. Kaethe gaped. "Don't worry," he said, stroking the flattened ears. "Of course they're yours. But—why not let someone hold one a while? Sometimes, Schatz, I think you can be a little bit selfish."

THE RIVER SPREE

From crossing to crossing, the longer she stayed away, the drabber East Berlin looked on her return. Monochrome and flat as a page. Home. *Mein Zuhause,* she said out loud, though not very loudly, as she stepped out of the Friedrichstrasse Station into a midday as colorless as dishwater. Sharp ashy snow bit her forehead. Twice, three times a year she returned. Any more often and the number of visas stamped into her passport would raise severe suspicion. The Vopos didn't stint with their stamps. Each one-day permit, with official signatures and receipt for currency exchange and times and dates of entry and exit scrawled over the proud sextant-and-miner's-hammer (signet, she thought), exhausted a full page. Sometimes she explained the biannual trips as a chronic student's research into the architecture of the late Baroque, sometimes as social calls on friends acquired during earlier study trips. She answered the interrogations with a nasal accent and cutthroat grammar. She had transferred from her American college to the Free University, she explained, on account of a fascination with German art. The young Vopos in their jaunty caps joked that she must have a Communist boyfriend. She was laden with heavy net bags lumpy with coffee and chocolate, nylon stockings, patent medicines, scented soap. A visitor from the West wasn't expected to cross empty-handed.

She saw no sign of Max among the clusters of men (long dark overcoats, rubber overshoes, thick welted gloves) and women (fake fur collars, mannish felt hats) hovering outside the station.

I've missed this place, you know. Kaethe wasn't talking to herself, but to the attentive listener lodged inside her—*Johanna* she called this person—though of course Johanna couldn't literally listen, being hardly more than a concept but however unformed still a close companion. This deep breath of relief she drew would be Johanna's introduction to East Berlin air. Unlike the West sector, this was no propped-up appendix to a distant country, but remained the real capital, the center, battered old Berlin-Mitte. The breath she drew tasted of brown stove-coal and motor oil and the wet, pearly imminence of more snow. Behind them loomed the arches of the old Reichsbahn, where flocks of pigeons wheeled in the illumination of enormous weather-smeared panes of greenish glass. Farther behind the station, the deep and narrow Spree river churned between steep stone banks, waves clashing like chunks of black rock. *See? What it's like. Not much to show tourists.* Plenty of open space, at least. No effort at "reconstruction." Icy snow-devils polkadancing through the jagged fangs of destroyed foundations. On the far side of the river stood Bert Brecht's theater, where the bard of proletarian rage had ruled absolutely, with the canny egotism of any desperate, exploitative tyrant or dried-out, plagiarizing writer. If she had not moved across the city, would she know her former idol was now so discredited?

Here the river curved through the dark heart of the city. To the north, and down to the south where it broadened into a vast inland harbor, the Spree (chunks of silver, obsidian, Prussian blue) joined and became an element of the Wall, daring boats, rafts, submarines, even swimmers to cross. Last year a six-year-old girl had drowned. The escape boat shot out from under her family, she drowned in this same narrow choppy water, screaming for help. Surely at that age expecting her pleas to be answered. The reporters wrote she was visible even without aid of binoculars, floundering between the slick banks; there was time for photos to be taken from the west side. And yet none of the watching guards had moved, none overcame his fear of the consequence of disobeying orders: this is what a political stalemate means. What would she know if she had stayed in the East?

She crossed Georgenstrasse into Friedrichstrasse, heading south toward Unter den Linden. From the shelter of the post office entrance a person in a long overcoat stumbled into step behind her.

You'll be followed, I hardly need mention, Max had said years before. Please, my dear, don't let it annoy you if our foot soldiers are inept. And don't embarrass them! It's hard to get good help these days.

Followed?

For the usual reasons, on the one hand. To wit: Who on earth is this Katie Shalke? As a loyal citizen and my invaluable daughter, on the other.

But if they know who I am, why do I bother with the passport, with the whole charade—

They? Now you're sounding like a boulevard press paranoid, Kaethe-cat. You know there's no single "they." We have layers, the world has layers, and we can be thankful for that much. Different views result from differing angles. Or do you want every Vopo fresh from the provinces to have access to your dossier? Checks and balances, Kaethe. As long as "the left hand knoweth not what the right hand doeth," and so forth . . . He had quoted the last in English; she caught an echo of her grandfather's accent. *And in the end, it's all for your own protection. Suppose you appeared to be persona grata here? How long do you think your pals in the West zone would put up with that?*

Her arms ached unbearably. She paused to drop and shift the bags from one side to another. Her follower today, about fifteen paces behind, looked to be a woman of fifty or so, with a lipless nutcracker profile, head protected by a large flowered scarf from the light snow.

"Allow a stranger to lend a hand, Fräulein?" Two fists, flexing in tight black calf gloves, lifted her sacks from the pavement. She smiled up into her father's twinkling, one-sided smile. "Oof, heavy!" He mimicked a stagger. "Bourgeois life must be treating you well. Oh, my darling. Darling Kaethe!"

She felt lightened by more than the weight of the bags. It was a struggle not to embrace him. The seams carving down his dark cheeks. She saw with a momentary pang that his hair had gone mostly silver. Like a Siberian fox.

"You're staring. Do my late hours show in this winter light?"

"No, no. It's just so great to see you. I worried you might have been held up—"

"You always think I'll forget all about you and leave you in the lurch, Kaethe-cat. But I never have, have I?"

They walked on in step, turning left onto Unter den Linden. This stretch of avenue, hemmed by the massive, pillared façades of the Humboldt University, extended by the courtyards of graceful Frederickian palaces, punctuated by damaged spires and cathedral domes, always suggested to Kaethe the essence of a previous Germany —a place serenely out of time, beyond the reverberating crimes and terrors of recent generations. Indeed, Max agreed. Ancient, this part of town. Bull's-eye of the old, star-shaped fortress built after the Thirty Years' War, long before the notion of "nation"... (Kaethe's mind wandered. The question was, when to reveal her news. Announce the dialectical change in her own life, the event that even now must be showing through as a blooming complexion and quicker smile, because Max interrupted himself to comment on how well she looked. When, and where, to tell him? The news curled up inside her like a glowing source of energy, keeping her fingers warm and eyes bright.)

There were plans on the table for transformation, he pointed out. Finally, out of the ruins, new State buildings, the world's highest TV tower—we'll see. Already the comrades enjoyed such major innovations as the new Interhotel, and this Lindencorso Café across the street, shining walls of glass, tubular steel tables inside, all the modern amenities, spacious and gleaming. They would take refuge there soon from the cold. But for certain kinds of conversation, fresh air was better.

Kaethe glanced back at their "escort." Don't worry about her, ordered Max. He knew that woman well, an old Stasi regular. She was paid well for street duty.

The students hurrying through the stone gates of the University looked like children invading a giant's house. Wasn't this university, too, she asked Max, in some degree of disorder? The former Nazi-resistance fighter beloved Professor Havemann, for example, kicked out for "criticism of the regime." (Would she know even this much if she had been allowed to enroll here? Would she understand the reasons better? Remember: like so many antifascists, Havemann in freedom chose *this* Germany, the socialist East.)

"A long, messy, unfinished story," answered Max. "I'd rather hear how your studies are going."

Kaethe fastened on the middle distance. She had feared an attack of nausea marring this visit, but the cold air—always colder on this side of the Wall—braced her. "With luck I'll finish in a semester or two." She could do it, she believed, now with a fresh and urgent motive. Not to live like her homemaker cousins-by-marriage, or risk ever becoming her own soggy mother: dependent on in-laws' charity. "Only there are constant disruptions. Demos. Hurdles. Distractions."

"Hurdles. Bosh. Life is all about hurdles. What distractions? You're a married woman now, Kaethe-cat, solid felix domestica, right? What could possibly *distract* you?" There was a raw, excited edge in his voice, a happy twitch to his smile as he observed her more closely. "Or should I ask who?"

A flurry of snow crystals struck her eyes. Here was the subject behind the subject: Max, not concerned about her studies, simply didn't want her to be married. That was all. Nothing personal, presumably; he held no particular grudge against a son-in-law he'd never met. Max Schalk, a busy man, had sent one formal note of congratulation to Achim Friedrich Johannes von Thall, who in turn asked less and less about her "family." And why should he? The mother long dead, a faceless father, and no roots anywhere beyond.

"I don't have a lover, Max. Believe it or not."

"My respects. You amaze me."

Nothing personal. Max viewed marriage as either a ruse or a self-deception, and he hadn't expected his daughter to persist in one or the other for so long. At first he'd treated "Countess von Thall" as a sort of a crass, shared joke, a conspiracy he'd had a hand in; later he wouldn't mention it at all. Max didn't punish her except by imposing a certain distance. For Kaethe the recurrent surprise was how *she* had managed in each long interval between visits to forget his disappointment. And this time again she sensed his flickering hope, that she was about to wake up to reality, acknowledge the true isolation the two of them shared.

"I don't even flirt much. There's no one around worth flirting with," she said. "All the men have turned political. Politics ruins them. They turn so monkish and self-righteous. Plug ugly."

He laughed out a white puff of breath. He stopped to hug her, and the bags filled with coffee cans banged her backside and she looked happily, in a sort of helpless triumph, into the blinking eyes of the babushka-spy. "You might try women, darling," her father whispered.

"Listen, Max—" I have something to tell you.

"Just joking! Never mind me. What's the problem, then?"

Somewhere a dog barked maniacally. This wasn't the right place. She would wait to tell him until they went back to the Lindencorso

Café. There in the full light and warmth he would welcome her news. She felt sure of this. She imagined how his expression would transform as the future sunk in. For a moment she was able to see past herself, into how this coming event, the *"Johanna,"* would alter his life too, and all the ways he saw himself. Even "von Thall" would seem to him less absurd. "Nothing. My kittens! For Christmas Joe gave me two kittens, did I tell you? And I'm not sure whether before I left I fed—"

"Well, well. Just look who's down below." He pointed. They had reached a small quay. She leaned over the low wall, saw slick steps leading down to a mooring of the sinuous, ever-returning river. A small barge bobbed on the current. Across a stone-flagged expanse beside them rose the reddish, blackened, curved stone walls of the Berlin Cathedral. Shell-blasted angels overhead. Their follower, crimson-nosed, snuffling and openly defiant, took shelter against a locked side-door of the church.

From the roof of the barge a black dog barked up at them, quivering, legs splayed. Might be a poodle, a standard poodle, said Kaethe—big and unshaven.

"Watch how his tail-stump wags," Max said. "Should he prostrate himself or attack us? He can't make up his mind."

Max grazed her chin gently, with his gloved knuckles. "Are the kittens all that's on your mind?"

"Oh. Yes. No—you haven't mentioned the writing. My scenes?" She lowered her voice. "You must have received them. In the mail pouch. Did you read?"

"Comrade Schalk! We thank you for the contents of the pouch. The pamphlet drafts and all that. Industrial research budgets are nothing new, but corroboration has value. As for the 'scenes,' yes, your YuSos are wildly funny sometimes."

She stared at obsidian water and quaking black dog, and pictured the mail-hole in the bole of a plane tree, near the tiger-land, inside the Zoo. She had no idea who the go-between was, or whether the "donkey" was permitted (required?) to read the pages she placed there. Putting a limit on what she could write. *Max, I have something to tell you.* "I can't imagine what use my stuff is to you."

"Plenty." He squeezed her waist, and that brought back her smile. Most of what she sent was a hodge-podge collected and bundled with her weekly letters. Drafts left around the basement meeting room, bits of recollected talk that might illustrate some trend or other, descriptions of APO demonstrations, even newspaper clippings. For all the furtive method of delivery (how easy to get used to a routine that felt like the resuscitation of some childhood game, and anyway she welcomed an excuse to haunt the Zoo) there was never a question of "betrayal." Of whom? Among her acquaintances, who was vulnerable? Not a possibility.

She had also begun a sort of impressionistic journal of daily life, a primer for someone on the other side.

"Did you read the . . . impressions?" The snow melted instantly on her face. She was blushing.

"Those fancy bits! At first I assumed they were additional reports. I worried you'd gone soft-witted, over there." He chuckled. The poodle, fallen silent but continuing to watch them, collapsed with its muzzle cradled on outstretched paws.

She thought about how hard it would be to capture that dog, the clothes-line cased in ice, that red-nosed woman behind them in the doorway—to freeze the frozen moment in words. She wanted her pages back. She would plunge them in the black river until every trace of ink rinsed away.

"To keep any sort of a record? Is that ever wise? You might as well join our friend back there, with her camera and dictation machine. Or is it make-believe? But I always thought the main purpose of writing make-believe was to make the teller stronger. Something like an acting career for the shy, you know. Except that heaven knows, Kaethe, *you're not shy.*"

Kaethe shook her heavy head.

"My dear. You've picked yourself a bed. So lie in it! Art for art's sake takes quite a stack of cash . . . "

She shivered. She suddenly feared looking old to her young father. Old, because of nothing finished or even much begun. Young goes to old, no warning, no second chance. A numbness began to seep in. The cold intensified as they stood still. Soon she would insist on returning to the café. And once there, she thought, she was under no obligation to tell him anything. Keep *herself* to herself.

"Ah ah! Careful now. Don't be sulky." He lifted her chin, squinting. An inspector's probing look. "You know why I'm talking to you like this. Don't you? Because it's a debilitating sort of individualism, in most cases. 'Art.' If you were the rare exception, Kaethe-cat, you'd have started much, much, earlier. And now, if you persist? After years squandered, along with any potential productive work—that's how it goes, you know—in the end what I've just told you will sound like the mildest, kindliest little bit of advice. You understand?"

She nodded.

"Now, what about translation? You could help me. The work's piling up over my head. All right, we'll talk later. Here's one more thought. If you did move back here, we have the Writers' Union, the cultural committees. . . . People do know me, after all. A matter of mutual respect. It would be . . . an entirely different situation. Will you remember that?"

"Yes."

"Promise."

Below them the dog yawned, offering his stark pink throat.

They ordered fresh bread rolls heaped with raw ground pork, garnished with onion and parsley. A local delicacy. This Lindencorso Café was a rich officials' hangout: Max bought a split of foamy Georgian bubbly, overwhelmingly sweet. The enormous space of occupied tables echoed with subdued voices. People here didn't look nearly as plain and poorly dressed as they had on the street.

In the warmth, sipping wine, her resentment vanished. How long might it be, until she saw him again? "Max. I have something to tell you."

"Spit it out!" At certain moments the American in Max still shone through. That grin in the rough, pitted skin. Outflung gestures confident of finding enough space.

Something shifted low inside her. Like a fist opening and closing.

"Wait, Max. Just a moment. I'm sorry—" She shoved back her chair. "Wait, I'll be right back—" Desperately, suddenly, she needed to go to the bathroom. Far too long out in the cold. She nearly tripped over the feet of the escort. Found the arrowed sign, the corridor, the door, pushed past the old woman in charge of soap and towels.

The cubicle door reminded her of schoolgirls' toilets, barely covering the hip region. Socialists have nothing to hide.

She tried not to moan out loud. Had that wine been so bad? Her gut twisted; cold sweat broke on her forehead. Brown boots passed back and forth under the door. Finished, she hurried to pull up her underpants. Max would be impatient. Quick glance down at an almost meaningless reddish-brown bloom in the crotch. A brighter swirl of pink adrift on the porcelain shelf beneath her. She rose and turned to inspect what had come out of her, holding the back of her hand against her mouth. Feeling nothing, or near to nothing now, no more than twinges, a ripple of emptiness. She made no sound, but forced herself to pull the cord to flush. In the efficient roar she closed her eyes and pictured the chop and tumble of waves in the Spree. Then she buttoned her clothes enough to go out and buy a "lady's wrap" from the attendant outside, to be tied into her already stained pants, as she had done many routinely inconvenient times before. Everything almost as usual.

"You took a long time. Feeling all right?"

"Fine."

"You look on the pale side."

"Please. We talked enough about me."

"What else? You were just about to say...?"

Comprehension can take a while. The jittery facts wobble before settling in. Her white plate wobbled in the light of a Socialist chandelier. You never lose by keeping silent, she thought. Only if you tell can you be accused of lying. Already a suspicion was creeping in: Had she lied to fool herself? The celebrations, much too soon. The disappointment as the story collapses. Disillusion. Rapunzel's gold dissolving back into straw. And yet, this ache in her swollen breasts.

"I owe everyone now." She was seeing the presents: a strand of dimpled, antique pearls from her mother-in-law, the scrappy pair of kittens she had dubbed Karl and Rosa, after the heroic founders of the Party. (Happiness sees nothing as sacred.)

Max frowned. "Owe what to who?" He reached for her right hand, and captured it tight.

In the new café laughter shattered off the walls.

Take your time, Kaethe-cat," he said. "Leave yourself time. You can tell me now or later. Whatever this is."

She looked up. His ruined face glowed, transfigured by concern. She loved him.

THE EYES OF
THE SHAHBANU

Freundin, Die Frau, Fuer Sie. Women's magazines, overlapped like fish-scales on the side of a Ku-damm newsstand under crackling clear plastic curtains, protected from thieves and the wind-hurled spring rain. Waiting for her bus, Kaethe stared at the nearly identical candy-garish covers. They all featured close-ups of the most recent bride of hawk-nosed, ancient-blooded Mohammad Reza Pahlavi, the Shah of Iran. A diamond tiara rode in Farah Diba's brown wavy hair; her neck and cheeks and red lips were as plump as a well-fed toddler's; her eyes, nearly crossed in an expression of inward serenity, had the firm sheen of chocolate glacé.

"Let's hope this Queen manages to produce what his Highness wants," said a woman who had paused beside Kaethe, "else who knows what sort of Oriental punishment lies in store for her. Poor thing! He didn't show much mercy with the first two wives, did he now?"

Their umbrellas bumped. Farah Diba, thought Kaethe, was a care-free, silly-sounding name, unlike Soraya, which had a certain tragic, astringent potential. *Farah Diba*—she looked like a schoolgirl playing dress-up. Where did she come from, did she like her life as a Queen, her husband's unfathomable wealth and unchecked power and incessant risk of assassination, their junkets abroad, where she would see herself on the covers of foreign magazines, more popular and gossiped over than a movie star?

"They're coming to visit us, aren't they. Next week. Well, everybody knows, it's in all the papers! The Shah and *Shahbanu,*" pronounced the woman with pedantic satisfaction. Kaethe glanced down at her, at the orangey Brillo-pad hair middle-aged Berlin women achieved with their henna and vigorous perms. "I'm going. Either to City Hall, or to the Opera. To see her! Just for a peek. Are you? I don't know why, the family's all Social Democrat—my old fellow never would have allowed me! But he's in the grave. And I'm retired. What else is there, I ask you? Anyhow, she'll have the royal ermine on her, and he's such a smart figure in his sky-blue uniform—" she shook herself, laughing. "I'll get that cribbly feeling all over. Something *different.* You know what I mean, young woman!"

"I hear there might be trouble," said Kaethe. The wrong bus came and went.

"Ah, the rowdies, you mean! Those hairy-all-over Communists, and their boss what's his name, the Red Rudi—"

"Rudi Dutschke."

"And him married to an American, did you see? How his wife can stand all the scraggly fur on his face, imagine those disgusting kisses, where I always thought the Amis were persnickety against germs! Have you seen the wild hair on their other boss now, Fritz Teufel— *Devil,* exactly the name for him—well, we've got him behind bars now. I don't let the rabble stop me, young woman. *So-called* students. Draft-dodgers! Hey, this is a free city, no thanks to them! Anyway, the mayor warned that pack. Just who is it pays taxes to support those parasites? Sex is all they study, they boast as much themselves, they're at it like rabbits night and day! I'm sure Mayor Albertz's men will be on top of the situation at every twist and turn—that's what we have the Political Police for—"

"Still," said Kaethe. "Even so." As she stared at Farah Diba's portraits (full face, three-quarter, the gold collar, the red dress) the Persian Queen's expression swam from Sphinx-like satisfaction into uncertainty. Apprehensive melancholy. Did Farah Diba, waiting on the Peacock throne for conception like a pile of twigs late to catch fire, now and then shiver at her own utter lack of power? The inability to control even her own body. The object. Her will and her individuality irrelevant to her body's purpose.

"And these vermin want to tell *us,* who lived through the Sovietskis murdering and raping and before that Hitler's gangs, tell *us* what democracy should be! Decency, public decency, that's where democracy starts! Am I right, yes? You should indulge yourself, go see their Highnesses! A proper young woman like yourself. Don't be intimidated by that rabble!" With a crisp wave goodbye, the woman stepped back into the flow of pedestrians. She hadn't been waiting for a bus after all. The city was full of lonely widows who accosted strangers with their pent-up need to talk. It was a form of begging where no coin changed hands.

Five days later Kaethe kept half an eye out for that wiry frizz of tangerine hair among the heads that trickled out of subway and S-Bahn and side streets, rising like water toward the Deutsche Oper. No face in the crowd looked remotely near pensioning age. The faithful Shah-and-Shabanu admirers, she guessed, had seen their fill at their Highnesses' earlier, tumultuous matinee appearance at City Hall.

Here people murmured to each other with grim-set expressions. They walked fast and with a purpose. These were not fans.

Theatre posters lining the streets announced the night's performance: Mozart's *Die Zauberflöte,* June 2nd. The Flute to be played to the fairy-tale Persian pair, this left a cloying spun-sugar taste in her mind. An apothecary clock showed the time: seven twenty-two. Curtain at eight. Soon the royal cavalcade, limousines and mounted police, would arrive from the west.

It was a fresh, rainless evening, the city's famous sparkling air artificially further lit-up by floodlights gilding the opera's high façade, and headlights of rows of police cars and motorcycles in the Bismarckstrasse—another of the city's improbably wide avenues never designed for traffic, so said Max, but for the triumphal processions of returning armies. Had Friedrich I, the Great Elector, foreseen tonight's rag-tag army of dodgers, peaceniks, polit-tourists and deserters? Dressed in patched jeans, sandals and a bulky sweater, Kaethe blended in. Only the police, with their epaulets, peaked white caps and rubber truncheons worn at the waist as smartly as dress swords, looked soldierly. She chose one officer to smile at, her old habit. His cheek twitched. Annoyance? He was handsome in a fascist sort of way. Walking backward, she pulled the new pocket Rollei from her knit shoulder bag and snapped his portrait: a test shot. No flash, the extra sensitive film came from Max; she had four more rolls. Now her subject's whole body twitched. Nothing more. He was bound by orders to stand in place.

"Shithead imperialist tool!" called a woman walking alongside. She was pushing a collapsible stroller with difficulty over cracks in the pavement. The large child bumped along in its cramped tube, sleeping slack-mouthed under a banner that read SCHAH=MÖRDER. Kaethe frowned; it seemed late for a child to be out.

Joe had ordered her to stay home. Where she went in the city for a few hours didn't strike her as his business; she hadn't meant to let him know. But after the news bulletins of the afternoon he had grabbed her house-key. "If you want to be a fool and run in the streets at night with the show-offs you can *stay* out in the street." He was all Joe these days, political, but his line had no sympathy for the anti-Shah demos. "Let the Persians ream out their own dirty stable. It's not a German problem." But what about the Savak then, she asked, the Shah's secret police in Teheran, kidnappings, torture chambers, shouldn't we students speak out, show our solidarity with the local, anti-Shah Iranians, against the visiting despot right here? "Hoping to change what? It's sickening, it's brutal, also it's their thousand-year tradition. Don't be so naive. As a movement we're squandering our *potential,*" he announced. "We already have the NATO weapons on our plate, Vietnam on our plate, relations with Israel..." He suspected ultra-right infiltrators of fomenting the demos. "They're aiming to marginalize the Left. They've found the perfect pressure point, to irritate and scare the working classes. *I forbid you to go!*"

Albus, all darting sapphire eyes and sharp nose scenting drama, slipped into the room. Righteous and furious, Kaethe had torn past them, out through the gate into the street, had feinted running in the wrong direction before she circled back for the bus stop and the ride into town. Now, with a spreading sense of warmth in the company of the demonstrators, hands linked with strangers whose set expressions had begun to thaw, the soft "du" passing between everyone as if they were all brothers and sisters from the same literal family, with one shared history, common memory—now she could admit Joe might have some logic on his side. So what? What did a single marching body count for out here—only a hundred and ten anonymous pounds, given the chance of arrest she wasn't so dumb as to carry any ID—among the thousands converging on the Opera? Zero. Besides, she had her own private logic for coming here. It was all a matter of balance. Everyone's life was, presumably. In the Saturday marketplace butchers and cheese-sellers weighed out the goods in a scooped metal scale, piled on the graded, opposing, balancing weights with judicious sucking of lips, and not so long ago any vendor caught giving false weight risked hanging, or having his or her hands and tongue chopped off, at least. She had Max to please, Max who might suspect she'd forgotten him, so long out of sight. She hadn't crossed the Wall since winter, on a dark, distant, snow-blurred afternoon in early January. Her letters since had been sparse and so uninformative he might think she had something to hide. But the pictures of tonight's demo, scenes and close-ups of faces he could feel confident about, would be a gift. He'd welcome her again.

"Shit," said the carriage-pushing mother. "Pigs leave us no room to breathe."

Official vehicles and limos and black marias and rows of foot-police occupied all the open boulevard space in front of the Opera. An apron of heavy iron-grille barriers funneled the arriving protesters onto the opposite sidewalk and held them well away from the colonnaded entrance—far enough, Kaethe gauged, for even the most energetically hurled tomato or bag of paint to fall short of the target. Behind the side-walk stood the planked barrier fence of a construction site, wobbling as people swarmed up for a perch and a view, squinting west. Barks of "Shove on, move ahead, give the comrades behind a break, damn it!" mixed with excited swelling choruses of "Shah-Shah-Charlatan!"

There was a change. Kaethe now hardly needed to make the effort to walk any longer; she was sustained upright and borne forward into the narrowing passage by the increasing press of determined bodies, and her fear of being squeezed too hard (not squeezed to death of course, these were her sisters and brothers, but the camera that her im-mobilized arms couldn't reach drilled like an auger into her ribs, and her shoulder was being bent forward by some body more massive than hers but equally helpless to shift)—the fear was counter-balanced by the extraordinary comfort of this inescapable embrace. She breathed in smells of hair and the spicy dry shampoo they all used between showers, men's acrid sweat and women's musk, damp wool, menthol-eucalyptus drops and garlic sausage and Rothhandle cigarettes, fainter whiffs of hashish and pine-oil cologne. There was no modesty here: the embrace rubbed and penetrated and alerted every part of her. A woman's pony-tail trailed against her lips. Bone and muscle slipped against her mus-cles and bones. Unmistakable was the soft resilient bulge of a man's crotch wedged between her buttocks as everyone slowly, slowly moved forward. She felt the bulge take on shape in the groove of her behind, expanding and hardening in exquisite, anonymous distinction.

A strong hand clasped her by the waist, to steady either its owner's balance or hers. Kaethe let herself lean back, lifted and incapable of falling. Smiling. At a moment like this everything was settled, all choices were inevitable, and what would happen had already begun. The man forced so close against her, saturating her clothes and jeans with his body's warmth, was innocent. He had nowhere else to turn. Banners crackled overhead. The choruses booming "Murderer, Murderer," and "Bring back Mo-mo-mossadegh!" struggled to stay synchronized. The royal Guests of State would arrive any moment. From the other side of the barrier, police in riot gear and their favored allies, the so-called Jubilee-Persians—an imported gang of Shah-supporting goons—were stabbing through the bars into the crowd with wood staves and nightsticks. "Back immediately, all of you! You're obstructing a public way!"

Between the barrier and the fence, the crush of demonstrators in front and behind, there was nowhere they could move. Whenever one person somehow managed to heave away from the jabbing sticks the whole crowd swayed, linked, a single enormous animal. As Kaethe rocked backward the right hand round her waist was joined by a left hand; its strong, crooked thumb drew circles, massaging her navel. The left hand traveled slowly, almost imperceptibly, down the slope of her stomach to her mound, already swollen against the tight-sewn welts of her jeans. There was nothing she could do. The unyielding length of this stranger's erection rested stiffly against her ass.

Her mind, and her body, and her eyes: all three were thoroughly and separately occupied, as if three selves of her roamed in this crowd tonight. Though she'd lost sight of the mother pushing the stroller— but surely even the most radical mother would have turned for home by now?—she kept on glimpsing, in the stark blaze of headlamps and roaming searchlights, unexpectedly familiar faces. Once she cried out in unthinking delight, convinced that she recognized a tall, beautiful man in a torn red sweater: *Chinese.* But in the ongoing din anyone's single cry was soundless. She also thought she saw members of the YuSo chapter, and fellow students from the Institute of Amerikanistik, and even a former dueling-society "brother"—once a guest at their wedding—from her husband's younger days. Her camera remained out of hand's reach; the stranger's arms pinned her bag to her side. The bulky, muscled arms protected her. Their owner steered a course as she took tentative steps, stage-doll steps along the invisible pavement, and all the while he stroked her hips and thighs and forward between her moving legs as if layering her with a weightless new kind of cloth. She was learning the personality of these hands. They expressed humor and insistence, experience and comradeship. *He is not a German,* she suddenly thought.

With the courage of outrage an officer vaulted the iron barrier, wedged himself miraculously through to the construction fence. "Down immediately! Private property!" he bellowed. Without waiting for response his truncheon swung against the ankles and shins of the fence-perchers; Kaethe heard the queer grinding sound of its impact on cartilage and bone as if isolated and amplified, well before the raw shouts of pain. Two demonstrators dropped like loosened fruit into the crowd packed below. A woman cried, "Leave him alone!" and "Why do the Shah's dirty work?" Uniformed reinforcements arrived. The crowd, though unable to give itself room to inch forward or back, somehow made space for the officers to pass down the line. First arrests. The hands on Kaethe's body froze still; the chest warming her back seemed not to breathe.

Her mind ran back down the Ku-damm and into the sleeping shadowing suburbs of Grünewald, to Joe, who had wanted to stop her from coming here. He was no one's fool. He had foresight and he cared about her. Out here in the first wave of the demonstration, as a nameless and unreachable no one, she could sense the depth of Joe's caring. How many people in the crowd had someone who'd tried to keep them safe? Away from his entrenched frown and the irritable habits of speech she understood his frustration with her. But he had forgiven and would forgive her again. He made excuses for her she wouldn't grant to herself. He believed absolutely, for example, that they had achieved a pregnancy, scoffed at her doubt, and he only blamed himself, he said, for not having kept her quieter, insisted she stay in and rest. He pitied but didn't mourn. Another baby was what he wanted. *Statistically,* he said, our chances now are better than ever. *Another,* he said. He had imagined the *lost one* in all the details of its history from kernel to fish to fetus, and then birth, growth. An infant's first smile, he said, was a reflex to satiety. Suddenly he knew this kind of thing. He was serious, and had more imagination than she.

A humming, buzzing rolled through the crowd, rising fast to a roar. She thought of how a torn-open hive of wasps must sound to a wasp trapped deep inside. She bobbed, pushed on the shoulders in front for leverage, for a shifting view of the Opera entrance where a chain of identical black Mercedes with opaque windows was drawing up, further obscured by the motorcycle escorts, and only the triumphant last-minute synchronization of "Murderer! Murderer!" from hundreds of hoarse throats announced the emergence of the Royal Guests from one of the limousines, that and a fizzing dazzle, in cold camera flashes, of diamonds and medals and baby-boy-blue satin. An entrance door opened and closed. Police dropped their salutes and turned back to the crowd. The street, all at once, looked much darker.

That was all: a sense of deflation and collective impotence. When Kaethe raised her camera, glum faces turned away. To be shut out makes people feel ashamed. Inside the music-fortress the orchestra was striking up the overture, uplifting the souls of Reza and Farah with themes of Papageno and the Queen of the Night. Had the Royal Couple in their blitz-studded hurry from limo to theater even noticed a few thousand demonstrators?

Who could swear they had arrived at all? What if there'd been no one at the center of the exploding white lights? The Shah and Shahbanu seemed no more real, to Kaethe, than the unseen incubus that had imperceptibly released its grip on her and vanished, leaving only a cool draft playing on her spine.

"Move on! What are you pack waiting for? No more mischief! Clear the streets!"

The attack was coordinated. Well planned. Policemen moved in military formation, banded in groups of five or six. She could observe that and make sense of it even while trying to run into the soft, heaving wall of demonstrators that blocked all escape. She noticed that the police barriers could be opened in only one direction, toward the crowd; the police, truncheons in hand, freed of protective duty, streamed through.

"Down!" someone commanded. "Sit down, all of us! If we simply sit, they'll see we're not aggressors! *Passive resistance!*" The call spread in English, *passive resistance,* and even as Kaethe squeezed herself down to hunker in a narrow space between other struggling bodies she found herself smiling at these sibilant, clipped accents. Playacting, she thought. Pretending to be Freedom Fighters, but for whose freedom?

Who has seen the victim? There's no Viet Cong here, no blacks in the back of the bus. *Bored crazy,* she heard the professor with white eyebrows say. *The State feeds them, buys their books, excuses them even from military duty!* He had left Berlin, and she was supposed to be transferring supervision of her thesis to a new instructor. *Berlin is pink fantasy land. They are all so spoiled!*

She was watching everything that happened through the limited porthole of Max's camera. Swinging it left and right. Snapshots. Two officers pulled a demonstrator to his feet. He tried to sink down again; they punched his head sideways, he bled in a sudden gush from one nostril, her finger clicked the shutter release, click again, as they twirled him around and punched at his kidneys, snapped on handcuffs. Hauled him away over ducking, swaying heads. Behind the paddy wagons, as she photographed, were four police mobile ambulance units. Demonstrators, both men and women, were being yanked up from the seated mass of *passive resisters* like long-rooted, stubborn plants. Smoke bombs were tossed, acrid smoke spread along the ground so there were tears and coughing and areas where little could be seen. The police stepping by and over Kaethe held truncheons at the ready, their arms quivered as if in fear or fever. They shouted an order before yanking someone up, before striking, and the demonstrators cried out with the blow and after, begging for themselves and their friends. *Stop this,* they cried, *how can you, look at her, let him go, she didn't do anything!*

By sitting they'd trapped themselves. Wrong strategy. Anyone now who tried on his own to rise up was taken for an aggressor, and attacked. Kaethe fumbled, changing film, feeling exposed for the moment, safer behind the camera. She glanced up to see a policeman carrying somebody over his shoulder like a rolled rug; it was the large child from the stroller, eyes wide open now. Looking down Kaethe saw a spackling of blood on the knee of her jeans, whose was it? Strange to wear blood not one's own.

A patch of clear pavement, small miracle, opened beside her. Someone writhed fully stretched, groaning, on the ground nearby. Finally enough arrests were opening up space. A packed paddy wagon backed and beeped and drove off. A departing ambulance struck up its jaunty siren: *Ta-tu, ta-ta!*

No warning, no order, no split-second intuition. She watched the camera ripping skyward through her fingers at the same moment as the blow burned through her shoulder and back—as if the pain itself was robbing her. She gasped but couldn't breathe to cry out. A hand wound itself into her hair like that of a strong and vengeful parent, raising her partly to her feet. And then light flashed inside her head, striking into every hidden place, at first ugly, piss-yellow, then flickering. Only after-fires flaring here and there, until absolute silence and darkness fell.

unscheduled trains

THE WAITING ROOM

Rahel sits straight as a concert flutist on her side of the humped, sherry brown, crushed-velvet sofa. The telephone system on the massive desk has been switched to *mute/record;* the white double doors normally open at this hour to the pension hallway and its traffic of guests are double-locked, and Boris lies stretched out like a taxidermist's nightmare, a hairy, structureless barrier, against the drafty crack at their base.

The afternoon sunlight levels judgment on Kaethe's skin, revealing age spots like drops of brown water. But Rahel's hands, pouring the ritual tea, are long and biscuit-pale with a clear gloss on the nails, for all the world like hands that have never scrubbed, cooked or served. Rahel's complexion, too, on the side of her face blazed by the window, is smooth, poreless and luminous as eggwhite. Short licks of hennaed hair arrow from the crown of her head. No glint of gray, of the thickened iron-wire hairs Kaethe plucks from her own comb.

The office doors shudder under a triple knock. Boris stiffens. Rahel and Kaethe lock glances.

"Don't pay any attention, Kaethe."

"But it's my *job* to." The pleasure of making this simple statement. "Under-manager" is her title, in this her first week as subordinate alter ego to the boss—so that Rahel will be less chained to the pension, and Kaethe, down to her last hundred marks, can stay on in the airy back room she is coming to think of as her own. Rahel has argued (as if argument was needed) that though the search may not have turned up much yet, it's far too soon to think of leaving Berlin. What Rahel doesn't know is how long it's been since anyone expected anything of Kaethe, how grateful she is for this job. An outward identity. The carapace most people wear and complain about.

"Your workaholic American side," said Rahel, "is showing. Do me a favor and learn to relax! Today is the Sabbath, come to think. Those guests have a nerve. Come. Enjoy your tea, and tell me more stories." Smiling, Rahel leans her head back, baring her neck. She has the elongated "wisdom" earlobes of the Ashkenazim but wears no earrings, no jewelry other than a hammered silver ring on her left middle finger. Not for the first time Kaethe decides that despite having somehow evaded the usual humiliations of time and decay, her friend Rahel—certainly *friend* at this point, despite the mystery of how and why—has the authority of her true age. It's the way she moves: unerring and deliberate. Or it's something around the eyes, Kaethe thinks. Before, in the dark interior of the pension, she registered Rahel's deep-set eyes as brown, or brownish-green like her own, but today's rush of light reveals, around the pinhole black pupils, irises of a dense violet-blue. A gemstone color.

A jay's feathers, her ex-husband once told her, are misperceived as "blue." In fact they are colorless, unpigmented, mere reflectors of the sky.

"You were talking last night," Rahel says, "about the demonstration."

"Oh, yes . . ." Sometimes she can't distinguish between what she might have told Rahel and what she typed in the uninterrupted stillness of her room.

"Were you badly injured?"

"No. Not really. But do you remember Benno Ohnesorg? I mean, the death of Benno Ohnesorg."

"Possibly . . . No. What a funny last name, though: 'Carefree'?"

"Mm, well maybe. He was a student. He was killed that night, here in Berlin. Come to think, not so far from this hotel. On the night of June the second. Nineteen sixty seven."

"My dear, in sixty seven I was light-years from this city, and never dreamed anything could drag me back."

"A fifteen-minute jog from here, maybe. Not far at all . . . He was shot by a policeman. An officer, not inexperienced but nervous, I suppose. He fired one bullet direct into the boy's head. Behind the right ear. Point-blank. The police weren't supposed to be carrying guns, so we had been told. . . . Rahel, is this is a new tea? It's smokier, stronger."

"Sunday tea. Go on about the boy."

"Anyway, all demos were negotiated in advance with the city authorities back then. Oh, we went by the rules, we always applied for our permits, God forbid anything spontaneous! No water cannons and no firearms, they promised. Umm. Ohnesorg was shot point-blank, in the head."

"He was a friend of yours, this Benno?"

"He wasn't my friend. I didn't know Ohnesorg from Adam. No one did, as it turned out. He was a newcomer in Berlin. A tenderfoot from the sticks. Didn't belong to the student assembly or any of the leftist cells. He was a theology student. That's right, theology! Maybe he just came to watch, out of provincial curiosity? After the police moved on us, a band of bulls—*die Bullen,* that's what we called the cops—happened to chase him down an alley. Of course they were nervous, like hounds whipped up for a hunt, scared of their masters and scared of the quarry and desperate for action, some kind of release. We felt so morally superior, sitting on the pavement with our hands over our heads. I didn't hear the shot. . . ."

"Yes, but what happened to *you,* then? You did get home eventually?"

"Hospital is where I woke up. All around chaos like a train wreck. My bruises were starting to swell, I could hardly recognize myself. The headache. Like they were still hitting me."

"Come. Don't exaggerate."

"I swear. That's how I remember. Eventually I was allowed to call Joe . . . my husband. Soon he stormed in, slammed both our ID's down in front of the head doctor and got me released from there. No charges, no arrest, no record. The *name* bought me free, of course."

"At least good use for it. He was furious, I take it."

"Speechless, at first. Then ice-cold. He washed me up, and he wasn't rough, exactly. He gave me whiskey and aspirin. He put me to bed and turned out the light without a word. I heard our crazy sentimental old landlady sobbing outside, her noise made my head hurt even more. I didn't, couldn't sleep. I lay awake till dawn."

"Adrenalin, it's normal after battle."

"Next morning I was off again. They say rescued horses try to run back into the fire, don't they? People on the bus stared and whispered because my bruised face gave away where I'd been the night before. I was an 'asocial,' practically a criminal. The newspapers' huge headlines blamed 'the student rabble' for everything. A policeman stabbed to death, they wrote, and innocent Shah-admirers stoned bloody.

"The University grounds were full of people camping. The lawns churned to mud. Starting that day we were locked out by official decree of the Rector and the Mayor—the whole University was shut down. Barricaded. Banners, megaphone announcements. Rudi Dutschke was calling for a march, and without a permit. The air was sticky, sort of brownish. 'A funereal atmosphere,' I said to a friend. He gave me a terrible look."

"You didn't know yet about the boy?"

"I had turned away from the newsstands, the first headlines. My eyes ached too much to read. That lasted for months, by the way."

"Well, your studies were done for anyway, I take it."

"For one reason or another. I never finished my degree. It was years before the Free University came back to any kind of real life. Everything changed from that morning on. In the aftermath of the Second of June we had street battles and arrests, how-to sessions on explosives in friends' kitchens, the assassination attempt that blasted away part of Dutschke's brain, crippled his speech. And he spoke so rousingly. . . . In that vacuum things escalated. Andreas Baader and Ulrike Meinhof taking the lead, the department store bombing, the RAF and the Movement of June Second, the kidnappings—"

"All long ago."

"But I remember."

"A theology student . . ."

"The gun fired less than two feet distant from Ohnesorg's head. One bullet. Fractured his skull."

"Yet the police weren't even supposed to have been issued guns."

"Some people swore it had to have been one of the demonstrators who shot him. A provocateur, pushing the conflict. A plot. Even though the bullet, the gun were identified . . . Later the officer was cleared of the manslaughter charge. 'No evidence of intent to inflict bodily harm by shooting,' was the Court's verdict. Amazing?"

"You do have to wonder."

"Ohnesorg was caught kneeling in the street. Unarmed. He was only trying to run away. He had never been involved. No one knew him, but ten thousand came to the funeral. From that night on, from the moment that cop took aim, he *was* involved."

"But dead, my dear. What matters less than politics, to the dead?"

"When they told me, I cried as if I knew him. Like a sister! I never cried like that in public before or since. But I don't think now that I brought up much honest grief for Ohnesorg. I cried because I was terrified myself, because the numbness was wearing off from the night before. Things were changing in a dangerous direction and I could see in people's faces how helpless they felt. The Free University was shut down and I was afraid to go home."

Rahel lays her hand on Kaethe's forearm. The touch is unselfconscious; this is the demonstrative physical closeness between German women that Kaethe admires but has never been able to initiate. "And when you finally did go home, what happened? I suppose after a day or so von Thall forgave you?"

"I hardly thought I needed forgiving."

"Remembering makes you tense. Maybe this will help." Rahel bends forward at the hip, her gaze gentle but probing. Unblinking. Now her two hands are kneading Kaethe's arms, which are bare up to the short sleeves of her cotton blouse. "Getting any better?"

Kaethe nods, silenced by a queer helplessness: part embarrassment, part lassitude. She's not used to attention, neither physical nor any other kind. She hasn't known attention for a long while. She can't resist. Firm, cool fingers reach inside the airy short sleeves to circle Kaethe's biceps and shoulders. Waves of simple pleasure rise up through her from the touch. The smell of the new, strange tea mixes with the rose-glycerin ointment and some other not unfamiliar scent, sweet and crisp and ephemeral, coming from Rahel's forward-pitched but balanced body, rising most strongly from the smooth valley between her breasts that float against a green silk shirtdress as if caught in silk sails. On this warm afternoon.

OBSTRUCTIONS

Kaethe wakes gasping, gritting her teeth as nerve pangs skitter across her lower back. Her mind races to capture the scraps of a quick-decaying dream. Suddenly the pain vanishes and she is in flight, confident of her power to fly, rising effortlessly to glide in the warmed upward streams of mountain air over the strips of fields and gorges around Glass River, looking down on the cabin-sized stump which is all the volunteer brigade managed to salvage of her grandparents' farmhouse after the fire that left so little by way of human matter (bones, real and false teeth). Cremation, a second, consummating conflagration, was the only funerary option.

In flight Kaethe sees the blackened cabin dwindle farther and farther away as if being sucked into a voracious little hole in the earth.

Dreams allow no thought, it's as if one of the senses were cut off. There can be dread but no anticipation. She soars over crumpled hills like waves and Atlantic white-caps like crumpled cerulean hills. Now a pair of large white birds, huge angular wings, cerise beaks, wind-puffed feathers, flank her one on each side, supporting her when she is tired. She wakes (a waking that's merely like the opening of nested Russian dolls) to find the birds swinging her down toward an island, kidnapping her toward a green glowing paradise. In dread she beats their nerveless feathers until with soft shrugs they let her drop and she falls, falls, falls; her back cracks against the sharp rock-ridge of a glassy wave.

Awake again, on the polished white-linen waves frozen between the black head- and foot-pieces of her Jugendstil bed. Or dreaming, perhaps asleep in Glass River? The pain of her fall ebbs like a slowing pulse. This is Berlin. Her own, temporary room, one of the finest the Pension Zur Kurfürstin has to offer. A queer simulacrum of home. She sits up into the waning light, clutching the sheet at her reflection in the armoire mirror. She remembers a well-publicized magazine photograph of an infant chimpanzee tightly clutching a terry cloth doll to her small barrel chest: *a simulacrum of the mother.* Hardly even a doll, no limbs, nor features, nor fur; the researchers couldn't be bothered. Now she remembers the magazine was *Life,* and where she last saw it: lining the bottom of a bootbox, randomly opened to the mud-smudged image of the chimp-infant. Of course it was the worried appeal in those close-set simian eyes like clouded black marbles that transfixed her, as she stared into the bootbox spared by fire. She had seen her own child only once, for one day, in the previous six years. Only twice since Unification. Well, no unification for Kaethe and Sophie. Having lived alone in the mountains for some time by then, she knew better than to cry.

The walls around the courtyard impose an early twilight. From the desk throbs an emerald pin-dot, signaling that the laptop computer, Lies's heisted gift, also merely "sleeps." Behind the laptop is a small stack of books, scrounge from outdoor dealers' bins: Goethe, Heine, Keats. The double-sided photo of Sophie leans against them. Face-water and night and day creams and hair tint, the pathetic arsenal ranged on a shelf between sink and mirror—all these objects are the markings of "home."

She has developed a specific routine: as a rule her duties as pension under-manager last from eight until four, allowing a retreat to this room for an hour or more of running words together on the nacreous screen of the laptop. A record of her search. But often an irresistible drowsiness cuts the writing short. She naps and then wakes, as this evening, without an alarm. Then she will go out. After a light supper in one of the chain cafeterias, she will take the train eastward, to volunteer until midnight with the mobile health services van. It was Pig-Ear who introduced her to the team. They are all glad to have "someone older than us, *sensible,"* around.

In the long, turning pension corridor two lightbulbs are dead; Kaethe strides through the dark patches, imagining an unwary guest tripping on the carpet edge, a sprain or head injury, a debilitating bankrupting lawsuit, herself long gone.

The spare stores are kept in the kitchen. Lies and Rahel look up from the table. Rahel's hands suspended in the act of peeling a pear.

"Sorry to disturb. I just want to grab a couple of lightbulbs." She smiles.

"Come sit with us a minute."

"I can't, you know."

"Oh, don't be so inflexible. What can we offer you?"

"A Vivamed," Kaethe realizes. Vivamed is an aspirin-caffeine compound. She is suddenly aware of a headache budding in the left hemisphere. Her vision on that side seems dimmed and in this new, monoptic view the room and everything in it shifts position.

Lies, expressionless, stands up to rummage in a cabinet.

"Here. Swallow." Kaethe receives a teacup of seltzer, the thick pill, a chair. Lies holds the lightbulbs. "You shouldn't go out tonight." Rahel pushes lightly at Kaethe's sleep-crushed hair. "Like this."

My hair needs cutting, Kaethe thinks. There are grease spots on my trousers. They must think I've been neglecting myself.

"For that matter, to be honest, these expeditions of yours are becoming too much. Look at how tired you are and you haven't even set out yet. What's more, you're simply asking for trouble in those districts of the city. Lies, not true? You won't find the girl this way. Come on! Your charity van must have a revolving clientele, night in night out. Same pack of prostitutes, junkies and beggars. And not one of them admits to knowing her. True?"

The headache precludes a nod. Kaethe looks at Lies, but there's nothing to read. Both women's faces shimmer slightly around the edges. "I thought," Kaethe admits carefully, "of trying something different. Tonight. Going to visit a person my daughter trusts, or did trust. Mathias Leytenfeger . . . I must have mentioned him."

"Oh, yes." Rahel sighs. She rises and moves behind Kaethe's chair. "But is it ever wise to stir up an old entanglement?" Crossing her arms down over Kaethe's chest she pulls back smoothly until Kaethe's head tips against her. "My dear friend. Listen! Give this business a rest, for a while, is that so terrible? You're only ruining yourself. You'll pay with your health."

"I'm sure Sophie's near here. She's somewhere in this city. I feel her."
Eyes half-closed against the ceiling light, she thinks, *I've had this head-ache before. The minute it's gone, I'll forget all about it.*

"Fine! If that's so, you've done all you can. What sort of penance do you think you owe? Your conscience should be clear. You've advertised; she knows where you are. She is an adult, not so? Who for whatever reasons of her own would prefer not to be found. And my dear, you know you are welcome to stay on with us as long as you like! And so, if and when the girl should change her mind—"

Penance. The word throbs in Kaethe's head, like the neon sign on a back-country Baptist church. Accusing and provoking. Shaming. She wants to laugh it off. But it's true that ever since arriving at the pension (or were there even earlier stirrings, during her last months on the mountain?) she has felt the contours of her own past shifting. Sometimes almost imperceptibly, sometimes with a violent lurch, as when a step leading downward is missing. Her self-conviction eroding. The habitual assurance that her instincts and decisions, however tough, have been justified, turns out to be the dry-rot of self-righteousness. Crumbling self-righteousness opens the way to regret. And regrets are inexhaustible, they expand, they harden and take on sharp edges. And all around stretches the shelterless land she never believed in. Guilt.

Kaethe squints into an apparently empty room. Now where has Lies disappeared to? Probably gone round behind Kaethe's back, too, out of sight; perhaps now leaning possessively against Rahel's shoulder, as the two are sometimes found standing. Kaethe, relaxing in the slow cir-cling pressure of Rahel's fingers on her chest and throat, remembers her most recent dream—the flight, the linked white birds—with a force that shakes her.

Penance, though? An ugly word. Suggestive of superstitious flagel-lation, as if harm done could be transferred, soul to body. Or sin diluted by pain.

TRAVELER'S AID

Her next awakening is tentative, her mind swinging in and out of sleep as if the night before—which remains a perfect blank, featureless as a snowfield—she'd drunk too much or taken an injudicious mix of pills. Lying curled on her side she contemplates the tall window, the abstract swaying angels, white curtains. The tiny green light of the computer winks its constant invitation.

The abrupt cooling of her back suggests more than dissolving memory. The invisible half of the bed behind her dips, shifts. Kaethe turns, nose crushed against the warmed pillowcase, taking in a scent of lemon verbena, French soap. Not the brand she uses. The polished white duvet rises and sinks with a soundless breathing not her own. All she can make out, down flat on the bedsheet beside her, unpillowed, is a claret-red blur. A rosy globe that seems to tremble around the edges.

Unnerved by her own imagination, Kaethe slides out and down from the bed. Her clothes from the day before lie on the desk chair. She steps quickly into pants, buttons the wrinkled shirt crookedly over her bare chest. At the corner sink, while trying to keep watch in the mirror that reflects a portion of wall above the bedstead, she furiously splashes cold water over her face and neck, rinses and spits a smoky, syrupy tang from her mouth. She has heard no sound other than splashing water and caught no movement in the mirror, but when Kaethe turns around again she finds the bed empty, sheer white on white, and no one but herself in the room.

It is a Monday morning. Mondays and Tuesdays are her off-duty days at the pension. As she passes the breakfast room's glassed doors the wall-clock shows eleven forty. What makes her sleep so late? What has happened to her inner magnet of day and night—the "circadian rhythm" that scientists have recently discovered to be controlled by photosensors located behind the knees, a freakish finding that conjures up for her a vision of gigantic grasshoppers, knees rearing up toward the sun? Perhaps her recent drowsiness is connected with the recurrent headache, she thinks, which annoys her this morning in a small way, like the buzz of a radio not switched all the way off. Perhaps the headache causes waking dreams as well. Hallucinations... but was that all that visited her, a mere hallucination? In the entry hall she ducks past Rahel's office holding her breath, escaping from sight-range as soon as possible, to fumble hurriedly with the locks of the main door. A sneak thief making her getaway. She's too confused to face Rahel, or Lies, with her boots and tight shorts and new, vulnerable, not-yet-healed navel ring, and hip young woman's carefully cultivated lack of expression.

Day or night, just about any craving can be catered to in Zoo Station.

There are banks, a busy post office, a catacomb of white-tiled underground baths deep as wine vats. Vending machines and machines to make passport pictures and instant business cards with fifty logos to chose from; there are florists and candy boutiques, gambling games that fold up with a hiss and a snap whenever a pair of green-jacketed police stroll too near, an off-hours grocery with a full aisle of schnapps and champagne, a white-coated apothecary as well as a potent assortment of drugs dealt from the backpacks and money belts of travelers just in from Ankara or Amsterdam, hunkered on their heels in the echoing vaulted halls. Off in a corner the modest sign of the Red Cross emergency asylum where Kaethe spent nights when she first came to this side of the city. Insomniac nights. Five marks in advance at the entrance. A darkened windowless bunk hall, a blind shooting gallery of cracking coughs and sudden angry cries. The blanket is thin, your own coat is warmer, the rest of your possessions become your pillow. Everyone shooed out by six A.M. sick or well. *Out with you Frau, this instant! Where would it all end if we made exceptions?* Kaethe has trouble believing that she once took shelter there. Now the small door to the asylum suggests the entrance to hell, or to a previous life. She wonders: Has Sophie followed her path this far, spent nights on an iron bunk?

She buys a tube of Vivamed and a *Tagesspiegel* newspaper and from another automat a city-wide transport ticket good for twenty-four hours. In the cosmetics shop she buys a reddish-brown lipstick and Radical Age-Erasing Miracle Foundation; in the public washroom she also dabs on the shop's gift-sample of cologne, which unfolds as a blend of sandalwood and lemon verbena. Wearing the makeup she looks tougher. A cinnamon smile.

Emerging into the main hall again, she nearly falls headlong over a slumbering boy wrapped around a raw-bellied yellow dog. Yin and yang. The boy without waking flings his head back to reveal a clumsily tattooed swastika under his soap-white chin. So, thinks Kaethe, here's your master-race, end of the century. . . . But in that second she recognizes that the sarcasm isn't her own, hears Lies's sharp-edged Berliner accent spit the same phrase: *Herren-Rasse! That's what the Amis consider themselves compared to us, like their soldiers wouldn't pull the wings of a fly. But know what, Frau von Thall? Humans are all the same. Right now the CIA runs a research station, where what their veterinarians do is break the legs of dogs, leg by leg, mutts no one wants of course—*

That is a ridiculous story, Lies.

I swear. I can prove it. Somewhere in California this is happening. They crack them as mean as they can, with no anaesthesia because that's the whole point—to measure how strong the pain is? And how long the pain takes to reach the top. I don't know scientifically how it's measured—but dogs make a lot of noise when they suffer. They're like people that way. So they get chosen!

There's no earthly reason.

Sure there is. Improved interrogation techniques. So the American Army will know more than any other military about how pain works in a prisoner. There's your master-race!

That's enough. Who fills your head with stories like this?

But Lies tightened and pursed her lips then, and chose to glare in the direction of the kitchen window. And Kaethe was just as glad. She never had warmed much to dogs . . . although Boris, dozing under the table as meaningless chatter flew overhead, was an exception. But then, Boris seemed a species unto himself.

Clocks, like dogs, are everywhere in the station. It's still too early for where she means to go. The paper's headlines have smudged in her fingers' grip. Too nervous to swallow any solid food, she orders a fresh-squeezed orange juice at the stand-up bar and looks from one clock to the next.

Blankengasse, narrow and old as a ghetto alley, which it once may have been. In the late afternoon a gully of shadows. A bicycle carries a Turkish matron in headscarf and pantaloons jittering over the cobblestones. A few thin men are returning from work, trudging from the trolley stop below the hill. About to pass Kaethe, one man (lightly tanned, silky beard more gray than brown) reflexively lifts his eyes.

Immediately, he knows her. There's no doubt, and she would know him for certain if only by the shiver that crosses his face, like a chill wind roughening water. And his glance sideways: as if looking for a line of escape.

All the openings she's rehearsed, and now not one word rises to mind. Her throat is swollen shut. Unthinking, she steps forward into the center of the street, as if to block his way.

"Good God." He stops. *"You."*

"Hello."

"What are you doing here? What in Heaven's name gives you the right? Here, with no warning? I swear—" He swallows the next word. Silence.

On this warm July day Mathias Leytenfeger wears baggy brown trousers and a blue collarless shirt. Worsted socks in dark leather sandals. From his right hand dangles a worn briefcase so flat it must be empty. She had forgotten this particular briefcase, and now to re-admit its existence creates a wake of other sudden, brilliant memories, like a comet's tail.

"But why—" He clears his throat. "So. You *are* here. Now why won't you at least look at me?"

So close, she forces herself to look up. The sky around his dark head is deep and dazzling. "Mathias, you look well . . ."

"No, no, give up, don't try so hard! It's not a compliment I'm asking for."

"But you look—I didn't expect you to be still so—" As he breaks into an exasperated smile her eyes blur over, distorting everything for her protection.

There's no distance between them. She feels his arms lifting, crossing over her, linking at the small of her back. The articulation of his wrists. She feels the surprising lightness of his beard and the steely press of his cheekbone against her temple, and is pulled forward tight against the shirt that smells of laundry bleach and Mathias's sweat, Mathias's solid curved ribs, the slip of his skin under the thin shirt in July. "The same," she whispers. It's at once a confession and a lie. "You're the same."

He leads her upstairs. Twenty years since she first gripped this banister. Today the oak stairwell appears neither more nor less in need of repair, as if the green and purple stained-glass porthole windows on each landing are able to filter out the glare of time passing. Then—on that first climb, she looking upward, trying to see into the darkness of a place she'd never been—he had propelled her, one hand on her waist, encouraging and reassuring, and as they climbed step for step he dropped his hand down slowly along her hip and caressed the soft crease of her thigh, releasing a sudden, paralyzing flash of desire so strong that she would have pitched backward, if there hadn't been this banister to grasp.

He leads. He pushes open the door. There's slanting sunset, a stir of dust, and the embedded reek of tobacco.

"You still don't lock the door."

"Maybe some day I'll come in and find a stranger waiting in ambush. The neighborhood's in flux. My Mr. Destiny. Or Miz. I wouldn't mind. Want tea?"

"Yes. I've become addicted." He is the only German she's ever known with no lock on his door. She'd like to tell him about Glass River, how its few inhabitants don't lock up either, that her cabin there latched with only a nailed swiveling chunk of wood to hold back the wind. That her space in America was no bigger than this: the room for sleeping and eating, his study next door, the grisly bath out across the landing. While filling the kettle he plugs in the hot plate, and she sits down, narrowly, on a corner of the day-bed. Bodhisattvas and elephants parade on the thin beige spread. The deep jingling down-sinking of the springs. How evocative this sound is—and how little it mattered to her, how her self-consciousness used to vanish in this room, how after a point, once their bodies tangled together slippery and straining, they both barely heard the jubilant alarm bells of the old springs.

What she can't quite recapture is her reason for coming here now.

"Well, Kaethe! Is it a new game, or the old one? Am I supposed to guess what you need this time? Naturally, what's mine is yours. Always was. As far as that goes nothing has changed. But if you want money... ach yeh, too bad. Money still shuns me, you see. Need connections? Negative. Folks find they are better off not admitting they ever knew me. Reputation? You saw the last of that. Although I did enjoy a brief nimbus of glory after I came out of jail the second time—in that touchy-feely euphoria after the Wall came down, as if I had actually contributed to deposing the old farts. Didn't last, though. Old Right, new Left, new Right—I've lost track. Plus ça change. To them all I'm a walking zombie. *Thaler, Thaler, du musst wandern.* You know, Kaethe, how it is? Here —take your tea. Are you comfortable perched like that? Otherwise I could clear off a chair. This is ban-cha. Japanese green tea. Breathe it in slowly. Delicate, hm? I'm an addict, too. We Ossis can get everything fancy and foreign here now. There's no more reason to want to leave East Berlin."

"Mathias... I'm intruding. I apologize. You're obviously furious. I should be off."

"Sure. Have you had a chance to dine in any of our new restaurants around here? I tell you, the best does come to those who wait. Chefs are better here than in London, or Paris. There's more respect for fresh ingredients when you haven't had them for forty-five years. The meek inherit the earth."

He settles on a sagging red-leather hassock, pulling the hassock so near to her that his knees, spread wide, bracket her own legs (jutting parallel, for this occasion sheathed in a black skirt) like long parentheses. She has nowhere to look, avoiding his direct stare, but to his handle-less tea mug, and his crotch, spanned by the rough brown fabric of baggy pants. The outline of his sex only suggested by the cloth but clearly remembered, now only a few inches from her.

"It's good, this kind of tea." The tea tastes like hot Nothing. Green water. Dries her lips and tongue with every sip. This close to him again she shuts her eyes, but the image won't go away of his long evenly pale penis, resting on testicles like full, ripe fruit.

And, too, she remembers how Mathias used to gather her up in his lap, rock her like a child, soak away her tears until his handkerchief was saturated, and then excuse himself quickly and briefly laying her down, to fetch a clean square of linen from the drawer.

"Okay if I smoke, Countess?" But before she can nod he is pulling the paraphernalia from his briefcase. As he goes through the deliberate ritual of stuffing, tamping and lighting, his fingers—the long, dark-haired fingers she has stroked, covered with kisses, sucked and bitten down on—all tremble slightly, as if some constant current of excess energy inside Mathias has found this relatively harmless way out.

"So, you have a new job?" She hopes, with a glance toward the brief-case.

"No, damn it. There are no jobs! I mean, this new Berlin is the Boomtown, the Second Coming of the German Miracle, but oddly enough we have on this side—because we still have sides, Countess von Thall, believe me—what? Fifteen, eighteen percent bedrock unemployment. Anyhow, capitalism in its wisdom has decided it's cheaper to pension me off than to employ me. Listen: I could never save a penny. Those scattered years in prison turned out to be my nest-egg. You see, I qualify as *regime-damaged.* You see, Kaethe? All's for the best. But I do work. Achtung, hallo, of course. We are *Cherman,* aren't we? I volunteer. Full time."

"Where?"

"A couple of church Youth Clubs. Anti-drug, rehab. Ah, the good old Lutherans. They forgive me and forget me, as long as they no longer have to foot my salary."

"I'm surprised we haven't run into each other recently."

"In a Youth Club? Really? You've been sniffing glue? Tasting a little Ecstasy? From the looks, Frau von Thall, the stuff must agree with you! Had any mind-blowing epiphanies? Any visions, recently?"

"Visions . . . why?"

"Well, world of wonders. She's actually blushing."

Her stone-pottery mug, half full of the desiccating tea, clatters on the bare floor. His cheeks implode skeleton-wise as he pulls on the pipe. Lips squared back reveal brown teeth curved up to the gums. The unfamiliar beard, this close, is much grayer than she'd thought, although dyed in ribbons back to russet brown with tobacco saliva. Crazy, she thinks. He is. Puffed full of hate. Rich with it. "Sorry, Mathias. I mean it. Sorry I bothered you. I'll be off—"

"Stay! You have absolutely no right to run off again. You were like that when I first met you. Dashing to me, dashing away, just like a restless little immigrant. More a clueless Ami than you ever could see. Your beginnings stuck to you. You thought you fit in with your aristo-gang.

But you were rash, brash and insistent. A liability, in society. In fact that was what I liked about you, but ... *They* knew. No matter how you pretended."

"Mathias." She balances her voice. "I'm going." Now he stands up, casually, to lean his back against the unlockable door. "Please. Why are you acting this way? I only came here hoping ... please. I came to talk about Sophie."

"Oh, I guessed as much. You think I'm hiding her. Sure, I've stolen her. Peek behind the curtain! Leytenfeger, the troll who stole the princess. Why not? All's possible."

"I didn't mean that."

"Are you afraid for her, Kaethe?" A sudden new note, a tremor of seriousness in his voice. "Afraid, I mean, whether or not she's in this city? Which is her territory, after all. What I mean is, afraid for her ... degree of resilience. Stability. Understand?"

"No."

"Since you called, I'm remembering things you used to tell me. About your mother, for example. And Max—what he did not to others, but to himself."

He continues to squint at her with a sort of challenge, as if acknowledging he may have gone too far, as if he (Pastor Mathias Leytenfeger, curator of dreams) can begin to see into her malignant lapses, murderous reveries, her imaginary rendezvous with the man at his desk. But how these have mercifully receded, since she took on regular work at the Pension Zur Kurfürstin! Maybe she can manage to shake the daymares, outrun them completely.

"I'm resilient enough, aren't I?"

"Oh. Indubitably. Teflon. PVC. Unbreakable."

"But I'm not now, Mathias. With Sophie, I'm at the end of my ideas. I've been to the police. Nothing. Her father has got a connection with the airports, the transit police are supposed to be looking out—"

"Ah yes, there was a *father*. So you two concede one another's existence?"

"He wrote to me in the States. That's how desperate he is."

"And you answered?"

"Not yet."

"Harsh. You still can't find forgiveness in your heart?"

"Listen to you!"

"Quick, another topic. So how is our old buddy Achim? I read he's in line for a Cabinet position. Technology? Your ex-Lord and Master takes after his Papa the Captain, *requiescat in pacem,* more every year. Must give the Volk shivers! And he's remarried, to King Midas's daughter? Perfect match. But that must sting, Kaetchen. When you think about the life that got away."

She meets his gaze, which is gentler than his voice. Clear hazel eyes, deep-folded, sprays of long laugh lines. How, in prison, had he found opportunities to laugh? "I've put messages to Sophie in the Personals. Contacted old schoolmates but they haven't heard from her in years and don't know who her new friends are. I've been scouring the city and spending nights with the medical van, listening to the kids talk new slang I'm learning, watching for her ... but nothing. Sometimes I feel as though Sophie is very close by, moving ahead or behind me the way a bird, a Drossel maybe, will hop for company through the hedges when you're out on a ramble. She is watching *me.* Mathias, you used to give me advice. It's funny: each time I thought about making this visit I felt more hopeful. Maybe she's contacted you? On the phone a few weeks ago you hinted as much—"

He stares. "What the devil makes you think she's even come back to Berlin?"

"Just an instinct. But now someone thinks he saw her."

"Who?"

"A boy named Pig-Ear."

"Hmh."

"Why should he lie?"

"Oh, who knows. Besides, after all the years apart, and then you disappearing to the States—how well do you even know her?"

"I don't know my daughter?"

"Not for me to judge."

"Listen: I *do* know her. You do, too! She started out brilliantly in school but later something happened. That all fell apart. By the time you lost contact with her—"

"No, no. You both lost sight of me. I disappeared behind cement blocks. The Stasi pen."

"By then she was back with her father, in the Königsallee. Starting gymnasium. But by then she had absolutely quit caring. Irrelevant, she said. She saw no use in studying."

"I remember: it stunned me: how like each other you two were becoming."

"That's not fair. Stop mocking me. She still had a good mind! And still read whatever she could get her hands on. But Achim couldn't control her—"

"Now there's one point the parents had in common."

"You knew he sent her away? Further west. To the Taunus Mountains. First he stole her, then he exiled her."

"Do you scratch your scabs just to keep the blood flowing, Kaethe? I've heard all this before."

"At sixteen she dropped out of school. Achim was livid. Insulted, humiliated. For all her courage she couldn't face him, I'm sure. She joined a Greenie commune, an organic back-to-the-land group. Dawn to nightfall in the fields. For fun they occasionally dressed up as skeletons to harass the local nuclear power facility. Otherwise Sophie worked as a shepherdess, which is not at all as romantic as it sounds."

"She liked it. I found some letters from her waiting, when I came out."

"On the one hand, I mistrusted that whole nature-worshiping, anti-rational movement. I hated to think it left her no more time to read, to learn. On the other hand I thought of her as at least *safe,* there. Mathias, my point is simply this: I don't think now Sophie would want to stay long outside Germany, in a place where German isn't spoken. She has a feeling for the land. Last I saw her—"

"Where?"

"In Munich. After Achim moved there with his . . . second wife. Sophie decided to join them. She signed on as sort of a caretaker-companion for their little daughter. Just over a year ago, we spent one day together . . . Sophie met me in a beer garden, in a Munich suburb. There was something changed about her—naive, or even simple. I kept wondering, were they exploiting her? Was she trapped? All the questions I couldn't ask."

"You're certain she's not still in Munich?"

"Impossible. Achim scoured the town. But in Berlin . . . Look, I know that nearly everything and everyone in this whole godforsaken country is registered, documented and cross-correlated up their behinds by its bureaucracy—but isn't Berlin still beyond their grasp, the one and only city where a person can dive under, drift and even start out new? It's also where her past is. Including . . . well, you too. Especially you."

"Me? I'll ask again, Kaethe: What do you want?"

"Your whole life you've worked with kids in this city. You have the knack. The kids here trust you. You know how they survive and where they run and where they go to ground."

"Sounds like rodents. So am I the Pied Piper? Fine! What if Sophie did come to me, why would I tell you? Should I have any faith in your motives for coming back here, for this whole handwringing scene? If she is near, does Sophie need *you?* Or do you need her as the only medicine that can cure your unbearable sense of failure?"

"You're wrong to blame me, Mathias. I was facing an impossible decision then." Whatever rivulets of doubt may have crossed her mind recently, here is no place to admit them. "I never took the easy way."

"Easily said."

"I didn't have the *time,* the luxury of debating. . . . Given what any of us knew then, I did my best."

"Good for you. Nowadays everyone's a victim."

"Could you move aside from the door? People are expecting me. I mustn't be late."

"Maybe finding Sophie here would be the perfect way to give old Achim an additional set of horns. Think that's what's driving you?"

"I think that you can't hate me enough."

"Ah . . . but do you want to make sure? Come here."

She takes three steps. To obey is to collaborate, to join him in a risk.

"Even closer . . . That's good." Mathias touches only her shoulder, as if it's a curiosity worthy of careful study. Smoothing her bra-strap through the fine cloth of her blouse, lifting and resettling her familiar talisman, the string of egg-like freshwater pearls. The back of his hand brushes her earlobe and her eyelids are heavy, she has to struggle to keep them open, and fails. His kiss falls slowly, the most gentle inquisition of their past, and the taste of his sour tobacco is as rich to her as the drop of water inside a morning glory, and she sees rain against her closed eyes, the great bruise-colored massed clouds raining down on a dry, scattered town.

We're so far beyond liking, she thinks. Nothing has changed. From the first meeting he belonged to me and I to him, our first look, the shock of recognition and greedy, hot-cheeked return. And from then on the pull never weakened. That was the astonishing part. Now the current of his power is running through her, familiar, deepening as the kiss shares and deepens. Incandescent. She had come so close to forgetting joy. The bliss of sexual immolation: how it simplifies and lightens the world.

He shoves lightly against her shoulders, forcing her away. "Better pay attention, Kaethe. Achtung! Don't lose your balance."

She lifts a hand to her face which feels damp and slack.

"Six years, Kaethe. That's not long, is it? Then why are we both so horribly much older? To see one's age mirrored in a former lover . . . a great perversity. But it was you who came here. I couldn't pass up the chance you offer. I only wanted to find out if you could still make me feel like a man. You understand, yes? You were always a champion of sudden urges. Here. My door has no lock, remember? You can leave any time you choose."

THE PARALLEL TRACK

From the Blankengasse she hurries southwest, under a sky shedding night while darkness's breath rises from courtyards and alleys as she descends, finding a zigzag route toward the center of the city. Her shoes slip and wobble on the rounded paving stones. She feels heavy and uncertain, overdressed and risible. A stranger. Uninvited. Old.

Not long ago she fell, was knocked to the ground somewhere close by in this network of streets. Now she fears the blows she missed then: vicious boot-kicks to the head, the abdomen, and in and between her ribs. She recalls salvation in the shape of a small, frantically inquisitive dog.

Tonight the van has parked in a construction lot off the Oranienburgerstrasse. Sodium lights splash orange-gold pools across the fresh rubble, illuminating the path. The unmistakable gamey scent of burning hash, become again as cozy and familiar to Kaethe these recent weeks as it was in her twenties, surrounds and proclaims the van. Clumps of young men and women (the expression "kids," like "boys and girls," is frowned on here) hunker on stones and mechanical equipment, waiting. Some hold each other; many hold pets (though no animals are permitted inside the van): a mongrel by its neck-bandanna, a cat in a piece of blanket, an alert iguana half-zipped into a leather jacket.

Once, when Kaethe was about ten, a traveling one-tent circus stopped for a few days in Glass River. She who had no money for the shows, managed to walk through their camp in the off-hours when the horse and bear and trick dogs were let loose to ramble, back where the exotic painted ladies and raffish, half-costumed clowns shared companionable smokes. She remembers scenting that nearly unimaginable freedom, that instinct for lightness, now, as she picks her way around the medical van's "clients" with their gaudy hairstyles and bright rings and chains. Most of these "clients" will ask for clean needles, condoms or both. Antibiotics, often. Vitamins. They'll want food, sounding simultaneously nagging and indifferent, knowing meals are another department, nothing to do with this particular van.

She ducks inside, gives her name to an unsmiling aide, wraps up in a starched, permanently stained white coat that covers her from black hem to pearl strand.

When a girl begs for powdered formula is it for a baby or herself? The volunteering doctors rotate. Some are hesitant with the "clients," too empathetic, pushovers. Some are experienced, some seem vengeful (about what? Kaethe wonders, tightening her lips to a smile of encouragement and endurance, she hopes, for a girl much younger than Sophie who is hoisted helpless in the stirrup chair). Some doctors mutter in outrage under their breath, as if to say: "Don't blame *me* for the mess you've made!" in a peculiarly German way.

Kaethe is turning back in on herself. Involuting. Since her recent time in Glass River she finds herself comparing two nations, cultures, collective natures (none of these words quite hits the nail on its Gorgon head) much as she did almost half a century earlier, when she first arrived here. Germans against Americans. Self-congratulating, bulbous Americans contrasted with intense, sharp-edged Germans. Bigoted, barking Germans versus rifle-toting, born-again football fans. Ideologically re-armed West Germans and braying, praying Americans in complementary uniforms. Against the rest of the world.

The van has two spaces: reception-dispensary, and "clinic": a space capsule of an examining room. Kaethe rolls bandages, counts tablets, fills out forms, does whatever she's asked and able. Holds the chilly hand of a client. Fends off inquisitive police. Catches blood, human tissue, soaked wads of gauze in a kidney-shaped steel pan.

Haddi materializes in the reception. *Take this one's protocol.* Someone hands her a clipboard. She's seen Haddi at the van before—as much as anyone ever sees of him. A wraith, hunched deep in his oversized gray hooded sweatshirt. He's a quartermoon of cheekbone and nose, a lock of colorless hair. She would swear that Haddi is under sixteen. Twenty, he says. No job, never had a job, no trade apprenticeship. Missed the start. "I got bust and sent to prison the first time when I was fourteen." Not for theft, he says. "Only needles in my friend's room. Cops are so out to get us Ossis." Is he paranoid? she wonders, but doesn't write down the question. Outside the rainshowers must have resumed; there are wet dark patches in his sweatshirt's hood and shoulders. He's shaking steadily, violently, his nose is running a clear stream, but he ignores his discomfort and goes on patiently answering Kaethe's questions. He whispers so low—shame? hoarseness?—that she has to bend intimately close, putting her ear inches from his streaming nose. He came out of prison clean, he says. It felt fantastic. He moved in with a girlfriend. "Only she started working the street. I couldn't take that. We fought." He ended up back on the street. But they have a baby girl, somewhere in foster care. "I'm trying to get myself together, lady. For the kid."

He looks around, bites his elfin child's lips. He can't sit still. She brings cocoa from the hot plate. "Busy night! Long wait, I'm afraid. And you, Haddi? Where do you live now?"

"In the holes."

She frowns. His speech is so hard to make out. Holes? *Doorways,* she writes in the protocol. "And so, where did you grow up?"

"State Children's Home. Up northeast. My own folks booted me out. The Homes were work camps. Prison was nicer. We all ran away soon as we could. When the Wall came down. Scampered West!"

She doesn't tell him what she knows herself about those Homes. She leans even closer, accepting the biting smell of stale vomit. He's only a child. One who spent years in prison. Who has a baby of his own. She shows him the pictures. "You know this girl? Ever seen her?"

"No. *Yes.* Ah. Ah! Can't remember."

"Haddi, wait. What are you here for tonight?"

He gives the first and only smile. It's a little sly, a little pitying. He stands. He is too heroin-sick to stand without gripping the table. He hasn't touched his cocoa. "My meth dose," he whispers. "Only now I can't wait, can't stay...."

Toward the end of the night she unclasps her string of pearls and dribbles them into the clammy, limp hand of a young woman who is leaving the clinic late, after official closing, toward the pulse of dawn. Sell them! I don't have a use for them. They're the real thing, Kaethe says, so don't let them go for the first price offered! The client looks drained, too exhausted to be wary of a trick.

Kaethe catches not the last S-Bahn train to run westward, but the first of the morning. No one on the platform but construction workers in blue overalls, drinking breakfast beer. This train, an automated announcement pipes, is a Limited Express for Zoo Station, it will not stop at stations . . . and . . . Kaethe hardly listens. She is glad about the speed. She dozes, has always rested well when on the move, carried forward without her own effort, rocked by a plane or train or car. As the empty train slows to cruise through a nonstop she half-wakes, slits her eyes at the change in rhythm, and sees the passing station: snack-kiosks, advertisements for cars and concerts, benches, and a trio of young people all dressed in white, standing, leaning together. A cropped, claret-colored head. Shaven boy in the middle. And a girl, arms held cradled out in front of her, long untamed hair streaming behind, mouth wide open as her head turns to reflect the progress and eventual disappearance of the nonstop train.

Kaethe leaps up, cries out. Her leg twists, collapsing her into a pole, like a drunk. In old times there were bells to ring, cords to pull, ways to stop a train in an emergency. Now she can't find a bell, nor any instructions. Instead there are placards recommending mortgage banks, travel agents, suicide-prevention numbers.

Rats. That's what she has just seen, long-tailed rats, two or three of them, quick and pale, running on Sophie's bare arms.

COUCHETTE

Kaethe wakes to a throbbing behind her left eye and bells jangling on top of a wind-up alarm. After banging the clock mute she rises on her elbows to check the unoccupied pillow beside her. Sniffs, but registers only her own warm mustiness. A few hours ago, when she tumbled in morning light half undressed onto this bed, the odor of lemon soap struck her full force. What's only seen may be hallucinated (example: a moving image seen from a moving train). A vision is only waves of light after all, but a smell has molecular presence. Any plain truth is a relief. Better than ambiguity. Relieved to know that someone, a real body, had lain in this bed (someone with claret-red hair) in daylight she fell asleep as if plummeting through clouds to earth.

The room is again hot. The long gauze curtains dangle like becalmed sails. To invite a cross-draft she wedges her door open with books. The corridor is silent. Late morning in the pension, after the guests have swarmed out into the city, is a time for repairs and recuperation. Kaethe, half-dressed, hunkers by the door to savor the cool air that seeps, as if from a cistern, from the depths of the building.

She thinks about the person who came in two nights ago. Who, if real, not only climbed into the bed—for how long?—but hugged her from behind. That had to be either Lies or Rahel. They both use the same perfumed soap, the same hair dye. Rahel or Lies.

She doesn't feel threatened. Why should they harm her, what does she matter to either of them? Kaethe isn't insulted—the act was too bizarre and pleading for insult. An invasion perhaps. A supplicant's embrace. Is she comforted, then? Is she flattered?

Who would she want it to be?

From far off down the corridor comes the echo of the main door closing. Once again, at the end of last night's talk Rahel insisted on taking over all the morning chores in order to let Kaethe sleep. Kaethe's response now is a mix of shame and gratitude. How does she deserve this spoiling? She can't imagine how the older woman soldiers through the morning's work without a few hours of rest. Though Rahel claims to have the gift of napping like an animal—for a few minutes at a time—her stamina seems to Kaethe supernatural. Like the power of a genie or zombie, raised up from the dead to labor for all eternity.

But in fact there is nothing of the graveyard about Rahel, whose ready laughter and luminous, rounded cheeks and vitality make her plump, young counterpart, Lies, the so-called Mädchen-für-alles, Girl-for-everything, look seedy by contrast. "Of course it won't have escaped you?" Rahel's voice, as it rang loudly in the dawn kitchen, now echoes in Kaethe's head. "By now you've long since noticed that Lies and I are . . . fast friends. Ach. She was a wreck when she came here. She stole, she drank excessively. I kept her. Now look how she's bloomed."

Fast friends. Lovers? Lesbians. Kaethe can picture them coiled together: four white entwined arms and two crowns of softly spiked red hair. Two women. One less than half the other's age. Kaethe shrugs off an atavistic twinge. Condemnation is fear and ignorance. She feels relief again: plain truth revealed.

It must be difficult, Kaethe muses, crouched in the breeze trickling from the corridor, wearing only underpants and an unbuttoned shirt. Difficult to run this pension side by side, one giving and the other obeying orders, one acting as mistress to her mistress—there must be trouble sometimes. But still, why should Rahel, already in possession of a young, compliant lover, cultivate the company of a middle-aged stranger from the United States? A customer washed up at her door? With a split-second shudder Kaethe can see herself through the other woman's eyes: tense, watchful, tight-lipped. Her bearing an unappetizing mix of half-shed gestures of the Prussian gentry, Yankee stinginess, and the eva-

sions learned under State Socialism. Why favor *her* over hard-working
Lies, whose long hours on duty are strictly enforced, no tardy mornings indulged?

Even so, an undeniable warmth comes over her at the thought of living inside this pension of women, which belongs solely to women,
where only women's passions and labor and intellect have any weight,
and the men merely come and go. It *is* hidden, a parallel world, she
thinks, a secret universe masked as an everyday hotel-pension. Here
behind the double oak door, among the flowers and furniture and prints
and paintings, the place is brighter and larger than anyone would guess
from the street. Sensual and safe. From her resting-place on the waxed
wood floor she looks across the room to the black desk with lily plants
carved up all four legs, and on it the laptop, Lies's extravagant gift,
blinking its perpetual invitation to confession with a sprite-green eye.
Now at least once a day she answers, pops open the shell, presses down
the faintly rustling keys to make words spring up among radiating
waves of green, pink, turquoise. "Psychedelic" is a term rusting away
in the junk-shop of the past, but how the acidheads would have been
turned on by this screen! Her initial unease with the machine was due
as much to inscrutable technology as to scruples about larceny, and
has melted away as she discovers ad-hoc ways of making it do what
she wants, while the only obtrusive evidence of previous ownership is
the single phrase inscribed in the first window, "I have made an irredeemable mistake"—unpunctuated, as if the laptop's previous owner
was about to specify his error or crime or act of omission, but now all
possible meanings are left hanging.

Tax fraud? Bad choice of mate or career? Incitement to murder?
Kaethe could erase the phrase, but she's come to see it as the laptop's
ritual salute, along with an upbeat welcoming bell.

She has grown completely comfortable with opening the laptop's
palimpsest of memories. It's her own memory she can't trust. Still, the
laptop is a keenly attentive, lightly humming listener. A wonderful
companion.

From inside that first entry window—the vestibule created by a
stranger—she's able to dive down to any of the multiplying boxes con-
taining her own words. *Tracks,* she calls the daily entries: intermittent
records of her movements and encounters and thoughts since arriving,
once again, in Berlin. She has yet to reread a single sentence and probably never will, but there have been junctures in her life when having

such a record might have boosted her luck, given her the power of full recollection, or even exoneration. Now and then she works on reconstructing a long letter to Sophie, begun years ago but destroyed before it could be delivered or even finished, a letter that first took shape on yellow lined school paper during the winter in Glass River. And other notes and letters are accumulating, all to people she has had no contact with for years.

Clashing church bells startle her. Ten notes, a motif from Bach. *A mighty fortress is our God.* Rahel claims to revere Bach, but there is never music in the pension. Rahel wonders why Kaethe doesn't have the intelligence to quit the search for a child who refuses to be found, and start creating an overdue new existence for herself. How many new lives do we have in us? asks Rahel. All the cells of the body are completely renewed in seven years. A seven-year cycle of rebirth. Is that why lovers, after seven years, will suddenly look on each other with appalled indifference? Strangers! But these cellular redivisions are numerically limited. There's a gene for death, in that sense. We're born into the mercy of our own annihilation.

Next comes the tolling of the hour. How the bimmel-bang of churchbells can drive a person to the verge of madness. Faith is a fortress without windows or gates. One . . . four . . . ten, eleven, twelve. Time to dress quickly, take her place in the office, greet the guests.

It's only the headache, she realizes, that keeps her pinned on the floor, avoiding any jarring motion or change in altitude.

lost correspondence

THE GLASS RIVER FILE

Schalk Farm, Glass River
December 28th, 5:45 P.M.

Dearest, dearest Sophie,

Is it possible that over three months have gone by since I last saw you? Since our day together in Munich. Our *good* day. Are you surprised to hear me say so, considering how I cried toward the end (Please don't stop reading, Sophie. I know you said let's not bother with letters for a while but I promise not to write the kind of thing that might make you uncomfortable.) Remember how warm it was that afternoon? The roses pouring their hearts out. You wore an enzian-blue cotton dirndl and we sat drinking beer with Schuss— shots of raspberry sirup—sharing the Spatenbrau garden with hornets and rowdy dogs and the oompahpah band. Until the paper lanterns went on and blue shadows covered all the tables.

Now, here in what's left of your great grandparents' farm, it snows and snows. Flakes big as roof shingles drifting past the window.

On the windowsill are two photos: the one our waitress took of you and me together. The other shows you with your hair radiating like a sunflower, and you have the same calm, intent expression that

I remember from back when you were four or five, Sofchen, when
we all still—

At a sudden crash she jerked forward. The pen skittered a loony
autonomous line. "Shit, shit, shit!" Kaethe cried, because as she scrambled to grab the chunk of wood smoldering on the floor, pains pierced
her stiff knee-joints, and her wool writing-gloves with cut-off fingers
refused to be unpeeled, and because already the pine floor itself was
beginning to smolder—and because anyone should know better than
to leave the stove door open, especially since the warming effect of the
revealed flames was an illusion that in fact sucked away heat.

The sound of her own voice braced her. "Ah, hell! Shit and god-
damn it—" Bright threads on her old gloves curled, the gloves sizzled
merrily as she hopped to the sink, juggling hot wood. Ran icy water
over wood and hands and sodden gloves. Laughing at herself, then
stopping abruptly, because there was no one to laugh along with her.
Of all the kinds of loneliness Glass River offered, this was her least
favorite: having no one to laugh with, to share absurdity with. By the
time she spoke to another person the incident would have gone stale.
Joe at the General Store would frown, would say, Kath, you're living
out there ten miles from nowhere on a farm that burnt down once
already—what, once isn't enough? But no: there was a storm picking
up, wind screeling along the mountainsides, and by the time she'd have
dug through and clambered over snow drifts to make that trek again
she would have forgotten this incident completely. And that, she
thought as the wood shrunk and blackened and her hands turned glossy
red, was why she lived here now. To have no one to talk to made forgetting that much easier. And you, she reminded herself, cupping water
and carrying and drizzling it over the scorch marks on the floor, are
simply a random mixture of reflexes and memories, and without the
memories practically speaking nobody. There could be a relief in that.
Her twinging knees made her feel old, body caving in, but why fear
age, let alone dementia? Old-timer's disease, like Reagan. Reagan's in a
cottonwool heaven, she thought, and blessed to be feeding carrots to
his horses in California, with no idea of what a president is let alone
that he was one.

Glass River, December 28th, 6:50 P.M.
Dearest—

Happy birthday, my beautiful girl! I know you said let's not bother with letters for a while—what is, is, and scratches on paper won't change it—oh Sophie, I understand you better than you think, how empty phrase-making exhausts you, how incomprehensible you find others' efforts to charm you, how much simpler it is for you to get on with your life without your egotistical family. You are a lot like me—but now I can hear my mother using that phrase and I shudder!

I think "a while" has passed, yes? Did you get the snapshots I sent, and recently a birthday package (and because it hasn't come back and I've heard nothing from Achim I assume you are still staying with them, in Munich)? But this is my first letter. There are things I need to tell you. Sophie, please don't stop reading—

She stopped. The fountain pen, battered gold and green, gouged through the second sheet of paper. To plead, parent to child, was backward. Inappropriate to say the least. She pushed herself up again and set a kettle to boil on the stove and got out the rum to mix a grog. She tolerated the penny-candy flavor because rum was a concentrated drink. Less weight to carry up the mountain.

Don't write then, she told herself: you can't even decide how to begin. The "salutation." So be it…Sophie, I salute you! On the twenty-eighth of December, your birthday. Exactly nineteen years ago a post-Christmas thaw transformed Berlin, a breeze from the west, and the curtains of the women's clinic's stone-framed windows billowed over my lying-in bed as I nursed you. . . .

Oh dear. Who was it once said that losses turn people sentimental? Certainly that's what happened with *my* mother—Baerbel, notoriously abandoned and mostly three sheets to the wind. Devoted to pop ballads and the melancholy revision of history. Of course torch singers all die from broken hearts. Or drugs or drink.

What is a birthday? By the evening of tomorrow the twenty-eighth won't matter. Always plenty to do here. The first year I was less afraid of bears and hurricanes and trigger-happy hunters than of boredom creeping in and taking over. "Being bored is the original sin"—Mathias said that. It's the sin against life itself, he said, the worst, we can forgive ourselves for all the others.

Oh really? Can we?

Tonight before the snow packs hard there's still the path to the wood-pile to shovel. Logs to lug in so they'll dry by morning. And basins to fill with water in case the power goes down. Dish of milk to set in the cellar for the wilding cats or whatever creature shelters there. I prefer to think cats. And my meal to make. Discipline. "Hunger comes with the eating, young woman!" Who said that? Oh: Frau Albus, right, good old Albie, wrong as usual . . .

She heard "good old Albie" echo with a surprising fondness, and wondered how long she had been talking to herself.

December 28th, Glass River
My one and only Sofchen—

Felicitations! Today is your birthday. In fact yours was a birth-night, 2:20 in the morning when you sobbed in your first breath, and as it's now almost eight at night here and you are six hours ahead—well, I'm a little late settling down to talk to you.

How I long to talk to you tonight. To talk about you, tell you some things you are, I believe, old enough to hear. To tell you straight and honest. It's time. I want to say "du" to you, again and again. DU

Have you had a birthday letter from Mathias? Are you two still in contact? Certainly for the three years when we were together he made a big deal of your birthdays. I envied his knack for creating the big splash—purple balloons sailing from our balcony like giant grapes, the Chinese firecrackers on the pond, the skating party at Sans Souci. You turned nine, ten, eleven. You bossed him around and he reveled in that . . .

Did you in those years ever daydream that he was your father? The assistant pastor who bicycled around Berlin in sandals, who taught you with riddles and songs instead of rules and orders. You called him Mati, remember? A sort of blend of the standard parents' nicknames of "Vati" and "Mutti"—as if you had a third parent, of a third sex.

No. I was the daydreamer. I wanted our lives to be "right," simple and defensible. I sweated wishes as if wishing hard enough could budge the past, could take two halves from two failed histories (my imploded marriage, Mathias's isolation) and bind them into a whole—with a child, the proof of union, cupped inside.

Be assured: he fell for you, and the fantasy, too. Mathias saw
himself in you—your lean runner's legs and dark hair coarse as
sea-grass.

She drained the last cooled drops of grog. The wind had died down,
allowing snow to collect in scallops along the individual windowpanes.
Nowhere in Europe so vast a silence. Like the deepest, unexplored bed
of the ocean. The stove needed priming. Moving about she felt the stri-
ations of heat and cold in the still air of the cabin.

Happy birthday, Sophie! You arrived in such a rush. We nearly did-
n't make it to the hospital. The nurse tried to "hold me shut" until
my Herr Doctor could arrive to preside over the course of nature.
I screamed to the chimney tops, they must have heard me in the
farthest corners of that ancient labyrinth of a clinic. Achim argued
and threatened them, he was fighting on my side again, and finally
you . . . emerged. A beautiful creature. Close wrinkled like a paper
flower about to bloom. Skin rosy peach, and long limbs even then,
all covered with a waxy scum. What a rush you were in from that
morning on! Howling in your cot until the day you figured out
how to pull yourself up on two shaky legs and move ahead.
   "Sophie." The morning after your birth I lay speechless (and
crudely stitched together, for all the joy a late firstborn takes its toll)
while voices battled around me. Which family name? Ernestina,
Luise? Crusty ancestresses all. An impatient nurse stood by with
a pen and the registration forms. It was Harro then who mused,
"Sophie." Wisdom: the far-seeing, the wide-eyed perceiver. I liked
that! You could say it was Harro who named you.

A tangerine flash across the windows, then complete darkness except
for the woodstove's shimmer. Kaethe stood with her knees twanging.
Power failure. No matter. There were always candles nearby.

Glass River, December 29th, 12:30 p.m.
Dearest Sophie,
   Last night I set out to write you a birthday letter. Reminiscing,
rambling, it all got away from me. Let me try again: all yesterday

and into this morning we're having a mammoth snow storm. I measured thirty two inches already: eighty centimeters. Surrounding the cabin (remember the pictures I showed you in Munich) there are normally bare fields, but now the drifts mound in gigantic sculptures like Henry Moore nudes. From as far away as the county road I can hear the wind blasting into frozen branches, like a string orchestra gone mad.

Those pictures didn't do justice to the farm. No wonder you weren't much tempted to join me here. I'll send some new ones, show you how the sky here in winter is deeper more dazzling blue than the Mediterranean.

The electricity is out, so I expect to be cabin-bound for a while. Please don't worry. I have chow for weeks and on the woodstove can always melt snow for water.

Oh, Sophie—when will I stop pretending?

This morning I woke with your voice in my head, asking the question you've never asked me out loud. Your natural question: Mamma, WHY did you leave? When we were together in Munich you came very close: the phrases you kept weaving in that afternoon were "after you left…" or "before you left…." (Though we have had many leavings, some rougher than others, you clearly meant the first, awful tearing apart. Your first loss of faith.) The question, "how could you have?" lay huge and unspoken, like an accident scene we had to detour around. Did you want to spare me the embarrassment of an answer, or have you always been afraid to hear?

How do you remember that leaving day? You were five years old. Six days a week you went to kindergarten. On that Sunday your grandmother had picked you up and brought you home with her. At lunchtime I joined you. I had brought you a present, a stuffed toy rabbit. I wiped crumbs off your cheeks. Come evening I did not return. There had been no hint, no anguished kiss, no whispered promises. Later, even as the adults packed suitcases and you were taken to Zoo Station next morning, they gave you hugs and sweets but no explanation: whatever roughly cobbled lies they may have offered must have bewildered you—you with your black, truth-seeking eyes. And *Mamma gone?* expanded into days, weeks, months.

A drop hit the page, blurring the ink. Kaethe looked up at the ceiling, where a yellowish, trembling line of water followed a crack in the plaster.

Guess what? There's an ice-dam forming on the roof. An ice-dam means the snow has iced over hard but liquifies beneath, say from the rising heat of a stove. Over time the top accumulates more snow and freezes in thickening, insulating layers. Meanwhile the secret melted water pushing everywhere needs to flow, will force its way into every cranny and crack until eventually it breaks through slate tiles, oak boards, horse-hair plaster, anything.

Before the good light is gone I'll have to bundle up, go outside, see what I can do about the roof. But there's plenty of time, hours before dark. First, try to finish this—

Only minutes ago I was on the verge of explaining *why,* as if the answer was clear to me all along and I simply required the backbone to tell you.

You were five. We had enrolled you in an "alternative" pre-school, surely you remember rainbows painted on the cement walls around the garden? You had a knack for slipping loose and wandering around the city. Anyway I was always a little relieved to see your ruddy fierce face among the other blander kids, whenever I came to pick you up. That day, in my hurry and utter confusion, I brought something to leave with you. A stuffed toy rabbit. For lunch we shared cheese on a roll, sliced tomatoes. You were chattering about your morning. Of course you had no idea what sort of day lay ahead. By then my hands were shaking; I noticed, brushing crumbs off your cheeks. All concentration, you stroked the rabbit. ("Small Hare," your father used to call me.) I said an ordinary goodbye.

Why?

Funny. My mind skips like a cracked record, it spins and spins, much too far back: to the scene of your "birth from sin."

Sophie, that was an Event! A social high-point according to the Berlin papers, and your introduction to the whole far-flung family. Your christening, the triumph of your grandmother's stubborn campaigning. We the parents had dragged out the decision, a benighted rite we agreed, too busy to organize a baptism and

disenchanted with the stodgy pastor who required that we swear
to raise and educate Sophie Friderike von Thall in the Lutheran-
Evangelical faith.

Achim was working twelve, fourteen hours a day. A few months
after your birth he had published a research paper in Robotics,
about key variables in machine recognition of pitch. And now,
finally, awards and recognitions were starting to fall on him like
shooting stars. We didn't quite have the Big Money, but he was so
certain of Wirtschaftswunder-sweepstakes payoff being around the
corner that our lawyer was drawing up a contract with old Albus:
to fund her as the "entitled squatter" who would buy the Königsallee villa from the State. And then deed it to us. Speculation in
the air. We had friends willing to bankroll.

And I was in love. After you were born, I stayed home. I thank
you, Sophie, for the gift of earth's gravity. Of knowing which way
is up and which way is down. For the first time ever I was bound
to the everyday suck and pull of the ground. Days melted together,
all of a piece. Having you released me from all the insoluble, sterile
questions about myself. Who was I? Irrelevant! But some instinct
in me resisted the idea of your baptism. Too much a ritual of giving away, maybe, of sharing a piece of you—your "soul!"—with
the clan, with Jesus himself, for that matter. Ana Luise's pastor
warned us, "If, God forbid, anything should take the little one
away, heaven's gate will be closed to her." Fine. Heaven's a boring,
stuffy place, I said. She'd like limbo better.

In your long christening gown you looked like a Moorish Infanta
to be painted by Goya. The gown was cut from my wedding dress
and sewn by Achim's old nurse and her sister. Ana Luise could
have afforded sprier help. Her fortunes were rising not only with
the flood-tides of her sons, but also with the public frenzy over the
recent unearthing of Count Ernst von Thall's wartime diaries, in
which your paternal grandfather comes across as a sort of poet-
soldier-hero: a German Abraham and Isaac in one. In that year of
terror and violence the diaries were a godsend to the establishment.
Your grandmother gave television interviews, lectured around the
country. . . . She arrived at your christening fresh from turning
down an offer of forty thousand marks advance from a publisher
known to support apartheid. Linking arms with me at the font she

trumpeted the Lord's Prayer vibrato, her eyes moist with fulfill-
ment. Later on, at the reception—the Bristol-Kempinski, you see
how you were launched like a debutante—she and I took turns res-
cuing you whenever you tumbled in that ungainly dress. Scooping
you up so your kicks and squalls sweetened to giggles. "The sisters'
cataracts," she whispered. "They don't sew quite as neatly as they
used to. But I can't 'replace' them. Isn't usefulness all that keeps
any of us from going under?"

Harro, the battered old atheist, ran your christening party like a
drum major.

There were over a hundred guests. (I scrutinized each man as he
entered, in the wild hope that one might be your grandfather Max
in a witty and skillful disguise.) Achim worked the crowd, bobbing
from one table to the next, bowing over dowagers' bloated hands.
You, darling, were toasted more than once as the "Stammhalter"—
the scion—as if your gender was immaterial, negotiable, and all
that mattered was for them to have another incarnation of the firstborn of the firstborn of the firstborn. Recorded so, back to the first
Crusades.

Exuding fumes of Mosel, Harro breathed into my ear between
speeches: "Rome." He had an ex-prisoner's insensitivity to "personal
space." You were drowsing on my shoulder.

"Rome didn't burn because some fatsoes at the top partied too
hard." Harro gestured with a piece of tartare-on-pumpernickel at
the bright, buzzing tables. "The Empire crashed because the whole
concept went kaput. By the year 400 no two people could agree on
what the hell 'Rome' stood for. Not for democracy, nor civic virtue,
not the old gods or the new upstart from the colonies either. Not
for a common culture. Not even self-defense. Entropy! All the real
power—" he shoved the meat dab into his mouth, "gone to the far
ends of the earth. Political extremes. You, Kaethe—right? You're
the only one in this capitalist bordello with any shimmer of what
I'm talking about."

I stroked your back, nodding. Flattered. "You mean skinheads
ruling Zoo Station. You mean Entebbe. Neo-Nazis in the Bundes-
tag. The assassination of the banker . . . Jürgen Ponto . . . ?" I paused.
We both waved to your uncle Leon, roaming between the tables
with his shirttail hanging out, disconsolate because there was
neither organ nor piano for him to play. "The Red Army Faction

attack on the embassy in Stockholm. Holger Meins beaten in jail—"

"Bah! You sorry for the RAF, girl? Them being neither a political fraction, nor an army, nor as God is my witness any legit shade
of red. What about their torture and killing of poor Schleyer? I
could have been him. Not ideologically: he had a Brown past.
Humanly, I mean. Same draft year."

Sometimes we blot out a sickening event. How else could I have
forgotten poor Schleyer? I had rocked you in my arms, evenings
in front of Frau Albus' little black and white TV, touched, like all
the public, by the kidnappers' photos of their industrialist lion in
captivity—his cheesy face thinned and saggy, the large loose lips
seeming caught between a Candid Camera smile and a grimace
of abject terror.

Kidnapping, Sophie. Our neighbors had resorted to setting up
inflated plastic people-puppets in their windows, to foil prospective
kidnappers. At the same time I gathered that on the other side of
the city Max was juggling informants, to stop up the RAF's bolt-
holes eastward. They were an embarrassment.

But for me in all that time, you were the unfolding drama and
reality, you were making me into someone new.

I couldn't fear kidnappers if I tried. I'd known so-called urban
guerrillas, these gaunt theoreticians. Some of them had been not
merely companions, but my first protectors in the city. We had lived
skin to skin. I imagined masked conspirators breaking into the villa
at Königsallee, carrying off the Countess von Thall and her child—
and then recognizing me. A reunion.

I felt no sympathy either. They'd had choices, made their decisions. The best of them weren't capable of feeling sorry for themselves.

Harro topped my glass; wine fizzed over my hand. "Lapis, eh?
Since when do you wear a signet ring?" He flashed his own, a
handsome bloodstone that replaced the ring ripped off his frozen
finger in Siberia.

"Achim's idea. In honor of *her*." I shifted you like a compact
white log to my other shoulder.

"Right, so. And may she be only the first of your brood!"

He pinged his fork on his glass; the room quieted halfway, and
Harro rose with another toast, a sort of meandering thanks from
an old P.O.W. for these gathered relatives, for the mild December

temperatures, for the success of Brandt's Ostpolitik as evidenced
by the quality of tonight's caviar. When he paused, the dismissal of
applause broke out, and Harro fell back beside me with a whoosh,
as though dropped from a B-52.

"It doesn't work, your analogy." With Harro I always ended up
arguing. "Berlin's not a Rome. Not even a capital. Berlin is over! It's
back to being a provincial, floating outpost. And it's cut in half, like
a worm in a laboratory dish. This side's only kept alive artificially—
pumped up with subsidies, and bonuses to anyone resigned to life
in no-man's-ville—"

"And the other side?"

I shrugged. Harro beamed at me, his eyes damp and drunkenly
knowing. The two of us, he signaled, we're different from the rest,
we've spoken other languages, lived as different people in other
worlds, but now we've made it here to the center. We belong.

You woke in a sweat. My sisters-in-law surged around, marvel-
ing that you didn't whinge—all their babies had cried on waking
from naps, and wasn't I lucky to have one so self-possessed?

I handed you to Harro, for safekeeping.

She had pulled her table a few feet out from the drip-line on the ceiling
and had set a plastic tub beneath it, and while she scribbled the drops
hit the water in a quick rhythm, with the timbre of plucked strings.
The words flowed faster.

You understand, Sophie, that not all of this is exact? You don't
expect me to remember your uncle's exact words, do you, or mine
—or at what point, exactly, he spilled wine over my wrist? But how
else can I get the truth across to you? Because *why I left* won't make
sense unless you can follow me into lost times—those hours with
all their warmth and color and skepticism, paired with robust confidence in our years about to unfold—

The paper dimmed, as if someone stood between it and the window.
Naturally there was no one. Outside a low-bellied sky, like a caved-in
tent, hung ominous as the skies that gather before a summer cyclone.
And inside, a summer-like heat. She could hear the rustle of wood
falling to ash inside the stove. And the drops from overhead hastening
to fall.

Kaethe went out, leaving the door ajar. Thirty-five degrees. A balmy wind-shift. She needed no coat, only the work gloves and boots. The stream of her urine drilled a glimmering gold well in the snow. She pulled up her thermals and, buttoning her jeans, lolloped over thigh-high drifts to the north side: to check on the roof.

Where the ice-dam overhung the eave it was twenty inches thick. Grayish blue in the sapped light. Like a deformity, she thought. A nasty growth. Time to break it open. Otherwise, if this was a true thaw brewing, the ice-dam would at some unpredictable point gush free, flood what little was left of her grandparents' burned-down house and worse: drown wires and lights, dissolve the sheetrock, swell boards and joists into crazy waves like sculpted water.

She knew where she had left the axe. A few feet out from the woodpile. The first storm always blew in before expected, before all tools had been stowed away.

Though this snow's surface looked consistent in its swirls and shallows, it felt erratic underfoot. Now she was able to walk-slide on top, but next step she floundered in a white pit, struggling to move invisible legs.

The previous February she had trekked up into the woods on her father's boyhood wooden skis, on one of the brilliant, sun-scoured days that follow a heavy storm. In a clearing where the snow rose high she came across a white-tailed doe, taffy brown and shaggy, lying rigid in its nest of snow. The doe had evidently been unable to free herself from the drift. A broken leg, Kaethe had guessed as she poled past. The intricate doe corpse looked smaller than in life. Coyotes or hawks had already begun to feed at the underbelly and the eyes.

No electricity, so no water from the pump. From now till morning only wavering candle-light, or no light at all. Twice last winter, between what he called "bouts of weather," Joe from the Glass River store had driven his snowmobile up the mountainside to her drift-barricaded door, to bring mail, eggs and bread and to check, naturally, on whether Ms. K. Schalk still figured in the township census (Entering Glass River, Pop. 187)—but there was no knowing whether or when he would come again. Hand-scooping into the snow around the woodpile, scanning despite the poor light for the telltale hump of a buried axe. She thought of how, were she to break a leg, or catch an infection, or knock over a candle in her sleep, she could die as unremarked as the doe.

True—although she could never pinpoint a moment of conscious choice—that she had chosen freely to come here. And then to stay.

But all her life and in much safer places there had been times when the immanence of her own death pressed like a hot, black chamber against her. That close. Nothing lay between but a split second of transcendent pain.

Up here, alone in the cabin, she felt the membrane between herself and nonexistence stretched thinner than ever. But she paid it no attention.

December 30th, 7:10 A.M.
Dearest Sofchen,

Morning, but I'm writing by candlelight. Outside no stars, total darkness still. Yesterday I interrupted my letter to you to clear ice from the roof but couldn't locate the axe and after I came back in and ate and returned to that ridiculously long, rambling letter I had lost the thread of what I want to say—

My mind keeps racing back to your beginning. On this date, twenty one years ago, you were all of two days old. Every four hours they carried you to me from a far-off nursery. From neck to toe you were swaddled. A mystery. Even your lavender mottled hands tucked into white mittens I removed. A little white knit cap pulled down over your ears.

Four hours was too long apart. You came to me famished and fretful, tossing your face from side to side in search of a teat, sucking with your rosy gums at the muslin mittens. Luckily I had milk to squander, and when you mewled it spewed from my nipples in fine jets; my breasts were big as sugar beets, hard-packed and feverish. The first minutes of nursing were painful—but that pain carried the sweetest, most welcome release, it blotted out all other sore places in body or mind.

Nurses paused to admire us. How unusual, they said, for a "late-bearer" to have so much milk! On a few occasions they brought me other babies, thinner and limper than you, the ones that were failing to thrive. How could I say no? My promiscuous breasts responded, obedient to small sounds and touches, and I lay feeding these nameless ones though immune to the pleasure—temporarily paralyzed, not to mention catheterized. A "late-bearer." Pared down to an animal self. The other two new mothers in the ward were at least fifteen years younger. They traded makeup tips and strolled around aimlessly, slack-tummied, on sturdy, fish-white legs.

Two-days-old anniversary. A day when your father and grandmother and assorted uncles and aunts and awed, bug-eyed cousins all squeezed into the space between my bed and the open window —how hot that hospital was, ancient coal boilers all fired up for winter!—and uncorked champagne. The nurses, charmed by Achim, sipped with us and winked and told naughty jokes.

When we did finally re-enter the world we were still surrounded by a kind of cushioning nimbus. Evenings, Achim came home early to play with you and before returning to his lab experiments he cooked me a strengthening dinner—Argentine steak, or scrambled eggs—and helped me bathe. Nothing was as before. I took this pretty much for granted. Amid all this change, it was days before I asked when anyone had last seen the cats.

Achim looked at the rug, compressing his lips—that stern expression you know well. "They pined for you," he explained. "Two and half weeks . . . you were never gone so long. I couldn't tell them why. They lay in your closet, wouldn't eat. Kaethe—don't look that way. They *were* getting on in age. . . ." He had kept the sad news from me as long as possible, he said, so as not to upset me. Or dry up my milk.

Her reservoir of body-warmth from sleep was used up: in the fingerless, now singed gloves her hand formed slow, clumsy letters. She pinched out both candles and stood up stiffly, propping on the table. Opened the stove's maw and jammed in another log—clean-burning birch, so the stove wouldn't need raking-out any time soon. But if she went on at this rate there'd be nothing left to burn in February and March but sticky, dirty pine.

"Improvident." Word with a sharp point, like a poker or a pencil. A fine Yankee word. Word favored by her grandparents. Improvidence travels well, she thought, a deep-rooted trait. She used to joke and tease Ana Luise over the older woman's compulsion to buy cheap, rotting fruit from the market—together they worked for hours cutting out the

good bits for the family dessert. Kaethe assumed that in time she would
absorb the example—become a hoarder, an enhancer, a magician, an
anchor, a competent mother.

Ana Luise would have had birch logs left over in May.

Kaethe unhooked the blanket hung across the cabin door, pushed
down the latch, stepped out on ice. The cold slapped her good and hard.
No thaw after all. Colder than yesterday, coldest all season. That was
why the ice-dam had sealed its leak overnight.

To the west lay two horizons: first, the nacreous slope of her own
mountain. Beyond, rising out of the invisible, minor valley of Glass
River, a scraggy-peaked quartet. Mountains white-skinned by snow,
furred with bristly brown-black forest. The surrounding sky was the
color of moldering steel: good for more snow, she thought.

Midmorning. She scanned the nearer horizon and its worm-trace of
buried road, and listened for the distant snarl of a snowmobile's engine.

Anxious. Unwilling to re-enter the cabin, and face the letter waiting
to be finished.

Why did I ever leave you? I could lie. To both of us. Say that a single
unpardonable injury sent me running across the border, with no
plan to return. Bridges burned.

Kaethe laid down the pen. Something shimmered at the edge of her
mind—an ordinary morning in the Königsallee, Albie's secret-fattened,
lowered voice, oily coffee slowly stirred. Confidences...

She shook her head crisply, as if to make memories tumble in fresh
combinations, like dice.

Sophie...do *I* know the answer?

Maybe its root burrows a long way back, into years before your
birth. How prettily I've been painting that event, joy and harmony,
as if to say there could be no reason for what happened later—it
only "happened," as a chunk of meteor happens to fall through a
roof.

But before...despite all our blooming prospects and constant
busy-ness in the booming "frontline" city, before was anything but
joyous. A long, childless marriage can go in one of two directions, I
think—either toward an extreme, twin-like closeness (pity the child
born late to that union) or toward slow hollowing-out, so that even-

tually there will be nothing left inside the shell of the marriage but a little emotional dust.

I don't recall any shock over realizing that he went to other women. He never much bothered to make excuses, hide notes, lower his voice on the phone. Whores or housewives, to him it was all so casual. For our generation, in a certain time and place, promiscuity had implied freedom, even virtue—and so what ground did I have, later on, suddenly to complain? It was an affirmation he needed, I told myself. And we had an understanding: he would never, "out there," fall in love. A promise, to protect us both. He even took the disarming tactic of informing me about the details of his sidesteps, as if candor would lead us to a deeper intimacy. And I colluded. He would crawl back into our bed at four in the morning and whisper how much better a fuck I was (though by the way, he said, the woman whose hospitality he'd ust enjoyed was rabidly uninhibited, one could learn a few things there).

We went our own paths, but even after a dreary trail of years of that kind of marriage I still had an idea about a limit, a closeness, with us inside and the Others outside. Admittedly, I began taking detours of my own, with no one worth mentioning or remembering. For balance. For what I thought of, then, as my self-respect! But I still owned virtue.

Whenever I returned after such an excursion to Achim and my resentful cats, to crazy Albus and Ana Luise and all the family: each time there was a little more separation, I could sense my increasing indifference to "home." That scared me. I was weightless, with no shimmer of an idea that anyone—*you*—would ever come to anchor me. But do you see, Sophie? That was still virtue, the honest, remaining piece of it—to be worried by my own indifference.

Astonishing, how much she had written. How quickly. Her handwriting devolved from a chubby careful start to this elongated slant, with crosses and dots flying high and wide like clothes tossed off in a high wind.

She was excited to be thinking in German again. A language penetrates the mind like water, imbues the one who uses it with untranslatable emotions and attitudes and insights. In American she was not the same person, though no more nor less herself.

She stood, stretched, wolfed down saltines and cheese and a winter apple (its skin puckered and leathery) from the cellar, where some live thing had pattered and hissed while she set down the offering of milk.

Looked down at the scrawled pages, then to the photograph of Sophie half-smiling, ringleted, enigmatic Apollo with her soft-swung lips.

These pages are not fit for a daughter. Was there no end to the harm she was capable of, for her own selfish needs?

But so long since she had written to anyone in any language at all.

Nothing to stop her from poking some or all of these pages into the stove. At any time.

April, Sophie. Crocuses butting up through frozen muck, clouds tipping snow-showers down your collar. In the April before you came, Mathias and I first met.

Your grandfather Max had invited me to the long-ballyhooed opening of the "Palace of the Republik," the DDR's copper-shimmery oceanliner of State erected directly across from the Cathedral. An equal though opposing ugliness. The opening hoopla was a big Socialist deal—delegations from all over, foreign wa-was, and enough vodka and caviar to fuel all the armies of the Warsaw Pact. This was years after "normalization," of course, and so I could often and without fuss fade from West Berlin into the Republic of Workers and Farmers for a daytrip—though still not bothering to inform your father. He was already shedding his liberal skin and metamorphosing into the cynical right-centrist he would become, like a Pinocchio with his nose half-grown.

Max had wangled three tickets. The third was for a friend of his I hadn't met, a guy, he said, who needed to get out and play more. Mathias Leytenfeger turned out to be a gangly, threadbare Lutheran cleric with a subversive sense of humor. I was used to Max's eclectic choice of companions. The three of us danced and drank pink Crimean champagne. The chandeliers sparkled like artillery fire over our hectic waltzes and polkas. Drunker couples crashed into us, laughing and cursing in German and Russian. My ankles were bruised; I danced even faster. Max swung me around that crazy floor. His eyes were bright and bloodshot. I'm overjoyed, he said, to see you getting on so well with my friend Mathias. We flew—my father's right hand clasped me under my breast; his hips, all experience, guided mine. It felt fantastic, I was simply a woman fortunate to be singled out: that was Max's way to dance.

Pastor Leytenfeger held his body away, dancing. I pulled him closer, both hands cupping the sinewy back through the thin shirt. Pausing in a corner of the hall I dared him to kiss me. Carelessly. Are you sure you want this? he asked.

Mathias's kiss burned through every barrier in my body: it made my palms sing, it burned to the soles of feet.

What can one kiss mean? But later that night I ran from them both. Why? Revulsion after too much drink, or a reaction to Max's cheerful remark? Was it my last hope of virtue? How did I know? I caught the last west-bound S-Bahn home. Back to the Königsallee. I *stayed* home: April, May, June. I clung close to Achim, insisted on joining him for every reception and dinner party, tried to see him with affection again.

I'd missed periods before, and been disappointed. It wasn't until near the end of July that I felt unmistakable changes, saw the signs. I should have recognized them sooner. But I had been trying hard to remain deaf to my body. Oh Sophie, it was another sort of possession I was guarding against. Not you.

Kaethe lifted her pen. The truth was, she had left in small steps. Piecemeal. When Sophie was only a toddler, her visits "across" resumed. She had brought news and photos to Max (they seemed to satisfy the grandfather in him completely) and with a sleepwalker's sureness found her way to Mathias. Cautiously, cautiously . . . This time as a young mother with a stake in propriety. She even made efforts to deceive Max's system of informant-protectors. Once there's a child the gates of marriage clang down, all the equivocations evaporate.

She believed in practicality, not guilt, yet it hung around like an unclean smell. Sophie stayed safe in the West, in so many good hands. The idea of guilt infuriated her.

In the winter she crossed over in the S-Bahn wearing a short puffy jacket, long woolen kilt, high-strapped boots. No underwear. As the train jounced she would suffer the rough friction of the wool against her naked bottom. She would unbutton the jacket. Flushed, raise her eyes to meet the gaze of any good-looking man in the car. Wanting them to know. Wanting them all, any man: to see, to touch, to share in her arousal. When she arrived at Mathias's place, breathless from the stair-climb, and pushed open that door with only a hole where the lock should be, he would hurry to greet her with a cheerful, chaste brush of his lips—until she took his hand and kissed his palm and drew it inside the folds of the kilt, which was fastened only with a large decorative pin. Through the short labyrinth of wool to her bare, hot skin. Until his fingers found the welling moisture between her legs, all prepared for him. His touch made her shudder, and sometimes nearly faint.

From beneath the floorboards she heard a rustling noise, a faint scrabbling. Well, you can come in from the cold, she thought. Down there (among rusted tools, piles of mildewed clothes and charred furniture) the persistent smell of urine was mild and tolerable, and so she guessed that whatever took shelter in the cellar found its own frequent way in and out—chinks though the unmortared stones of the foundation.

She had never been "in love" with Mathias. It wasn't the kind of lust she was used to, either; it was a diffuse craving, almost melancholy, and insatiable. She would lie undressed on his couch, not listening to his pained, post-coital struggles with conscience about what was right, or terribly wrong. His skin had the creamy sheen you see on adolescents. The more he agonized, the less she needed to; he had scruples enough for both. She would reach for and stroke him, his back and bare thighs and narrow buttocks until he shivered and tried to trap and push away her hands, until he had no choice but to turn back to her and do what she wanted done all over again.

> You were five. I don't know with any certainty what sparked Achim's jealousy. Or when. At home it seemed he saw only you; he had stopped noticing me except to try to plant another child, or give a lecture on my uncontrolled spending. I would ruin us financially, he said; I fell for trashy temptations with no care for the consequences.
>
> But life was being good to him that year. An appointment to the Technology Office of the Berlin Senate, and if that didn't yet bring quite the recognition or the money destiny owed him, we had, I thought, enough. Meanwhile the city was growing by leaps and bounds, sending pirate glamour-shots out over the TV into Czech and Polish and DDR state-built apartments, and luring a

booming supply of refugee labor. Money sloshed around Berlin like suds in our new washing machine. Absurdly easy to borrow for a new car, a vacation in Tuscany, curtains and a sofa set for the villa guaranteed to be ours, one day soon.

But once he became sure he knew all about me and Mathias, everything must have fallen together for him. Your father is a scientist, after all. This was the Occam's razor the scientist had been hunting for, slicing across all his mere mounting suspicions with one explanatory stroke. I came home one evening and found him in a tight-lipped rage. Drinking scotch whiskey. I figured he had discovered my visits across the Wall.

His first accusation—"She isn't mine, is she? How could I let myself be fooled for all these years?"—took me completely by surprise. "Don't give me that look! Sophie—she's someone else's bastard." Ridiculous: anyone could see you had his gestures, his lanky bones, not to mention his flashes of temper. I was about to laugh at the absurdity but he went on: "You're quite inhuman. You've managed to keep your filthy secret. . . . Well, what did I ever hope for, from a tramp like you? You fascinated me—but I never could figure you out. Someone able to change her country, language, family loyalties, all easily as a set of clothes. A betrayal like this must count as small potatoes, Kaethe Schalk."

I was bewildered. I saw he wasn't joking. I could only stare. "What an ice-cold piece of work you are," he said. He smashed into picture glass with his fist. He said, "Let's admit it, we've both known long enough. *I* am infertile. Only, I wanted, wanted so much to believe in the outside chance, in my one baby! You took advantage. You let me love her. You set me up."

Better let me bandage that cut for you, I said, but he squeezed his fist tight, for the satisfaction of seeing dark blood well out of his knuckles.

If only, Sophie, if only! I should have let him go on thinking I'd lied that way. Then in his fury he would have thrown you and me both into the street, right? His pride would have trapped him into doing what he dreaded most: letting us go free—and all it needed from me was silence.

I was stupefied. Anxious about you who were much too close by, playing with our landlady in the back of the house. I forced my voice low: reason and restraint. How that must have infuriated him! "You've changed sides so often," he said, "you're washed in all waters. Don't think I'm not aware. *Shit*—do you even know who that child's father is?"

In my own outrage I stammered, insisting on innocence (knowing I was hardly innocent) throwing out counter-accusations (what difference did they make?). I needed to clear my name, Sophie, to convince him—but of what? Your genealogy? Your notarized pedigree? Of course not, because you were—are—*you,* and that should have been enough. Convince him of my virtue? Exactly. My past, ours, the chaste ideal that I clung to before your birth and after. I needed Achim to know there had been such a time, lasting long after his affairs began.

He hurled words like rocks. My attempts at defense only convinced him of my treachery. After that night, he became just as suddenly, strangely quiet. Weeks of mutual silence. In a way I felt sorry for him. Watching him drag out after a full day's work to one of the prostitutes in the Tiergarten or to a colleague's love-starved spouse. While I stayed home, close to you, as far away from him as I could. I slept on the floor of your nursery. Perhaps you remember...

A month later, as I passed the open bedroom door, he spoke my name. I went in to him, in the dark. And left an hour later convinced that with this act of coupling and forgiveness the worst would be over. That next day we would find ourselves able to talk again. With honesty. Figure out what should come next. What was left.

Next morning, a Monday, he left very early for work. Soon afterward a grayish man like a small, chubby rat, vaguely apologetic, stood at the door. "Countess Thall?"

"That's me." What was he selling, I wondered. He handed me a smudgy typed paper. All seals and signatures: he watched, as official witness, as I read the summons to my divorce. The preliminaries had been dispensed with in judges' chambers. "The aggrieved party—Husband and Father—petitions for sole custody of his child, Sophie Friderike von Thall. You are summoned to final hearing on the matters of Divorce and Custody in two weeks."

Two weeks, Sophie, is not much time. In two weeks everything can happen. I'm trying, you understand, to explain.

Achim took you away with him to your grandmother's house.
I would be free to visit you there. I hardly protested. Two weeks:
I had little time to spare for mothering.

I bumped into things. In a blur. I cried, although at that point
more from the burn of injury than the ache of despair. At night in
the villa I hurled his books and ashtrays at the wall and screamed,
and closed my eyes passing your room. But during the days I pulled
myself together, I became as duplicitous as your father would have
predicted. I appealed to his brothers: Achim is stressed, I said, over-
worked, you must talk him out of this craziness. I phoned Harro
in Bonn—an emergency, please come to me at once! Every noon-
time I turned up at Ana Luise's to spend my hour or two with you.
I played Duty, and Fortitude, and Faith. She, on her side, spoke not
a word about the separation—she might have been baby-sitting at
my request. We even continued our clandestine ritual of savoring
the occasional smoke, though it no longer tasted right to me, and
your grandmother watched me through her practiced exhalations
with sad, ruminative eyes.

Oddly, the part about Faith was true. In my heart I didn't believe
the threats in the summons would be carried out. They were a public lashing, a matter of pride and punishment. For good or bad this
marriage wouldn't end, not so; certainly, I wouldn't lose my natural
right to my child.

Meanwhile I was running all over the city, looking for help,
for a lawyer. But too late, as most of them were quick to say. Von
Thall? The same as Ernst, the war hero and pacifist? The same
family that served Frederick the Great? Defend you against the
von Thalls? And the child in question, you mentioned that one of
her godfathers sits on the Constitutional Court? I regret we can't
accommodate. . . . Sorry. This office is simply too busy.

"Getting down to brass tacks," said the one lawyer willing to
listen, "you're still a foreigner." He was a fat man but baggy like
a deflated beetle, past retirement age, with mustard stains caked
on his vest. "You have no personal source of income? Not one
dime, lira, piaster? Your past is—well, I ask you. Less than trans-
parent. No?

"Let's face facts," he said.

Neither your uncles nor their wives found a spare minute to
return my calls.

I was surrounded by traces of Achim. They lay scattered all over his mother's house, in the messages colleagues and friends left with Albus, in your babbled daily stories. I looked for him. I missed him! He was my partner after all, we shared *you,* he was the one I could turn to when the demons were snapping at my heels. He used to like to tell me: "Whatever happens, Little Hare, don't forget we're in this together." But now he stayed hidden from me: his exit had been thoroughly prepared.

I went back to Szredskistrasse for one evening. To Max. No weeping permitted in front of Max. "I want your advice," I said. He shook his head. He used to keep his hair short cut, bristly like Bert Brecht's, but now it flopped long and gray and thin. "Keep your chin up, Kaethe-cat. Don't let me find out you crawled in front of them." If only the jurisdiction were here, in the People's Republic, he said, he could arrange certain things, protect the kid and me. Socialist justice would protect a mother and child. But I'd made other choices. His arm didn't reach. Together, that night, we killed a fifth of vodka. Until noon the next day I was too drunk to leave. "Ach, Kaethe-cat—you know where you're welcome, at least."

After that visit, as if in quarantine, I avoided further contact with Mathias.

On the Sunday, Harro arrived. Sober, and somber. In no doubt about his influence. His career, like his oldest nephew's, was soaring; he acted the diplomat to the core. He went around to hear Achim's perspective first, then to his sister-in-law. Monday afternoon, his last few hours in town he picked me up in a cab.

We drove to the golf course in the American Zone. Golf—the quintessential capitalist-exploiter pastime. Not a sport; more like a jaunt in a coolie's rickshaw, I said. "Are you sure this is a game you want to learn, Harro?"

"I am learning it," he said. "Golf has its charms, Kaethe. Ha! Watch this!" Rain was falling mistily all over the sterilized grass. He swung a club and clots of mud jumped up like locusts, half-burying the pockmarked ball. "Shit. But since Western businessmen don't go to Turkish baths anymore, golf is where to do business. Also it gets me out for a healthy stroll. My heart's a mess, they tell me."

I carried his clubs. We squelched from hole to hole in the whispering rain. There had always been a special connection between us. Only a year or so before, Harro had urged me to stand for election. Wasn't I a well-informed female, vociferously opinionated—and wouldn't that be excellent, in politics? The party (any party!) was starved for women candidates.

"Business," I repeated. "Then I suppose this is a kind of business now? Harro—you know what Achim's doing."

He turned to me and all the folds of his face settled, illegible and glistening wet. A former Gulag resident, indifferent to weather. "Ach. Let the man go. He needs that now, see? A guy needs freedom sometimes—after his pride's been hurt."

I tried to explain more. That I'd done no real harm, whatever he said or believed. This was a hasty mistake. We walked on.

"It's your duty, Kaethe. If you truly love him . . . don't fight it."

"But that is crazy. And Sophie—"

"For the love of God, Achim is my brother's oldest son. Sophie is his only child! You think we, all of us together, won't give her everything a girl needs?"

Was this fair, I asked. What about me? No one would speak to me. The planned divorce had been prepared—somehow, through someone—without my knowing.

"What did you expect? Advance warning so you could make the first move? The Queensbury Rules? Come on, you're smarter than that. Since when does fairness play in?" He reshouldered his bag of clubs. Clapped his arm across my back, turning us to retrace our path. "Don't ask me, Kaethe.

"Hey, hey—you know I've always been partial to you! But, totally beside the point. Blood's thicker than water. Har!" We were both soaked to the skin. Drowned rats.

Hunger drove her up from the table. Persistent pangs she could no longer ignore. When had she last eaten? A cup and snow-scrubbed plate in the sink might have been left from the night before. On the sill beside her daughter's photograph the wind-up clock ticked with the soft rhythm of a player dealing cards. Three forty-three.

Since she had begun to write the letter, time seemed to be continually accelerating. Years ago, in Berlin, she had joined a gym (free trial day) crammed with steel and rubber machines (had also paid a rejuvenation-quack for vitamin B injections, had dyed her hair) and though the gym routine soon bored and repelled her, the electric treadmill gave a peculiar thrill. Ground rolling backward, tactile hills humping and flattening at the pressure of a thumb. The pace ratcheting up—and yet the runner stayed fixed in her assigned space. So with the letter: time rushed faster and faster, and although she was going nowhere, was stationary, virtually sealed in the remains of the farmhouse, the writing was bringing her closer to Sophie. She was stripping down. It would be hard to stop, now. Paradoxically, the more she showed of herself, the clearer and closer her daughter appeared. The colorless down along Sophie's cheekbones, and the strong wrists, and the luxuriant curve of lips that seldom smiled. Kaethe could almost see her now.

She ate while rereading her words. A pair of withered Macouns, a chocolate bar, a cup of milk. The milk, although kept cool in a lidded box shoved up against the drafty front door, wouldn't stay drinkable much longer.

Those last six days, before the date set for the hearing. Terrible, chaotic, like some natural disaster. Like a firestorm or flood. There's no memory that leaves me feeling more shamed—that hot, nauseated response—and yet I don't see what I could or would have done differently. I can't blame myself! But I still feel humiliation.

There were urgent conferences with the lawyer. My sole defender. He was long in the tooth and short on tact, as he himself said, and his career already a mound of dead-ends: he had nothing to fear from the high and mighty von Thall tribe. "Not a prayer of you gaining custody," he said, "not as your circumstances stand. Don't argue!" He hammered it in that I was a commoner, a foreigner to boot. His job was to see I got the money due me. If they were going to treat a woman as a vessel to be tossed away when no longer useful, well hell, Countess—they better pay like they broke a Ming vase.

I nodded comprehension. Nothing made sense.

Arriving to fetch you at kindergarten I learned I needed signed permission from the father. I spat. So much for the Anti-Authoritarian movement, sisters. So much for solidarity.

Ana Luise had withdrawn deep in her house. When I came for my visit with you, all out of breath and uncertain, the doors stood ajar and you sat alone in the dining room, practicing writing your name.

One morning I spied Frau Albus out on the garden walk, tugging and pushing an enormous, leather-strapped, pre-War suitcase toward the gate. From the window I watched her flail like a dung-beetle wrestling its ball, glancing up nervously, as if afraid I'd explode at her, prevent her leaving. Where was she off to? I wondered. In all Berlin she knew no one but us.

I went to bars. I drank standing up, alone, hard and fast, like someone taking the water cure at a spa.

I told the lawyer—Behrens, yes, that was the old man's name!—that I wouldn't accept a deal. Would not lie down and let their shoes march up and down my spine. I would fight to the end: loser take nothing.

Saturday. He knocked, let himself in. He, Achim. Morning. He woke me. Let's take a walk together, he said. Out where it's quiet. Let's walk along the Charlottenburg canal.

On the path we met no one. Black ducks, exhausted by a summer's parenting, dozed on the steep banks. In late August even the easily agitated fronds of weeping willows hang absolutely motionless over their hazed mirror of water.

Simply walking beside him I felt a crazy kind of gaiety begin to bubble up. Be patient, I told myself, wait until he finds a voice to speak in. My stride stretched to match his. A person wakes up from a long nightmare in stages, I realized, like a diver rising through the ocean, pausing to avoid the bends. Achim thrust his fingers through mine and squeezed. His two gold rings were the only jewelry I wore.

We were still husband and wife. In that fact, after over fifteen years, nothing had changed.

Husband and wife: there's a kind of homely magnificence to the idea, to the accretion of years and routines, the secrets and closing-off of others, the very *Bürgerlichkeit* of it.

Had he heard from Albie, I asked, and to my surprise he said no

Kaethe laid her head on her arm. Hiding her face from the empty room. Overwhelmed by the forward rush of memory.

On the canal path, Achim stopping her with a touch. His kiss hardly

surprised her. She had been conjuring it, the reality brought tears to
edge her closed eyes, she raised the stakes with teeth and tongue, pressing her hips against him until they both rocked and swayed. Wanting
to be folded inside him, her husband, safe and at peace. He was brother,
parent, child-maker. He knew her.

"We were the Great Idea, remember?" He gave a small smile that
was both sentimental and wry.

"Aren't we still?"

Walking on, then. Clinging. I don't feel sure of anything, he con-
fessed. He had thought he needed the separation—well all right, a
divorce—to heal himself. Kaethe was the stronger of them emotion-
ally; it had to be hard for her to understand his doubt, insecurities poi-
soning his mind. But he did love her. Already in the time apart he had
craved her terribly. A humiliation. No other woman could do this to
him, and if that was part of his illness—

She said, who has been talking to you? There is no illness. She
stepped off the path and slipped inside the airy green tent a weeping
willow forms; Achim followed. Kneeling she unbuckled his belt and
stroked his heavy erection and her skirt was up twisted around her
waist and her pants blissfully torn, and in seconds he was inside her.
Tears in his green eyes as he moved above her. Canal grass beneath slid
like silk. So we can call it all off, she whispered. Come to our senses.
Give ourselves time. Oh yes, he said, that's what we must do, yes. . . .

Sophie—after that walk, I told Dr Behrens not to waste another
minute on the case. It would be canceled. I was trusted, that
Saturday afternoon, to take you out to the lake for a swim. On
Sunday I brought you a toy rabbit. Then I went home and waited
polished and perfumed for Achim to fetch me for dinner, where
we meant to talk matters over. Waiting, I drank white wine and,
when that bottle was empty, turned to Max's gift, the Russian
vodka. The next morning, two of your younger uncles shouted
my name, pounding on the door. They poured me full of coffee
and Vivamed, got me dressed and washed, and drove me to the
courthouse.

I don't remember this part. You understand? It was pitch dark
in that old hall, dark as in the whale's belly. Who else was there?
Did I say any word other than yes, or no? There were affidavits dissecting my character and unfitness as a parent, from people I had

thought I knew. I saw photographs of me I never knew existed: saw myself obliviously walking toward that sign, in four languages: You Are Leaving the Western Sector. Right up through the previous week someone had followed and photographed me. I heard the accusation "malicious abandonment of the family." Other than that, I heard nothing! All that's left printed on my mind now is a moment afterward: the two of us, freshly divorced, standing in the daylight again, hesitant, outside on the curved courthouse steps. What does one say? Achim reached me his white flag of a handkerchief. He said, There, that could have been worse, no? We had a decent judge, at least.

I was bloated from earlier weeping. Shaking uncontrollably. A common symptom of hangover, as anyone might have thought, exacerbated by lack of food. But in fact the shaking would continue into the next day and the next, intensifying until it felt like my muscles were trying to break my bones.

Listen, said Achim. I want to thank you. For not—for being . . .

I looked away so he wouldn't continue.

He was free! He talked about plans to take you, Sophie, for a short holiday with friends in the south country, away from the city smog and heat—for that matter, well, what was I doing for the next week? Did I want to come along? Always room in a Bavarian farmhouse for one more.

No.

Well then . . . you will come say goodbye to her! We don't have much time before the train—

He was ebullient, radioactive. Nothing made sense.

No.

Why? You can't be that selfish, not tell the kid *goodbye*. What will she think?

I turned my back. Covered my face. Maybe I was still able to say: she shouldn't see. She shouldn't have to remember me this way.

Kaethe dropped the pen; her numb writing hand reluctantly uncurled. She stretched arms and legs straight up and out like a marionette. A marionette struck by a recollection of her own mother. Baerbel on a summer morning, in her all-purpose single room in the Pittsfield lodging house, ironing a dress. Baerbel barefoot, wearing only her plain nylon slip. Her shoulder blades sliding like cuttlebones. A woman so slight, big-eyed, that she could be taken for her daughter's schoolmate. (And where was Kaethe? Drifting around the room, scrutinizing everyday objects with hands clasped behind her back, as if some rule forbade her touching objects that lived with her mother in exile.) As Baerbel ironed she continually shook water from a bowl onto the wrinkled blue cotton with a practiced flicker of her fingers, as if dispensing benediction. The snout of the iron hissed each time it ploughed a fresh furrow in the cloth. We do the collar first, Kaethe! Then each sleeve, back and bodice, for last you save the skirt, like so.... She had sewn this dress herself. Forget-me-not blue. A new pattern from Kresge's five-and-dime. Smocked and sashed, it defined Kaethe's twelve-year-old body almost too knowingly: Who would believe her, if she tried to pretend it was store-bought? That sunny early morning Baerbel chattered and laughed, ignoring clumsiness and silence, as if she wanted to teach her daughter more than how to show good posture, choose a pattern, iron a dress.

Neither knew how little time was left for teaching. By September she would be gone. Buried in a Pittsfield grave, although no one really knew her in that town.

In warmer weather Kaethe slept on a cot in the second room, the former front parlor, also spared by the fire. But once winter sunk its teeth in, her mattress and quilts occupied a corner of the stove-heated kitchen. One doesn't need more than one room.

Her lair. On New Year's Eve morning she rose as usual, stiffly, rocking up on all fours like a tortoise, shaking off the fragments of dreams. As the quilts slipped sideways the cold made her gasp, shudder and laugh. A familiar enemy, it focused her. This was the same intense cold she'd survived in Berlin.

Ravenous, she trimmed the mold off a loaf of rye bread.

She flicked a light. Still no power. Outside, the risen sun struck fire from carpets of ice, burning her eyes. If only she could X-ray through this snow, find the ax.

She touched the piled pages on the table. So, then. The story, such as it was, to an end, such as it was. But for what reason? Who in their right mind would send such old news? Even she wasn't crazy or selfish enough. A child of no matter what age has no protection from a parent's testimony. But if she never meant to send the pages, why hold back, why leave one small incident out?

Because it remained inexplicable and terrible to her. Beyond the rest.

On the iced-over step she fell, hard. Hip, it was. Elbow. She tried to scrabble up, remembering a fairy tale about a prince having to scale a glass mountain for his lady-love: how he slipped and flopped and stumbled around (as Kaethe did now, on the motionless sea-swells of frozen snow) in front of the whole tittering kingdom. Each time he slid back and toppled again. Whack, on the bum! Proving his love by the very impossibility of his success.

At least she knew where the axe was. On the cusp of the New Year, a thaw had breathed on the hillside, shrinking and clarifying the drifts, so that now, in the rich red afternoon, the shaft of the axe shimmered like a shadowy homunculus inside its own miniature glass mountain. Only ten yards from where she sprawled, with the ice already beginning to melt beneath her. Soaking, too, into the roof of the cabin, where inside on the ceiling a wobbling vein of soiled water had re-formed.

Batter the axe free with a good hardwood log. Next, climb to within striking distance of the eaves and hack at the ice-dam until the water gushed free. So simple, what she had come out to do, after the letter a return to more normal tasks. But how to reach the axe if she couldn't get up on her feet?

She began to take account: of the fire in her hip, and a stinging inside her sleeve—but it was her left ankle, numb until the moment she put an ounce of weight on it, that kept her from standing up again. She lifted the thick-booted leg in her hands, angry. Shook it lightly, as a parent shakes a stubborn child. Starbursts of pain.

Crawling, then rising on her knees to wield the log, she eventually won the axe. Fell back far too tired to think of how to reach the ice-dam. Black clouds were merging like flocks of giant rooks in the dusk. By the time she had pulled herself back over the stoop of the cabin, a new skin was congealing on the ice.

Her grandparents' radio still worked, though Kaethe had long since stopped listening to it because the weather forecasts, usually woefully wrong, dulled her better instincts. There had of course been a phone, too, in her grandparents' time, but both poles and wires burned in the fire and she had refused the company's offer to replace them. She liked this irrevocable silence. It was far more habitable than the silence made tentative by a phone that doesn't ring. This evening was the first time her mind turned to the lack.

Half-crawling—*robben* was the German verb, taken from the way seals flipper-haul themselves on dry land—Kaethe arranged things as best she could. Pushed the blanket back up against the door, peeled off her jacket. The uncountable strands of pain—different decibels and timbres clashing throughout her body like maddened instruments in an orchestra—absorbed her attention so thoroughly that she had to stop after each few moves and recollect herself. It was as if her mind withdrew some distance and listened, fascinated, for some pattern in the chaotic din. She noted her luck, in that the useless ankle and hurt hip were both on the left side, so she could manage, balancing on the right, to draw herself up semi-erect with the help of furniture. She cleaned her lacerated forearm with the warm snow-water kept in a pot on the stove. The sharp bite of iodine brought a little relief and focus. She swallowed down four aspirin before confronting the problem of the boots. They were rubber, loose-fitting, yet for all her will and mental remoteness from the pain she couldn't begin to budge the left one. She saw the risk of fainting with her swelling foot still trapped, and chose to cut the boot off with slow grinding kitchen scissors. Exhausted, she lay back to rest a moment on the floorboards.

Through all the cacophony of pain came a light scratching noise from the cellar below.

"You're on your own," she said, "whatever you are." She wouldn't be going down there, maybe not for some time. No point hoarding milk till it curdled, though. She would drink as much as she could and set a bowl on the cellar's top step, under the hatch-door. She looked over to the bucket catching drops from the ice-dam; it was near brimming, too heavy for her to lift to the sink. Nothing to do but watch new leaks like fat brown water-snakes coil down one window frame. They might or might not dry up again with the nightfreeze.

What she could do was shove two more logs into the stove—worry tomorrow when her leg felt better about bringing in more—and in laborious dragging trips across the floor stockpile apples and aspirin, chocolate and water beside her lair. The final trip hauled to the mattress a big untippable crystal ashtray, a gift of the Grange with her grandfather's initials inscribed: the best she could do, for a bedpan.

She inched in under the quilts. "Comfortable" was a meaningless word; she lay in the oscillating cradle of pain. The light diminished to an ink wash. A candle would be recklessly dangerous. Grimaced at irony: living here, she didn't have to justify the care she took to survive. A long night looming. Her pain had shifted amplitudes: now the ankle merely jabbed, while her hip boomed like chords played by an enraged, autistic organist. "Leon," she wondered out loud, "what in hell has happened after all these years to Leon?" No more sounds came from below. Nothing to hear but the sucking pops and hisses of the burning stove. *This,* she thought, *having all the food stashed around the lair, taking off to bed at four in the afternoon instead of working, this is like some childhood escapade. Self-indulgence!* She put a hand up to her cheek, and the satiny slickness there surprised her.

Her letter ran on, unstoppable. The paper, an endless foolscap, unrolled in images, not words.

Telling the picture of the time after losing Sophie. Of Kaethe von Thall, stripped of motherhood, as bars are stripped from a court-martialed soldier's sleeve. Only hours into the country of divorce, shell-less as a peeled egg, returning to the villa in the Königsallee. While she'd been at the courthouse someone had gone through these rooms and efficiently removed the few objects of material worth—silver bowls, a painting, an antique desk. Who? A burglar with a key, a brother-in-law? Kaethe prowled the hall, sitting room, bedroom, kitchen, the half-stripped nursery, back and forth. She paced like the haggard lioness in the Zoological Garden, her daughter's favorite. Rain fell, night fell. She had never ceased shaking and now she began to groan, then to howl. No one would hear. Albus had moved out, and the villa stood far back from the street in its sound-absorbing garden—a grassy, weedy tangle of a garden something like a little girl's coarse, unruly hair.

She screamed until her throat seized up. Her throat ached as if it was bleeding from a hundred small rips, and the blood tasted like steel between her teeth. And still she went on screaming—she had after all no particular plans for that evening, there was really nothing else to do—even when she produced only the rasp of air. If she paused she noticed herself rattling like an addict, like a crate of glasses in an earth-quake. She curled up on the floor and screamed to keep herself company. A part of her, lucid and deep and cold as the devil, watched all this with detached interest. Her fingers slid down plaster. Difficult to

hold on to any wall. To walk upright. From one room to the next. No
one came. In darkness or in light to locate the telephone. Lift the
receiver, drop it. Scream a while. Still only your word against theirs,
the lucid devil said, but if they find you raving like this they'll have their
evidence and put you away, you'll never get another chance, never! Lift
again. Hit numbers at random. Which day is this? Pretend to know.
Scream. Try again.

The next day or the next a voice pours out of the black dots in the
receiver. A sweet poison spray of a voice. Whose? She holds her breath.
Fights to hold on to the eel-slick receiver. And then fear squeezes the
last breath out from her body, a sinewy fear like the swift embrace of
sanity itself, and she wants only to speak, to say her name and where
she can be found, and please, please, not to be left alone any longer in
the dark—but she can't speak. How is speech made? There's not a word
in the empty room of her mind. Not the most private language. Finally,
struggling like an animal desperately ambitious to become something
more noble, she creates a sound: uugh, uagh! A sound like that.

A shaft of snow-dazzled sunlight teased Kaethe awake in her cocoon
of quilts. For a moment, forgetting, she took the usual quick inventory
of what seemed slightly more than the usual aches and pressures of
sleep, and her hunger, and a complaining bladder. Then she moved, or
tried to. Gasped as pain slammed down around her. Manacles around
her hip and leg.

Her fingertips managed to reach the ankle; it felt swollen and hot.
Maybe broken, she admitted, and possibly the hipbone too was cracked.
The admission brought a certain relief. Nothing could be worse, and
yet the sun was shining on her face, she had slept deeply and all even
the fanciest hospital could do for an injured bone was hold it still—as
she, all night, had done.

She ate one of her apples slowly, extracting the juice, and swallowed
three more tablets.

What she dreaded was soiling her bed. Eventually by millimeters
she hauled and pushed herself to the edge of the mattress. Ended,
swearing and weeping, with her aching, pounding pelvis positioned
more or less over the monogrammed ashtray. Tears of exhaustion fell
on her braced hands while the familiar odor of her own urine rose,
sweet and acrid. And frigid air broke through the gaps in the quilt—
had the temperature outside dropped so, she wondered, or was she

starting a fever, or had the wood-fire died down already? In this ebullient sunlight it was impossible to see the outline of flame around the
stove's closed door.

The journey back across the mattress cost all her strength. She
was aware of thirst but far too tired to drink. Sleep, again. Sleep to
heal. Lucky, lucky, the one who can sleep! *Taler, Taler, Du musst wandern* . . . Sophie loved that nursery song. Drifting, she remembered the
longest sleep of her life. It had followed her nerve-crisis (she called the
incident that, rather than "breakdown," an ugly, mechanical term) in
the Königsallee villa. The telephone call she had eventually managed
to place, choking over her own sounds, was to the Sophien Kirche in
East Berlin. *Leytenfeger is not in yet, but we expect him tonight,* a professionally soft-voiced stranger answered. Kaethe left only her first
name and added thickly, "Please."

The man who later stepped through the unlatched, wind-banged
front door was also a stranger. He wore a white jacket but she didn't
believe this man with sunken, liverish, watchful eyes could be a genuine medical doctor. *Everything will be fine,* he said, *Max sent me.*
Mathias? She asked, gazing up from the floor. *No, lady: Comrade Max.*
He had then taken a syringe from his briefcase and swabbed her bicep
with a mumbled reassurance.

The injection, as she would discover, plunged her into dreamless
sleep for three days and two nights. When she finally woke her hands
were steady and her ersatz-doctor gone, though not, judging by the
unwashed dishes and stubbed cigarettes left behind in the kitchen, gone
long. She saw minute details vividly. Her mind felt as chill and purposeful as the knife the stranger had left on her plate used and dirty
and which she reflexively wiped clean.

She hated the house and everything in it. The air itself seemed to be
pushing her out. She packed only one small bag.

Once again she rode the S-Bahn beneath the center of the city.
Another sandy-haired peasant-soldier waved Kaethe Schalk into the
DDR. She dragged up the seemingly endless hill to Szredskistrasse.

Her father stood in the open door. "You lost, then. I am sorry."

"I tried. But Max, he pretended—"

"You were the means, not the end. Logically, he had to betray you."

"I'm sorry."

THE QUINTUPLE
DEFINITION

The result of betrayal may be injustice. Injustice can lead to a betrayal. But they're not the same thing. A slippery, leering, violent word. Meaning?

Now she would have time to reflect .

BETRAY: *vt.* *[L tradere, to hand over]* 1: *to help the enemy of (one's country, etc.)*

Well, if that's all that's involved . . . A country, a geography, a population. One can betray north to south, west to east, ruling class to working class to nomenklatura. Heads a traitor, tails a patriot, same coin. Is someone who doesn't claim a country or standpoint incapable of betrayal? The so-called Cold War (a joint theatrical production) created a bustling labor market for spies and traitors. Also spy novels, double-cross movies, Russkie routines for comics. In an open economy you move to where the jobs are. In communism you work where you're told. Isn't it much the same thing?

As a young woman Kaethe Schalk used to deposit letters and photographs in the boles of trees in the Tiergarten, in public trash cans, inside trashy magazines "discarded" on the bus. It was a game, and a way to keep her beloved correspondent aware of and interested in her ongoing existence. Besides, how can there be "betrayal" to your own father?

Was it so different (a few months after her flight from West Berlin, after she moved back into her father's apartment) when the summons came to present herself to a certain office in Magdalenenstrasse, number twenty? She felt neither singled out for honor, as some confident Party member might have, nor frightened out of her skin. She felt nothing, only the click of surprise that confirms the coming-true of a thing you had dismissed as your overheated imagination. Max didn't ask where she was going that day; she didn't tell him.

All the connecting rooms of Erich Mielke's office were blond. The long curved caramel desks, longer conference table, locked wall cabinets, secretary who wore a pert microphone fixed in her honey yellow curls by a steel tiara. Mielke lived there, everyone knew that. On the other side of one of these bland blond walls the chief of the Ministry for State Security had a bed, ample stash of food, bathroom and TV. Pitiful, she thought, for a man in charge of over 30,000 workers in this one kilometer-vast, high-security complex alone. The whole proud, waxed and polished anachronistic setup, tube chairs and kidney tables, looked pathetically modest compared with the office of even a mid-class manager a few train stops to the West. Still, Mielke wasn't the only Stasi boss who had literally moved his whole existence into the depths of the gigantic warren of the Ministry, as if into a bunker, as far as possible from the people he guarded.

"Come in, step closer! I've looked forward to meeting you."

"Here I am."

"Indeed. Looking quite your father's daughter, Frau Schalk."

"Thank you."

"Give my regards."

"I certainly will."

"Unfortunately, his moon's in Pluto currently. Kapisch?"

"Will he be—"

"Please, no questions here. You have chosen to reside permanently in the Democratic Republic. Looking forward, at long last, to exercising the full rights and responsibilities of citizenship? A mature decision, not coerced but made of your own free will?"

"Naturally, I—"

"Naturally. Your homeland! The spiritual homeland of all lovers of peace and justice. Please, please, sit! Make yourself comfortable! Sit yourself down, Frau Schalk."

She did so. The phone rang. There was a bank of phones on his desk, like saddled horses in a corral, waiting to serve. Erich Mielke, a bullish man in a droopy, too-big suit, a bullheaded man with a face in-folded like an ancestor-carp's, picked up a receiver and grunted noncommittally. "Excuse me, Frau Schalk!" He hurried from the room, shutting the door behind him.

And now she felt the sweat start on her palms. This was terribly wrong. The whole business had felt skewed from the moment of the summons, of course. Why would a man of Mielke's prominence— number-two man in the State, some would even say, first of the Erichs —want to interview a return-nik, one of the double border-crossers, indecisive dual losers, disillusioned by the sharper edges of Western competition? She had guessed Mielke's motive to be the one he'd just acknowledged—curiosity about the daughter of a comrade and sometime rival. A wish to check over Max Schalk's sole bit of "family" in person.

But what was this test? Why leave her alone in Mielke's blond office? How many remote eyes were watching her? Did they expect her to lean forward to decipher the notepad on which the Chief had been doodling, or to open file drawers, or expose the safes concealed in the walls? She hardly dared draw a deep breath, or shift her gaze from the prayer-like contemplation of hands. Within this walled city inside a walled city there were other living quarters, so she recalled having heard, besides offices and bureaucrats' studios. There were interrogation rooms. And jail cells.

"His star is in Pluto." What was the exact phrase? A metaphor. How unusual, for a Party functionary to speak in metaphor. Pluto meant that Max's career was in darkness, at least temporary eclipse. Why? Presumably, because he was the antithesis of an Erich Mielke: not earnest, hardly credulous (least of all about himself). And for many years now, she suspected, no longer a believer, though he kept the shape of his old beliefs nearly intact like a shining, intricate chrysalis, and only a magnifying glass would show the tiny aperture through which the living, intelligent creature had long since escaped.

Months earlier she had assumed her return East was purely welcome and even gratifying to Max. Only now, hunched here in the central com-

mand of the Stasi, did her perspective wheel and shift—suddenly she
saw the liability she posed for him. Her clumsy invasion. Her egotistical blindness to his predicament. How swiftly he'd decided to take in
this prodigal daughter whom he had already for years managed to
shield from certain consequences. To Erich Mielke, for example, the
comrade "Countess Thall" must look at best a dilettantish pseudo-
agent. At worst a traitor, a septic splinter pointed toward the heart of
the apparatus. A danger demanding prompt attention.

"Are you a Party member?" He had returned, to stand behind her.

"I was FDJ! Over there. Socialist, Free German Youth. But I'm
afraid that here I never found the opportunity..."

"You better make up for lost time."

Nothing further. A few days later it wasn't Mielke but a letter signed
"AO in absence of EM" that offered her the position of simultaneous
interpreter for certain sensitive functions in the Magdalenenstrasse. She
thought of the cellars of the complex. Sorry, she wrote back (doing how
much damage to Max?): a recent illness ruled out full-time work.

The next letter from AO was almost affable. He (Kaethe always read
AO as male. Anton? Axel? Ariel?) proposed part-time work. Good
English instructors were always in short supply. And would she like
to be nominated for the Writers' Union (which could use a few fresh
faces), while contributing the occasional "unofficial" sample of her prose
to the Ministry? Who would say no?

And so, as in years past she had written her rambling letters to amuse
Max, she now reported via AO to Erich Mielke.

The Ministry first presented her with lists of names to identify.
Mostly people she had never heard of and never would. A few she knew.
Traps! The transparency of their game was reassuring. The doddering,
deaf couple on the ground floor was listed, as was Mathias of course.
Also Max himself. (Either AO or EM was thick as a brick.)

"You cross into the Occupied Zone next week with permission to
visit your daughter. Sign below for travel money. Appended find a list
of questions pertaining to the class enemies Achim von Thall, Ana Luise
von Thall, Harro von Thall and their named and suspected associates.
Any and all members of the SPD or other political organizations. Your
report is expected in this office within eight days."

BETRAY, 2: *to expose treacherously*

She lived quietly. Her instinct was to leave as little trace of herself as possible, and to carry as little as possible with her. At the State Konsum stores she took pains to give exact change, hardly noticing the empty shelf space, the unsatisfactory and declining quality of the goods available (malt coffee as in postwar years, bread expanded with straw or even stray pebbles)—or if she did, then with a sense of release from the burdens of constant choice and greediness. A sense of home. The cobbled back courtyards of Prenzlauer Berg held smells of diesel and soft coal and lye and sweet whiffs of human waste from the failing plumbing. She slept in Max's front room on a sofa that she made up neatly the moment she rose; all her possessions were stored beneath its skirts. Two or three times a week she dropped in on Mathias, whose attitude was so patient, so tender and forgiving of her moods and silences that she sometimes wanted to physically hurt him—punch his chest or slap his face, say—simply to see rage rise before he could control it. She called him "Priestling." Sex was one of the few things she looked forward to. The harder he drove at her the better. In earlier times she'd had no pleasure from that extreme fucking, and now he needed her coaxing assurance, to trade the hammocky mattress for the unyielding floor, then to let himself go into that rigid flesh-hammering abandon that dissolved all bonds between them, except this one.

She seldom stayed the night with Mathias. And she never brought work to do there, or spoke of her activities beyond the English lessons she inflicted on tone-deaf middle-aged men in the Magdalenenstrasse. Her drafts of reports and translations remained secure in Max's apartment.

It was common knowledge, simply human nature, for "informal collaborators" to take full advantage of their leverage, spiking mundane encounters with mischief, settling old scores. But Comrade Schalk had no motive and no stomach for treacherous exposure. She felt neutral to the point of transparency. All the things that mattered were beyond her grasp. The "reports" from *Tarantula* (her leggy cover name) to AO were as dull as she could make them, as eventless as real life had become. Tarantula was the opposite of a Scheherazade: spinning endless tales in order to bore the master to sleep. She cast the doddering pensioners as street-sweeping civic heroes, while she and Max conversed nightly on abstruse points of Marxist-Leninist doctrine. She sketched obligatory horns and pointed tails only on miscellaneous von Thalls, whom she couldn't avoid encountering on her rare, supervised visits to Sophie.

On the day Sophie started first grade, carrying the gigantic, festive cornucopia of sweets that is meant to sugar the bitterness of separation and of growing up, Kaethe wasn't there. Come summer she wasn't there for the emergency tonsillectomy either—arriving afterwards, too briefly, to sponge tears off the cheeks of a seven-year old who couldn't speak. She missed the swimming lessons and the first two-wheeler and school Sports' Day. She heard the nicknames of various other women— "Aunt" Sabinchen, "Aunt" Pippa, "Aunt" Franzie—who evidently stayed for longer or shorter terms in the Königsallee, but when she arrived there Sophie alone would open the door and the only signs of a third occupant were rearranged furniture, a fancy home-baked torte, or, in the bathroom, alien pantyhose hung up to dry.

Where was Frau Albus? Albie, Sophie volunteered, had of course returned home to the villa again. But she was growing so forgetful and troublesome and actually rude to the guests that Achim despite great difficulty had to find a special old people's place to take more care of her. Papa never had time to spare—but maybe Mamma could take Sophie to visit old Albie? Maybe. Kaethe shuddered. She wasn't sorry for Albus, who near the end had run from her, denied her like the rest. But she thought of the power implicit in "putting someone away." Only the powerful could slough off whoever had grown inconvenient—and consider it natural, and right.

Achim's unseen women haunted rooms that used to be hers. She imagined them goggling at her from behind curtains and doors like hyper-feminine imps. The sense of being an intrusion from the past, a leftover, functionless appendage, made it hard for her to unbend with Sophie. Facing her daughter's quicksilver smile brought an obscure but paralyzing sense of shame. Sophie was precociously kind; she brought out her drawings to show; someone had been teaching her manners. More like two schoolgirls, Kaethe thought, who can't dredge up much in common to talk about, than mother and daughter.

Once as she was leaving Achim appeared from his "home office," the rooms that had been Albus's domain. Kaethe immediately assumed that he must have kept a listening post in the back of the house through most or perhaps all of her previous visits. For two years she had felt immune to any strong emotion. Now to see Achim so close and unexpectedly, to automatically accept the hand offered in a friendly, casual gesture, flooded her with feeling. Outrage, she thought. Or fear. Or disgust. He said, "I hear you're doing well. You've found work, over there? That's great. . . . I want you to know," he added, "how proud I am of you."

She asked less often for permission to visit.

Her own father, by contrast, under whose roof she again lived (and did this dependency partly explain why she saw herself as merely an older girl, beside Sophie?) no longer invited "geisha" to stay the night. Not because he felt too old to enjoy women, she guessed. Although age in any aspect was one of Max's forbidden subjects, she figured her father at not much over sixty. Physically he might pass for a decade younger, with his fluid, loping walk and the range of expressions (inherited by his granddaughter) that gave color and emphasis to his dry speech. And yet something had changed, or was about to. Max went late to work and returned early; he seemed invigorated to find her at home or, if she came in late, he sulked behind clipped sentences. With bachelor pride he cooked the recherché specialties (aphrodisiacs?) that geisha of various ethnic origin had taught him over the years. She was the beneficiary of them all—as if after wandering away from his wife and child, and treating subsequent women as expendable conveniences, Max was finally anxious to invite someone into his life.

Now she, not Max, was the one who veered between sarcasm and indifference. In rare moments, having caught her own acidic tone, a suspicion crossed her mind about how one person could, over time, fundamentally alter another. An instinct for generosity could be drained, by steady exploitation, down to stingy mistrust. Her father took no notice of her new brittleness.

"Max and I have the perfect arrangement," she told Mathias, slyly. "The ideal marriage."

"Max tolerates you because he needs you. Or he will, soon."

"Why?"

"They're closing down his shop. This is the eighties, isn't it? Apparently even the government wants to cut down its cholesterol. A lean, mean, Security machine." And so it was from Mathias, who picked up all kinds of rumors and early warnings through his parish work (*you Lutherans,* she told him, *acting like catacomb Christians in imperial Rome*) that she learned why Max had lost his appetite for work, and what he did in the few hours he still spent at the Ministry. One by one, he was letting his men and women go. Shipping files into eternal storage. Presiding over the dismantling of his own organization, of his now unsupported, superfluous projects, his own history.

What next? She couldn't envision Max idle, or sweeping public gutters like the deaf couple on the ground floor. Could no more see into his future than into her own. Had he suffered some "treacherous exposure?" Not that she sensed, watching him.

Max's prospects preoccupied her; she hardly wasted a thought on her lover. And so it came at first as an utter, incomprehensible surprise when one late afternoon, as she was hurrying up the stairs for the usual hour or so with Mathias, a neighbor blocked her way and whispered, *Don't go up, Comrade, he's gone you know, don't ask where, they came for the Herr Assistant Pastor at five this morning, banging and barking to wake up the dead—*

The next day she would instruct her cadre of plump, balding, chanting English students while listening past them for other, fainter sounds. Wondering whether Mathias might be only long minutes away, a ride downward in the *paternoster* to a cell somewhere submerged in this same fortress in the Magdalenenstrasse. And that night she would tell it all to Max, and he would say, I'll see about this! Meanwhile, he's better off in the hands of those comparative amateurs in Magdalenenstrasse, than the institution at Hohenschoenhausen!

Despite early assurances, in the next days and months Max wouldn't succeed in finding out the cell's address, the official charge or the trial date. He was irate, humiliated. How much was his stock still worth, in the information bazaar? There were no more bags of oranges, his complexion looked blotchy and five teeth had to be pulled. He and Kaethe had each other completely to themselves.

BETRAY, 3: *to fail to uphold, e.g. betray a trust*
Cynicism, so Mathias had remarked shortly before his arrest, is a kind of living death. (Stop laughing, Kaethe. *Will* you stop laughing at me?)

BETRAY, 4: *to deceive, seduce and then desert*

She felt no personal responsibility for Mathias's predicament. False arrests were commonplace (often prescribed by Mielke's office as a sort of prophylactic), a routine public hazard, sort of like being caught in a trolley's faulty door. She expected that some day soon Mathias would pop up from the system's underground, scuffed and angry but essentially intact.

He would have no reason on earth to blame her. He knew nothing of her occasional reports to AO, which had nothing of interest to say about "Mathias Leytenfeger" in any case. Since his disappearance into the Magdalenenstrasse maze, however, she considered herself suspect by association, and sensed a sharper edge behind AO's requests, and paid more attention to the quality and veracity of the information she passed on.

"To deceive, seduce." How close the two are. Almost synonyms.

"Seduced and abandoned . . ." An old-fashioned phrase, reminiscent of a culture of silk petticoats and horse-drawn carriages and insurmountable class distinctions. A phrase that by now had lost its meaning? Perhaps her mother, Baerbel, would have heard "seduced and abandoned" as something other than quaint. Baerbel, after her seduction and before her handsome Allied soldier's defection, had led her little girl out to beet-picking in the fields around the DP camp, in the breeze of hope at the end of the last World War.

But the phrase in no way applied to Kaethe. Could she recall a moment when Achim had seduced her? Or, for all the corrosive stream of banal infidelities, when he exactly abandoned her? In the court—in that sombre Socratic cave where what she came to call *the losing* took place—it was Kaethe who had covered swollen eyes when the judge read the charge of desertion.

Seduce. Betray. How often the act of sex, for all its honest hunger, involves a betrayal. Betrayal of memory. Or betrayal *by* memory. She would have Mathias to thank for the insight.

Assistant Pastor Leytenfeger had been a guest of the State in "investigative custody" for three months, and then sentenced by a laconic Comrade Judge and Doctor of Jurisprudence inside a scant hour, and was serving out the additional imposed six months when Max got wind of his impending release. One day in advance. Neither father nor

daughter considered it prudent for her to meet the ex-prisoner at the
gate, nor could they know which one of a score of locked steel gates
he'd walk out through. Instead, Kaethe went around to the dusty,
mildewed flat in the Blankengasse and scrubbed every surface with too
much harsh bleach until her eyes stung and brimmed.

When Mathias walked in (carrying only the scuffed leather briefcase he had grabbed up at his arrest) he found a woman speechless, in
tears. His doubt—if there had been any doubt—fled through the
opened windows. His anger—if there had been anger—burned down
to ash. He wound his arms around her, awkwardly. Their foreheads
and chests bumped, as if neither had ever embraced another person. As
if this was the first time. "Where's Max?" he asked.

"Max, he's coming of course, he's out buying coffee and a cake," she
finally mumbled. Mathias kissed her eyes, licked them as if greedy for
salt. He was much thinner than she remembered. But not weak. He
lowered her, laid her down gently on the still damp, bleach-reeking
floor. Unbuttoned her sweat-limp blouse. Lifted the flowered *hausfrau*
apron, unzipped the black serge trousers. "You're crying. You're crying. I never expected you would cry," he said. The thinness of his torso
made his sex seem absurdly large. He prodded, demanded. Starving.
And as he entered her she felt the sure bloom of his pity and absolution,
inspired by the explosive heat of her own desire.

Only later that afternoon, adroitly sliding three jewel-bright, gelati-
nous slices of Obsttorte onto Mathias' chipped and stained plates, while
aware of the secret irritation of recent love—the semen slowly drying
on her inner thighs—did the wondrous simplicity of the matter strike
her. There is nothing a mother would balk at, to keep and protect her
child. Like any good animal she would kill without a second thought.
To seduce, betray? That's not even a crime.

And so it was almost three years after the *losing,* on a visit permitted for
the purpose of belated celebration of Sophie's eighth birthday, that
Kaethe Schalk succeeded once again in seducing her daughter's father.
Because some stray scruple rendered her unable to touch Achim (or
even directly to meet his gaze) in the now elegantly refurbished
Königsallee villa, the trysting-place she chose was a remote basement
bedroom in her former mother-in-law's house. Leon's old room, from

his extended adolescence. Achim knew why they were there, he was eager and unprotesting, a small unquenchable grin of triumph kept disfiguring his face. Her eyes never closed. Later she would remember all that her eyes took in of that room: two high, barred windows. Do-it-yourself bookcases screwed to the wall, filled with pictorial biographies of composers (all gifts, some from her) and floppy, moldering sheaves of sheet music, and model airplanes encased in excessive gobs of hardened glue like very large insects in amber. A *Playboy* calendar frozen at Miss November, 1976. A bust of Beethoven, the familiar gift-shop genius, dressed up in dusty sunglasses and a Red Cross ski patrol cap.

She had been granted a "family hardship" pass to West Berlin for four days. Four days was a fortune in time, but not much for what she needed. For a seduction. How long does it take, is it possible, to win back the confidence of someone who, having lost his desire, has tried in every way to destroy you?

Max knew why she went back. He was standing by. How much of his dwindling political capital her "hardship" pass had cost, he naturally refused to say. "Political capital"—a ridiculous phrase, Kaethe thought, for Communists to use. But these days nothing was shameful, no one cared. . . .

Achim finished with a grimace, a strangled moan. He let his heavy sweat-slick head fall full weight on her breastbone. She had forgotten this gesture. His breath scraped raw as if he'd been running up a steep slope. He doesn't take care of himself, she thought. She envisioned his premature, sudden death. There was no comfort in it, on the contrary: Sophie would only pass deeper into the family. They might try to forbid completely her disruptive visits. Watching the gray sticky sleet collect on the window bars she asked the man whose body weighed hers whether Sophie could come to a movie next day. He raised up, startled. Yes, she said in an indifferent drawl, for once only mother and daughter. *Mary Poppins,* after all, downtown at the Zoo theatre. To make it harder for Achim to deny her, she held his gaze for the first time that day. His green eyes stared, clouded and confused.

Sophie had a child's uncorrupted love of kitsch. The movie entranced her. "A spoonful of sugar!" she sang afterward over and over in the numbing cold rain on the Ku'damm, hanging on the crook of her mother's arm, and only Kaethe had felt dislocated by this German-dubbed, Hollywood version of an English tale. A random yet inspired choice: the mysterious governess who spirits children away from wealthy, cozy hearth and a masculine home, up into the air, safe under her umbrella, to soar over all earthly obstacles.

Remember you said how much you want to come with me? To over there? Where you can meet your Opa? Are you sure? Absolutely sure?

Yes. (Singing, and swinging.)

But if I take you—

Yes!

We have to stay a while. It might be a long time before you or I can come back to . . . to here.

I know that! I'm not stupid, Mamma!

They didn't soar. The car, a low-slung black Peugeot, picked them up in front of the Café Kranzler. The driver wore a peaked cap, the car's plates bore the magic "cc" of diplomacy. It was growing dark; cold rain froze as it touched the pavement; the streets were emptying fast. Their car crawled slowly through Kreuzberg, old merchants' neighborhoods degraded to foreign workers' dormitories and then to boarded-up shells as they approached the squat and ugly fact of the Wall. Nothing casts a sharper shadow than high-powered searchlights. Kaethe held her wristwatch up to the white glare but the rapid pounding of her heart affected her focus—was it five-thirty or six-thirty, and how soon after a reasonable restaurant-supper interlude would suspicions rise, and phone calls begin, and the Allied border guards be set on strict alert?

Anhalterstrasse to Kochstrasse. Looming ahead, sparkling cheerily through the sleet-smeared window, the familiar entrance to Checkpoint Charlie, where West imitated East—twin glass observation turrets faced each other, along with double walls topped with barbed wire and rotating searchlights. Twin sets of machine guns aimed down on the paved, shared no-man's-land between them. She had always shuddered when passing through this space. It lay featureless and clean-swept as infinity.

"Your passports, please." The American soldier took the offered papers, barely glancing at them, and swept a light through the car's interior, across Kaethe's face, down her body to folded hands. "Good evening, Ma'am." The light sped back to her face. "Couldn't find worse weather for driving in, could you?"

She nodded, speechless.

"Ask you to step out for a minute, sir?"

Only the chauffeur was escorted into the glass-walled cubicle, where other guardsmen waited. Kaethe prayed to the sleet, the ice, the exotic gallantry of Amis in uniform. She was practiced in deception, in fact capable of enjoying it, so why this sudden anxiety about her own voice—fear that it would break, betray them all?

Right now Sophie lay only inches away from her, curled in a nest beneath the rear seat. She had a tranquilizer in her bloodstream, and for comfort a tiny flashlight in her hand.

"You have a good trip, Ma'am. Mein Herr, you take extra care of the lady now, streets are in terrible shape over on Ivan's side. Have a safe trip!"

He waved them through.

Across the no-man's-land. And a few yards farther, on the East side, their perfunctory welcome was a scrabble through the trunk for whiskey or existential literature. Then the barrier arm rose like a salute, and they drove on into the gentle velvet darkness of East Berlin.

Human-smuggling was a steady service business. Recession-proof. Humans are ingenious, and will gnaw away at obstacles with a perseverance that drives their guardians to distraction. More than twenty years after the rise of the Wall, and despite sealed borders, tens of thousands continued to flow into Austria, Finland, and above all to the financially generous "Life-Start Centers" of the Federal Republic. (Leech Centers, sucking out our blood, said Max, who was an expert on the subject.) But who would want to smuggle, or be smuggled, from West to East? What nonsense! (More souls take that route than you'd imagine, said Max.)

Betray, 5: *to reveal unknowingly*

Sudden wind shook the loose windows in their sashes. A thunderstorm, she exulted. Rain to quench this insufferable heat.

But wait: here was the ghost-glimmer of snow. Winter-blue.

And the banging came not from the windows but from the door, invisible behind her. Someone didn't know better and believed it was locked. She tried to call out, *whoever you are, please come on in!* but the impatient knocking canceled out her reasonable voice. And the mere impulse to stand up sent liquid snakes of pain coiling through her legs. She collapsed back on herself in defeat.

She lay in a rush of thick, cold sweat. A drawn-out scraping sound replaced the banging on the door, and now and then someone outside called "Katie! Katie, are you in there?" She realized she couldn't see clearly. Her eyelids were gummed over, stuck together although she struggled to open them the way a person struggles to wake herself out of an interminable dream. Sightless, she could still smell the room: a pungent, horrible reek, worse than it had ever been on her mother's most abysmal drinking days. She could also feel: the scroll of paper, limp as cloth, gripped in her hands, and, moving along her left arm, once again a queer, rhythmic prickling as if from clustered needles—or the prongs of dolls' forks, she thought. It didn't hurt exactly, and didn't frighten her.

Like a rifle shot the door cracked open, followed by a blast of wind, and this did frighten her. The floor beneath her vibrated under the intruder's rapid, heavy steps, and her mind partly cleared, as if rising through layers of the imprisoning dream. *"Katie.* Oh, my God. Is it you? You down inside those blankets? Can you hear me, Katie Schalk? My God—it is *freezing* in here! Colder than out in the open. How long's this stove been out of commission?"

"Go . . . away." She knew the man's voice. The owner of the store. "Joe," but not her "Joe." A large, blustery man with vestiges of handsomeness who practiced flirting with the summer-wives. His parents had shared a church bench with her grandparents. And what was Joe up to here now? She poked the quilts down an inch, raised her head an inch. One sticky eye finally surrendered a peephole. A figure in workboots and parka was dragging in logs, striking matches, preparing to burn the place down. "You. Go—away."

"Now listen. Katie." Instantly he crouched directly over her. "Know what tipped me off? No smoke out of your roofstack! I thought, either she's run out on us again or something isn't right. Now I'm getting this stove in gear and thaw some of the ice out of your bones and—"

"Bone."

He pressed a cup against her mouth. Water spilled down as if her lips were carved soapstone. "Joe," she brought out. "I broke bone. My hip."

"I dare say. And then soon's the medic from the fire station can get himself up here—I already radioed—we're taking you down to County. You need—"

"No. Can't go. Can't move."

"Let *us* worry. Hey—mine is a sorry rattletrap but Ted Leblanc's Ski-doo, he has got all the latest equipment, stretcher board and Velcro ties. I'm not saying it's gonna be any picnic getting you down the mountain but—"

"I stink, Joe. You know. Room stinks. Disgusting. Too embarrassed. Go away."

"Oh, hey. Not your fault! Anyhow . . . it's not so bad in here."

She didn't need to see his face, to know that he was lying.

He couldn't sit still and wait. He rummaged around the room. She had no means of stopping him. He funneled more water down her throat and then a diced-up apple along with crumbled crackers, and even another pair of pills. She coughed; she felt giddy. Was it this small meal, or the excitement of companionship that had suddenly pushed her body's pain way down to a background, hive-like hum?

Joe laid three fingers, like a vow, on her forehead. "You've got some fever there."

"Maybe so." A mental shrug. What was fever? She was *safe*. Not alone. Could see the new fire leaping in the open stove. She wanted to talk, to babble for the sheer pleasure of it, the amazing gift of speech shared. She wondered: Had the pain backed off for good, because her bone had partly healed already? "Joe? How long, you think? For bones to heal?"

"My guess? Like just about everything else, a break starts mending from the moment after whatever happened. Long as it's kept still. And set up straight. You don't want a bone mending but set in all wrong. Then they have to crack it all over and start from scratch."

"Ah."

"Hey. Those old-style tracker skis leaned by the door. Is that what tripped you up? You been out on those planks? Must be your Granddad's, with those funny leather straps. They're easily twice too long for you."

"Not Grandfather's. My own father's skis. When he was a boy, here."

"I've heard about your father, here and there—Mike, was it?"

"Max. Heard what?"

"Well—a hard guy to win an argument off of, for one thing. And after the fire, folks were wondering whether he'd come back. To claim."

"Never told."

"Never told you about the fire? Well, at least he left you the key, right? It's a damn good inheritance, Katie!"

"Seventy."

"Seventy acres? When you were a kid here. I saw *you*. You'll see what you have, I promise, once you get around to building a new house here. For that, I could help steer you to a loan."

"Loan? No. Thanks. Can't pay back."

"Oh, hell. Kate Schalk." He blurred, retreating into the distance. Again she felt ashamed. Her stench unfolding in the fresh heat, and even she wasn't immune to it. How many days?

"What day is today?"

"January . . . fourth. Hey. Hey, there! Who've we got here?"

He came back, to dangle a squirming black spider in front of her one opened eye. "This your little kitty-cat?"

"Oh—give!" The creature dumped to sprawl on her stained mattress. All legs, black with white-dipped paws, grown to somewhere between kitten and cat. The familiar tines pierced her arm, withdrew, sunk in again. "I like cats. This one has been keeping me company." Ah—her tongue was thawing, with practice. It felt less thick.

"Better company than the coyotes, I guess. What in hell's holding up Leblanc?" He was restless, he roamed.

"I had two cats, once. Karl and Rosa. Litter-mates. Spoiled to death." Lightly she stroked the oily black fur, feeling the liquid adjustment of tiny, perfect bones. "Karl and Rosa disappeared. Something happened. For years, ten or twenty, I didn't think once about them. Just decided not to think. Ever done that?"

"Want to tell what happened?"

"My husband—he was a scientist. Writing a paper, 'A Theory of Perception,' well, now you can find it in textbooks but then, it was failing. He needed an organic model to give final answers for his thesis about the transference mechanism—in ears. *Then* was middle of Christmas holidays. Every place, every source, was closed. But he had a deadline, and a job at stake, and a new baby to support. See I was away then. In the maternity hospital. Cats have the most fabulous ears. Know that? The beautiful whorls, to trap, and echo surfaces, to amplify. That's what he often admired about Rosa and Karl. See? Look how beautiful this one is!"

"He used your cats—for their ears?"

"He had a deadline. He would not have let them suffer. They trusted him. He took them to the laboratory one night, while I was still away. But the cats were old anyway, he said. They'd had good lives."

"He *told* you all this?"

"Oh, no. Never admitted. I maybe had an instinct. But I never spoke about them. Even our landlady—didn't *mean* to tell me. But he had allowed her to help him. To catch them. And she had a crazy way of talking. Wouldn't know a secret if it fell on her."

"But then you—just forgot?"

She pulled the sheet up over her mouth. She thought: ah, you can't imagine. I chose not to remember. It was too enormous. Unfathomable. I put it away. Until now. I did the best thing for us all. I was practical. I had a newborn to care for. . . . No, she thought. I forgot Karl and Rosa because I didn't need them anymore.

And again: but wasn't it soon after Albus told me, that I began to run away again? Going East. To forget.

The half-grown kitten stretched beside her flicked its signal-flag ears, shiny brownish-pink inside like scallops. It had ribs fine as fishbone. Purring, it kneaded her arm in an ecstatic rhythm, as nurslings do.

Joe cracked the door and peered out. "Coming down thick, Katie. Damn. He better hurry. Snow's piled up to the windowsills. Wait'll you see."

"Is she some kind of writer? Look, Joe. What language you think this stuff here's in?"

"Leave her stuff alone. Come give me a hand. Open the stretcher!"

"And then?"

"We'll just roll her up in the bedclothes, as is. Use the sheet like a sling. They can deal with—the details, whatever—once we get her there."

"Jesus Christ."

"Got something you can give her first?"

"I'm just the EMT, man. No morphine on board."

"Hold on, then. Don't touch her yet! Here, Katie, hello, hello, time to wake up again—"

He woke her, wouldn't let her stay hidden, and this time it was whiskey, the sugary sting, that flooded her mouth. She coughed, and drank again. With one eye she blinked at Joe, in awe.

When her body was lifted from the soiled bed to sway for a moment in mid-air the pain burst free like water from an ice-dam and crashed through every part of her. She cried out to be left alone, through the noise of it all. Joe grimaced under her weight, his face zooming close, as to steal a kiss. "Steady, girl," he said.

THE BERLIN FILE

All the intense efforts of the von Thalls to repossess their grandchild—overtly through Ana Luise's public moral standing and the brothers' legal connections, covertly through Harro's commercial and diplomatic corps cronies—hadn't budged the Pankow authorities. Of course not, said Max. The Socialist justice system relishes any windfall opportunity to wring Bonn's nose. These are embattled times: harvests blighted by Chernobyl, crowds of so-called dissidents shoving their way out through the loopholes of Western embassies.

Max himself could still rely on a few supporters in official positions, solid as cement blocks in fact, men and women who knew they owed him their livelihoods if not lives. In East Berlin, said Max, my granddaughter is as safe from her weight-tossing, aristo relatives as if she lived on the dark side of the moon.

Max's flat was where they lived for the first months. A reunion and revelation, grandfather and granddaughter face to face for the first time. For Kaethe, the expression of fealty for his cunning and generosity and power, for Sophie's safe deliverance to her. Max seemed fascinated by Sophie; watching her he would lapse into a sort of frowning, astonished reverie (the prodigiously emotive face giving the lie to his flat, monotone voice). But her games disrupted him. They required chalk-marks on the floor, the scraping repositioning of furniture, explosive bursts of song or incantations. Max had never (as he pointed out to

his own daughter) been constrained to live for any length of time in
such claustrophobic proximity to anyone so young.

Sophie took her activities down to the courtyard. The enclosure was
crumbling cement and cobble and mossy hard-packed earth. The lives
of a few shrubs, shaded by four five-story-high walls, hung by a perpetual thread. Here she brought wounded, verminous birds, sickly
hedgehogs and rabbits—Kaethe would look down from the balcony
and sigh to see her daughter's head bowed over another foundling—to
be bedded in cages and crates she managed mysteriously to acquire. She
nursed them on bread scraps and milk from a dropper. Almost always
they died.

The move in spring to Mathias's flat initially gave everyone a sense
of relief and release. But for all Assistant Pastor Leytenfeger's talent for
self-effacement, the place remained small; he and Kaethe could only
snatch an opportunity to be alone together when Sophie was out playing somewhere in the streets. Mathias fretted wordlessly through her
absences. Kaethe sensed a reproach, as if, of the two of them, Mathias
made the better mother. Over time it crossed her mind that perhaps
his infinite attentiveness to the girl, open admiration (such as no real
mother could allow herself) served to balance out, in his heart, the
weakening of the bond between him and Kaethe. Lust was the bond,
she had always believed. Stronger than separation, imprisonment, or
virtuous resolve: their mystery of sexual complement. The deepening
spiral from desire to satisfaction to greater hunger. *This,* he said once,
embracing her hard, *can't be sin. Should it shake my faith that I've lost the
sense of sin in you? In me? Instead this—this strengthens my faith.*

Apart from that bond, she believed, they might as well live on separate continents. And so she enrolled unenthusiastic Sophie in the swimming team, in skating classes, and set herself the ever-new task of
seducing Mathias, until all anxiety and mistrust and street-noise were
washed away in tides of pleasure. And so in the small flat she and Pastor
Leytenfeger and the girl-child too kept up a tenuous balance. In retrospect, it looked a lot like happiness.

The von Thalls, after their legal humiliations, backed off. Naturally
they sent Sophie elaborate packages and absurd, excessive gifts, and
there was the commotion of a phone call every few weeks, and even
occasional paternal visits: excursions out for cream-torte, chaperoned
by Max's old babushka-wearing colleague, and permitted by a Kaethe

who reveled in the chance to flaunt magnanimity. Achim took less advantage than she would have expected. Each time he did turn up to see his daughter (teetering uncomfortably in Mathias's threshold, eyes drawn to the small hole left by a missing lock), his face looked more haggard, his midsection softer than Kaethe remembered. The usual pressure at work, he said, running his hand through long lank hair. *You don't know what I go through to make time to get here....* His voice held an edge of distance, also a plea for pity that made her flinch. They avoided each other's eyes. He paid no support for his child, nor did it occur to Kaethe to expect money.

Kaethe noticed his gold Swiss watch, the sort of silly excess they used to revile together. She dreaded these brief meetings, which left her raw for days.

A few months after her twelfth birthday, Sophie received a first formal invitation back to West Berlin. Her paternal grandmother had passed away.

The Family Hardship Travel Laws showed special sympathy for the bereaved, as if the Party ranked leave-taking from the dead higher than rendezvous with the living. In the case of a close relative's death, a temporary travel permit for the West was as good as assured. Ana Luise's funeral service was scheduled for April 19th, in the Church of the Nazareth. Her interment would be in the nearby cemetery, in Grüne-wald. Kaethe held the announcement—a large, bone-white square of vellum with an oppressive black border—addressed solely to Fräulein Sophie von Thall, in her hand. *Meister Leon von Thall will serve at the organ,* it said. *In accordance with the wishes of our departed, beloved Mother, musical selections will include* Wachet auf, ruft uns die Stimme *and* Ich will den Kreuzstab gerne tragen. Well, Mathias noted, they can't go wrong with Bach. And I hear the Nazareth has a magnificent choir.

They debated. Kaethe tried to convey an idea of Ana Luise: a tall, gaunt old woman, clumsy and often impulsive, who had been noble in a way that had nothing to do with pedigree. (Aren't all old women somehow noble? said Mathias.) The visit was a question of reverence, of rising above bitter mortal bickering. Sophie would be safe for a few days *across,* they decided. She was too old to trick, or keep against her will.

Kaethe dragged around heavy with a confused sadness she could neither admit nor shake off. Hard, to be unwanted at the funeral of someone whose smile once ignited your own, whose affection you had once taken as your natural due, who begged you to call her "mother." Hard to accept and hard to comprehend. West German newspapers published eulogies, letters, remembrances of both the Countess and her late husband, the brilliant humanist and war hero, Captain Ernst. Someone, anonymously, mailed a stack of these to Kaethe. She felt slighted, good-for-nothing, shunned or, worse, discarded—a wallflower, left out of the solemn, meaning-filled Totentanz.

April seemed a hard month to have to leave the world. A series of strokes, the tabloid *Bild* revealed, had battered the popular matriarch. First speechless, then paralyzed, in April she mercifully *passed*.

Kaethe packed a black sweater and skirt for Sophie, and borrowed black oxfords unfortunately a full size too large ("stuff paper in the toes!"), a five-hundred-gram bar of grainy Czech chocolate, and a pretty volume of German poetry in the old, thorny script, something a child could soothe herself to sleep with. Published 1941 in Leipzig, the book sampled Goethe and Rilke, Storm, Keller and Hölderlin. No Jews, she presumed, riffling the pages. Heine was present only by association, through his duplicitous enemy, the monumentally untalented von Platen. ("Sofchen, remind me to buy you a Heine of your own when you get back.")

Harro met his grand-niece at the station, to escort her over. Kaethe saw him only from a certain distance—beneath luminous strips of white hair long as an orchestra conductor's, his complexion looked sickly and congested as a prune. He wore a supple black merino wool coat and polished black shoes, and turned slowly on his axis, searching for a child, not recognizing the mother. Kaethe, flushed and stony-faced, couldn't know this would be her last glimpse of Harro, no more than she knew, as Sophie brushed a kiss past her mouth and then ran down the platform to meet her great-uncle, that the vellum announcement invited Sophie to more than a funeral. The family occasion sparked by Ana Luise's death was to mark the start of Sophie's new life, as planned in tight-lipped secrecy for this eventually certain, though unpredictable, date.

After three days the hardship pass expired. A phone call came for Kaethe via the disabled "hero of the Revolution" below, heralded as usual by a shout from the middle of the street. Sophie's voice crackled over a tenuous wire, shrill with warning. She begged without tears.

*Mamma! I really have to be with my Papa again. He needs me, too. Don't
blame me* ...

With that, there was nothing more to fight for. Sophie Friderike von
Thall would stay, for some unknown period of time, with her father's
people in the West.

To be a parent is to be always on watch, an *unofficial collaborator,* never
again able to completely let go. One's attention may seem to wander to
war or weather but stays tethered to the child; nothing is quite real
unless it affects her. The bliss of parenthood: self-forgetting. No more
anxious measuring of one's own worth, intelligence, achievement, love
spent and love denied ...

Sophie left her mother's makeshift care at twelve. For daughters in
particular, Kaethe reminded herself daily, twelve is a year of storms,
collisions and upheavals. At almost the same age, Kaethe had slipped
free from the stiff, chilly embrace of her grandparents' household. And
surely, she told herself, Sophie was going *toward,* not away from—she
had gone to seek her father, and aren't all girls likely to do that? Hadn't
joining the lost father once been Kaethe's heart's desire too? And
wouldn't she have gone straight to Berlin and Max Schalk if she could
have, instead of detouring through the musky classrooms and dormitories of Gore Academy?

The consolation that Kaethe clung to, through her sorrow and anger
and bewilderment, was that her own child had a mother to come back
to. Sophie, once the bedazzlement wore off, would want to come back.

Twelve is too soon. Being assured repeatedly that the child is physically
thriving and blooming, hearing the child describe herself as "just fine,"
though "different from before," doesn't begin to heal the raw, suppurat-
ing place where flesh of one's flesh has been ripped away. For Kaethe
there was no time to develop the new vanities and projects that normally distract a parent from the stealthy departure of a growing-up
child. Sophie vanished from one minute to the next. In the wind-rush
of a West-bound train.

The parallels, the irony of her loss, drove her into silence. Few people
knew; she wished no one did. She developed a brusque tone of self-
mockery. A farcical grimace as a greeting. If the two men still close to
her sometimes viewed this duped mother with reservation—there was

always the unshakable though unspoken *turn and turn about, now you know how he felt*—for Kaethe the comfort-blanket of self-pity was out of the question.

Again, as in the time before she smuggled Sophie through the Wall, she lived mechanically. Marched from one indistinguishable day to the next. She taught her English classes at the Ministry, where enrollment shot up as her reputation for rigor increased. The reports she submitted to AO became more plodding, factual—even witless, like pages from the diary of an idiot, because she could no longer perceive any relative significance in the ebb and flow of events around her.

In imagination she traveled with Sophie, through letters.

There were leisurely months of summer vacation on the exclusive North Sea island of Sylt, which Kaethe pictured as a wonderland of blondness: blond butter and blond eggs, blond sand and roof-thatch, bare-bottomed blond children splashing on the shingle, and standing out against it all, like a single poppy vivid against a wheatfield, fiery Sophie. There was the return to the villa in the Königsallee, recently completely gutted and remodeled. There was a skiing vacation at a semi-private little Austrian castle—the Jagdschloss Inntal—renowned for its unpretentious perfection, where the international guests all bore "predicates" before their family names, and sons and daughters guaranteed to be "from the same drawer" were tossed together for fun and horseplay from an early age onward, in hopes they would eventually mate. There was a five-day board meeting in Bermuda to which Sophie flew with her father, for the sophisticated adventures of piloting her own moped, and stroking a sea-turtle with her salty brown hands.

Whenever a letter came (Sophie's squarish handwriting, some letters plowing eagerly forward and others, more reluctant, slanted back) Kaethe felt her heart rise and want to burst inside her. An uprush of anticipation, expressed in her hands' tremor as she peeled apart the glued edges. Like a lover's billets-doux, the envelopes were objects in themselves. Unopened, each had the power to excite and assuage her simultaneously, to sharpen desire and at the same time bring peace.

Every month or so an envelope jutted from the letter-box. Sometimes there was no real letter inside at all, instead a colored-pencil drawing of, for instance, an Alpine valley scene, or a brown, spikey-feathered pelican on a pier, signed *love and kisses to everyone, your Sophie v. Thall*. The written word didn't seem to come easily to Sophie. This struck Kaethe as a disturbing turn in her development, although Mathias

pointed out that when Sophie had been with them Kaethe had tended
to brush off school results, as well as complaints about *Schalk-Thall's
lack of diligence* and reminders that sixth-grade recommendations for
or against eventual university acceptance entered a pupil's permanent
file.

"But she was only going through a phase. The school was so stuffy.
They're requiring 'pre-military' now. Sophie was rebelling. It's natural, I did just the same when I came here," said Kaethe, revising herself
into a classroom insurrectionist. "She needed to make her own choices.
Would you want Sophie growing up repressed?" She recalled Parents'
Night lectures at the Rainbow Antiauthoritarian Kindergarten. "A
child's rebellious spirit ought to be celebrated. It's healthy!"

"Not healthy in Germany," said Mathias.

For two months, no envelope came.

"Misdelivered, I'll bet," said Kaethe. "The post office has gone to the
dogs. No one cares about doing their job anymore." More and more fre-
quently, unpermitted "sponti" demonstrations would suddenly clog the
streets. Teenagers yowling "We want freedom!" and "Gorbi Gorbi
Gorbachev!" As Max said, what did they know about the Russians?
Boom-boxes blared Pink Floyd and the Rolling Stones. There had been
violent clashes but no mass arrests. Not yet.

"Yes, letters get lost. Or shredded by the censors."

"Stop, Mathias. For Christ's sake! Why do you always say the one
damned thing that will unravel me?"

"You said she's doing fine. And do you have to swear so much? No.
Kaethe . . . I'm sorry, Kaethe. I know how this all—now listen: Have
you thought about going over again? You *could* go over. You're not like
us."

"Ah. So you don't want me around anymore."

"What?"

"Now that she's gone."

"That's utter nonsense."

"You're hardly ever home. Last weekend Leipzig. Dresden the week
before."

"That's because—that's the work I've been asked to do. It's temporary. I'm *obliged,* especially since the Church has taken the risk of keeping me on. Kaethe, Kaethe, you know what I feel for you."

"Oh, yes."

"I'd like you to stay here. I'm simply thinking of you both. You need to at least be near Sophie. She needs to know you are near."

"Even assuming they let me out—"

"They'll let you. Max will handle it."

"Oh? Have you *seen* Max recently? He doesn't get around much. Does anyone even still listen to him? Come on, say you haven't noticed. No. You know as well as I do—if I go across one more time, they're going to say good riddance. Same as with Biermann and Bahro and the rest. They'll lock all the gates behind me." A pause. The picture sprang up of a future back in the West—more than ever as a satellite to Achim. But miniaturized, hovering on the edge of his glittery life. And what sort of example to a daughter would she be then? Renting a shabby room equipped with an electric heater and hot plate. Like her own mother's last room. Taking a flex-time office job. Always at the mercy of Achim von Thall's orders and convenience. Tethered by a long line. "He'd be ecstatic. It's what he wants—it's his whole goal, to rule over me, make me a kind of chattel. It always was—" She stopped, struck by a weird insight: that a woman in her situation found more freedom under this State dictatorship than in the West.

"Oh, nonsense!" Mathias leaned out the window, as if to fly. He knocked his pipe dottle into the street. "Over there you can have any life you want!"

"I agree. I'm just over-sensitive. It is nonsense. I get on your nerves. So you think I should go?"

"Yes. You *belong* close to Sophie!"

She did go. Packed up, lugged her bags back to the Szredskistrasse and her sofa-bed in Max's front room. He greeted her with an abstracted kiss, without surprise, as if she'd merely been off on a weekend jaunt. It was good to be under his roof again, she felt. Unseen. She was glad to discover that her impression of Max's apathy had been wrong; either that, or he'd found new interests, new wind for his sails. Often as she woke in the morning he was already on his way out, his briefcase bulging like the outward proof of a vigorous mind.

Max came home one evening and threw open the windows to invite the traffic sounds from below. He switched the radio to a Shostakovitch symphony.

Kaethe grinned. "Is there any *louder* composer than Shostakovitch?"

Max sat down with his back to the desk, facing her. Not smiling.

More a mime's stylized grief. "They've taken him in again. Your friend."

She balked an instant at the word "friend." "Who? *Him?*"

Max nodded.

"When was this? Where?"

Max leaned very close. "You haven't heard? The Zion congregation. Protest. Demands. Mass arrests. Well, the Party's nervous. Twenty-fifth anniversary of the Wall celebrated, meanwhile our population hits an all-time low. Economy's bad and pressure rising. The churches are behind it all, they're convinced. Well, we'll see who's let go tomorrow. As for *him,* however . . ." Max drew back. "Second time generally goes harder." He fixed his eyes on her, unblinking, even as he held a match to a cigarette and pulled the smoke in deeply. "But you knew that."

"What are you trying to tell me?" She much preferred the smell of Max's Egyptian cigarettes to that of Pastor Leytenfeger's pipe.

"The implication. If he has realized you're a UC. An Unofficial Collaborator."

Kaethe blinked. They never spoke of their work. Their employers. Now so casually he has exposed her. The room swam behind Max's ever-changing face. Whole structures crumbled in silence. "You mean that he might think—he might blame me?"

Her father shrugged. His gaze wandered to her sofa; stowed beneath its skirt were a VEB typewriter, a few books, a box of clothes, stacked notebooks and loose papers.

"I should write to him. You have channels, right? At least to explain I had nothing to do with—"

"Please, no." Max's eyes widened, until they were huge and round as a those of a cat entering a rat warren. "Don't even think of it. To write to him would not help any of us, just now."

But she did write; she wrote to AO. No risk there, her supervisor would long since be informed about this second arrest of her lover. Sometime-lover. Former shelterer. AO by now had a record of all her relation-ships, her successes and failures, evasions and oversights, weaknesses and addictions—knew pretty much more about her than anyone could conceivably want or need. From the beginning, it hadn't been the lives of "others" she spied on and detailed and delivered, as much as her own. Was that the State's purpose, then? Sometimes she speculated that from all the miscellaneous data of her past few years AO could read a pattern that she, being too entangled, was blind to—and she thought about corresponding with him in a new way. A tide would turn; she would ask the questions. AO would send her answers.

"What could the charge against Leytenfeger be?" she wrote. "From what office? As you know I lived with Assistant Pastor Leytenfeger, and saw nothing out of the ordinary. No dubious acquaintances. *I* had no suspicions. As you yourself know best," she added. Let AO assume she was keen to justify herself. She hoped he was in a position to also somehow convey to Mathias her history of uselessness to the Ministry. Her beautiful, blessed uselessness.

A certain closeness—an odor of intimacy—arises out of a long, frequent correspondence, no matter what its ostensible purpose. For years now, except for the cautious and anodyne letters to Sophie (for who else might read them?), she'd had no correspondent but AO. Paradoxically, the reports to her "manager" felt safe from prying eyes. . . . Going by the regular deposits in her Volksbank account, her recent work for AO had been judged reliable, insofar as a heap of unsifted facts can be relied on. But how could she rise above reliability, to break into AO's silence and merit an answer? By telling the truth? (Truth doesn't preclude humor. She imagined AO, like many solitary analysts, to have a dry but ticklish sense of humor.)

No answer.

On November 10th, 1989, she wrote again.

We don't have a television. So I missed Shabowski's inconceivable announcement yesterday. Whatever he said in his interview that led people to jump—literally—to the conclusion that the Wall, like the emperor's robes, is nothing but a figment of the bureaucratic imagination. (Tell me: will Shabowski be called to account? Was he tricked, as most of us think—handed the wrong bulletin to read over the air? Drugged, maybe?) Anyway, I missed yesterday's Wall-smashing. Slept right through it. Woke to the festive racket of beer bottles smashing on cobblestones. To the hangover, too.

Were *you* there, AO?

When will things go back to normal? Will there be elections soon? Arrests? As we Berliners say, "the porridge is cooked hotter than it's eaten." Folks from our neighborhood talk about going across but only to sight-see. To boast that they've been. Not to *stay*. Basically there is a sense of disruption, dis-ease. Strangely,

it reminds me of the days right after the Wall began to go up—
the same nervous scurrying, hoarding, leap-frogging rumors.

Not that I hear anyone laying much blame on that border guard
who opened the Brandenburg Gate barrier yesterday, rather than
fire on the people. Our Republic has come a distance. You, AO,
you must be proud. I hope so. We've had far worse, temporary
crises.

Can you tell me how the Leytenfeger case progresses? Again
I assure you that whatever his flaws the man is Communist to the
core.

As a footnote I should mention that if the free-travel edict does
look likely to stay open a while, I may consider making a short
family visit, myself.

She waited. In her own way (everyone hummed and stirred in their
own private way) she shared the euphoria. Surely the breach in the Wall
meant that she could expect a call any day from Sophie. Would they
meet for tea at the Hotel Kempinski? Or would Sophie hop a trolley to
visit her, and Max? All barriers broken.

Instead she received a special delivery letter from Herr Dr. von
Thall. No handwriting. Typed. Initialed by a *Sekr. Frau Koch*. The letter explained that owing to Sophie's inadequate school performance
and other self-destructive behaviors persisting despite the efforts of a
highly recommended (and expensive) psychologist, Sophie *at her own
request* had left Berlin to live among cousins in a wholesome country
environment, removed from the conflicts and pressures of the political
city. To a village folded in the Taunus mountains, in fact, a landscape
Kaethe might recall . . . "Sophie shows improved insight into her own
needs for peace and loving supervision and the fixed routine of her
uncle's household. She will doubtless soon be in contact." This letter
signed off with: Best regards.

Kaethe could hear Max rummaging in the bulb-lit, interior kitchen.
He had been roaming the West for the day, had brought home hothouse
Dutch tomatoes and Israeli garlic bulbs and a voluptuously misshapen
Italian cheese. A week's pay's worth of delicacies.

Kaethe refused to go over. Was waiting. For what?

Her next report began: "To be a parent is to be always on watch, *an
unofficial collaborator—*"

Shortly after the breach of the Wall, before the democratically ratified
(on the promise of an unprecedented Eastward transfer of wealth)
rebirth of the "single German nation," and in the very hour of Mathias
Leytenfeger's release from Hohenschoenhausen detention (he had
heard rumors of a shake-up and was hoping for freedom generally but
not that morning, was no more prepared than the head-scratching
guard who approached his cell, still rereading the order) on that morning Kaethe Schalk sat swaying, perched on her suitcase, in the corridor
of an overbooked train moving west from the inter-German border,
savoring a sweet Stuyvesant cigarette, staring out at the unfamiliar lar-
gesse of billboards and fatness of cows.

The von Thalls now in possession of the Taunus castle met her at
the station. They were not uncivil. The brother reminisced about student hijinks in Berlin; his Dutch wife dandled their sixth child on an
improbably slim hip. They all seemed distracted, terminally busy.
Kaethe was offered a chair but no food or drink. An older child was
sent to fetch Sophie.

Two days later she wrote a letter. She wasn't sure the recipient had ever
existed. If he did, he now only had power to listen, not to harm.

From: T
To: AO
Subject: Observations in the Taunus
     My daughter is a head taller than any of her cousins. Taller than
me. Not yet fifteen, but already not exactly a child. I couldn't stop
staring. I felt embarrassed by the beauty of a young girl, even or
especially when she's my own. Long willowy waist, and those
endless legs . . . But she is thin. I know what shape she should be.
The relatives complained she's a picky eater, won't touch meat or
eggs—but who knows what they give her? Still, she has energy.
We tramped across the fields surrounding the castle. I was here
once before; I recognized the sky. (Skies are individual everywhere.)
Every so often she would lope away, to do a handstand, or throw
sticks at the sky. I asked, Are you content? She said, Did you notice,
here on Uncle's farm the animals have grassy pens, the chickens
scratch in the grass, but down the road they keep chickens caged

in barracks. They're bald, feathers rubbed off. The eggs drop
away through bars. I'm thinking how to let them all out. The
smell makes you want to die. . . . Mamma, are *you* content?

I asked her: could you want to come live with us again? That is,
with me and Max? No, oh God, I really hated the school there, she
said, and ran off for a while, whistling. When she came back she
whispered, You could come live *here,* Mamma. I avoided the trap
of Sophie's black eyes under the long, arced brows. I looked around
the cleanly harvested field, last year's barley stubble patrolled by
crows. Suddenly she started giggling, shaking her head as if I'd
already given some funny answer. Her hair lashed her cheeks. I
said, Oh, Sophie, this is no place for you either, why don't you at
least go back to stay with your father? Sophie stopped twirling
around. He's getting *married,* Mamma. Finally he found a wife.
Hasn't anybody told you?

I'm back in Szredskistrasse now, AO. Home. . . . Despite everything
I have such a feeling of relief, release. That visit was the beginning
—we spoke—and what we didn't have to say counted even more,
and Sophie hugged me goodbye at the station. Why did I wait so
long? I ask myself, what sort of—but there were many reasons,
and it's no help now to Sophie, my asking, is it? I'm peaceful! It's
true that peace only comes from being able to love, finding the one
who can break down your barricaded heart. Now I think it's best
to give Sophie a space of time to reflect, and then I'll go back for
another visit, maybe invite her to a restaurant, we'll continue this
way and maybe soon, who knows. . . .

And you, AO? I wish you would send me more than occasional
acknowledgments. I want to know: are you well, healthy, suffi-
ciently protected? What is your position now? Can you be feeling
the same threat that the rest of us, your network and reporters, do?
Things falling apart.

Are you still there? Reading? This flood of Wessi capital, flag-
waving cash, before we idealists can work out the questions of
our bloody history. They'll want our heads on a stick, won't they?
(I don't mind. It's my father I worry about. He's older. Working
harder than ever these days. As if possessed by the devil. Isolated,
I'm afraid, in every direction. Please, please, look out for him.)

From: T
To: AO
Subject: Request for Contact

I am sitting in a café I don't know the name of. I have just come
from the Prenzlauer Berg police station. The occupying West is
so polite! You understand. I believe you do understand perfectly.
Can't find any letter-paper however. You won't mind that I scribble
with the waiter's pen on the back of this handbill advertising ten-
day vacations in Rio and Mexico City. We never *dreamed,* here.
But perhaps you are by now in Rio or Mexico City? Unless you
somehow confirm receipt of this scrawl, I won't write again. It's a
futile habit. How fast everything went down, Westward Ho! Poor
Mielke, making his teary farewells to the "people he dedicated his
life to defending." Ah, damn! Only now it occurs to me—how
slowly my head works today, after answering too many questions
from the police—even if Magdalenenstrasse were still up and running, there's no one for whose *sake* to write anymore. You don't
answer me for Mathias's sake. For my father's sake? He is disappeared as I presume you know. One way or the other. Dead, they
want me to think. Nonsense. Not Max. (*Jamaica,* I imagine. He
talked, recently, about the Caribbean.)

I am certainly not writing for my sake. Though it's true I'm
broke, no check has come.

Are you gone too? Did you ever exist? Are you made up of nothing, or compressed out of many people? Perhaps the woman in the
babushka is a part of you?

I have no place to go now and no money. (AO, flip this page over
and look what these vacations cost. How does advertising bring
these dreams any closer to us, in Prenzlauer Berg?) You know that
for a few days I have been away. The second visit to my daughter
since the Wall-breach. I had to make another try. But I waited outside the gate in Taunus for three hours. The boy came out. Sophie
won't come down, he said. She's been sick.

No one is to be believed.

When I came back, I went straight up to Max's—our—apartment. A uniformed Wessi blocked the landing. I backed off, nearly

fell. My dumb first thought: *Scheisse,* it's my turn. My own overdue arrest. But no, it wasn't that. And they won't tell me.

And now I can't think where to go. Where to put my travel bag. Not in the apartment, because cops are posted, to protect the "evidence." Don't leave the city, they say, until the investigation is complete. Then I will be free—to go where? Back to the Taunus?

The family. The more I plead, the more they turn her mind against me. You're not helping *her,* so the Dutch hausfrau informed me: that last visit left her quite upset. She wouldn't eat or speak to us for two days.

No rights. No one to ask.

Max is gone.

It's five-thirty, professional girls are trickling into this bar. Dollfaces, a lot more cheerful and confident than the old-time geisha. Could I become a geisha? Too old. But imagine this: to be paid money, in exchange for being touched and held.

Please confirm receipt or I won't write again.

Dear AO

Subject: final letter from T

Another picture for you: a city fumbling into the thin air of freedom. A woman waked from a long walking coma, during which she presumably appeared functional, and no more close-mouthed or mistrustful than the average member of post-Stalin post-Ulbricht society. She woke to find herself in familiar surroundings: the same flat she had shared as a schoolgirl with her father. The same clawfoot tub in the kitchen, the w.c. in the outer hall—never renovated, since he refused to let workmen in to modernize and no doubt wire the place with electronic antennae—but the flat now opulently furnished with antiques and Bauhaus sculpture, African zebra rugs and Moroccan hassocks, the booty and tributes of her father's long career. All this was hers to enjoy alone—though with the change of regimes and helter-skelter sell-off of DDR State-owned property probably not for much longer. She anticipated eviction. Meanwhile there was no one to prevent her painting *Unrecht! Unrecht! Unrecht!* across the walls. The dripping, black-angry letters could have been taken for a political statement, like the slogans students decades earlier had splashed on the walls of the Free University, or like

the banners waved from the windows of the occupied Stasi Headquarters by rampaging citizens only a short while before. But they
were private, in the sense of being a message only to herself. About
the forgetfulness of those who have power. The stealers. About
emptiness, an ache nothing can dull or soothe, time least at all.
Unrecht = injustice, but she is aware, as an experienced translator,
that the two words weigh differently: the German being starker,
emphatic as a blow, with no hope of revision.

She could run to ground, though. Erase everything. The "opening" brought her a spate of dead letters. Death notices. A paid-up
tax bill. As a small inheritance, perhaps a place to go.

the as-is condition

OUTSIDE

Drive southeast out of the city, general direction Dresden, or northeast toward Danzig, into the tart green, rain- and wind-swept Brandenburg flatland, and you can buy fresh-laid white eggs, plucked and scalded chickens, succulent pears, apricots and cherries for a song. Recently hard to come by on the other hand are wheat, barley or feed corn—the automated, capitalized farmers of Lower Saxony and Bavaria have trumped the eastern sand-scratchers out of the "united" market, and even if the survivors of collectivization could produce Western size and quality, where are the highways and container-trucks to take their stuff to market? Since unification the fields have gone from their age-old symmetry of furrows and seasonal growth—the visual matrix of farm-land—to a monotonous chaos of thistles and brambles, haunted by tramps and crows.

Rahel drives east in a rust-fringed, oil-belching '84 Opel Kadett—not because she has calculated how prices for produce must rise for anyone who powers into the small, weedy farmyards as a "Mercedes-Wessi," but because she has a miserly streak about machines. Good times or bad, she has never been tempted to squander money on the merely functional.

Even in midsummer the farm wives still wear their old-style, lumpy layers of plaid and flowered cottons and wools, underskirts and skirts and apron-dresses. Headkerchiefs and mucking boots. The men (but men are seldom seen here) wear blue cotton worksuits the color of an October Baltic sky. To Rahel all the faces, old or young, look confoundingly alike, as if carved by an unimaginative sculptor from an inexhaustible supply of weather-faded wood: flat-planed faces, button-featured, with trenches of mute discouragement curving down from the corners of each mouth. Rahel considers the possibility that they are in fact all related. They certainly don't look related to her.

The countrywoman's stock form of greeting is a sharp nod and an assessing glance. Rahel returns the head-bob, adding a citified smile that disarms no one. Boris, leaning out the open window of the passenger side, pants and drools dismissively above a growling, hackled, milling pack of yard dogs. They are undersized mongrels, a reversion to the canine mean, nothing like the bizarre first-generation crosses of the city, such as Boris himself.

For Rahel life has become a void, as boring as the void. She can calmly recount her past because it seems to have happened to someone else. She pitches herself into the future like a numb drunk careening downhill. The future of others is what draws her on, while her own remains featureless and meaningless. Movie fans, she tells Kaethe, are bound by the compulsion to see how other lives play out, watching the melodrama of emotions as you'd watch the cycling licks of a fire in the grate. (But you wouldn't stick your own hand in fire, would you? How? What for?)

Rahel can muster an interest in dissecting her motives (boredom, sensuality, the gratifying paradox that the more thorough one's indifference to people, the greater one's influence over them). These are the mechanical watchsprings of her actions. She has long since shed any sense of real involvement, or culpability.

She rarely sleeps. Why has it become so hard to find the narrow passageway to unconsciousness? She used to take sleeping pills and mild paralytics (was a frequent research volunteer in Dr. Kropf's Somnotherapy Clinic) but by now even the private-label herb schnapps that topples troubled guests (Kaethe, for example) like a blunt hammer, leaves her sharp and dry, alert as ever. Also unlike everyone around her, Rahel in her all-too-few hours of oblivion never dreams. Not one dream since the death of her cancer-raddled son, soon followed by an event almost indistinguishable in the tumbling, grieving wake of the first loss: her husband's fatal skid against a street trolley at an icy Hamburg intersection. Lies, who used to confess her dreams in pillow-babble: "Imagine: last night my mother came and hugged me!" Or: "I had that nightmare about how you were leaving me!" or "And then Boris turned into a fiery monster, and chased me into the lake" has been warned no longer to irritate her employer with these clichéd, self-referential fragments.

Mornings in the kitchen with Kaethe, however, Rahel can't hear enough about her new friend's waking dream: night journeys in the city.

Looking at Kaethe, who does Rahel see?

A cat's cradle of contradictions, was the first impression. As if the newcomer amounted to what physicists call a "sub-stable" system. Rahel noted a diffident assurance, a vulnerable strength. This improbable Countess von Thall seemed oblivious to her limp (a deft, circling motion that conjured up a peg-legged old sailor) and Rahel (while imagining a parrot perched swaying on the new guest's shoulder, ruffling out its wings for balance) admired her refusal to accept fact. She also liked this guest's bony, brown face of a sports figure or wayfaring tramp, while deploring the hair dulled by brown dye. A traveling suit of green linen and silk looked wrecked by wrinkles and stains. Still, Kaethe moved in the American way—decisive and rangy, not hemmed in by walls or crowds—so that beneath the rumpled clothes Rahel made out a muscular, sturdy body that had somehow escaped the spongy ribs and broadened pelvis usual in middle age. There were scars, old ones and fresher, but no slack flesh or immoderate bulges.

A pension-owner has the instincts of a tax collector: in a glance she can tell who is buffered by wealth and who is on their uppers, who pretends to money he doesn't have and who is trying to fan away her own rich reek of money. The Countess wore no jewelry except for a plain blue signet ring, its soft gold dented by wear. Her shoes looked cheaply glued, not sewn. Rahel had planned to put her in the room adjacent to that of Lies, the chambermaid: both rooms long and narrow and utilitarian, with a coffin-sized wardrobe at the foot of the bed and a wash basin by the head. As they proceeded through the corridors, Rahel repeated her standard patter. Unlike most people at the end of a long, cramped journey Kaethe gave off only a light spicy smell. Like earth, just before rain hits. Rahel, beaming professionally and amused inwardly by the fancy of the teetering parrot, brushed lightly, intentionally, against the newcomer while rebalancing a suitcase. She felt a surge of curiosity and desire rise up in her, a sweet and cleansing cloud. It thickened in the back of her throat, making her swallow hard.

That early on, in that very first hour, Rahel followed an impulse that could have passed for partiality or even pity—though it was not pity, and moreover why would anyone have a twinge of concern for this evidently practiced traveler? Rahel's impulse was to lock all doors, leave on all lights, stand guard. The impulse was to hold and enfold the new guest, if only from a distance. Keep her safe from some imminent, unnamed source of corruption. So Rahel on a whim put her new arrival in the finest room, Rahel's personal favorite, the far-removed, ebony-furnished, airy and quiet chamber where, if lucky, one could hear the Drossel sing. All for no extra charge.

And now, toward the end of summer? Rahel still hasn't completely pinned the other woman down. Contradictions continue to unfold: the almost exaggerated play of facial expressions is a standard American trait (any German five-year-old has already learned to be more self-censorial and impassive) but Kaethe von Thall's spontaneity ends at her eyes. The eyes are extremely deep-set, as if turned unapproachably inward. In broad daylight the irises are bright chips of green and russet brown, but at all other times they look to Rahel nearly black, and somber, as if regardless of what story Kaethe is unfolding or smiling over, the eyes remain fixed on some sorrow beyond distraction. These eyes, like a blind person's, still can make Rahel catch her breath. She is also intrigued by the other woman's speech: her German sounds outdated, purified of slang. On the other hand it's peppered with unorthodox twists of phrase, so that Rahel finds herself anticipating the next queer but apt coinage. They are, she decides, not the literal translation of Americanisms, but reflections of some inner image-language without sound or syllable, that mediates between the spoken ones.

At the first farm she buys a half-dozen jars of thistle-honey and a small crateload of pear schnapps and a crescent of trimmed-off, desiccated cattle hoof for Boris to gnaw on for the rest of the drive. (Although the hound has been panting out the window into the breeze as usual, he is suffering a touch of carsickness. This is plain to Rahel, just as her malaise would be to him.) There is nothing fresh to be bought from this miserable outpost but a lone bunch of salmon-pink, heavy-headed gladioli, found propped against the house's wasp-ridden wall. She pays four West Marks (still thinking of the currency as West, even though the Eastern alternative is long gone) and lowers the long blooms like an unconscious child gently into the trunk of the car. The gesture revives a memory of her most recent return from the Brandenburg heath. An afternoon late in July. Arms full of prickling daisies, she entered the pension kitchen.

"Such a hot day to spend driving." Kaethe embraced her, took the flowers, plunged them into a vase. "So how is it your skin stays so cool? Even now you feel cool as a stone. As if you lived underground."

"Because I keep calm. Never any excitement."

"Oh no, Rahel, I don't think so."

"Of course. Tight and emotionless, like a little fist."

"A fist . . . ? Oh, *Faust,* is that it? Sometimes you do remind me of the Doctor. The way he was in the first part, before he cut the deal with Mephisto. So bored with books and cleverness. But wasn't he looking for temptation? To say, *Verweile doch, du bist so schön!* What exactly *was* their deal?"

"What Faust promised the devil *exactly* was, 'Should I ever say to the passing moment, "Oh stay, you are so beautiful!"—then you can throw me into bondage, and let my funeral bells ring out—'"

"Still doesn't make much sense. Why should the devil take his soul at the moment he finds something to really care about? That's backward, somehow."

"But look how Goethe subverted the old, moralizing story! His *Faust* was a real mensch, much smarter than the fairytale character. He dickered, split hairs, he held out. He never did make a closed deal—it was a *bet,* an open-ended toss of the dice that really depended on his own appreciation of whatever the devil would manage to tempt him with. So the dice were loaded—and he didn't think the devil had much to offer. Did they teach you kids old Johann Wolfgang over in the workers' paradise? Did you ever read his *Theory of Color?* If you believe in genius—"

"No. For me Goethe is too . . . huge. Huge and perfect. I like E.T.A. Hoffmann. And Gerhart Hauptmann, and Tucholsky—the clowns and comedians. And Heinrich Heine. I'd rather read Heine any day."

"Ah, minstrel Harry, the perpetually self-regarding, insecure Jew.

Like all brilliant comedians, a sad figure. Had himself *baptized,* did I
mention? And his dying in the Paris 'tomb'—too painful to bear. But
do you know, I found some pointers that he had good friends in this
neighborhood. In the 1820's quite the chic address. It's pretty clear he
would have visited this house—"

"Here!"

"But I haven't run into his ghost yet. Have you? I'll tell you which
ghost I'd like to let a room to—Walter Benjamin, the critic who did so
much to polish up Heine's reputation. You've read Benjamin? Do you
know that charming essay about his Wilhelmine childhood, about the
excitement of leaving the Berlin flat for summer vacation? Lying in the
darkened nursery, knowing next day was the Big Day because of the
light strip burning late under the door, while outside the grownups
murmured and packed. Next morning they'd all be off to Zoo station,
for adventures in the sun. . . . It's charming, a perfect somersault of
memory. But ironic, isn't it? Thirty years after, when Jewish children
in Berlin lay listening to their parents whisper as they packed the suitcases, it would mean a different sort of journey."

"Walter Benjamin. But he ended up a suicide."

"Yes. September nineteen forty. In the harbor town of Port-Bou,
with a visa for the States in his pocket. Makes you wonder: can a sudden influx of hope be dangerous, even fatal, like a rush of oxygen into a
diver's air-starved veins? His last piece of writing—while interned in a
French work camp—was an essay called 'On the Concept of History.'
Difficult subject to approach from inside a internment camp . . . Before
that, he had been rediscovering, or reinventing, Baudelaire. He had an
enormous heart for other poets. Goethe, as well! Has it struck you,
Kaethe, how often German Jews have been ahead of the pack in picking and defending the best German writers? By the way, you are part
Jewish, aren't you?"

"Me? Oh, Rahel, if you had ever met my Lutheran grandparents.
Or my mother! I remember her pale frizzy hair. Her eyes, before she
drank so much, weren't so much blue but clear, like pools of water.
Hah! *Jewish?* Not a prayer."

At her last farm-stop Rahel buys two dozen brown eggs and an oily
smoked ham, newspaper-wrapped bundles of scaly Bosc pears and sour
green apples and the small, tightly folded rosy-violet prune plums that

remind Rahel of a woman's most hidden part brought to light. "Today I'm going to bake a cake from these," she says, offering a ripe plum back to the farm-wife's thumb-sucking daughter, "for my best friend, who's had to live too long in America, where they only bother to grow the gigantic, picture-perfect fruit. All flashiness, no taste. Nothing as good as this."

Best friend. At Rahel's age, the phrase is an anachronism. Also a lie, with its implication that Rahel enjoys a circle of friends, candidates from whom to select, imperiously and capriciously (as this drooling, grubby child may do at school among her peers), a *best,* a favored intimate. But she savors the phrase; it warms her and gives a pinhole glimpse back into the heart of long, long ago, before anyone ever turned away forever, when innocence and possession were two sides of the same coin. "My best friend adores these," she repeats, allowing the silent little girl to probe solemnly in the newsprint package for another plum.

Giving Kaethe the job of under-manager was an inspired move. It freed the guest from pressing money troubles while binding her; now it keeps her obliged and close and available while Rahel takes more time for herself, for jaunts such as this, out to the Brandenburg heath. And with each day of work Kaethe's return to America is pushed farther into a hazy future.

"It's obvious you belong here."

"Where? In the Pension Zur Kurfürstin?"

"Well, that goes without saying! But I meant, in the city. Berlin fits you. How could you feel natural anywhere else? How could you ever have wanted to leave here?"

"Where I no longer have so much as a mailbox, and the only people who call me by name are you and Lies—"

"And the Shimizus. Don't forget the Shimizus." A Japanese couple and their three bamboo-slim daughters, all with surprisingly muscled arms, have taken rooms for the summer while working in the Charlottenburg garden-café as a string quintet. "And plenty of others. Kaethe, I'd say you sound sorry for yourself. So discouraged this morning? It's the wind, Kaethe, the wind has turned and is blowing out of the northeast now, and that ruffles all our nerves. Here, come sit, put your head back. Let me smooth your hair for you. Let me rub your temples."

There is only one salvation Rahel believes in: the salvation of the senses. Spring, summer or fall, her need for another excursion into this thistle- and pine-studded heath builds up inside her until concentration on any- thing else is impossible.

Here she is whole, not a half-living creature. Here it seems as though all mirrors have been smashed. The highways are crumbling, the wind- brakes self-seeded, and as she walks in diamond-hard sunlight or under scudding mackerel clouds all that falls comes around young again, inviting consummation. There is no death-ending, only transfigura- tions. She finds a lesser but similar relief in the drawings and the furni- ture-sculpture she collects. And it's the same with sexual pleasure. Another transcendence. God, she has thought, watching Lies surren- dering to her ministering hands, the girl's chubby face twisted in a grimace that mimics pain—to be able to give one's self away so. To cut the anchor-cables. Rahel knows that even in these moments she exists primarily as an observer: Lies's pleasure is more real to her than her own. Lies with her head driven back into the pillow, flushed web of veins below the surface of her cheeks. The white quartermoons of her lidded eyes.

But that all seems quite long ago. These days, the more time Rahel spends in Kaethe's company, the more her hired girl, Lies, manages to exasperate her. Their long domestic harmony, a couple-arrangement that worked so well because it assumed so little, has recently been eroded by brittle nerves, unjust reactions and snappish remarks. Imag- ined through a third set of eyes (Kaethe's? And how much has Kaethe seen, and seen through?) the love affair embarrasses Rahel. It's ludi- crous, labored, deformed. She wants to repudiate it. To fly away, become someone else, disembodied and dignified, who has never lain waiting (an aging, raging insomniac) in a chambermaid's narrow bed long past midnight, waiting for the girl to come in from her club-crawling, techno-dancing nights. Who never discovered and took in Lies at all. Meanwhile Lies sends her sullen, assessing glances. For once Rahel has to struggle to hold her own glass-smooth expression, to hide her sud- den distaste for this young girl—a physical nausea over having taken *too much* of Lies, more than her fill—and her longing for a way out.

And yet it was Kaethe she quarreled with, only the day before.

"It's the wind from the northeast, that ruffles all our nerves. Kaethe, come sit, and let me—"

"No, please. *Don't*. I can't stand to be touched."

"Are you having your days? Is that why?"

"My—? Oh, how one forgets. The 'days'. No. I'm long past that whole business."

"Actually, I thought so ..."

"Rahel. You're wrong. I don't fit in here. I'm not even sure anymore why I came."

"To look for *her,* of course."

"Maybe that was an excuse to myself? A virtuous smokescreen. So I could revisit the scene of ... Oh, there were so many, you pick a scene. Or, maybe I wanted to trouble Mathias again. Good! Probably that was the real reason. See, my friend? I'm getting the hang of your way of thinking. Anyway, I'm thinking of giving up. I'm thinking that you've been right all along. Sophie isn't here, probably never was."

"Have you heard from her father recently?"

"Not directly. Nothing new. But he checks up on me, expects to know every step I take, whom I talk to, what I learn—of course I don't answer much. There's no trust between us. Still it's funny, the super-manager he's become. He's delegated the Sophie-problem to me, and demands my report."

"So you two *do* talk."

"Only letters. Only recently."

"Perhaps working up to some sort of forgiveness."

"Forgiveness? You've seen his letters drop through the slot. Each one typed and signed *in absentia* by his secretary, Fräulein Koch. Could you ever let an employee know so much about your private life?"

"Aristocrats are used to parading naked in front of their servants. Reticence is bourgeois."

"And it's always this Fräulein Koch who answers his phone and takes messages. Come to think, her boss could be dead and I none the wiser."

"Possibly he's afraid of you?"

"Oh, please ... Rahel, did I tell you how once, for a moment, I imagined I saw Sophie?"

"You did."

"How I'd been looking so long and hard that I hallucinated her. It was early dawn. Who knows what I saw. I've been seeing all kinds of odd things this summer."

"You're losing weight, dear friend. You run around too much."

"That's what you always say. In fact I do nothing but sleep in this place."

"And still you're tense, at your wits' end. Kaethe—you wouldn't think of going back? To that burnt-out shack in the middle of nowhere?"

"Not now."

"Ah, good! I was almost afraid—"

"But later on, where else? First I should search Munich. Where she was last seen, after all . . . I understand so much more now. The kids from Prenzlauer Berg, the kids at the medic van, they all tell me Munich's where they want to go from here as soon as they can scrape up the cash. There's a huge 'scene.' Makes Berlin look like the provinces. Munich's rolling in loose money, you know, movie money, rag-trade money. . . . They tell me there's a ring of warehouses surrounding the town, bankrupted real estate. Nowadays anyone can hide out in that maze, find shelter and money. Tend bar, trade drugs, sell sex, pony drugs up from Ankara and Sofia—well, *Sofia,* it's a fact, that's the hot source, so the kids tell me. See, Rahel, I'm not living in Never-Never-Land. Maybe I used to try to strike deals in my mind—*please let her still be like this, like that, exactly as I remember*—but at this point I don't care what she's doing. How she is holding her life together. I simply want to find her."

"Ah. So you don't make deals, Kaethe. Fine! What's more, you don't care what deals your child is making?"

"No, I don't."

"What's happened to your imagination, I wonder?"

A justified question. No hurt was intended, Rahel assured herself. But Kaethe looked as if she had been slapped without warning. Her eyes went dull. She stood up and turned her back on her employer and began scrubbing on breakfast dishes as if she would grind them into sand.

Here is the plumcake Rahel plans: slices of fruit spiraling out like a chambered nautilus on rich, crumbling shortbread. Overlapping new moons of the tartly sweet plums. Garnet-dark juice under the skin bleeding into the translucent green. All of it shimmering, sealed in agar and sugar. Pungent, sweet-sour. How can Kaethe resist? Then the spurting satisfaction of the first, tart bite.

Rahel has no intention of letting Kaethe Schalk leave her protection, let alone set out for Munich. Why go? In order to meet the same or greater disappointment? Whom would she turn to when money ran out? Count von Thall? Would he fob her off—or worse, insist on inviting her to his home, to a festive menu of humiliation personally served by that blond icon of the boulevard press, the present Countess?

When Rahel was a mere girl she embraced the notion of "individual fate": a unique unfolding of events that, at least in retrospect, suggests a meaningful direction. But now she sees fate for the cheap rattletrap it is, merely the jolting twists and doglegs of a city tour bus. Playfully, she sometimes adds a detour or attraction of her own—the proprietress of a pension, especially one catering to artists, musicians and other suggestible souls, is rich in opportunity. "Call it my creative outlet," as she once explained to Lies.

With Kaethe she hasn't been able to resist. Kaethe, more than any guest Rahel can recall, has offered herself for redirection. And yet, she realizes (driving back now over potholed roads toward the dark mass of Berlin on the western horizon), it's as if she has lost her timing. Her hand is slipping. Often, whatever she has tried to arrange for the guest from America has gone slightly, unintentionally, crooked. Kaethe mentions that the herb liqueur brings sleep, but also headaches and even memory loss. All Rahel's sound advice—to give up the hunt for a child who doesn't want to be found, and instead develop some curiosity about one's own future—seems to drive Kaethe farther and deeper into desolate parts of the city. Even the light duties in the pension seem to weigh her down with petty insecurities. She doesn't think she's worth paying; unless Rahel wordlessly leaves the wage envelope on her bed, Kaethe tries to hand it back.

"Boris? We could simply invite the woman to leave."

Boris, stretched out in the back seat now with the hoof-paring pinned upright between his paws, cocks his ears at the low, buzzing sound of his mistress's voice.

"I've put too much effort into her already."

Why this one in particular? Not exceptionally charming, nor, despite Rahel's wishful and generous assumptions, particularly insightful or well educated. *It's because she's the mirror,* Rahel suddenly thinks. Look how we've both gotten along: as migrants, belonging to no one nowhere. On parallel roads. Our children fled. She's my could-have-been . . . and I'm hers. Despite that limp she takes no notice of, she's still chasing after something, still believes there could be who knows what, an answer, a balm, a revelation—

But the girl? Forget her. Doesn't deserve spit. Wherever she is, she doesn't give a damn about her mother. "It is too infuriating, Boris!" Infuriating, to see Kaethe doubting herself more and more as the search comes up empty. Blaming herself. At her age the girl should realize how limited her mother's choices always were. No one is much of a free agent. History flows around us and through us, like water.

But some children crave revenge. Every time Kaethe has gone looking for her runaway, the result has been another cut to the heart. The child plays the cheese. When someone is caught in her trap, the child rejoices.

All the mother's stations: Berlin, Taunus, Munich. All her defeats.

But supposing. Suppose she does find the girl again—

"They'll leave, then. Together. It's not that I'm envious, Boris. But the girl will hurt her. Break her down. And I can't bear it, I can't stand by."

The hound makes his guttural, questioning whine.

"Boris! Or, what is the choice? Say we don't invite her to leave! We could make her complete. A full partner. Unencumbered. I write fifty percent of the Zur Kurfürstin over to Kaethe Schalk. Why not? Give half to her outright! Expect nothing more from her than a good half of the work. *Yes,* and for that . . . half of the existence. Fifty-fifty. Side by side."

And what about Lies? Most likely problem-Lies would solve herself then, too. Hasn't Rahel taught her pride? Confronted with the oppressive situation of two employers (two middle-aged ladies) she would choose to leave within a day. She would see no shimmering Rahel to mourn, only a solid Frau Loewnfus to wave goodbye to, as Lies returns to her own kind, her peers in their opaque and stubborn city lives.

It's the best that Rahel can give her.

Filled with a trembling excitement, she opens the deadbolt of the main door with three rotations of the heavy key. Bags and packages hanging from her arms. Unlocks the second lock. Boris, rude and thirsty, squeezes forward through her legs. The hallway gleams from a fresh waxing. She hurries, slipping and surprised by the tug in her cheeks of an insistent smile. In the kitchen she plunks down her packages. Purple plums rotate jauntily out across the table, to be caught just before they tumble.

"Lies?" she calls a few times. And also, "Hallo, Frau Schalk, are you in?" Formally, for the sake of propriety toward guests who might overhear from their rooms. No one answers her calls or knocking. She tries the latch, finds Kaethe's room locked. Standing at the dark door, in this unlit far end of hall, she senses the chill an empty room gives off. A draft of desolation.

And Lies's narrow chamber, to which Rahel always carries a key, is even emptier. Bare, although not swept clean. The only traces left of the maid are a dusty sock in the bottom of the wardrobe, and a thin silver nose-ring on the floor behind the bed.

WITHIN

How absentminded, to have pocketed the pension keys. Not so much a sign of nervousness as of a hunter's narrowed focus. Normally before going out Kaethe would hang her two keys, solid iron rods, on the master-board in Rahel Loewnfus's front office. Now they clang like warning bells as she jumps down from the rear trolley car (having waited till the last possible moment, the car already jerking forward again) onto the cobbles of Senefelderplatz. Closest stop to Prenzlauer Berg.

Thirty meters ahead, Lies strides doggedly uphill in the moist August heat. She seems reassuringly oblivious to Kaethe, who nonetheless dawdles for some additional minutes behind a yellowing plane tree and a municipal recycling bin. Beyond these objects, along the avenue, there is scarcely any camouflage—and that is another lingering difference between the two parts of the city, Kaethe thinks. In the East, even after fifty years of begrudging peacetime, few trees have grown back.

Lies marches in a purposeful no-nonsense rhythm, as though thoroughly familiar with the neighborhood. Once it was Kaethe's neighborhood, the place where she had lived longest, a place she might now and then have termed "home." (Although sometimes home, like happiness, reveals itself only in retrospect.) The developers and prize-seeking architects who have swooped like starving locusts over privatized blocks only a few trolley stops south and west have as yet overlooked this quarter. Formerly grand houses stand in a state of suspended decay, somnolent in the gold-slanted sun—because although it is early in the day yet, the morning rush hour has ended. East Berlin workers, keeping blue-collar time, set out at sunrise. The only promise of activity Kaethe notes is fresh scaffolding for the planned rebuilding and regilding of the dark, plummy-brick synagogue.

For a time, this was also Sophie's neighborhood. Here is the kiosk where she yammered (never for long, Kaethe recalls, setting out again to follow Lies. Sophie's wheedling was contained in the glow of commanding black eyes, the self-parodying pout of the lower lip) for the treat of a watery, ersatz-vanilla ice. Here is the park where she used to linger, pet-hungry, to play with other people's dogs.

Eight, when she came through the Wall. Then nine, ten, eleven. Almost the complete span of girlhood. But in Kaethe's memory Sophie hardly changed at all during those years—except over the final few months. Around her twelfth birthday, quarrels had flared (over what? Friends, curfews, schoolwork?), alternating with searing silences. Stifling silence in a cramped flat. (Mathias tried to joke them out of it: Can't one of you give an inch? It's like living on the Maginot Line around here . . .)

Lies's march-step doesn't flag despite the steepening hill and the bulging hiker's pack strapped to her back. She is wearing a cropped, sailor-striped tee shirt, new athletic shoes, and the white denim shorts Kaethe remembers from their first encounter. Her muscular rear winks with each stride, like the automatic *follow-me!* signal of a white-tailed deer. Either the shorts have stretched or Lies has shed some of her chubbiness over the summer. She looks stronger, physically more resilient. Less of an indoor creature.

Sophie used to play outdoors even into winter, in these streets, dusty parks and inner courtyards.

And why, Kaethe asks herself (just as Lies, suddenly only a block and a half ahead, hesitates before veering into the street on her right), why did she never apply to the authorities for a flat of her own? Merely because the process was famously exhausting: standing in lines at all the possible offices to sign on to long waiting lists? Or because she shied from becoming that much more visible, knowing from her own freelance work at the Magdalenenstrasse that a person's vulnerability to chance or malevolence multiplies with each new file, in each additional bureau? Or—the true answer—because only by living with others

could she keep her pent-up greed, her unslackable thirst for Sophie, in
check. What damage might she have done to Sophie if the two of them
lived together, alone? Shut out the world completely.

Knowing where Lies will emerge on the next street over, she chooses
her own shortcut, via a right-hand needle's-eye passage with only a
sketch of sidewalk. It was always a favorite hideaway of Sophie's, and
today, when everywhere in the city the air is uncharacteristically heavy
and humid, like a sulphurous bathhouse, this old alley remains five
degrees cooler. The humped cobbles in perpetual shade glisten under a
lingering skin of dew. Summer flowers in windowboxes, bolted petu-
nias and geraniums, still bloom over sparse withered leaves. And here,
too, she takes flinching notice of the hovering citron-and-black insects
called "bees" by the undiscriminating Berliners—although Sophie,
explorer and observer and collector, long ago taught her to be more
accurate with names. These are neither bees nor wasps, but hornets:
irascible, underground-dwelling creatures. Their sting packs the hot
punch of a bullet. This August they swarm in such inescapable hordes
as to excite newspaper headlines, edging out such current topics as
the new Swiss pet-cloning company that promises sentimental million-
aires a perfect young replicate of arthritic, dying Fifi, and the unending
sputter of bizarre, death-dispensing sects ("religionoids," as Rahel calls
them) by coincidence also often Swiss....

Some reporters suggest that the "bees" smuggled themselves in with
the two-legged refugees from the *used-to-be* countries whose current,
quick-changing names no one can keep straight, but Kaethe prefers the
theory of Lies: these poor, bewildered hornets have all been dug up
from their sandy tunnels, *uprooted,* by the unparalleled excavation of
the city. They swarm among humans because they have nowhere else
to go.

At the end of the alley she peeks out like a nosy neighbor, on the
lookout for Lies.

Time and distance are exchangeable. Aspects of one essence. It's a
homely truth—did the schoolboy Albert Einstein, she wonders (later
great-uncle to one Esra Einstein, with whom Joe von Thall once shared
a lab bench), get a kick out of trailing acquaintances around Stuttgart
or Zurich? Only two hours ago, while clearing away the breakfast, she
happened to witness Lies slipping out of her room—preoccupied with
pressing the door shut soundlessly, turning her chambermaid's duplicate key—but now Kaethe has been following Lies by train and trolley

and on foot far enough to feel as though a full rotation of the earth has passed.

When she checked her room nothing appeared to be missing except the pension's thin scratchy washcloth and her half-bar of spice soap from the sink. Maybe she already used up the soap, and left the cloth in the laundry? But other things have slipped away recently (she blaming her own gaps in concentration): a gray sweater she knit in Glass River, a gauzy neckscarf that was the storekeeper's last-minute goodbye present, twenty marks from the pay envelope left on her bed and, only a few days before, the hardest loss—a dented green lacquer fountain pen that Max had owned since before she was born. A baton for his thoughts. He had liked to roll the pen between his fingers as he talked, used it to punctuate the air when he made his points.

This morning an absolute certainty gripped her: young Lies, amoral as a jackdaw, had stolen not only the washrag, but the scarf, the money, and even the green pen. . . . Moreover it was a real, breathing Lies who had held her and stroked her spine while she lay half-anaesthetized by Rahel's murky sleep-aids. . . . Kaethe turned all this over in her mind and could wring no reason from it. She heard the girl scuff away, down the corridor. In a hurry. Because Rahel had driven out to the country before dawn, taking the hound, there was no one to prevent Lies leaving. The front door clanged shut. Her heart thudding, Kaethe followed. Lies's mind might be a topsy-turvy maze, but it should be easy to find out where she was going with her fresh theft. Jackdaws have nests.

Why hasn't Lies come into view yet? Kaethe weighs her choices: turn back and try to retrace Lies's own steps, or press forward, in the risk or hope of intercepting her. She doubles back, into the chill breath of the alley. Again she has a poignant sense of diving back into the long ago, because everything here—pigeons purring, vermilion roof tiles, smell of moldering leaves—reminds her of Max's railroad flat.

Lace curtains billowed and snapped in a cold November wind. Rain squalls had swelled and blackened the parquet floor. She nodded. Yes, she did understand why the front-room windows were found standing wide open: in life, the man dead at the desk had been mordantly sensitive to bad odors. And although opportunists labeled him insensitive and ruthless, he had in truth always been personally scrupulous, and hated to offend anyone close to him.

And so why? *She couldn't stop asking herself. Disbelief slammed up against certainty. She felt herself turn cold under the investigator's blue stare.*

Would Max have arranged his own death (for that hour on that day, in the flat only she had a key to) as if to make sure that she would be the first to find him?

Three or four hornets, like an escorting honor guard, stitch through the air around her. Their wings fan her fingers, legs, cheeks. She forces herself not to strike out.

"Through my years of public service, Frau von Thall, I've learned there is no shock as devastating as the death of a loved one. Moreover, a freely chosen death is the hardest to bear. Your poise is exemplary. It's fortunate you returned from the West when you did. We appreciate your coming straight to the station here. We have been searching throughout the Republic, literally from Kiel down to Wasserburg, in order to notify you. Perhaps now you will be able to shed additional light on this situation. There are, naturally, some questions. . . .

"We saved a few items for you. Do you recognize this pen? Fine, old-style workmanship. Here, it's yours! Apparently he was holding it in his hand—until. . . . Dropped on impact. The hands by the way stained purple. 'Gentian violet'—a common farmer's cure for infection, the lab men tell me. Indelible. Doesn't hinder us, we have taken a clear set of the deceased man's prints. Yours, too, by the by, are everywhere. Unfortunately, there's no set matching those of the deceased in any of the archives. Max Schalk apparently was never fingerprinted—or, as is not unheard of, he managed to purge his own records. . . ."

One of the insects alights on her left hand. She can feel its six deliberate, sticky, minuscule pads moving along her ring finger. Looks down at its size and bright color, brighter even than her signet ring, which clearly is the attractor. She shakes her hand violently, repulsed. Two more hornets join the first. Probing, exploring.

Here is a duplicate of a letter, evidently written by him and addressing you, which I found lying unsigned on the desk. Would you read it, please?

Dearest Kaethe-cat, now that such a journey is *möglich,* our
way back to the Neue Welt wide and inviting as the Yellow Brick
Road, I need to update you about current *Umstande* in Glass River.
First, the rather tragic news—

It was less than a page, straight to the point, written in the ad-hoc American/German creole they had come to speak together. The farmhouse had burned down, riven by lightning, cremating the elderly Schalk couple

*to a fine ash. Fortunately, there appeared to be no mortgage or other liens
against the place, and therefore . . .*

A rather breezy tone, not at all the dark desperation of a suicide, the
policeman pointed out. But probably written on an earlier occasion.
Same pen, but different shade of ink. Family business, this matter of a
derelict property Herr Schalk had recently inherited in the United
States . . . hardly a man's likely last words. Nonetheless Frau von Thall
would understand that the authorities retained the original note in their
file.

*"Property in the U.S.A., Frau von Thall? I'm astonished your Herr father
hadn't already told you."*

*She shrugged. Astonished? No. Pure Max, not to breathe a word to her.
Not to run the slightest risk of her leaving him at a time that didn't suit him.
Now see who has left whom. . . .*

*"Frau von Thall? I know what an ordeal this represents. But we have
been keeping the body . . . your father's presumptive body—cooled. Temporarily preserved. We need you to come and conclusively identify—"*

*"Oh, no. No, you can't ask me to. Didn't you already say, 'Schalk's flat,
Schalk's own desk, who else could that be?' No. You don't need me. And you
can't expect—didn't you say there is . . . that the body you found has no face
left? Nothing?"*

*"A Soviet service revolver is quite a powerful weapon. But there are
bound to be other marks, special characteristics a daughter would be sure to
recognize."*

*"So. What does the face-part look like? Pulped? Sheared off? It was you
who found him, right? Did you have to touch him, to turn him around? Did
you see only a bloody blank crater, or—"*

*"Frau von Thall! For your own sake—for both our sakes. Please, keep
your dignity."*

*She felt the stiff mask that sealed her face finally crack to a smile. This
District Captain wore the sylvan fawn-and-hunter green uniform of the
West Police. In November 1990, to see Wessi cops manning the Prenzlauer
Berg police station was nearly as surreal as hearing them tell her that Max
Schalk, with all his vitality and vanity, gift for forgetting and habit of
survival, had of his own volition blown away his face and life only days
before . . . in the midst of the reunited city's ongoing tumult and elation. On
the same day that Kaethe, perhaps infected by the public spontaneity, had
again boarded a train bound for the Taunus region, to return without invitation to the Jagdschloss in the hills.*

The hornets scramble for position on her hand. An irritable vibration on her skin, like low electric current. Against all good judgment, she breaks into an awkward run.

"Was Herr Schalk a victim of depression? Inclined to anxiety? Despite public joy over Reunification, we have been finding certain individuals, especially elderly males, prone to nervous symptoms."

"Max was not elderly."

"Had anything occurred on that day that might deeply upset him?"

"I don't know! I was gone, understand. I had already left the city."

"We believe you, of course. Our colleagues in the transit police corroborate your itinerary. . . . But can it be your father was despondent over your departure?"

"No. He had no idea I was leaving the city. He would have—he presumably expected me . . . home, that evening. Neither of us went out much. I meant to call once I arrived at the farm, leave a message for him with the neighbors, but then, what with my daughter, it slipped my . . . there's really no excuse, is there? But that's how we are, he and I. We were. Together, every night."

"Ah, yes, your daughter. The granddaughter of the deceased. And has she been notified yet, will she be joining you here soon? A memorial service can be arranged but the mortal remains will not be released until after completion of our investigation. Similarly, the Schalk apartment and any possessions other than those which you've just been handed against receipt. Meanwhile if you have any procedural questions . . ."

No. No to it all. No and no and no and no and no.

It's the sun's warmth that agitates or intoxicates these beasts. They fly and crawl faster the moment she's back on the open avenue. One or two have landed in her hair now, causing only the slightest scalp-tingling sensation, a nerve's mere whisper. JND, she thinks, the "just noticeable difference." Difference between knowledge and oblivion. What you don't know can't hurt you. Pain, as everyone knows, is all about anticipation. *Stupid, keep a grip now, don't run!* It is extremely important to avoid exertion, in this heat, and also to keep a sense of humor. How funny it seemed to her, even back when she was a PhD candidate's wife-and-typist, for scientists to try to pinpoint and quantify something even philosophy can't grasp—the border of awareness, the JND.

Traffic is picking up, she notices. A few scrap-metal Trabis (holdouts, ghosts from a lost world) are parked along the curb. Hornets mill in the gutters. Ahead, farther up the hill, a shimmer of pedestrians. But no Lies. The earth might as well have swallowed her—or more likely one of these shuttered, unrestored houses lining the side street. She imagines the maze of courtyards, life and clutter concealed behind their blank, locked gates. She stops still.

To run and shake her head and arms like a madwoman is worse than useless. Sweat crawls down her skin like clustering insects and releases the flowery odor of her soap, her shampoo. So what if she is stung? This absurd predicament has the dreamy conviction of the climax of a nightmare. The rule is to submit: stop running, let the dreaded, inevitable thing come to pass: only then can you break through the dream-barrier and wake up.

Down the street, a gate cracks open a foot or so. Two figures glide out with the particular fluidity of youth; one is tall, bristle-headed, his extreme thinness advertised by black stovepipe pants, the other is short, wraith-like, huddled in a hooded sweatshirt despite the day's heat. A series of stabs suddenly flames between her second and third finger. The boys sprint off, one glances briefly back over his shoulder—and she sees Pig-Ear, his silhouette at least, in the peculiar high-peaked ears. As if dismayed by her sharp cries, the hornets, too, rise and zigzag away. Her first instinct is to tug off the irresistible ring. Crimson red in the pale web between her fingers are three innocent-looking small dots.

"Oh please, be home! Are you in there? Please, open! It's *me,* I need help, I only need to come in for a minute, please—" She pounds with her right fist on the unlocked door.

"Kaethe?" A drawl of incredulity. "Can that really be you again, Kaethe?"

"Yes!" Would she impersonate herself?

The door swings open. "My God. Truthfully, I never expected . . ." He looks rumpled, as if he'd slept the morning away. A book in his hand, index finger marking the present page.

"An emergency. So sorry. Seems I just keep turning up on your doorstep like a bad penny." She laughs. Mathias gives a look of puzzled suspicion. "Bad penny" is an English colloquialism, she realizes, and senseless in German. She holds up her hand, plumped and congested as a homemade sausage. "Luckily I happened to be in the neighborhood. Look—it's only a few bee stings. But hurts like the devil. So I thought of you. Maybe you can spare some ice?"

He has always relented on such moments. She only needs to confess a weakness. He invites her to sit on the elephant-drape cot and presses her shoulders back to the wall and thrones her offended, still-swelling hand on a cushion. The icepack, wrapped in a dishtowel, is so ferociously numbing that she has to close her eyes in gratitude.

He asks why she's in the neighborhood. She talks about Lies the jackdaw, who stole the green lacquer pen. An outrage! Mathias shakes his head. She only recognizes what she has been hoping and not admitting to herself when he says, "Oh, poor Kaethe. You don't give up, do you? But it would be almost miraculous, if this Lies led you to her. What connection could there be between your chambermaid and Sophie?" He strokes her upper arm steadily, with enough pressure to distract from the throbbing from elbow on down.

There *is,* she thinks, with a spurt of triumph. *I* make the connection.

"Feel any better?"

"Yes. Well enough to be off again soon. Mathias, you should have been a doctor. Instead of a pastor without a congregation."

He shrugs. As long as she is needy there's a truce between them. "Who'd have trusted me with a congregation? Atheist that I was."

"Oh, come *on.*"

"What's so funny? All right, atheist with his fingers crossed. Marxist-existentialist-Christian, if you like pedantic pigeonholes. Knee-jerk subscriber to the God-is-dead theology of those days. Sure, I studied theology. It stirred me up, the Big Questions. Maybe I liked the rebel swagger of saying 'God' to the functionaries, you know? Those were the old days, the lockstep Ulbricht days. How many other ways were there to challenge the system, to think about the next, necessary steps, what was just, what a *real* revolution from the basis would require? Say, a revolution such as Jesus had in mind, see?"

"I never heard you talk like this before."

"Because we never talked about ideas, you never asked a single question."

"I was terrified you'd *start in* on me! About how on account of me you were damned through eternity. That kind of thing. Moping."

"Moping? If I moped I had other reasons. For the first time I was sorry to be such an outsider. I wanted to be able to offer you . . . things. And Sophie, too. *You* know. A life like Max had. Here."

"I should go now. I'm ruining the bedspread." Drops of melted ice water are dappling the elephants.

"Not unless it's to see a doctor. You better come with me! The swelling's worse. Even your face is flushed."

"I'm all *right*. Have you forgotten me? Never a day sick, no allergies, I recover from bumps and bangs in no time."

"Oh, yes. Quite a toughie. But this is looking serious. Maybe an allergic reaction to those hornet stings. I remember in prison, in Hohenschönhausen, we watched a guy die from a spider bite in the neck. Swelling closed off his windpipe. No one had a knife for the emergency hole-punch, needless to say, and by the time we inmates got the Vopo's attention . . . Allergies can develop late in life. Sensitivity builds up without any symptoms at first. Then—acute systemic reaction to some agent that person never suspected before. Swelling of the airways. Heart failure. This kind of reaction, Kaethe, if not treated in time, can be fatal. Believe me."

Oh, she thinks, such melodrama. There were moments, in the wild first phase of attraction, when his dramatizing moved her. Then, her heart melted in an admiration laced with envy. She thought of him, Mathias the practicing Christian, as having a more finely tuned soul than anyone she had ever encountered. A soul one could learn from. Or even move into, as into a capacious, expectantly empty house.

But now she merely thinks: nobody in this city wants me to find Sophie. Not Rahel, not Lies, and not Mathias either. Why not?

A small, craven, irrational fear rises: that all these friends are trying to protect her. From what? What could be worse than not knowing?

Her head floods hot. No pain there, though. It's the heat of energy, ideas and resolve tumbling through her mind.

"For heaven's sake, Kaethe, will you sit back down? Keep the ice pack on!"

"It's getting late. I have to be somewhere. I'm not your prisoner." No answer. She matches his cold stare as if unashamed of her lack of tact. As if she has nothing to hide. "I know why you're angry with me, Mathias. Want to know what I think?"

His eyebrows climb in sardonic invitation. He's communicating as Max used to, with mute mimicry, as if to outfox a transmitter hidden somewhere in the room.

"You've convinced yourself it was *me* who set you up. Had you sent away, that second arrest. Right?"

"The *second* time?" He regards her with interest.

"Yes—because I'd already moved out, and we were not on speaking terms, and so that second time must have seemed . . . Either someone convinced you, or you had already figured out I was a . . . because at some point you must have realized I was . . ." Her throat thickens. She has never said the words before. To no one, never.

"As close as jam to bread with Uncle Mielke himself? That you were UC? 'Unofficial collaborator,' Max Schalk's über-dutiful daughter? Stasi-baby?"

She shrugs. Her throat too tight for speech. But she wants to argue that he is wrong to impose even this brief shiver of shame on her over her former dealings, both inept and necessary, with the Magdalenenstrasse.

Incredibly, she hears herself say the words, "Everybody did it."

"Oh, sure they all did. Sure! Everybody but the chump pastor, is that right?"

She can't fathom his return to good humor. "I had to stand by Max, you understand? Support the Party, or appear to, so they wouldn't mistrust him on my account, and also for Sophie's sake, so there'd be no problem when it came to high school, and how do you know that my— my letter-writing, my work, didn't help your situation, too? Maybe it all would have gone worse for you, if I had played high and mighty and been seen as trouble, instead of—"

"Sacrificing yourself as you did. Dirtying your conscience so I could remain pure. Oh, my darling. My sweet little Judas goat." To her utter surprise he leans close and prints a firm kiss on her forehead. "Could be, Kaethe . . . but no, it wasn't the *second* arrest I so much owed to you, as the first. Shh! You had no notion of what havoc you were creating, did you? Your haphazard notes on my dull—to you—comings and goings. On our cozy vodka-lubricated evenings with your father. Until my arrest, and cockeyed trial, and there I stood, guilty of fomenting conspiracy against the State! Of the usual joker's deck of crimes against Socialism. Although they knew, certainly my Comrade interrogator knew, that all I had ever wanted or worked for was that it should happen, make socialism *real*. . . . No, shh, shh! You just sit back, now. There's something else you may as well hear. . . . Yes, I think you're right to say that in the long run, everybody did it. For everyone the Stasi eventually found a fitting need, a weakness, an irresistible reason to collaborate. They found one for me, too. I played my part. UC."

"You?"

"Yes, yes, yes. I'm sorry to keep laughing, but can't you see this is a little bit ludicrous? This look on your face—so shocked. You know the story about the blackmailer who's bamboozled by a counterfeiter?"

"But you didn't have any family. No children. What hold did they have over you?"

"Ah. Ah. Don't think I want to dig into that."

"Was it about me?"

"In fact: no. Not directly." A cat-like smile she can't recall seeing before.

"Well—but what was your assignment? I can't imagine. Who were you supposed to report on?"

"On my pride and joy, naturally! The parish youth group. After all, we attracted any number of hotheads. Malcontents, scheming to jump the Wall."

"Oh, Mathias..."

"Myself, I never had much sympathy with the ones who simply wanted to save their own hides."

"No, well, neither of us did..."

"Though Max was even stricter on that score. Our disagreements showed up more sharply toward the end. Like bones in a starving animal. As things fell apart. I was heavily involved in the movement for open elections—and I don't mean the goulash-for-votes travesty we ended up with—but your father had a more radical vision. I used to needle him, call him an old Trotskyite. Well, you know, at the start we became allies, worked to organize the Opposition together, but later I could hardly follow him that far into nostalgia for past follies—"

"Max. You both together in—you and Max?"

"Of course. Max, my Virgil in the underground! My guru. But I could have sworn you had at least some glimmer..."

"*Nothing*. No. But how? Since when?"

"Ages ago, Kaethe, your father came to me as a stranger. To the Sophien Kirche, for advice—'pastoral guidance' as we call it. What he really wanted, I found out, was the fresh, bloody argument. A mentally well-armed opponent. But it wasn't long before I accepted him as my teacher. The Great Reformer, eyes wide open. Honestly, I loved him. We worked together, undercover, years before you and I met. That's *why* you and I met, Kaethe—how else could Providence have pulled such an improbable trick?"

"You worked with him. In secret. Against Honecker, Mielke—the whole raft of bosses. And neither of you trusted me enough to tell me?

I was the blind dummy. But you loved *him* and trusted him so much that you turned Stasi?"

Slowly, he rolls down the dishtowel-icepack. Wrinkles his nose critically at the sight of her mottled forearm. "I can't love him anymore, Kaethe. I'm the piggy who built with straw. My cover is in shreds. There's an open file on me in the Gauck Commission: 'Stasi collaborator.' No parish then, and not trusted to work now! No. If I saw him today, I'd walk in the other direction."

"You would?" She pauses, thinking, studying the familiar lines of his narrow face. "So do you believe what I sometimes do? That maybe Max is still alive? Holed up somewhere? In the Caribbean maybe, didn't he always talk about going there if things got any worse? I can see him in a beach shack, sunburnt brown as cork, fishing for his supper. . . . Mathias, listen: there are days I'm sure he's alive. I'm not superstitious but I feel his presence. One always could. There's a charge in the air, electric, unusual things happen. The way they used to, around Max! I see his kind of people, you know that sense one gets. . . . There was a man next to me in the plane, for example, when I flew in. And I see this man in the street now and again still and we never speak but he's aware of me—also I think I've ended up with something that belonged to him, this thing called a 'Thought Book.' What if Max is alive, still has an organization, and sent him—"

"An angel, to watch over you? Beguiling, Kaethe. I wonder: Is that how monotheism got its start? With the yearning of lonely children for the dead father to be merely off on vacation, to send benevolent emissaries—"

"Oh, stop."

"Then you stop clinging to the impossible! Schalk is dead. I'm sorry, it's a fact. He shot himself point-blank."

"Or faked it? Do you know they made me look at a body? I told them, yes, that's my father, just so they'd let me leave. But all I saw were those grotesque, purple-dyed hands. Why would he do *that?*"

"Gentian violet's a disinfectant, isn't it? Your father started life as a farm boy, remember. He'd know that."

"I don't follow you. . . ."

"An attempt at cleansing, perhaps? Combined with—given the stuff's lurid green stain—confession?"

"That is the most far-fetched—"

"An attempt at atonement? Ah, Kaethe, Kaethe . . . his troubles are over now. Listen: does it matter at all to you that I may face trial again?"

"Don't act so dramatic! That won't happen. Too much time has passed."

"Depends what's in my Stasi file."

"Mathias . . . do I have a file?"

"I'll bet. I'd take poison on it. But go ask the Wessis. Go to the Gauck Office. Take a number, shuffle up in line to read your own biography."

"And Max has one?"

"Good God, yes. One? A dozen? Probably enough paper to burn down the Reichstag all over again. And that's after his best efforts to erase himself. . . . Oh, Kaethe, look at me. You don't know, do you? You've been away so long! Up on your American mountain, as out of touch as Sleeping Beauty . . ."

"Don't know what? There's still something else to know? About you, or Max? Funny . . . I always thought I was the one with secrets. The manipulative one."

"You should see yourself, Kaethe. You look really strung-out. That close to the breaking point, I'd say. Why do you push so hard? With that limp—yes, of course I've noticed—how many hours are you on your feet? It crazy, this obsession. The chances of you finding her this way are essentially zero! What you need is—But why am I telling you what to do, when did you ever listen? Weren't you on your way somewhere? Don't be late. I'll pack up more ice for that hand and you can—"

"Not yet. *Tell* it, Mathias. Finish what you were about to say."

Mathias looks away, then back. For once she can read nothing in his eyes.

"It's about my father?"

"In nineteen fifty-three."

"Ah. Well, before I even came here. Prehistory. Stalinist ice age."

"Old hat, yes . . . But you see, the story—I should say indications, *pieces* of a story—only came to light less than a year ago, Kaethe. To light, yes, that's what it was. I heard—that there had been bones unearthed, in the course of reconstruction work on an old restaurant formerly popular with the Pankow crowd. Out east by Weissensee. Human bones, dug up in the cellar. Later I wondered why I didn't guess immediately. I should have put it all together—during our early meetings in the Sophien Kirche there was enough he alluded to. He told me more then than ever afterward. I suppose it was still fresh, eating at him, this story he 'merely proposed, for the sake of argument'—"

"You're not making sense. Fifty-three. What happened in fifty-three?"

"Uprisings, all over the DDR. June of that year. Thousands on the march, Max said. They were dead serious, chanting slogans like '*Ivan raus!* Give us free elections!' It was deeper and broader and better organized than the top Party men admitted. From Stettin to Karl-Marx-Stadt workers were laying down their tools—or shouldering them as weapons. Ulbricht panicked—God knows he had reason to! Soviet soldiers were called in quickly to crush the cells of rebellion. Some of those Communist soldiers refused the order to fire on fellow workers. Out in Magdeburg they were tried for treason, summarily executed—"

"What's any of it got to do with Max? *He's* never been near Magdeburg!"

"The bones *I* mean—they added up to only one man. Dug out of a cellar. This cellar is in Weissensee. Under a lakeside café-restaurant. Country peace and quiet—you know, a pretty getaway spot, with the willows sweeping the shore. Only thirty minutes from here. The skull's teeth correspond to dental records on an employee of the Ministry. A paper-pusher, no big fish, by any standard, but other documents show that this man apparently took advantage of his privileged status. Traveled over the border suspiciously often. Was carrying messages. Not for some principle, simply for West marks. Bribed by Bonn. He had a girlfriend up in Hamburg who he was gaga over, that probably made him easy pickings."

"So what?"

"He was caught running a packet in the summer of fifty-three. Chaotic, desperate times. As Max once said, history's like billiards, you can only try to nudge the game your way. We—the DDR, I mean—had to draw a line. Set an example. Someone ordered the man's trial for treason."

"So. Bad luck. He was made into an example. A show trial?"

"On the contrary. Quite private. In that cellar. An example only to those colleagues on the inside who would be sure to hear through the grapevine, and take the matter to heart. Our clerk was left blindfolded throughout. According to the written report he begged and babbled and apologized down to the last second. Poor sod. Not too bright, couldn't believe what was happening. There was a raucous party going on overhead in the restaurant. Right after the execution—by *Genick-schuss,* the classic military method, one bullet to the base of the skull— the presiding judge invited his aides upstairs for a hard-earned meal. However, there are always loose ends. One last man had to stay sober, had to stand witness. Remain below to countersign orders and fill out the death certificate. To straighten up the premises, and compose the final report. Kaethe? Do you understand the story I'm telling you? Do you understand why?"

She nods, but won't look up, nor ask who that last man was.

BELOW

Kinship among the children of monsters.

Presumably neither Caligula nor Caliban, Bluebeard nor Hitler, sired any offspring. Where all energy is devoted to destruction, sterility seems the logical correlate. But there are exceptions—Henry fathered Elizabeth, Tatiana brought a fond sparkle to Stalin's eye, and a schoolroom's worth of fresh young souls sprang from the loins of Idi Amin. Some monsters do beget children, and they, sooner or later waking into the clanking carapace of their history, are going to perceive themselves as outsiders no matter what they do or where. For them, what is "normal" human society? Kaethe Schalk, hearing her name echoing from above and behind her, tripping down a long, green-tiled stairwell into the darkening street, finds herself thinking of these beggared princes and princesses as her scattered siblings. What tales would the children of monsters trade, if they could find each other?

Some monsters attract pity in proportion to their awful isolation. This is the King Kong effect. Movie audiences shed tears of sympathy for the enraptured, incoherent gorilla clutching the miniaturized, wriggly Fay Wray. Children, especially, are tuned to respond to the subtlest signs of a monster-parent's loneliness; for them, pity is made out of the same raw material as love. Loneliness: pity: tenderness: love.

The Genickschuss. *For a suicide, an unusual angle of approach. When*

seen from behind, it is almost bloodless—a small point of entry, easy to over-
look at first. What strikes the observer (who approaches cautiously, pausing
to let his policeman's light play all around the room) is the attitude of the
man at the desk: his head skewed sharply to the right and tilted back, as if
gripped by a startling, new idea. The observer notes a service weapon (nickel
a dozen since the crash of the USSR) lying under the chair. The door to the
flat had been found securely locked. There are deaths, and there are deaths.
This time the observer is repelled but also impressed: it can't be easy, it takes
real discipline, to deliver that shot to one's own head.

Max would have known how.

"But I still *love* you, Max!" She shouts it out in the street, breaking
into a run. Embraced by the evening air of Prenzlauer Berg, which is
all that's left of Max Schalk. And don't fairy tales teach that true love
never dies, but instead transcends all doubt, shape-shifting? Isn't this
exactly the crucial test? That true love will leap in your heart even when
the beloved appears gruesome, monstrously formed? She's not running
away from anything now, only toward the raspberry horizon, sunset
glowing at the end of Mathias's lilac-shadowed street. And why believe
him? How, after all these years, could Mathias on the one hand boast of
having been Max's high-minded co-conspirator against Party and State,
and on the other hand insinuate that his "teacher" had helped to assas-
sinate a small-time traitor? Or at least (for Mathias didn't literally
accuse Max of having pulled the trigger, the charge was broader, less
refutably brutal) had served as an official witness. Sober from start to
end, eyes wide open to examine the neck-shot, as delivered. Why believe
him, the self-confessed weakling, a Stasi tagalong himself, the soured
ex–assistant pastor Leytenfeger?

Because some part of her mind accepts the picture. It fits, like a burglar's all-purpose tool it tumbles every lock. Shines light into musty old
questions. Such as: Why did Max Schalk, at a certain time in life, give
in to the potentially all-around dangerous impulse to summon his half-
grown daughter to Berlin? Why not earlier? Why couldn't he wait any
longer? Was it fear—not for her, but for himself—of continuing alone?
With what nightmares for company?

And it's true that there must be files. Sufficient remnants or reprints
of the mountains of evidence that the Ministry for Enlightenment raced
to destroy during those frantic days of November 1989, when for two
nights Max didn't even come home. Files on Mathias Leytenfeger, files

on Max Schalk, and a file, if not destroyed, that details nearly forty years of the life and work of colleague "Tarantula." What would she see in that mirror, if she were perverse enough to want to look? But as Mathias said, people have been lining up for years, former Stasi victims avid to read their own files—to revisit the worst of times, to savor the corrosive blend of old and newly bared betrayals. Once they hear it's all written down somewhere they can't rest. For some seekers, the most crushing revelation is to find no file at all—not to have been *seen,* or considered worth a second glance. But *she* was seen. Never, she promises herself, I'll never read that trash.... But *if,* who would she find?

Running for any distance strains her calcified hip. She can't ignore it anymore. This annoying da-dump da-dump rhythm of a truncated waltz slows her down but nothing hurts exactly, not her jolted arm either, though it pulses stride for stride, hot as molten lead. If Mathias wanted to chase after her now he could catch her easily. But there are no footsteps other than hers. He has said all he has to tell, now. She can still feel the surprising pressure of his last kiss on her forehead. A hard benediction. Pastor Leytenfeger's last kiss . . . *He won't* (the thought strikes Kaethe like an aftershock) *ever come looking for me again.*

When summer draws to an end in Berlin night falls fast, without ceremony, like black rain. Reaching Ebersfelderplatz, slowing to a walk, she sees daylight fade to the horizon, in a hurry to leave town.

Is there any sense in returning to the side street where she last glimpsed Lies? She circles back there on a forlorn hope, like a predator mesmerized by the broken scent. For someone not quite steady on her feet the street is a shadow-trap, dark except for a brilliant bolt of moonshine down the hump of cobbles and bars of soft incandescence spilling through curtains and shutters. Sounds from indoors: a man's relaxed laugh, a child's piping protest, the hearty coaxing of a TV announcer. Never, not even living alone on the mountainside in Glass River, has she felt so far outside. Limping along moonbeams' reflection between lamp-lit windows. Living rooms, lamps and families are available cheap to just about anyone. There's shame attached to not having them. A begging question.

How funny, Kaethe thinks: to be lost in your own old neighborhood. Granted there have been changes—new street-lighting reveals ebullient graffiti and fruit-filled Turkish shops, chic pubs and restaurants, even a flock of the deluxe Mercedes taxis, lined up for the late-night ride back to the hotels. Swaggering groups of twenty-somethings, immigrants and tourists, outfitted in Swatch watches and Levis, hike the post-Communist jungle trails, joking in their native Latvian, Bulgarian, Minnesotan. Finally, along with the rest, she washes up in the vast stations of the Alex. Alexanderplatz. Once and future heart of Berlin. Everything pumps and crosses here, as it did in generations before. Faces swim by, expressionless urban masks, such local archetypes that she's momentarily convinced *I know him, I once knew her. . . .* Elderly couples, leaning on canes and each other's bony grips, triumphant in their survival, push past youths whose green-dyed mohawks undulate at each step like Roman plumes. For long minutes Kaethe can't tear her gaze from a slender Turkish girl, a woman around her daughter's age, wearing the pleated, sheltering headscarf and long, formally tailored coat. Her brown-at-center irises are rimmed with sparkling Bosphorus blue. These extraordinary eyes swivel back warily at the admiring stranger. All of us, Kaethe thinks, a little dazzled: the ugly and radiant, the guilty and guileless, all pumping through the Alex.

The elevated S-Bahn station is a lofty glass palace. Newly opened, fresh-built and smelling of mortar and sawdust. Except for illuminated emergency posts (the fire alarm, the train brake, the S.O.S. button), it's a perfect imitation of the airy station-architecture fancies built at the turn of the last century. Has any other civilization ever spent so much to resurrect its more naive past?

Glass invites the eye to roam. All around, the city lies like a body framed by a curtainless window. Huge pale gashes in the earth, illuminated by high-intensity halogen spotlights. The construction schedule doesn't respect night: high cranes still swivel, as if performing the formal dance of their namesake birds, all the way out to the horizon. Kaethe looks straight up through the plain glass to the starry night, thinking: *all this country wants is to build, bury and build*. Exhaustion rains down on her like starlight. She's all used up. So they were right, the chorus warning against staying out too long, walking too far, pushing too hard. Now you either sleep on a station bench or give up, go home. "Home" where? Tonight, she realizes, home simply means the Pension Zur Kurfürstin, where Rahel Loewnfus will be waiting up with her smoky tea and sardonic good humor, dismissively tut-tutting any apologetic guest who stumbles in late.

A yellow train pulls in on the opposite track. As it departs Kaethe straightens up, facing the platform that is only twenty feet distant although unreachable across the canal-bed of tracks. And there stands a fellow-traveler she recognizes immediately, a man wearing a raincoat with the belt tied rather than buckled. Her seatmate from the flight in. As if half-sensing someone's concentrated attention, he brushes Kaethe with a fleeting, impersonal glance. How can he not recognize her? Has she become only another anonymous, dried-up Berlin drudge to him?

Or does he know her perfectly well? *Don't start,* she warns herself, *your old friend the assistant pastor was right about one thing, you have to let go of this idea of a messenger from Max, of some benefactor whose business it still is to watch you, watch over you—that is an addled fantasy. . . .* She notices that he has slung on one shoulder the telltale black nylon padded case of a portable computer. A brand new machine. Someone in his sort of work will have long since cashed the theft-insurance check and written off the lost laptop, in which she only ever found one fragment of a sentence. . . .

But the Alex district, for all its stratospheric hotels and office towers and giant-screen movie theaters, remains part of the East. She has an urge to call across the tracks: people here are still hungry, mein Herr. Watch out for pickpockets, thieves.

The businessman's frank expression borders on ingenuous, is certainly not reproachful toward her. Why can't she shake the hope that he has some purpose connected with her? What if she calls across: "AO," easily taken as "hallo." But now he pulls a square of paper from his jacket pocket and consults it briefly. For a second his raised, thoughtful eyes meet hers. Then he glances around for his bearings, and dives for the stairs leading down to the street, shops, and the underground trains.

Kaethe, on her side, does the same.

She follows him into a train without noting the direction. Their next station is Potsdamerplatz. These few square miles around the Potsdamer, once the most heavily fortified part of the Wall and since '89 the most radical amputation, excavation, have now been nearly sewn up. *Risen up, from the ruins . . .* so went the old DDR anthem they sang in school, but now in Potsdamerplatz one's lips can't even form the letters "D-D-R." She follows her businessman up flights of makeshift stairs.

Like a medical wonder from the laboratory, like wounds repaired

by antiseptic skin, the street level has been newly covered with rippling
water fountains and exotic bamboo groves. A golden walk-in casino is
shaped like a gaping giant clam, and a mall three stories high, packed
with neon-rimmed franchises, stays open until all hours, democratically, to delight the new-minted East German consumer—not exclud-
ing the homeless hag who straggles slack-jawed from display to display
with nothing in her pockets but lint.

Kaethe hurries behind the man in the raincoat. The crowd surges
over a temporary bridge of thick planks spanning a construction site.
Her businessman halts unexpectedly for a look down, and so she too
squeezes between the ranks of observers pressed up against a steel rail.
From the abyss below comes the usual smashing and hammering of
metal on metal. It's like an amphitheatre with a submerged stage: random halogen spotlights bathe the rapt features of the almost all-male
audience. How men love to watch other men build things, she thinks,
and then looks straight down herself into a pit far vaster than anticipated, as many stories deep as the nearby tower-buildings are high.
Tunnels slope away from stacked, unfinished platforms, cutting under
and over each other in all directions. Silhouetted figures in worksuits
and hard hats flash and vanish into lights that dazzle off stone dust and
sprayed cooling water. The lights hide more than they reveal.

"Oh, brother," says a Berlin-accented voice close by. "Fantastic, how
deep those engineers can go. It's a second city down there. Bunker city!
Only who wants to live in a hole?"

"Want to bet? There's some moved in already. Asocial types. Illegals.
East-refugees. Fixers. All the dregs."

"Headcases," the first voice agreed.

How deep is it? The gawkers can only argue, because the incalcula-
bly deep base of the pit lies invisible beneath a pool, or underground
river, of black water.

Distant black water and nearer white light gleam through cracks in
the bridge's boards. Kaethe's feet tingle, as if drained of all warmth
on such a summer's evening, and this is where her fear of tipping over
into the pit settles—in the soles of her feet. A sickening, resurgent
sensation.

Someone flicks a cigarette butt over the railing. It disappears long
before reaching the bottom.

Then a crumpled wad of paper pinwheels downward, unfolding

itself like a big white flower into the limelight of the pit. She glances with a start across the crowd to her seatmate from the plane—and sees among men in suits, tee shirts, leather jackets, the beige raincoat turning away. Superstitious after all, she runs, bumping against irate pedestrians. Crosses against a red light. The driver of a double-decker bus leans on his horn.

Stupid! she calls herself, angry and helpless. Now there's no one to follow. Like Lies, like Pig-Ear, like the scrap of paper he tossed away, he has vanished. But not before showing her that one small sign. Giving direction.

Alte Potsdamerstrasse, Bellevuestrasse. Supercilious prostitutes, posted along the deep shadowy parkland toward the Brandenburg Gate, turn to watch her progress. Their muscular legs in gold and silver stockings shine out between the black platform boots and edge of leather miniskirts. This is their territory, they have a legal right, their tasseled bags hold the health certificate for both johns and cops to check out, along with condoms and lipstick and pre-moistened towelettes. *Keep walking,* their long stares say: *don't dream of stopping here, you're bad for business.* She changes her mind; heads south again. Not hiding the limp. Her toes rubbed sore from the uneven gait. Her good arm holding up the bigger throbbing one. Much like a goggling late-night tourist she peers all around her as she walks: she is looking for a way to go down, a way to slip under the earth. But beside every entrance to tunnels, scaffolding and fenced-in pits loiters a laconic guard, unmistakable in his tilted, brimless cap of the Security GmbH, rakish as a foreign legionnaire's. The guards' very presence emboldens Kaethe. Keeps her walking. (Stresemannstrasse, Kathenerstrasse.) Where there are guards there will be something of value, a place worth reaching. A warm, safe, windless corner, maybe. A safe dark nook in a city beside itself with resurgent glory and anticipated glamour, this *legitimized* city which over the course of the summer has been sweeping its stations and parks clean of disorderly strays and fixers, punks and beggars. Soon, winter will come. And nobody will say or care where the riffraff has gone. *They shove off, that's how those people are. . . .*

And supposing she abandons the search, only for tonight? There's still a chance to grab the last S-Bahn back to the unrenewed, almost frowsy, unguarded West. Back to Rahel, in her timeless oasis of art and rational civility. Then—but then she might never return here. Because tomorrow all the chances will seem used up. All trails followed, all questions disposed of, the downward pirouetting scrap of paper a laughable excuse for hope. *I'll tell you what I know about hope,* Rahel once said. *Hope is crude, tough as sinew and hard to slap down. You could be Job, bad things fall on you until you're drowning in dreck, and you shout, That's the limit, damn it, now I'm going to give up hope—but you can't, because it won't give you up! Eventually you almost get used to carrying it, like any other passion or infection. But one day, nothing special, you wake up and—pouf! It's gone, like a drinker who skips out on the bill. You're free. Do whatever you like: pray, curse, stand on your head in the corner. Nothing you do will reignite hope. It's as if the gods took back fire. Everywhere is cold and dark. "Hope" is a word you soon will hardly remember.*

The tunnel entrances are high and wide. Inviting. But guarded, and cordoned off by saw-horses, or, in the case of older, more established excavations, by chainlink gates. How can she, how does anyone get in? Bribery? She counts her cash under a street lamp, shivering although the night is not cold. (Exhaustion can chill a body, of course, as will going long without food. But she tries to quell the shivering, because it wakes up the pain in her arm.) Forty marks, she has. Forty marks certainly won't buy a working man's job security. Plead, beg, tell the unlikely truth? They'll hoot, call her crazy. Could she dart past a guard and try to outrun him—galumphing in the dark?

As in Zoo Station, a sudden repugnant softness underfoot. Again she has almost stepped on a body, this one slumped on the ground with his back against the steel fence. Snoring. Stained pants, shabby shoes, quarter-inch gray whisker-sprout. Steel-rimmed glasses in the old Honecker style have slipped forward on his hatchet nose. She lifts up the "Security" cap that has fallen between his knees.

Though the gates are chained shut there's a gap. She's narrow enough to push through.

She carries the guard's service flashlight, too: long and heavy, sturdy German quality. She hopes the batteries are fresh.

Inside the tunnel entrance is packed sand, swept clean like a park or courtyard, dry and firm underfoot. She taps along downhill in moonlight quickly, eager to be out of sight, trusting her instinct for balance. Turning one corner brings a complete absence of light—a blackness like the vacuum of outer space—until she switches on the beam.

Nervous, jumping haloes of pristine light.

The tunnel appears to branch and branch again. All on the downhill slope. Since childhood she's often been praised for her sense of direction; now edging forward—again casting back to the simple, practical advice offered in fairy tales—every hundred meters or so she scuffs a heel-mark into the sandy floor. The sand is dull gold, extremely fine grained. The walls have been flattened and shored with fresh milled planks. What will eventually take shape here, she wonders: a parking garage? Train tracks, or the tangle of giant cables and pipes that make up a city's subsurface roots? For now the cool air smells only of minerals, fresh and moist, and every surface the light glides over looks pristine and scarcely touched, like a just-built house awaiting its first inhabitants.

Her heart races a half-beat ahead of the pulse in her dangling balloon of an arm. The heavy exhaustion of earlier night has vanished. Despite a nagging thirst (sharpened by the tantalizing smell of invisible water) she feels ready to march like this for hours (intrepid explorer, in a rakish, oversized cap). How late can it be? "Tonight," she says out loud with an exuberant swing of the light. "Tonight I'll reconnoitre. Take a first look around." Her voice rings richly; the tunnel has the acoustics of a recording chamber. "I can find a way in again tomorrow. It's not so hard."

A whistling answers, a breathy, multiple alarm. Shadows bob at the corner of her eye. Kaethe stops. Forgets to breathe. Floats the light-halo up and around, just snagging the hint of a fast humping undulation, fleeing ahead out of light's range. *Rats.* And what could be more natural, in these tunnels? But how closely have they surrounded and followed her, scuttling near her feet, below the range of the narrow beam? How many? "Of course you are rats! Keep running rats, hello, company of rats! Here I come, ready or not—" From now on she will talk to herself, babble any stream of nonsense, to warn the rats to keep a distance.

Aiming the beam close the ground, shuffling in its wake. Until at the opening of the next branch it catches a too-symmetric indentation. Beam wavers, moves in closer. The first distinct, clear print. She is Defoe, no longer the original lone wanderer on the beach of this inland, underground desert. It was not a tunnel-workman's boot that made this mark. Finer, curved parallel lines, something like a scallop pressed into the sand. She wonders how old the print is. She sets her own foot beside it. If from a woman, then someone bigger than she. "Or a small-footed man," she informs the rats. "A man or boy. Wearing gym shoes." She pictures Haddi, for some reason, among all the three and a half million people in the city. The light-beam jerks—her involuntary apprehension, or expectation. Does Frau Defoe have company then, beyond the rats, down here in the tunnel. *A stranger is just a friend you haven't met yet.* The motto Grandma Schalk once forced her to cross-stitch on a hoop, only to rip out and embroider again . . .

"Well, good. Enough for tonight. All right. I will come back soon. With supplies, water, rested. Tomorrow—" Never, not even lying crippled in the cabin in Glass River, has she felt so available to the whim of an intruder. Although here, isn't she the intruder? But hardly a threat, with only the flashlight for a weapon. She turns back, in the direction of the entrance, looking now for her own marks, exclaiming steadily to impress the susurrant rodents. Retracing her way out.

A barrier stops her: a wall of sheer, brilliant light.

"What the shit! Lady, who are you? How d'you *get* here?"

She is voiceless.

"Lady, could I have the courtesy of you answering? What the shit do you think you're *doing* here?"

He lowers his beam, like a fencer lowering his sword-tip.

"You're no shit Security guy, that's for sure."

Her eyes are beginning to readjust: she can see that he is freakishly tall, even for a German youth. High-domed shaven skull, decorated with another homespun tattoo (a star, a runic sun?) at the hairline. Jaw like a dogfish and broad, flat lips. Some teeth gone. Long, dirty scarf coiled around his neck. Studded waist-tight leather jacket, black jeans a size too small for even his skinniness. In his right hand a black rhomboid of a gun, the style the police wear on their belts. Unlike the flashlight, the gun is still pointed toward her head. She forces herself to look downward. Humbly. Between them, nuzzling her stung hand (which though fiery to the touch has gone wonderfully numb) stands a muscular, reddish dog, bowlegged and as tall as a calf. The bearded terrier head too large for its quivering body.

"Can you talk? What's your game? What's up with the bozo cap? Lady, you don't look exactly like a homeless Mutti. You sure as shit don't look like a hooker! But loony? Lemme relate: you skipped from the asylum."

"No. I'm no more crazy than . . ." What? Than I ever was? Than you appear to be? "I happen to be looking for someone. Obviously, there are . . . people, down here. Maybe you can help me find—" never has she woken up to find herself locked deeper inside a dream.

"Help you find the way to the top, you mean. Visitors verboten! You are totally *lost,* lady. There is no one hereabouts who anyone, except the Protectors of the Peace, would come looking for." Though she can't completely make out his expression the sneer in his voice rings clear: an experimental testing of her nerves.

"So there are others? You're not alone down here, right? If there's any possible chance you might know my—a girl named Sophie . . ."

"Ah. Female, eh?" He pantomimes hard thinking, stuffs the gun into an inside jacket pocket, shrugs. "There's not a lot. Don't know any *Sophiee.*"

"Here . . . Look, shine that light here, I happen to have a photo on me. . . . There. Of course, she will have changed some. See? Well? You look as if . . . yes?"

"Nah. No clue."

"*Yes.* I can tell! Look at me straight! Listen, you: you won't get away from me. Where are these others? Where is Sophie? Believe me, I only need to see her for a moment, to *talk* to her, I don't mean to make trouble. . . ."

"Ach. Nah, I don't like the concept. Looking at you, you're not, well, you're no spring chicken. And it's a distance. Honest, lady. No Sunday stroll."

She pauses. Draws breath. "For God's sake. I've been shifting for myself on a mountain in America for five years. I can hike."

"Camping in *Oosa* . . . ? Fantastic. No shit." He shrugs. "So, so . . . But you walk in front, lady. You lead." He shines the light ahead of them both. After a few steps she hears his suspicious questions from behind, "What's the deal? You twist your ankle coming down here?"

"No. I just walk crooked."

He continually strafes the rats with his halogen beam. Seeing them scuttle he laughs: the powerful light works like a whipcrack, making the rats surge ahead faster, hustling, mewing and whistling, leaping over each other with the peculiar waddling, humping motion she noticed before. They are a jumble of colors: brown, black and beige, also dappled, and pink and white. Their long, ring-scaled tails drag through the sand like fun-fair snakes. The rats, her companion admits (sounding to her like a landlord soft-pedaling a drawback), can be a problem—they're always out for food, especially in a pack they'll turn aggressive, go after someone who is alone and nodded off—but that's where a dog like Rotzi here weighs in for gold. "My dog crunches a rodent's back quicker than you can spit. What he's bred for, see."

"I see." Kaethe nods. She cannot imagine the giant, uniquely misassembled Rotzi, loping along beside them, having been "bred" for any conceivable utility. "How many are living down here?"

"Hounds? Permanent? Maybe ten, twenty. Some just don't want to go back up sun-side anymore."

"People, I mean."

"If you're asking *people* . . . No clue. Depends."

Is my girl one of them? Kaethe could ask. *Is she here?* But the words stick and won't come out. If he were to say no, cut the last thread of connection, how to go on? But what choice does she have? "Is it much farther?"

"Shit. You're tired. I knew it."

"No! I am thirsty, though."

"Hold on!"

She turns around to him. Her own light shows a frown of concern creasing his tattoo. He yanks off his backpack and digs deep: the pack yields a liter bottle of water, he wipes the uncapped rim against his jacket sleeve before handing it to Kaethe. She drinks, hearing Rotzi pant between her swallows. The water tastes of fresh geraniums, dribbles down her chin and neck. "Thanks."

"Pals call me Professor. Ha ha."

"Thanks. Professor. Is it much farther, now?"

He laughs again, the wind rushing in and out of his lungs, like someone who'll take any excuse to laugh. *"You,* lady," he says. "You nag like a little kid."

The tunnel grows narrower, and steeper. He leads. Underfoot the rubble-strewn slopes pitch upward then down again. Oktoberfest ride, she thinks, Tunnel of love. Her thoughts arrive in discontinuous snatches, giddy, almost surreal. Underfoot, rivulets of water begin to appear, flowing criss-cross in shallow eroded ditches. Ground slick as runny eggs. Once when her feet slide in the muck her guide kindly grasps her elbow, the swollen one. She chokes back a cry of pain. Once again she trips, recovers and points her light straight downward. A metal-covered pipe or cable lies across the sand floor. "What is that?"

"Power. Freebie from the Kraftwerk. Little do they know." They proceed, Rotzi bounding ahead at the horizon of light, his misshapen head swallowed by velvet blackness.

At some point the tunnel walls have darkened, greenish with oxidation, framed by boulders and huge worn beams. This section, she realizes, is old, much older than the post-Wall construction. And so there must be other entrances, she thinks. Hidden. Unguarded. But where? What part of the city are they moving under now?

Professor stops abruptly, as does she. There's no way forward. They confront what looks like a trash mountain—dirt and rock, piled two- or three- stories high.

"Did we take a wrong turn?" She forces down an uncoiling panic.

"No. Here is where we climb," he says.

Now his light rises, plays over foot- and hand-holds that have been notched lightly into the hill ahead, mere indentations to an uninitiated eye. At a height their beams can just reach, she can see the black oval of an adent, a miner's low, framed opening in the tunnel-face.

"See where we're going? Okay so far?" he asks.

"Sure. I think so."

Rotzi canters up the rubble-slope first, scrabbling confidently. Professor jumps at the wall next, climbing like a squirrel but pausing at intervals to shine down his light and pantomime to Kaethe exactly where her best next holds will be, in which sequence. She's pouring sweat, agonizingly slow with one useless arm, fighting back the panicky fear that Professor, tired of waiting, will disappear and leave her stranded.

Now the slope is opening out, less steep than it looked from below. *This isn't so hard.* Like climbing a long, winding staircase, on two feet and one hand. Macchu Pichu, she imagines. The pyramids. Angkor Wat. Places privileged tourists climb.

She moves up by Professor, intending to rest beside him belly-down on the high sill. All of a sudden, instinctively, she claps her good hand over tight-shut eyes.

He says, "You see why we can't have the whole world wandering in."

Each time she opens her eyes they fill and brim with shocked tears, as if she were staring at the sun. Below and stretching outward is a wide lake of light, day-bright, shot with color like oil-threaded water. After a while she begins to make out the distinct white dots of flashlights, propped upright like single blooms in vases. Other, more subdued and enduring sources of light are propane gas rings, glowing at intervals throughout the space. Space. Storage vault. Cavern. A dome, like a train station, with many exits and entrances. The purest light of all pours from halogen bulbs in steel cages—she recognizes these industrial lanterns from the Potsdamer construction pit—pinioned to the old retaining planks. Here and there a human figure moves, silhouetted along with other, four-legged shapes as well. There is a murmuring wash of sound that Kaethe can't sort out. Suddenly, as she edges forward, it swells to an earsplitting pitch. This is the howling, barking, yipping banshee racket that any pack of village dogs sets up at a stranger's approach.

Rotzi crouches, trembling, then hurls himself into gravity, claws rotating for traction on the steep slope in front of them.

"Follow me, lady." Professor descends before her on a system of narrow ledges, reaching back his long arm.

To take a homely, familiar object or situation, and turn it into a fabulous intensification of its possibilities. This is what children do, playing: in nameless games using one old shoe, a battered hubcap or a beribboned branch. It's what painters do with light.

And so there are certain elements Kaethe recognizes, approaching now on level ground, as the opportunistic props of play: the makeshift pallets on the sandy floor, the woven market baskets, lids secured with knotted string, the cardboard boxes lined with rags for bedding.

In contrast to other regions of the tunnels, there are organic smells here: damp fur, the malodorous tang of blood, spoiling meat, sweet trace of buried excrement. She sees the dogs everywhere, sprawled in the sand or roaming loose. Only a few nuzzle up to Rotzi in greeting, while the rest keep their indifferent distance. She is aware, too, of a variety of people standing or hunkering nearby—of varying ages, but most look tribally related by piercings and tattoos and chains. She hardly pays them any attention. Her eyes are fixed on a tall figure in the center of the visible space, near the source of most intense light. The lanterns here seem to be aimed as accurately as possible at a cot-sized rectangle of white linen sheets draped over wooden crates. This arrangement, flanked by a pair of open, old-style strapped suitcases, is again like a prop for the imagination, a metaphor roughly sketched. The tall person moves around it with the cool economy of authority. She—it is not so much the shoulder-encircling, partially braided hair that convinces Kaethe that this is a she, nor the ankle-length wrapped cloth, more like a Buddhist monk's robe than a skirt, but the feminine curve of hip and haunches that even her pouchy military jacket can't disguise—she, then, squats down with limber ease to reach both hands into a basket. Kaethe is close enough now to see what she lifts out: a liverish mottled puppy, softly wrinkled, round as a soccer ball. Only when someone hands the woman a small rubber-capped bottle does Kaethe become aware of various observers, or assistants, circling the makeshift table. Having laid the puppy to squirm on the sheets, the woman selects a large plastic syringe from the shining array of instruments in one of the suitcases. All the time, while judiciously filling the syringe and prodding open the reluctant animal's ridged pink maw she is flicking back her ropy screen of hair and braids in an habitual gesture than makes Kaethe wild to grab the hair-screen and loop it up and out of the way of the work, to free the child's face, as any mother would do.

Kaethe is sure her presence has been registered. She doesn't feel ignored. To Professor she murmurs, "What is she called here?"

"'Blackie.' She calls herself." His voice rises shrilly over an outbreak of yapping and echoing sharp snaps. "But we most of us just call her the Doctor. Kind of obvious?"

This time, as the Doctor turns to exchange one pup from the basket for another, Kaethe catches a green glimpse, between the swirling braids, of a gauzy scarf knotted high and tight around her throat.

Kaethe dodges around bystanders and dogs, trying to suppress the limp while holding her darkened throbbing hand protectively at heart level. "Sophie?" Peering into the amphitheatre of propped flashlights. "Is it you, Sophie?"

The braids decisively swept back by a large hand, chalk white in its tight surgical glove. The high, broad forehead, smooth arched heavy brows raised as if appreciating a perpetual joke. "Good Lord." The carved, swung lips parted in a half-smile. "It's not possible. Finally, and here. You found this place?"

"Yes. Sure. Wasn't so hard." Like a blind beggar with her one outstretched hand.

"Oh. Oh, Mamma, it *is* you—"

And before she realizes the girl is coming, Kaethe is buffeted backward, then feels strong arms closing around her, so that at once she stands still and upheld, breath in-drawn, submissive. Dizzy. Slowly she draws in the rich unforgettable odor of her girl's musky hair, of lingering August sweat on Sophie's skin, of disinfectant and a trace of spicy soap.

"I thought you might not . . ." but she can't think of what she thought, or find any words at all. Meanwhile Sophie is swiftly peeling off the gloves—each finger lets go with a rubbery pop—and then drawing her hands down Kaethe's cheeks, softly and methodically, as if brushing away minute crumbs. With the light dazzling behind her it's impossible to read her expression. ". . . That maybe you didn't want to be found."

"That is true. Right. Not by you. Not by the police you sent ferreting. Not by *them*."

Them means the family, Kaethe assumes. "But you're not . . . angry at me, for being here? You didn't try to run off, or hide."

Sophie gestures, a wide sweep. "Busy. Too much work. No one else can do it. Can't just disappear from here."

Kaethe draws back, to study her. Sophie doesn't wear metal studs or a visible tattoo, but even when she smiles fully, as now, a vertical cleft remains between her heavy brows—new, deep as a scar from a knife. Around them the small group has drawn in closer, young people diffident in their curiosity, absently fondling the dogs or gazing up into the uneven shadows, appearing not to listen in.

"Something changed." Sophie lowers her head, and her voice, so much lower than her mother's voice to begin with.

"How?" How do you resist, in front of strangers, the need to go on touching, pawing, covering the lost one with kisses? And even that doesn't take the edge off the hunger. Starved.

"For a long time it was better not to think about you. That's over now. Lies came asking around and found us; she talked about you arriving. Explained how your days go. Working, staying on in Berlin, and that kind of thing." Sophie tugs at the knot on her scarf. "She delivered all your presents." The fierce smile flashes again.

"My presents . . . Oh, *Sofchen*." All at once comes the hot pricking of tears inside the champagne-cool light. *Where have you been? Why does your speech sound so awkward? Who, besides me, has hurt you? Have you found anyone to turn to? To trust?* Instead she asks, "Lies? The girl from the pension? Is Lies down *here*?"

"She's coming tonight again. To stay longer now. To help out. She is

... Lies is the one, to come, to care, you know ..." Sophie shuts her eyes for a moment, twisting a ring woven of horse-tail hairs. She sighs, as if language were a tiresome burden.

"Lies is your friend, you mean. Yes? Your—girlfriend." Kaethe speaks lightly, bending to pat a shy dog. *Rahel, remind me once more. All closeness takes courage.* Quick as shiver comes the recalled sensation of a caress, a woman's unhurried, lingering kiss, deepening layers of softness. The slick little jewel teeth, the small lips and tongue probing, shameless as a baby's. *A little warmth is plenty to hope for. What difference, where we find it?* She adds: "So I introduced you two, in a way—is that it?"

"Yes." A pause. "That is true."

Then what is this twinge? Is it still the old jealousy over you, my possessive hunger? "If I can't have her, nobody will?"

"You sent her." Sophie smiles.

Oh, Achim, you with your suspicious pride. Your talent for scathing condemnation that I remember so well. When did you find this out about our girl?

"These presents, Sophie ... so you have the sweater I made? And you have your Opa's pen?"

"All the things Lies brought. Opa's old green pen, of course!" She slides her fingers into a pocket of her flak jacket, and with a flourish pulls out the pen. But its gleam is obscured by the darting, large head, body and scaly tail of a fawn-furred rat. After pausing to inspect Kaethe with one red eye it quick-claws up Sophie's hand and sleeve, into the braided forest of her hair.

Kaethe cries out. Sophie echoes her in alarm and revulsion. "Oh, Mamma ... What on earth happened to your poor hand?"

Mamma. That name spoken. She's glad no one seems to notice her joyful, welling tears.

The wasp-ravaged hand has merged with the forearm, all taut as a blood sausage. A repellent magenta color. Sophie, unflinching, holds it in her gloveless hands. Surely and gently she probes the whole aching limb. Strangely, Kaethe feels no apprehension, only a sort of relieved surrender.

"Sofchen. I need to ask you one thing." Despite a tightening of the girl's features, a deepening frown-line, Kaethe hurries on. "Why didn't you ever come back? To us, to Max and me. We waited. After the Wall opened, and after you had long since left *them*. Why always run to strangers?"

"Always afraid of your anger."

"Oh, no. My sadness, possibly. There were times I must have been dreary to live with."

"Anger, Mamma. Rages. What you said, cold and despising: 'Sophie pretends to us all, Sophie has no gratitude, Sophie ingratiates herself with her Papa and only wants to have him to herself.'"

"Never. I never thought so. Not one moment. Nothing like that."

"But you *said* so."

"No—"

"Over and over. 'Sophie won't stay. Sophie's too fancy for us here.'"

The group of helpers around them has dispersed. Sophie drags a basin close; prepares soapy water from a kettle kept simmering on a nearby hot plate. Kaethe's gaze wanders over thousands of glittering mica chips between her scuffed, mud-crusted shoes. Periods of sheer blankness, she is remembering. Trying to see into the black spaces between what has been and can be remembered: the past, her own story and others, that she has been reconstructing and typing into the laptop, back in the pension.

How like Max she is! Both of them, geniuses at stuffing crimes into some strong-box of the mind. Inured to the sickly smell leaking from it, as some people ignore or even cherish the stink of their neglected bodies. It is true that there are days, weeks and months she can't remember. Beyond her reconstruction.

Some tears burn; like acid, they bite the wide open eyes.

"If it was like that, Sophie—why did you leave his house in Berlin? Not even finishing school. Staying would have been better. I'd have more chance—"

"You know. He sent. She, not the wife yet, sent the bad girl away. To Taunus."

"So. You were a regular Cinderella. That's what we all guessed."

Sophie grins up at her. Dazzling. "Not a tragedy, Mamma. The Biosphere farm, later on? A co-op, they did some of everything. Not only a job, a full apprenticeship. Animal husbandry! State certification."

"That's great, Schatz. I didn't know." She winces as a swab crosses her hand with iodine. "But why leave there and go to Munich, if you were happy with the co-op?"

"The farm had to be sold. On the fields a company built a discount market. Where to work? Time to try to live in the world—that is, Papa's world, theirs. Yours too."

"And?"

"Terribly hard. Same as before. Terrible."

"You seemed all right when I visited you. Sophie? Did something happen? An incident? With his other child. Or with your pets. You must have had—"

She waits. No answer. Sophie, breathing slowly, cradles the mis-shapen arm as if to heal by the weight of silence.

"No incident. Aimee—the sister girl. She died."

"What did you say? She *died*? That's not possible, no one told me—" But who would have, and why? "Aimee." Her mind gropes for an image and comes up with only a snapshot, flashed one afternoon in a beer garden by her daughter, the proud older half-sister. Kaethe hadn't much wanted to look: it was a confident peach of a child. Bright blond hair drawn back in barrettes. Mischievous eyes. An innocent. One found nothing to dislike. *"How, Sophie?"*

"Car crash."

All the thoughts colliding in her mind: about the tests Achim had once undergone, the verdict of near-infertility, her reaction, quickly stifled, when she first heard about his second triumph over statistics. "Aimee." They all collapsed to one: "Did you see it happen, Sophie? Were you there? Did they blame you?"

"No. Nothing like that. She had gone with a friend's family for a ski trip. Autobahn. 220 kilometers per hour . . . that's too fast."

Now, after a careful dabbing dry, Sophie is stroking her arm. Kaethe blinks. Her swollen limb glistens under an icy gel. Cool anaethesia, spreading in toward the bone. Deftly, Sophie wraps it in thick, conceal-ing bandages. Then arranges a gauze sling around Kaethe's bowed neck. Places the arm inside. "Feels better, does that?"

Kaethe nods, speechless.

"Now you've come all this way, would you like to see more of the camp?"

Barely concealing pride, hugging her flak jacket, the Doctor gives a tour of the features of what Kaethe has begun to interpret as a sort of field lazaret for animals, the strays taken in on leashes or under the wings of human strays. Stacked on metal shelves, desks and tables are bags of cotton and gauze, antiseptics, de-wormers and diuretics. There are the propane cookers for warmth and to sterilize water and formula bottles, pallets of pet food all stamped with the wholesaler's label, a set of top-flight Henckel scalpels and scissors, clamps and sutures. Sedatives, salves, an array of prescription injectables. Sophie handles them all confidently, explaining their purpose. These are mostly tools and medicines she learned to use initially on the Taunus farm her father sent her off to; later, on the commune she chose for herself.

Not only dogs have been brought in through the tunnels for treatment. There are also scabrous cats and verminous kittens in the baskets, an iguana shivering with infection, and a yellow-eyed crow whose wing-joint has been ripped away. The Doctor's services aren't charity —her patients' keepers deposit their payment in a trash can with dangling padlock near the work area: coins and bills in various currencies, phone charge cards, uncanceled theater, train and lottery tickets, cans of soda and pet food and evaporated milk, chocolate bars, fruit.... Kaethe accepts a wedge of black bread and an orange. Hands the orange back to her daughter for peeling, her own good hand shaking with hunger.

The rat, balancing cleverly (domineeringly, to Kaethe) on Sophie's shoulder, accepts a segment of fruit in its deft pink paws. As it turns to seek shadow, Kaethe sees the furry brown testicles dragging behind, nearly as big as the creature's head. "He's very—tame, isn't he? And what do you call him?"

"'Rat.' That's what he is. He doesn't want a name."

"Sofchen—" She will repeat it again. Those two syllables. To say them is like throwing a whistling line back over time, and pulling up the past. "Sofchen! What *was* the bad time, exactly? Won't you tell me? When was it? Have you been ill? What exactly went wrong back in Munich? Did *they* do something to hurt you? Were you ashamed, and thought you had to hide from them? Can you tell me? Sophie, I'm here, please."

But the Doctor shakes her head. Instead—returning to the problem of the crow, holding and swaddling it so firmly that it begins to calm itself, nattering *chk-chk-chk*—she talks about these particular sheltering caves. She explains that no one knows who started this current colonization. The youngest drifters, mostly without valid IDs and so not eligible to use any but the most violent and vile shelters—run by profiteers who collected a stipend per-head-per-night from a purblind State agency—these so-called "Tremper" have organized the place. In their way. There is potable water. Power has been grafted in by stolen cables. At any rate the present authorities up on the sun-side haven't caught on to the caves' use, or maybe the charts and records of their existence have disappeared? She describes how under Berlin there are any number of these high-ceiling chambers, they must form part of a much older system, long predating the opening of the Wall. For years this space was used by the Stasi to eavesdrop with super-keen electronic devices under West German military posts. ("See, Mamma? They conveniently left behind all the furniture, and these hand-carts for transport, and over there that junk-pile of fat earphones and oscilloscopes.") And decades before that, the Gestapo's lines of communication and command had run uninterrupted by the bombs raining on the sun-side. "Professor thinks there's bound to be a rubble-blocked connection to Hitler's bunker, somewhere down here." And a few thousand years further back, Sophie surmised, in the Age of Bronze, these tunnels served as the entrance passages to even more remote tombs where warriors, female heroes too, lay buried in jewel-crusted armor. . . . Constant temperature. Everlasting repose, while the city above roils in its revolutions and crimes, wars and storms.

"The Brixen Maiden," says Kaethe, and Sophie flashes a knowing smile.

Sophie, though, evidently has not shut herself off entirely from the surface-land. Her skin is the color of cured wheat, with the raspberry tinge across her cheeks as when she was twelve. Evidently she comes and goes; it is possible to come and go. "From now on we'll have time—we'll take time together," says Kaethe. Ample time to talk, she means. How long might it take, after all, to complete the wonderful task of finding Sophie? She can contribute this and that, meanwhile. And pitch in with the work here, as well. Nothing is wasted: the med van was good practice. She feels buoyant, already healed, reprieved—it's the restorative food, and the icy gel drawing poison from her hand under the bandage, and the sense of time and therefore consequence suspended, down here in the caves.

"Yes, but look at you now, shaking with tiredness, and do you realize it is six in the morning?" the Doctor exclaims. There are no proper beds free down here. Also, the stung hand needs antibiotics not stocked down here. And Kaethe also should not forget that Rahel will be worried and upset, and missing her at the Pension Zur Kurfürstin, especially once she finds that Lies has moved out.

In argument, Sophie's voice falls lower, extraordinarily gentle and persuasive. (Yes, this is the cadence of reason, the remembered burr of Achim's voice. Kaethe can hear his exact inflections again.) There's an easier shortcut up, she explains. And be sure to take a taxi. Absentmindedly Sophie unfurls and rebraids her hair, then loops the braids together, freeing her face as Kaethe wanted to do many hours before—piling up a lopsided crown of braids, ends woven into beginnings. "Mamma. The expression on your face! We'll be all right. Go back, get some rest now! Don't worry about anything. It's all fine. It's good that you came."

Professor and Rotzi step in from the shadows on cue, as if whoever has escorted a newcomer into this place is obliged to lead her out again.

But Kaethe hangs back. There's still so much that she wants to explain, confess to Sophie right now, tonight—but what, exactly? How Sophie more than ever resembles her father. Broad shoulders, strong, flat back. Achim's high-beaked nose. His iridescent skin. His habit of standing tall, nearly at attention, and gazing determinedly out into the distance, while secretly adrift in the tumbling clouds of his own thoughts.

And so Sophie is uniting them again. As ever. *Achim* . . . Kaethe can see the traces of her young husband, now living in Sophie. He's in his daughter and now in Kaethe too, moving in her mind and memory, never far apart from her. From now on she will always be able to see him so. This leap and twist of the heart, as if beginning to fall for Achim von Thall all over again! *Innocence,* she thinks, meaning what she offered up to him. Meaning what they gave each other for safekeeping, without a second thought. The treasures, as Albus knew, that once overflowed. Not lost. Not losable. Merely left in the other's trust.

It is wrenchingly hard to let go of Sophie, of rough hair, warm cheek and waist, fingertips. To back away, out of her reach. "Till soon, Sophie?"

"*Tschüss!*" The gay Berlin goodbye—tongue-tip sound of a kiss in mid-flight, a sweet essence of adieu. "Till soon, Mamma."

The ledges on this side are less intimidating to climb than they were to descend. Starting up, Kaethe can see clearly every stone and shadow, the hard-packed shale and crumbly spots where a visitor's boot has landed too hard. The effort of climbing distracts her from the minor but pervasive sadness of one more separation, however temporary. All Sophie's words echo as if just spoken in her mind (the low lilt, elliptical phrases, direct intent) and yet she can't remember much that she herself said. Did she remember before leaving to send her thanks to Lies— the thief, the raven, the messenger?

Soft clots of silt pelt her head and climbing-arm like first drops of rain. If anything she dreads more the descent on the other side of the high opening: the slimmer foot- and hand-holds of the pitch-dark tunnel-face. *But let's take one obstacle,* she thinks, *at a time.* Her heavy keys clank in her pocket like church bells. . . . Their homely sound conjures up her room, the Drossel's song, the sea-sway of white drapes, the glowing inner shell of her laptop. *Everything is written there in the stolen computer—and once you've read, Sophie, then you'll begin to understand.* The only part she hasn't filled in yet are these last hours: today and tonight. Should she? Maybe the time for writing is over. From now on, who will need such a record? Now there's a future to consider. . . .

Under her toes and scraped knees the sand begins to hollow out and drizzle away grain by grain. She grabs for purchase higher up the ledge. One shadow bouncing above her is Rotzi; the other, moving deliberately as a lizard, is his young master. Clearly Professor has greater confidence, on this return journey, in her climber's agility. The slope, he has pointed out to her, is not so formidable as it looks: maybe thirty degrees at most. He turns his head, his teeth shine dimly downward. She grins back up toward him, even as her good hand closes on nothing but a fistful of sand. The fine stuff already cakes her torn, stubby nails. Both her knees are slipping, accelerating sideways.

Another grip, frantic and determined, catches a curled lip of rock. One more foothold. And here, thank God, the next.

The higher she climbs, the more overwhelming her temptation to look down again into the lake of light. Some of the people below will be leaving with their stitched-up or medicated animals, others will settle on pallets and bedrolls to sleep now for a few solid hours. She is fighting a desperate longing to take back with her one more glimpse of Sophie: who has perhaps returned to work, or stands with braid-heavy head thrown back to follow the slow progress of her mother. Or lies already curled up in blankets, waiting for sleep? Meanwhile, the higher Kaethe climbs, the denser the stark upward shadows cast by the terraces. Vertigo gapes behind her. To look back down into that crystal abyss might disorient even someone far surer of herself at this point of the journey, someone fully rested, with two good hands.

It's all she can do, inching up toward the last dark ledge, to keep looking ahead.

ACKNOWLEDGMENTS

To friends and colleagues who have read this novel in any or all of its
its nascent forms, and offered frank reactions, questions and encouragement, my deep and lasting thanks. Their company includes but is
not limited to: Alexandra Broyard, Margot Livesey, Trish Hoard, Mike
Mee, John "Ike" Williams, Sam Vaughan, Wolfgang Heuss, Chuck
Schwager, Wilton Barnhardt, Jack Shoemaker and my estimable agent,
William B. Goodman. The unwavering support of my family helped
bring this book through to light.

In addition, I owe a considerable debt to the authors of certain non-
fiction works that were consulted (and in many cases greedily devoured)
with regard to the novel's political and historical background. Especially worth noting in this context are *Geschichte der Deutschen
1949–1990* by Eckhard Fuhr et al., *Berlin—Hauptstadt der DDR
1949–1989,* edited by Bernd Wilczek at al., *Lirerarischer Fürher Berlin*
by Fred Oberhauser and Nicole Henneberg, *Fürher durch die Geschichte
Berlins* by Werner Vogel, *Chronik des Mauerfalls* by Hans-Hermann
Hertle, *Das Ministerium für Staatssicherheit* by David Gill and Erich
Schroeter, *Getrennte Vergangenheit, Gemeinsame Zukunft* (DTV series,
various editors), *Die Familie in der DDR* by Wolfgang Plat, *An
Uncommon Woman* by Hannah Pakula, *Spymaster* by Leslie Colitt,

Witness in His Own Cause by Gustav Just and *The Origins of Modern Germany* by Geoffrey Barraclough.

That said, *Broken Ground* is a work of fiction. Any resemblance between its characters and living or dead persons, other than those public figures correctly named, is purely coincidental.